"A mesmerizing adventure with star-crossed lovers who will leave your heart pounding."

—Helen R. Myers, Bestselling Author Of *Night Mist*

WAVES OF DESIRE

Linda ran and splashed into the waves until the water reached chest level. Giff stared, noting the way the plain black bathing suit clung like a second skin. He felt another flash of arousal.

"I won!" she said.

"So you did," he said, running into the water. As soon as the waves reached waist level, he dived into the water, letting it wash over him, cooling his body. He swam underwater until his lungs screamed for air, then surfaced, shaking his head.

In just a moment, Linda bobbed up beside him, a smile still on her lips. "You're a great swimmer."

"I swim better than I cook."

"I've already suspected that you're a man of many talents."

The pull of the waves brushed her against him. He reached out with one arm and caught her around the waist as his toes searched for the sandy bottom. He could barely stand there, but he braced his legs, pulling Linda against him.

Her smile faded; her eyes darkened as her lashes lowered. He also felt the sexual energy that seemed to flow between them.

"If I kiss you, as I wish to do, this afternoon will not end with swimming."

VICTORIA CHANCELLOR

FOREVER & A DAY

LOVE SPELL NEW YORK CITY

LOVE SPELL®

November 1995

Published by

Dorchester Publishing Co., Inc.
276 Fifth Avenue
New York, NY 10001

Printed in the United States of America.

To those in my childhood who shared the unbelievable with me: Laura Haller, John Miley, and Mr. Eakles
And to my critique group, who said,
"Just finish the book!"
Thank you, April, Becky, Georgia, Guy, and Rob.

Special thanks to Karl T. Hagen, whose second language is Old English, and to Anthony McGowan, who knows all about past-life regressions.

Forever & A Day

Chapter One

Destiny is no matter of chance. It is a matter of choice: it is not a thing to be waited for, it is a thing to be achieved.
—William Jennings Bryan

June 7, 1995
Coastal South Carolina

Linda O'Rourke swallowed a lump of fear as she looked up the dark, narrow stairs toward the closed door of the third floor attic. The mottled, pea-green walls seemed to heighten the gloom, much like the sky before a dangerous storm. The rest of the house was bright and cheerful, but early afternoon sunshine didn't venture this far inside. Light from the bare bulb in the hallway crept only halfway up the steps, stopping as though an invisible curtain kept it away from the top.

There's nothing up there. You're alone in the house. Go up the stairs.

There were 18 steps, she knew from her childhood, when she'd skip up and down, singing out her numbers. She no longer wanted to skip up the stairs. She didn't want to be here at all. But she had to face what had happened behind that closed door to her grandmother's attic 14 years ago.

Before she could change her mind, she ran up the stairs, reciting to herself, *There is nothing up there . . . there is nothing up there*. She grasped the brass doorknob. The metal felt shockingly cold, despite the sweltering summer heat outside. She wanted to draw her hand away, but didn't. She wouldn't give in to the fear, she vowed.

It's okay that the knob is cold, she told herself. *These older homes were built to stay cool, even without air conditioning. That's why it's cold. You're facing a childhood memory—nothing supernatural. You're a grown woman now. You can handle this.*

She opened the creaking door, then paused, held her breath, and took in the sight. Built-in wooden shelves lined one wall, filled with shoe boxes, clear plastic storage containers and various odds and ends. She smiled when she recognized a pink plastic Barbie carrying case and a box of colorful building blocks. Nostalgia for all that was good and simple swept through her. For her, being a child during the summers in South Carolina meant not having a care in the world.

Two old chests sat side by side at the end of the room. A scarred and faded blue chest of drawers stood alone near the door, filled, Linda imagined, with out-of-season clothes from at least 20 years ago. Her grandmother wouldn't discard such essentials, which could be needed again . . . sometime. She'd filled a three-story house with items from a lifetime, things she hadn't used in years but kept anyway. Now that her grandmother was gone, it was Linda's job to go through them.

She let out a long sigh. Although she'd visited her grandmother many times in the past few years, Linda hadn't been brave enough to return to this part of the house. The very thought of climbing those steps had terrified her. She'd imagined all sorts of dire consequences from returning to the attic. She shook her head at her childishness. The terrors were only in her mind; the attic looked and smelled exactly the same as when she was young—a lonely, dusty place where memories were stored.

She eased inside and cautiously stood in the middle of the unpolished floor. Nothing eerie happened. She felt the tenseness in her shoulders ease, her breathing return to normal. Facing the past hadn't been nearly as difficult as she'd imagined.

Sunlight filtered through yellowed sheer curtains on the two dormer windows and dust motes swam through the rays as though happy to be released to play. Each summer, Linda and her parents—and sometimes Linda's best friend, Gerri—would drive from New York to South Carolina. Then Mom and Dad would return home, to busy lives and careers, while Linda would stay and play away those hot months, returning only when her skin was as brown as tanned leather, her curly hair streaked gold by countless hours in the sun, and her feet calloused from running barefoot through the sand.

Grandmother had left her the beach house last February in her will, but Linda wasn't yet sure what she would do with the isolated property, since her life was in Chicago. She had to decide what to do with a lifetime of memories and family treasures. And she'd tackle the past that haunted her still, she thought, staring at the faded brown card table that still sat under the dormer windows. If she closed her eyes, she could imagine herself and Gerri sitting there, their hands poised over the Ouija board, anticipation written all over their 15-year-old faces.

That fateful summer, they'd "met" an English officer, William Howard, who had died in 1815, a man who had instantly caught Linda's girlish heart. She'd been fascinated by his stories, touched by his short and tragic life. In single words and simple sentences, spelled out precisely on the board, he'd described the cold, wet fields at Waterloo, the artillery fire and the screams of the dying. He'd spoken of bravery, ideals, and sacrifice, and of defeating a tyrant. To her, William was everything that was good and heroic.

But then they were interrupted by someone—or something—that spelled those awful words. *I am Mord. Kill, kill, kill.*

Ever since that frightening night, she'd felt that

her brief "relationship" with the long-dead officer was not finished, as though she should come to terms with the attraction she'd felt, even without seeing his face. Gerri didn't seem so compelled by William, or even by the events that had scared them away from the Ouija board. She seemed to have the ability to put the past behind her, to shrug off the unexplained as simply part of life that had no explanation. Linda wasn't so lucky. Sometimes she wished she were naturally more of the pragmatist and less of the romantic.

As a teen, she'd made up elaborate stories in her mind about William. When she grew older, she'd second-guessed herself and wondered if he was a figment of her and Gerri's imaginations. In an effort to solve the mystery, while researching her dissertation in England, she'd searched for his name in the military lists of Waterloo.

And discovered a startling fact. He *was* real, as real as any man who had ever lived. And yet he was dead, and she could never meet him. She still felt close to him in her dreams, which had turned into erotic interludes as she grew older. Although they'd never actually finished the act of making love, they went far enough for her to awaken breathing hard and fast, her body sweat-dampened and aching. If only she could meet a real, modern-day man who excited her the same way as her fantasy lover. If only she and William had lived at the same time . . .

But they hadn't. It was an issue she'd never been able to resolve, in part because she wouldn't dare touch a Ouija board. She was more afraid of the evil that had interrupted her and Gerri on that fateful night than anything—even finding out more about William.

Linda crossed her arms, rubbed them against the coldness that seemed to come from within. Just the thought of the Ouija board brought chills to her skin, despite the warmth of the attic. She wasn't afraid of much in life, just snakes, unbalanced people with weapons, and evil entities.

The sound of a telephone ringing made her jump. Since her grandmother couldn't abide answering machines, Linda knew that she'd have to hurry to catch the phone. Only her neighbors in Evanston, who were watching her house and watering her plants, a few good friends, and the college dean knew she was in South Carolina for the summer. Since the number was unlisted, it could be an important call.

She ran barefoot across the floor, but had to stop for just a second. The attic looked calm, peaceful, without even a hint of strange occurrences. So why did it seem that the room was no longer a playful sanctuary, but a prison for something that needed to be locked away—something dangerous that she should never have known? It was a memory blown out of proportion by the years and her own imagination, she wanted to answer. But was that true? She didn't know. Shaking her head, she took one last glance around and shut the door.

She hurried down the narrow stairs toward the light below with the surety of a child running over familiar ground. The phone continued to ring.

Was this the fourth or fifth ring? Slightly out of breath, she grabbed the door frame and catapulted around the corner, into her grandmother's bedroom, and raced for the phone on the nightstand.

"Hello?" She knew she sounded out of breath, but she welcomed the interruption, the chance to hear another human voice.

"Linda? You sound like you ran all the way from Chicago!"

"Gerri! I was just thinking about you."

"Yeah, I figured you were."

"Psychic vibes, right?"

"You don't have to sound so skeptical. You practically broadcast cosmic energy, you know. I picked up your signal all the way in New York!"

Linda laughed. Only Gerri could joke about their psychic connection—something she considered to be quite real. "I didn't realize I was *that* powerful. Maybe I should get an FCC license."

"Maybe you should."

"I'm so glad you called." Linda sat on the quilt covering the double bed, immediately sagging toward the middle.

"Seriously, I was worried about you. Has anything happened?"

"No. I was just . . . looking around."

"In the attic?"

"Someday you're going to have to explain how you do that," Linda said, all thoughts of joking gone.

Gerri paused for a long while before answering. "I know you hate it when I say things like this, but

I felt you were upset . . . or in trouble."

"I'm fine."

"Don't kid your best friend."

"I'm not. Everything here is great," Linda said, ignoring her earlier feelings of fear and dread. Ignoring the chill she'd felt when she thought about the past. "I have a schedule all worked out, room by room. I've given myself plenty of time to go through Grandmother's things."

"Okay, I'll take your word. But I still think something's wrong."

"Nothing's wrong," Linda said, glancing up as though she could see through the ceiling into the room overhead. "I'm going to have a great summer."

"Well, if you're sure . . ."

"I'm sure!"

"Then I have some news."

"What is it? Good news, I hope."

"Absolutely. Are you sitting down?"

"Yes."

"I got engaged last night."

"Gerri! You don't mean it!"

"Yes, I do. Jon proposed. I know this happened fast, but he's just as wonderful as I told you after our first date. He's everything I ever wanted. Charming, sexy, handsome, kind, successful."

"Sounds like the ideal man."

"Oh, he is. I can't believe I was so lucky to find him."

"Hey, he's the lucky one," Linda said with a laugh. And she meant it. Gerri was a truly kind, intelligent and loyal person. She was also drop-dead gorgeous, with a slim, athletic figure and straight, almost black hair.

"I wanted to tell you the good news, and also that we've decided to visit Jon's parents in St. Augustine to tell them next weekend. If you're going to be at the beach house, I thought maybe we could stop by so you could meet each other."

"That's a great idea. I can't wait." Linda felt tears of joy build behind her eyes, but she told herself not to cry. Gerri would be convinced that something was wrong, since Linda almost never cried. Today had just been so damn emotional. Her best friend getting married made Linda think of her own single status, her upcoming 30th birthday, and her inability to find a man with whom she was willing to spend the rest of her life. Not that she didn't look. And date. And hope. Somehow, the relationships just never seemed . . . right.

They aren't William, added a little voice inside her head.

"Don't worry. Someday you'll find your own Mr. Right." Gerri must have heard the yearning in Linda's voice. Either that or she'd picked up some more "vibes."

"Well, I probably won't discover him locked away in one of Grandmother's boxes. By now, he'd be a bit moldy."

"Very funny." Gerri paused. "I can't wait to visit," she said, her tone more serious.

"Do you know what day?"

"No, not yet. Why don't I just call you from St. Augustine and let you know?"

"I'll try to work you into my schedule," Linda said with good-natured sarcasm.

"You'd better. If you approach cleaning out that house like you do constructing a history course, you may end up with more junk than when you started."

"I resent that," Linda said with mock outrage.

"Yes, but you don't deny it. I've never seen anyone who found dusty old relics and boring diaries so fascinating."

"It's a dirty job—"

"Yeah, I know." Gerri laughed again. "I'll call you in a week or ten days and let you know our plans. I've never met Jon's parents, so I don't know how they'll take the news."

"They'll love you. You're a dream daughter-in-law."

"Spoken like a true friend."

"I'll talk to you soon. Give your fiancé a kiss for me."

"Only on the cheek. I'm saving the rest for myself."

Linda laughed and pushed herself off the bed. "Have a great trip. Call me soon."

Gerri said good-bye. Linda held the phone to her ear, even after she heard the click on the other end and the dial tone. The house suddenly seemed too quiet, now that the laughter and conversation had faded away. She suddenly wished that Gerri was here with her, spending time together as they had when they were younger. They could bake brownies, watch talk shows and comment on the problems of others, laugh about movies or discuss politics. They'd stay up late and eat popcorn until their stomachs ached, then open the window upstairs and drop water balloons onto the deck.

Yes, that's what they do if Gerri was here. But she wasn't. And they weren't teenagers any longer. Linda reminded herself again that she was here for a reason: to go through her grandmother's things and decide what to do with the house. That was why she'd taken the summer off from a teaching job she loved, spending time in South Carolina instead of England or France.

At least she'd taken the first step. She looked upward toward the attic, glad she'd forced herself to walk up those stairs and open that door. In a few weeks, she'd tackle the things stored on the third floor. For now, she'd leave the dust motes to dance in private and the memories to stay right where they were.

Gifford Knight stepped through the glass doors of the airport terminal and was immediately assaulted by the heat and humidity of Savannah. Shuttle vans and taxicabs idled at the curb, contributing to high temperatures and air pollution. Sweat formed, dampening his forehead and upper lip. Giff thought the perspiration was probably caused as much by anticipation as by his inappropriate clothing.

He should have planned better for this trip, even though it had been an impulsive decision. The sports coat, black shirt and lightweight wool slacks, comfortable for the cool temperatures of San Francisco, trapped the heat of the southern climate. Even the air seemed heavy. He should have remembered that from his previous trips to the South.

His thick hair, left long like so many of the creative movie people he'd dealt with recently, clung to his neck. He hadn't even tied it back. He knew he looked as out of place here, in this historic Southern town, as he felt. Yet he would gladly pay the price if coming here meant finding the woman he was destined to love.

He hadn't liked California—was glad to leave it. The only reason he'd gone to Los Angeles in the first place was because a studio had offered to pay him quite a large sum to consult on the historical details of a script in production. As soon as he'd finished, he'd driven up the coast to San Francisco, hoping it was more to his liking. But it wasn't. At times it seemed he didn't really have a home. England was just a memory, really.

Giff lifted his face to the sun, breathing deeply.

Too busy. Too populated.

The exhaust of cabs and cars blended with the fragrance of lush, semi-tropical plants and pine trees, but that wasn't the scent he sought. For the past several months it seemed as though *she* was trying to reach out to him. He didn't know her name or where she lived, but she existed, just as surely as he'd lived and died many times. So had she, although she probably didn't know it. He would explain everything to her, when the time was right—if he lived that long.

Just a few days ago there had been an increased urgency to their subconscious connection. So he'd followed his instincts to the Atlantic coast, seeking a place caressed by the fresh smell of the sea, an isolated area of picturesque, older homes and part-time residents.

He remembered fragments of dreams as a young man of 20, brief images of a lonely stretch of sand that nestled between ceaseless waves and wind-tossed sea grass, of light and laughter that called to him across countless years. Images seen through her eyes, emotions shaped by her life. Soon he would find her. Soon he would make her his own, forever.

The shuttle to the rental car lot pulled up and he entered the air-conditioned darkness, grateful for the modern convenience. Nodding to the driver, he settled in a bench seat, his black leather suitcase and matching, odd-shaped bag beside him, and wished he knew exactly where he was going. And what he would find when he arrived. But then, the thrill of this discovery exhilarated him liked nothing else he'd done before.

He saw the driver, a middle-aged man with wrinkled skin and a bulbous nose, eye the long, cylindrical bag.

"You're a hunter, huh?"

Giff looked at the bag, knowing what the man thought. That he carried a shotgun or a rifle. But the man was wrong.

"You could say that," he replied, looking away from the driver's curious glance and out the window. It still amazed him how Americans accepted the carrying of weapons, as though a gun could keep one safe from all the dangers of the world.

In such an open society, they were probably the least suspicious people in the world—except for residents of New York City.

The driver remained silent for the rest of the short trip, taking the hint, Giff thought, that he didn't want to talk.

After locating his rental car, Giff drove north on 1-95, passing the turnoff for Hilton Head Island about an hour after landing in Savannah. He kept on driving, the black Cadillac matching his mood perfectly. Dignified and quiet, it purred along the highway, eating up the miles, leaving his senses free to concentrate on his destination.

He was getting closer, he thought, feeling the rising excitement that only came from the quest. Sundown bathed the world in a pink glow, and suddenly he realized that he was not getting closer. He slowed the car, trying to feel the direction, trying to find his goal. Ahead, an exit loomed, indicating a route east.

Yes, closer to the ocean. Closer to the lonely beach.

Giff drove through Charleston in the darkness, tempted to stop for the night but feeling more focused on his destination than ever before. Elation ran through him like a steady current of electricity, and he felt the energy that made him different, that some said made him more than strange. He didn't care.

He was close. Tonight, his instincts wouldn't fail him.

The crescent moon rose above the treetops as he drove through the national forest.

Go slow.

He eased off the accelerator, letting the car glide silently through the blackness. A sign loomed into the headlights, indicating the town limits of a nearby small community, population 1,253. Giff braked, pulling to the side of the road.

While his hands gripped the wheel, he closed his eyes and concentrated.

So close. So lonely and sad.

He opened his eyes and smiled into the night. Faintly, he saw the neon sign of a motor court ahead on his right, flashing "vacancy." Sure of his goal, he eased ahead, toward the sound of the surf and the destiny that awaited him.

If he was right, if she had called to him, then he only had ten days to find her. And maybe only ten days to live.

If he had eyes, they would now be open. If he had lips, he would curl them into a smile. But he had neither, suspended in this nothing place between heaven and hell, between the reality of earth and the eternity of space.

Mord had sensed the ripple of energy when the woman approached the place of her greatest fear. She'd been close, so very close. But she hadn't touched *it,* either not aware or too frightened. He knew her purpose in returning as clearly as if she'd whispered it to him. She'd been drawn back to the house by death and fear, two powerful enticements.

Already the excitement began to build. He had plans to make. He'd draw someone close, someone who would innocently touch the board and release him from this limbo. Someone unaware of the threat, who would let him seep into his consciousness, slowly, surely, until nothing human remained.

A male body, he thought. Because at this moment, if he had flesh and bone, he'd feel the blood soar through his veins, the rush of sexual excitement that was so much a part of being human. He'd become so aroused that he'd want to bury himself in the woman while she slept, terrify her with his presence. She'd never know what possessed her.

It would be joyous, to fulfill his own fantasies. But he couldn't, not yet. Not until he had a body and a mind that could be bent to his will. The damned laws of his black, formless universe limited his power to a mere fraction, to subtle suggestions most humans believed were their own ideas.

Humans. Weak creatures though they were, he enjoyed living in their world. No, more than that. He craved it. Craved their appetites, fed on their fears. He reveled in their pain, took delight in their confusion and suspicions. They were a virtual feast for his desires.

Too bad he couldn't stay in their world forever. Too bad their very appeal would eventually drain him, send him back to this place until one of their souls called him forth again.

Mord searched the energy for the man. A faint ripple was all he felt, which meant he was close also, although not yet near the woman. *Come closer, little man. Come and meet your own true love. Come and meet your destiny.*

Yes. Mord thought, *come and meet me.*

If he had a mouth, he would have laughed. *Soon*, he thought. *Soon I'll have it all . . . again. For now, dream of me, fair maiden. Think of me . . . and remember.*

Linda awoke in a panic, sweating, pulse racing, muscles primed for flight. She listened. Except for her labored breathing, the house sat quietly in the darkness. From outside, she faintly heard waves beating against the shore and the breeze blowing gently, just strong enough to stir the tinkling wind chimes on the deck. Inside, she tried to calm herself, but felt an irrational fear that something terrible crouched just outside her consciousness, ready to leap into the open when she least expected it. When all remained quiet, she turned on the bedside lamp and pulled the sheet up with her as she leaned back against the headboard.

Then she remembered—she'd had the nightmare again. Even though she was safe in her bedroom, she felt a chill that had nothing to do with the summer night. Coming back to this house, visiting the attic, thinking about Gerri, had brought forth the fear. She closed her eyes, unable to keep the memory from playing like a familiar yet terrifying movie.

The Ouija board pointer jerked, throwing Gerri and her off balance and rattling the card table. "What in the world!" Gerri exclaimed, her eyes round as she stared ahead. "Linda, what's going on?"

"I have no idea." The pointer darted back and forth, finally beginning to spell. Inside the attic room, a chill penetrated, bringing with it a metallic smell, laced with just a hint of acrid smoke and damp earth. Both girls went as still as statues.

Linda called out the letters. "I . . . A . . . M . . . M . . . O . . . R . . . D." She paused, shivering beneath the chill that had intensified in the room. "I am Mord," she whispered, then the pointer went crazy, going again and again to "yes."

"Linda, I'm scared."

"So am I."

"We should quit right now."

"I want to know who this is, and what happened to William."

"Let's just leave."

"Not yet." Linda shivered again, then asked, "Is William there?"

The pointer jerked wildly to "no." Linda asked, "Where is William?" and silently mouthed the reply as it was erratically spelled. "Dead," she whispered when the pointer ceased moving.

"Did you kill him?" she asked on a hunch.

"K . . . I . . . L . . . L . . . K . . . I . . . L . . . L . . . K . . . I—"

That terrible spirit, or whatever it was, had radiated evil. The chill had invaded the room, flashing images of horror and death, smelling of blood and gunpowder. Right after the awful event had occurred, she'd tried to tell herself that what she and Gerri had experienced was nothing more than mass hysteria brought on by their overactive imaginations. Sometimes she'd just about convince herself that wood and paper and paint didn't make a device that let you communicate with the dead.

That things really didn't go bump in the night.

Then, weeks or months or even years later, she'd have the nightmare again. She'd be shaken, stay up late, and refuse to sleep. She'd tell herself that nothing supernatural had occurred. Surely these experiences had a basis in reality, perhaps in reading an article that the conscious mind forgot—or, as her parents used to say, eating spicy foods too close to bedtime. They hadn't believed in the supernatural. An overactive imagination, her dad always said. Her mother called it silliness. Whatever it was, Linda had no idea why it both fascinated and scared her.

Glancing at the bedside clock, groaning when it registered only 3:17, she wondered if she'd be able to go back to sleep. She lay there for what seemed like an eternity, staring into the darkness, trying to unwind and failing to relax her tight muscles.

Hot chocolate was the answer, she decided a few moments later, the cure to whatever ailments one might suffer in the middle of the night. She threw off the sheet and swung her legs to the floor, wincing at the sound of creaking boards. As a child, if she'd gotten out of bed in the middle of the night, she'd crept softly to keep from waking her grandmother. She kept telling herself that now there was no one to hear the sounds of the old house, or even care what she did inside the privacy of its walls.

It took several minutes to find the can of cocoa, to heat milk over the gas stove her grandmother never would replace with a newer version or, heaven forbid, a microwave. Linda smiled at the thought of her feisty grandmother refusing to use all the appliances and gadgets her family had tried to foist on her over the years. Tomorrow, Linda vowed, she'd make a trip to Mr. Watley's grocery for some food that was easy to fix. Maybe even splurge on some of those modern conveniences if she felt like driving into a town large enough to boast of an appliance store or discount house.

Finally the milk reached the right temperature and Linda made the hot chocolate, breathing in the rich smell and wishing she had a big, fat marshmallow to float on top. She blew on the mug, wrapped her hands around it and walked to the French doors leading to the deck. The night tempted her with thousands of stars and a sharply defined half moon. Faint light skimmed across the waves. It was safe on the beach. This wasn't New York or Chicago, where a woman couldn't get a breath of air in the middle of the night. Slowly, she turned the dead-bolt lock and eased open the door.

The sound of the surf and the smell of the beach assaulted her, while the breeze molded her long, white gown around her legs and plastered it against her stomach. Her nipples puckered with the coolness and she grasped the hot mug, drawing heat and comfort from it, sipping the rich chocolate. The night, which had seemed so calm and familiar while she stood safely inside the house, took on another persona.

Wild. Free. She had the strangest urge to rip off her gown, to run naked into the waves and revel in the mysteries of life.

I'm not a history professor, she longed to shout. *I'm a Druid Priestess, a pagan witch. I'm not afraid of anything, of anyone, dead or alive.*

But she didn't She put the mug down and stood at the railing, holding the rough wood until splinters pressed into her palms. Her eyes focused on the waves, on their rhythmic caresses against the sand, and she wished she knew how to free the wild spirit that swelled inside her.

It wasn't until she blinked that she saw him, appearing at the water's edge, maybe 50 feet away. He wore black, with very long dark hair ruffled by the wind, streaking across his face so she couldn't see his features. He was nothing more than an outline, illuminated by the moon and faint light from her windows, and it took her a minute to know he was real.

He did nothing more than stand there and look at her, but somehow, it seemed the most threatening thing in the whole world. In her fantasy dreams of William Howard, *he'd* been on a beach, returning to her from the war. His face had always appeared vague, as though she looked at him through heavy, wavy glass or rippling water. She'd never seen his features. In her dreams, she'd loved him passionately, fiercely, eternally. But those were just dreams, made real only by her girlish fascination. She was a woman now, facing reality. Watching a real man stare at her.

And then the panic hit, the fear that she *was* alone, vulnerable, standing on a deck without neighbors or police or even a gun nearby. That this man, whoever he was, could run up the beach and be on the deck before she had the opportunity to dash inside and bolt the door. And that even a lock couldn't keep someone out if they wanted in badly enough.

He look a step toward her.

Her heart seemed to leap inside her chest. She backed away from the rail, resisting the urge to run, afraid to look away from the stranger on the beach. He stopped and stood like a statue, with only his blowing hair giving away his status as a flesh-and-blood man. A man who could be a rapist, a murderer . . . or just an innocent insomniac.

Whoever he was, he wasn't the man in her dreams.

When she bumped into the entrance, she jumped, looking away from him finally and focusing on the lock. Her hands trembled and each breath made her chest ache as she stumbled inside and shut the door. The dead bolt slid smoothly into the latch. The sound of the sea and the smell of the beach were locked out, along with the stranger who'd stared at her as she had stared at him.

Linda backed away from the doorway, then fled across the room to the fireplace. She didn't turn on the light; she was afraid he would be able to see her through the windows. Fumbling in the dark, hands shaking, she grabbed the handle of the poker. It felt cool and solid in her hand. She pulled it from the holder, hefting the weight like a sword.

No one tried to get in the door. Slowly, Linda backed from the room, bumping into the recliner and ottoman. She ran up the steps to the second floor and through her doorway, pulling down the shades and drawing the curtains closed in the childishly decorated bedroom. Only then did she risk turning on a light. After laying the fireplace poker within reach on the bed, she huddled beneath the gingham covers as though she might be safe if only he didn't see her. She listened to every sound, half-expecting a turn of the knob or a creaking board.

Nothing stirred. Gradually, her pounding heart slowed and her breathing returned to almost normal. But she couldn't force herself to turn off the light. It burned, bright and constant, until the sun rose over the Atlantic and she fell into an exhausted sleep.

Chapter Two

A strong passion for any object will ensure success, for the desire of the end will point out the means.
—William Hazlitt

"Anything else for you today, Linda?"

She looked at the apples, orange juice, canned food and chocolate-chip cookies, wishing for some microwave dinners that she could nuke—if only her grandmother's house had a microwave oven. She really should drive to an appliance store and get one. Maybe tomorrow, if she managed to get a good night's sleep tonight. Last night's horrible dream and the unexpected man on the beach had caused her a sleepless night and "the jitters," as her grandmother used to say.

"No, that's all, Mr. Watley."

The small, cinder-block grocery was the closest store to the beach, and had been here for as long as Linda could remember. As a young child she'd come here with her grandmother, then when she got older, she'd ridden her bike over the two-lane blacktop. It was comforting to know that other than a few more wrinkles on Mr. Watley's pink-cheeked face and the greater variety of candy at the checkout counter, very little had changed in over 20 years. That fact helped calm her nerves and introduced normalcy back into the morning.

She paid her bill and said good-bye, turned with a smile on her face, and almost ran into the customer behind her. She gasped, taking in a deep breath. One hand went up automatically to steady herself, coming to rest intimately on the solid chest of a man who smelled of her deepest, darkest fantasies.

Her purse strap slipped off her shoulder and the grocery bag tilted in her arms. His hands reached out to steady her—strong, tanned hands that seemed to scorch her flesh. She closed her eyes, feeling a jolt of dizziness that passed quickly but left her with a shock of intense emotion so strong she couldn't even identify it. She opened her eyes, realizing that she came barely to his shoulder.

"Allow me."

His voice sounded soft but strong, a deep, lulling timbre that reminded Linda of the resonance felt and heard from the bass notes of a pipe organ. For some reason she didn't want to look up from the loose, gray-striped, cotton shirt that appeared much too sophisticated for South Carolina, afraid of what she would see—and feel—by gazing into his eyes. Never before had she experienced such an unsettling reaction to a man.

But such apprehension was ridiculous, nothing more than a holdover from yesterday afternoon and last night. She was standing in Watley's Grocery in the middle of the day!

She blinked, then let her eyes roam up the open neckline of the collarless shirt, past the tanned expanse of his chest and neck. His jaw looked solid and chiseled, his lips sculpted but not too full, his nose classic. His dark hair was thick but not too long, swept back from his forehead and curving over the tops of his ears like a lazy black cat. But his eyes! Dark, bottomless brown, they burned into hers with what she briefly thought was an intense spark of recognition.

She must have been mistaken. She'd never seen this man before. If she had, she would have remembered. The only stranger she'd seen lately was the man on the beach last night. His hair had been longer, and maybe he wasn't as tall as this man.

His eyebrows relaxed from a scowling position and his nostrils flared. He looked as though he wanted to say something important, but he remained silent, still holding her enthralled by his touch and his eyes. Even though his hands were warm, she felt a shiver run through her.

"Linda, you okay?"

Mr. Watley's question startled her. Of course she wasn't okay. She hadn't been since she set foot in her grandmother's house the day before yesterday. And now she'd literally run into this man, quite possibly the best-looking man she'd ever seen.

"I'm fine, Mr. Watley. Just clumsy." Even though she willed herself to look away, her eyes refused to break contact with the man still holding her arms.

"It's my fault, I'm sure," the man said in that remarkable voice. "I stood too close."

"You can let go now," Linda whispered. "I'm okay. Really."

He eased his hands away in a way that reminded Linda of a lover's caress, as though reluctant to let her go. The warm sensation remained, however, spreading throughout her body. She finally managed to tear her gaze away, feeling the blush that was no doubt creeping over her cheeks, embarrassed by her unusual reaction. He must think that she was a real airhead, since she'd seemed so girlishly impressed by his looks and his presence.

"And who might you be, young man?" Mr. Watley asked, peering over the tops of his bifocals.

"Gifford Knight." He answered Mr. Watley's question, but looked at Linda as he spoke.

"The writer?" she asked, awed that this could be the man who wrote the most vivid, stirring historical novels and biographies she'd ever read. He captured history as no other author, making readers believe that they had actually traveled back in time and were living the lives of the characters. He was famous, a person who appeared on morning television shows and best-seller lists.

"You know my work?"

"I've read every book. They're wonderful." The

words slipped out before she could think. She wanted to impress him with her maturity and sophistication, but all her social skills and good sense seemed to be on temporary vacation.

"Thank you." He continued to look at her as though he'd just discovered a valuable treasure. That was ridiculous, of course. She knew she didn't inspire that type of reaction in men with her pleasant, but not what she'd call beautiful, face and rather short, ordinary body. Normally, she considered herself attractive, but today she didn't look all that great, due to the sleepless night and the stress of returning to her grandmother's house. But even as she tried to ground herself firmly in reality, she found her mind racing for topics of conversation, just to talk with him a while longer.

"I especially enjoyed the series on England's colonialist period. I've used it as a recommended text," she said in a breathless, throaty voice that didn't sound at all like her normal tone.

"You're a teacher?"

"A professor of history . . . at Northwestern University, just outside of Chicago. Linda O'Rourke."

"Linda," he whispered. "Yes, that suits you."

"Excuse me?"

His expression changed, going from intense to charming in the flash of an eye. "Dr. O'Rourke, I'm pleased to meet you." He raised her hand and kissed her knuckles, a courtly gesture. She wondered if he used it on all females. Did every woman have the same reaction to him, or was she just different?

"Why are you here?" she asked in a whisper as he released her hand. But then she realized how rude—how silly—her question sounded. It had popped out of her mouth before she could stop. "I'm sorry, I didn't mean—"

"That's quite all right. I'm here doing some personal research."

"For a new book?"

"Quite probably not."

She realized he had a slight accent, an upper-class British inflection that added to his mystique—and his attraction. She'd kidded Gerri yesterday about finding "Mr. Right" among Grandmother's boxes. But not in her wildest dreams had she anticipated finding a potentially perfect man in Mr. Watley's grocery store!

"And where're you staying, Mr. Knight?" Mr. Watley asked with a defensive attitude that Linda found charming. Two gentlemen, albeit one who must be 70, facing off over the damsel in distress. She barely suppressed a smile at the idea. She must have been immersed in history texts too long.

"I rented a house on the beach this morning."

"Then you must have just arrived," Linda commented, hoping she didn't sound too interested, too intrigued, just because he was the sexiest man she'd ever met. "I mean, you weren't here last night." *You weren't the man on the beach last night,* she prayed silently.

"I drove here early this morning." His words seemed somehow intimate, for her ears alone.

"Maybe we're neighbors."

"I imagine we are."

"I'm staying at my grandmother's house. It's the light blue two-story with the dormer windows in the attic."

"I've seen it."

He must have seen it as he looked at rental houses. He fell silent, staring at her, making her feel so self-conscious she wondered if she wore the effects of last night's scare like a badge. She wished he'd volunteer the location of his house, but she wouldn't dare ask, and had no idea which houses were even available for summer rentals. And she mentally chastised herself for being so interested.

"May I walk you to your car?" he asked politely, his arm already touching her elbow.

"Yes . . . of course." She glanced away from his eyes to smile at Mr. Watley. "Thanks. I'll see you in a day or two."

"You make sure you do, young lady," he said with a hint of threat, looking at Gifford Knight, "or I'll come searching for you."

Linda wasn't about to castigate him for being cautious. Protectiveness seemed to be a trait of older men, those with whom she worked and those she knew socially. They all wanted to safeguard her. She wondered how in the world she gave anyone the impression that she needed to be looked after.

She stopped abruptly. "You forgot to get whatever it was you needed," she told Gifford Knight.

"I can come back later."

"Please, don't go out of your way on my account."

"It's no trouble."

She started to say something else, but then Gifford Knight steered her toward the smudged glass door of the small grocery. She mentally shrugged, wondering at the eccentricities of the literary elite. They were reputedly even odder than the academic elite. "My car is the blue Oldsmobile over there," she informed him.

"A sensible choice."

She thought she detected a trace of a smile, a bit of sarcasm, but wasn't sure. When she glanced around the parking lot, she saw no trace of another vehicle besides Mr. Watley's old pickup. "Where's your . . ."

"I walked."

"Then your house must be close." The words slipped out before she could remind herself not to pry, not to be rude to this distinguished literary figure.

"Not far. I enjoy walking."

She took another look at him, standing tall beside her. If his hair were longer, his clothes darker, he could have been the man on the beach last night. But that was being too suspicious. Besides, the man hadn't harmed her last night. It was her own nervousness, her nightmare, that had caused the panic. And if Gifford Knight were the man on the beach, he would have said something, wouldn't he?

"Yes," she said, distracted by the many questions and emotions running through her mind, "so do I." She opened the door, then searched in her purse for her keys.

"You don't lock your car?"

"In front of Mr. Watley's grocery? I hardly think it's necessary."

"Perhaps not," he said, taking the bag from her arms and putting it in the back seat. "But it doesn't hurt to be careful."

"I appreciate your concern, Mr. Knight, but—"

"Please, call me Giff."

"Somehow, that doesn't seem right. I mean, you're a famous author. I . . . well, I don't know you well."

"Then we'll have to get to know each other better."

He said it as a statement of fact, despite the polite wording of the reply. Linda felt a shiver run through her, but whether it was from awareness of him as a man or a famous person or something else, she couldn't decide.

"Perhaps a walk on the beach?" he suggested when she remained silent.

"Yes, perhaps." Even as she gave that tentative answer, his choice of "the beach" made her remember last night. The fear. The panic. And she looked at him again, wondering how she could be both suspicious of and attracted to such a extraordinary man.

"Do you prefer dawn or dusk?" His voice was soft, seductive, and Linda felt herself being pulled toward him as though she were in the powerful undertow of the sea. She tried to imagine meeting him at dawn, but the vision blurred until she saw them together, entwined on cool sheets, watching the sun rise over the Atlantic.

"Dusk, I think," she said, feeling her cheeks turn warm. She prayed he didn't notice, or, if he did, that he wouldn't comment.

"Then perhaps you would allow me to prepare dinner, maybe something on the grill."

"A cookout?"

"I believe that is the common term," he answered with a smile and that subtle sarcasm—no, teasing—that she was just beginning to identify.

Should she? He was the most exciting, most intriguing man she'd met in a long time. Maybe ever. Yet she didn't know him.

"I'm perfectly safe," he said patiently, smiling, as though he could read her mind and understood her trepidations. The man fairly exuded sexual chemistry. How could he expect to be considered "safe"?

"Do you come with references?" she asked. Luckily, he couldn't guess that she was only half kidding.

"Do you really need them?" he replied easily, looking down at her, intent again.

She searched his face. He wasn't the man on the beach. He was a noted historian, an author of international renown. "No, I don't suppose I do." She slid into the driver's seat.

"Then come by around seven."

"Where?"

"To the house I rented." He gently shut the door, then stepped back from the car. "Two down from you."

Linda thought for a moment, trying to imagine the homes near her grandmother's house. A picture of a realtor's sign in front of a quaint, rose-colored Victorian cottage, complete with ruffled curtains and a heart-shaped welcome sign, sprang to mind.

"Not the Mannington place?"

He smiled slightly. "I believe the realtor may have mentioned that name."

Linda grinned at the image of such a darkly intense man occupying the cozy, fussy, gingerbread cottage. It struck her as hilarious that if the interior was decorated in the same style as the exterior, Gifford Knight would truly be a man out of his element. She laughed, harder and longer than she had in forever, until her ribs ached and the laughs subsided into jerky little hiccups. Her laughter was no doubt a relief of nervous tension, but, she thought, still rude.

"I'm glad my humble home delights you," he finally said with that trace of humor.

"I'm sorry, but I just imagined you . . ." Linda said between chuckles.

"Yes, it boggles the mind. Seven, then?"

She wiped her eyes, still smiling, nodded and said again, "I'm sorry."

"Don't be," he said, his expression surprisingly tender. "I haven't seen anyone laugh like that in a long while."

"Even if it was at your expense?"

He leaned closer, capturing her hand through the open window of the car. "For you, dear Linda, nothing has too great an expense." He kissed her fingers again, his expression sexy and threatening and exciting. "Seven. Then we'll walk along the beach at dusk, and you can tell me where you've been all my life."

"Mr. Knight, that sounds amazingly like a come-on."

He straightened, his smile fading. "Trust me. Nothing is more important to me than learning everything about you." He paused, making her wonder at the kind of man who could radiate such charm, such power, that she was willing to forgo all her caution while at the same time he urged her to be careful. "Until this evening, Linda." And with that he turned, walking away across the parking lot with controlled grace. He looked as out of place as a shark in a dolphin show, yet she'd been drawn to him as though she'd known him forever.

It must be his books. She'd read them all and surely had learned something about the man. Before meeting him, she would have assumed him to be older, less intense, but with a sharp mind and vivid imagination. Certainly not sexy! Yet despite the intensity, he seemed polite, even courtly. And Mr. Watley knew Gifford Knight was interested in her. She was safe. It was just that nightmare last night, then the scare on the beach. Her nerves were unreliable, stretched to the limit, but she instinctively felt she could trust him.

Tonight, she thought with a small shiver, she'd learn if she really could believe in her instincts.

Giff dropped a match into the coals, watching the flames spread over the charcoal with a fervor matched only by his pursuit of destiny. Undulating waves of heat, pushed on by dancing fingers of orange and red, covered the bottom of the grill. Soon the coals would burn hotter than the fire, until there was nothing left but ashes.

His composure, his concentration, had almost gone up in flames this morning. The instant she'd turned and touched his chest, he'd experienced a lifetime of emotions, from exhilaration to excitement to a sense of completion that left him humbled. That he would feel a sense of rightness when they met, he'd never doubted. That he would crave her with an all-consuming physical and emotional desire, he hadn't expected. Their past hadn't developed to the point of passion; either that, or he didn't recall such intense emotion.

Linda O'Rourke made him burn more than he would have believed possible only days ago. He'd known her presence was strong; it had called to him across an ocean, across a continent. But this need, tempered by tenderness and caring, was something entirely new. With her innocent face, rippling, soft brown hair and sea-green eyes, she'd become a flesh-and-blood woman in the blink of an eye. A woman he wanted on more levels than he'd ever thought existed.

He should have remained more detached, more focused. But one touch of his hand to her skin and he'd been lost to a passion that burned as quickly, as fiercely, as the coals. Now he must go slow, as difficult as that seemed, to present himself as an eligible, interested vacationer so she would find him attractive and desirable.

Very early this morning, he'd walked along the dark, deserted beach, unable to rest when he was so close to his destined mate. She'd called to him, although she didn't know it. She'd been upset, so nervous and restless that she'd been staring at the ocean when she should have been in bed, fast asleep. Yet when he'd first seen her, he could only stand and stare, which had alarmed her. And then he'd taken a step forward, unable to stop himself. She'd fled inside, more scared than ever.

Because he needed to build her trust, he couldn't tell her that he had been the one who frightened her. So before meeting with the realtor, he'd cut his long hair and discarded the black clothes he preferred. He'd let Linda believe the man on the beach was an unknown element, while Gifford Knight was a known entity, a respected writer who found her utterly charming.

He poked the charcoal with the long metal fork, stirring the embers into a frenzy of swirling sparks, and smiled. If it were in his power to control fate, their love would finally be consummated. No longer would he suffer from eternal frustration and denial. This time, this life, they'd be together. And nothing on earth or in hell would keep them apart.

The early evening breeze shifted the gauzy, blue and green cotton skirt against Linda's legs as she walked toward Gifford Knight's rented beach cottage. She'd considered two other outfits before deciding on this two-piece dress, which was casual yet feminine. Her hair also blew in the wind, untamed except for two combs holding the curly mass away from her temples. Elegant hairstyles were hopeless, she knew, yet she wished for once she could look a little more sophisticated, especially for dinner with an author she'd admired for years—a man she'd just met, but whom she felt a deep yearning to know much better.

She shouldn't be so excited by a simple, neighborly gesture of a cookout. Okay, so he'd seemed very attracted to her. Maybe he was that way around all the women he met. Maybe he was a natural flirt, or had been taught to be inherently gracious to everyone. He was certainly polite to Mr. Watley, even though the grocer had been slightly suspicious of the tall, dark stranger.

Well, maybe Mr. Watley had a point. Perhaps she should have thought twice about such an intimate, isolated occasion for a "first date"—if she could even call it that. Her gold and white sandals dangled from her fingers as her steps slowed, delaying the moment when she would knock on the door of the Mannington cottage. She needed to see if her eyes had deceived her this morning, if Gifford Knight was really that compelling, that mysterious and sexy.

She looked over the sandy dune to the house, smelling the unmistakable aroma of steaks charring on a grill. In response, her stomach rumbled and her fears began to dissipate. There was nothing sinister in having dinner together. He wasn't the man who had frightened her last night, since he'd only arrived that morning. They were two adults. She could always say "no" if things progressed too rapidly. He was a gentleman.

But the problem wasn't him, she finally realized. He might be a gentleman, but could she act like a "lady" when faced with his sexual charm? Instead of going on forever with her doubts, she put one foot in front of the other and trudged through the thick sand, up the wood steps, and followed her nose onto the gingerbread-decorated deck around the side of the cottage.

"Hello," he said before she had a chance to speak. He was also dressed casually, in white this time, which made his tan skin and almost-black hair even more striking. His shirt fit loosely and reminded Linda of a pirate. His cotton slacks were pressed neatly, creased and spotless. And his bare feet were tanned, long and elegant.

"Good evening." She smiled, moving closer to the grill and peering at the steaks. How had he known she wasn't a vegetarian or some finicky eater who was too concerned with cholesterol to enjoy red meat? Had he taken one look at her less-than-skinny body and decided she liked food a bit too much? Or, she wondered, grinning inwardly, could he really read her mind as she'd suspected earlier?

"They look wonderful," she said, tearing her eyes away from the searing meat. "I'm hungry."

"So am I," he said softly, smiling intimately. She blushed as she imagined him nibbling on something more personal than steak. He didn't seem to notice her newfound tendency to turn red at the drop of a hat. He reached into a silver wine cooler and produced a bottle of chardonnay. Without asking, he poured a glass for each of them, handing her one so their fingers had to touch.

He was doing it again, she realized. Effortlessly pulling her toward the magnetism he generated. So smooth, so seductive. A woman could get used to this type of attention without ever considering that it was fleeting. That he'd probably be gone in a few days or weeks, at the most, leaving her wanting what no one else had ever been able to provide. She'd had several relationships with men, starting in her freshman year at college, but each had left her feeling vaguely dissatisfied. The men she'd chosen had been nice; she'd shared many interests with them. She could talk to them for hours, go to parties, dinner, movies. It was the true intimacy that she'd never felt with another soul. The kind of sharing that she'd read about, that she'd imagined with William. Perhaps that kind of bonding wasn't any more real than some historical legends or religious fables.

She didn't think of herself as gullible when it came to people. She wasn't weak-willed. Friends didn't talk her into doing things or going places against her wishes. Yet from the moment she'd met Gifford Knight, she'd felt her free will slip away, almost as though they were two magnets being pulled together by an unseen but very real force. It was upsetting to feel swept away by something unusual, but she wanted to pursue a relationship or at least see if the attraction was as mutual as it seemed.

She wondered if he had any inkling of how much she'd thought about him since this morning.

If he had orchestrated this attraction . . . well, it would be frightening to think a man could intentionally exert such control over another person.

"Thank you," she said, taking the glass, brushing her fingers against his and feeling the current that sizzled as surely as the steaks on the grill.

"I'm not much of a cook," he said, putting down the meat fork and moving closer to her.

Her blood pressure seemed to rise. She resisted the urge to step back. *Try to act sophisticated,* she told herself. "But you're a terrific writer."

He smiled and stopped the movement of her glass toward her suddenly dry lips by placing one hand gently but firmly on her wrist.

"Let's make a toast."

She tilted her head and smiled back, lowering the wine. "To?"

"To us. To the start of a beautiful relationship."

He hesitated before sipping, looking at her expectantly, as though he thought she might not drink to such a strong sentiment. But she would fool him, she thought, raising her own glass slowly. If he was playing a game, she would be aware, watchful. If he wasn't . . . Lord help her.

"To us," she whispered, taking a sip, letting the glass rest against her lower lip and imagining a lover's kiss instead. The wine tasted cool and crisp, quenching her thirst but leaving her hungry for other delicacies, reckless and dangerous fare. "Can I help?"

"Thank you, no. Everything is ready. Just relax and enjoy."

She watched him efficiently turn the steaks. He

brought steamed broccoli and baked potatoes to the table, setting them in the center with smooth efficiency.

The patio table was set with china on a pale pink linen cloth, and she was sure the flatware was sterling. It must have come with the cottage, she guessed. Even though the sky wasn't yet dark, candles burned in hurricane lamps, giving the dinner a romantic twist. The whole evening seemed too perfect, too contrived, yet she didn't know how to voice her concerns, or if she was being irrational.

"Don't look a gift horse in the mouth," she whispered as she watched him walk outside, carrying a basket of fragrant, warm rolls from the kitchen.

He smiled slightly. "I'm sorry. What did you say?"

She flashed him what she hoped was an innocent, big smile. "Nothing. Just talking to myself."

"Ahh, I see you also like intelligent conversation."

She laughed at his joke. "You do it too, then?"

"Sometimes. Writing can be a lonely profession."

"So I've imagined." But she also envisioned his non-writing hours filled with other pursuits. Taking glamourous women out on the town. Arranging other candlelit dinners. *Stop it,* she told herself. She wasn't the jealous type. She couldn't imagine what was putting such thoughts into her head.

She felt shaken by the new emotions flashing through her mind. She wasn't sure she could get through dinner without saying something too revealing about her attraction to him. She felt as though her nerve endings danced along the red-hot grill, constantly being singed by his nearness.

But somehow she managed to sit down, spreading her napkin over her lap and looking at him across the table. Shadows from nearby trees floated over the tablecloth. Candlelight danced across the planes of his face, deepening his eyes, giving him a mysterious quality that caused her heart to beat a little faster. She told herself that he was naturally sexy, not acting out some role. By the time he opened a bottle of red wine, to go with the steaks, and poured some into her glass, she'd convinced herself that her fears were unfounded.

Go for it, the little voice inside her head urged. *How often does a man like this come around. Once in a lifetime, if that often?*

"How do you like South Carolina?" she asked as he passed the basket of rolls.

"Very much," he said. "This area is much as I expected. I'm enjoying the beach a great deal."

"Do you swim?"

"Yes, usually in a pool. I haven't been in the ocean in years."

"Then we have something in common," she said, accepting the bowl of broccoli. "Since you're supposed to swim with a buddy, perhaps we could go together."

"I'd love to be your swimming buddy," he said softly, taking the bowl from her. His eyes burned with the flames from the dancing candlelight. An accompanying warmth spread throughout Linda's body, so warm that she didn't believe even the cold water of the Atlantic could cool her.

She looked away from his eyes, spotted the butter, and reached for it instead of Gifford Knight. When she had her response to him under control, she met his gaze again. "Did you visit this particular location on the advice of someone?"

"You might say that." He looked at her over the rim of his glass. "Someone I've known for a very long time."

"Recommendations from old and dear friends are the best," she said, not quite understanding the little thrill of excitement his words caused. Perhaps it was because he gave her such undivided attention. He didn't stare off into the sunset as he spoke, or fiddle with his flatware. He looked at her as though she were the most important, most beautiful woman, he'd ever seen.

Utter nonsense, she wanted to say. But his gaze held her attention, and she wanted to believe what his eyes conveyed.

"My best friend—someone I've known a very long time also—just called yesterday to tell me about her engagement. She'll be visiting me soon, I hope."

"My best wishes to her," he said, lifting his glass in a toast. "When will she arrive?"

"I'm not sure."

"I don't want to be too selfish, but I'd hoped we'd have some time together," he said softly. "I want to know you much better."

Linda stared at his long fingers and manicured nails, wondering how they would feel on her skin rather than against the wine glass. "Hot" was the only word that came to mind. She shifted in her chair, aware that he was waiting for some reply.

"I . . . I'd like that too." *Weak,* she told herself. *Why didn't you admit you'd like to grab him across the table? Send food and dishes flying as you repeat the scene from* Bull Durham *in the kitchen—only you wouldn't pretend he's Kevin Costner. No, this man is better.*

He smiled as though he knew her dilemma. Then he cut a piece of steak and placed it between his even, white teeth, chewing slowly, his closed lips barely curved.

She wanted to know what his mouth tasted like. She barely managed to take a bite of her own steak. But then he didn't say anything else that provoked naughty images, and she managed to concentrate on her meal without experiencing any more strong urges to make love on a table, countertop or floor.

The food was delicious: steaks grilled medium well, baked potatoes with butter and sour cream, and the vegetable she suspected he'd prepared from a frozen food package. It didn't matter. He'd gone to the trouble of fixing the meal, sharing it with her, and that made it special.

He served coffee from a carafe after the meal, declining her offer to help prepare or serve the brew or dessert. Some pink, green and white petit fours rested on a paper-doily-lined silver tray, looking almost as tempting as Gifford Knight. She wondered where the tiny cakes had come from. They obviously hadn't been purchased at Mr. Watley's.

"I admired your accent earlier," Linda said, looking back at Gifford Knight. "Is it British?"

"Yes. I thought I'd lost most of it. I've been away from the Mother Country for years."

"I've known British people who have lived in the states for forty years, yet they sound as though they've just stepped off the double-decked bus in Trafalgar Square."

He smiled. "You're right." He reached across the table and selected a little pink frosted cake with a white flower and green leaves. He put it on her plate, then took her hand.

Her heart skipped a beat and her skin felt overheated. "So you are from England?" Even to her own ears, her voice sounded slightly breathless.

"I was born there. My father was an American, my mother English."

"I was in England six or seven years ago, but I never got the chance to see much of the country."

She felt his hand tighten around hers. "Why were you in England?"

"Doing research for my doctoral dissertation."

"What was your subject?"

"The political conditions in Europe at the time of the Napoleonic Wars."

"A worthy topic."

"And an exhaustive one. I hardly had time to sleep, much less act as a tourist."

"Then we must go back."

We? She must have heard wrong. Or he'd made a slip of the tongue. Even knowing that, her heart did a little lurch. To go to England with this man . . . She took a bite of her dessert, then a sip of coffee.

He eased his hand away, smiled, and sipped his own coffee. Watching him, she wondered again if he knew how much he affected her senses. She'd certainly never felt anything like this overpowering attraction.

A gentle breeze drifted off the ocean, rippling the tablecloth and blowing Linda's napkin from her lap.

"I suppose that's nature's way of telling us night is falling," he observed, gazing at the darkening sky.

"It is getting late. If we're going to walk at sunset . . ."

"Let me clear the dishes away."

"I'll help," Linda volunteered, picking up her napkin and rising from the chair.

"It's no trouble. You're my guest. I'll only take a minute."

He collected the cups, saucers and dessert plates and excused himself, disappearing into the house. She watched the light come on in what must be the kitchen. Ruffled mauve curtains framed the window, and a lacy shade hid all but his shadow as he worked at the sink. Linda smiled again at the image of such an intense, sexy man occupying a fussy Victorian cottage. She pictured him as more the weathered-wood, stark-architecture and leather-furniture type.

As if Gifford Knight could be cast as a "type." Conversation over dinner had confirmed her earlier thoughts; she'd certainly never met anyone else like him.

Linda walked to the rail, crossed her arms and leaned against the ornate white wood. Although the sky was not totally dark, the sun had set behind the tall pines lining the roadway west of the house. Waves crashed to shore, tinted pink and lavender from the twilight glow of the sky and wispy clouds overhead. Gulls danced along the shoreline, chasing tiny creatures before they burrowed into the sand. And the wind, the ever-constant wind, whipped through the sea grass from the north, carrying with it a hint of a chill. Far out to sea, it looked as though a storm brewed in the thick, dark clouds.

Something soft draped over her arms, and two strong hands grasped her shoulders from behind. Without looking she knew his feel, his touch. Heat penetrated the thin cotton of her skirt and blouse, even though his body didn't touch hers. She closed her eyes, letting a strange sense of comfort wash over her, reveling in both the excitement and the serenity he projected. No one had ever made her feel this special, not a lover or parent or a friend. No one had ever seemed so mysterious and disturbing.

"How about that walk along the beach?" His question was a whisper along her neck, a tingling of nerves already sensitive. She shivered involuntarily, and he responded by draping her more completely in the soft, warm fabric that smelled of Gifford Knight.

She looked down at the pearl gray sweater he'd

placed over her shoulders and arms, stroking it, holding it close to her body, even though his heat warmed her more thoroughly than any piece of clothing. "I'd like that."

He gave her shoulders one last, slight squeeze, then stepped back, letting out a long-held breath. He was obviously fighting for control as much as she, Linda thought. At least one of them was sensible. If she alone were to choose, no telling how the evening would end.

He took her hand, again enfolding her in warmth, and led the way down the stairs. He seemed tense, yet moved with that inherent grace Linda recognized as supreme confidence. Here was a man at home anywhere, a man who made his own rules to get what he wanted from life.

"Wait." She stopped and pulled off her sandals, using his arm for balance. He smiled while he watched her and she smiled back, feeling young and carefree for the first time in months.

"I wish I had a camera right now. I'd preserve your memory for all time, with the sun barely gilding your hair and your eyes hinting at mischief."

"Oooh, it's blarney I think I'm hearing," Linda replied in her best Irish brogue.

"You learned that from some relative, I'd wager."

"You'd be right," Linda said as she straightened and wiggled her toes in the sand. "My father's grandmother came over as a bride just after the turn of the century. I barely remember her, except for the brogue."

"You should go to Ireland some day. It's beautiful."

"I'd like to. Maybe another summer when I'm not teaching."

"Do you live in Chicago the entire year?"

Linda nodded. "I've taught every semester since I was hired at Northwestern—except this one. And yes, I live in Evanston, a suburb about twelve miles from downtown Chicago, but I was born in New York."

He walked beside her, his slacks brushing against her gauzy skirt, making her very aware of his presence. "Do you own a house in Evanston?"

"I have a duplex, half of a wonderful old house close to the university, complete with leaded glass windows and a turret room. It's brick and stone and those scalloped wooden shingles. I know it sounds totally atrocious, but I love it."

The conversation seemed to be one-sided, so she decided to ask him a question for a change. "So, where do you live when you're not grilling steaks on the beach?"

"Here and there. I keep an apartment in New York, but I don't spend much time at the flat. How long have you been a professor at Northwestern?"

He really didn't want to talk about himself, which was odd, Linda thought. Most authors she'd met were more than willing to tell you all about their brilliant backgrounds, their literary successes. Gifford Knight seemed much more private—almost evasive. "I've taught there since I received my doctorate four years ago," she replied.

"Do you enjoy teaching?"

"I love it. I've taught every semester except this summer. Of course, that means I have to cram the rest of my life into my breaks, which makes for a very busy schedule."

She felt him slightly stiffen beside her. Or maybe she imagined it. He asked smoothly, "Busy?"

"My grandmother has been ill this last year and I came to visit her whenever I could. She died in February." Linda paused, fighting against the sense of loss she still felt. Her grandmother had been such a wonderful person, a person who knew how to give and receive love. "We were very close," she said softly.

"Yes, I know . . . how that feels, I mean. I'm sorry about your loss. My mother passed away three years ago after a long illness."

"I'm sorry." She knew how it felt to be alone now. Even though her mother was alive, she was too involved in her career as a classical musician to "just visit." Linda, on the other hand, loved to talk and shop, spend hours over coffee and conversation. Her mother never did understand such a waste of time.

They walked in silence for a while, the waves continuing to pound against the shore, but no longer tinted by the colors of sunset. The sky transformed to indigo, with Venus and several stars already out. Even the gulls had grown quiet. Linda didn't realize where they were until he stopped and turned to face her. The light from twin spotlights she'd had installed this afternoon illuminated them from a tall cedar pole on the deck, showing a small section of beach and the steps leading to her house.

"Thank you for a lovely evening, Linda," he said, raising her hand again to his lips. His eyes closed briefly as he kissed her fingers, shadows from his dark lashes sweeping his high cheekbones.

"I enjoyed it very much," she whispered, moving closer, again drawn as though a magnet. "You're wrong, you know. You're a wonderful cook."

"The only other thing I prepare well is eggs," he said, looking into her eyes with a force that left her breathless.

She moistened her lips, wanting to kiss him more than anything she'd ever desired before. "Then perhaps I can sample them sometime. I like one egg, over easy."

He lowered his head until his breath whispered against her lips. "I imagine that if I were to fix you breakfast, dear Linda, we would both be terribly famished. And one would not be enough."

And then he kissed her with the ease of a man who had kissed her dozens of times before, with skill and passion. She melted against him and he responded, wrapping his arms around her, pulling her tight against his hard, aroused body. Her hands snaked around his waist, her nails digging in to the muscles of his back. In response, he slanted his head, molded his lips even tighter and stroked her to the point where she made breathless little moans that were the only way she could tell him how much she wanted him.

When she thought she might lose herself forever in that one kiss, he broke his lips away, still holding her close. She listened to his heart pounding near her ear as she rested her head on his chest. She felt a shudder ripple through his body as he let out a sigh that spoke volumes about what they'd both obviously experienced. And she knew something had just happened that would change her life.

"Linda . . ."

"Please, don't say anything."

He held her until his heartbeat started to slow, until she could take a deep breath. Beneath her fingers, he was lean and strong, making her feel cherished and protected. But it was too soon for more, she knew. To encourage further intimacy was crazy—but still . . .

"I believe we know each other well enough now for you to call me Giff."

"I believe you're right," Linda whispered, leaning back, looking into his darkly handsome face. "It was a wonderful evening, Giff."

"Yes, it was."

She eased away from his arms and he let her. Without his heat, his presence, she felt alone and slightly chilled, especially where the wind cooled her heated skin. When she started to remove his sweater, he stopped her, taking her hands in his. "Keep it. You'll be cold."

"I'm only walking a few steps to the door."

"Keep it." And he kissed her again, this time quickly but with a familiarity that caused her heart to race. He tasted of sweet icing and coffee, and of other things so tempting she could only imagine what it would be to taste and feel them.

"Good night, Linda. I'll see you again tomorrow."

She hugged the sweater close and smiled. "Good night."

"I want to make sure you get safely inside."

He gave her an amused look when she continued to stand at the steps, making no effort to go into the house. Her body didn't want to leave him, even though her mind told her that going inside was the right thing to do.

"Go to sleep, dear Linda, and dream of me," he said softly, but with a commanding, deep tone that caused every nerve ending to tingle.

She felt her breath catch in her throat. How could she not dream of him? He filled her senses: his smell, his touch, his passion. So she smiled and turned, running up the steps so she could stop at the deck and see him again, standing on the beach with the tide coming in.

Strange, but he stood in about the same place as the long-haired stranger last night. She shook her head at the fanciful thought, then fumbled for the key in the pocket of her skirt, unlocked the door and slipped inside.

She hugged his sweater close and watched as he finally turned and walked away, hands in his pockets, away from the circle of light and into the darkness. But she breathed in his scent and remembered, even after he was gone from sight. And knew that she *would* dream tonight, dark and sensual dreams of a man unlike anyone she had ever met before.

* * *

If he had hands, he would have rubbed them in delight. Everything was progressing according to the master scheme. The spell, after all these centuries, still worked.

The ill-fated lovers had found each other. Mord sensed their awakening needs, took pleasure in their mutual desires. They were healthy, strong adults, and it wouldn't be long before they would want to seal their bond with sweaty abandon. They'd fixate on each other, grow obsessed with the object of their desire. Their level of frustration would rise, feeding his own powers, giving him the strength to influence their thoughts, their fears.

He needed more strength. Soon, he'd need to break out of this void into their reality. He'd need a good strong body, but for now he could guide them with suggestions so faint they would never know his influence.

Until it was too late.

The secret to gaining more strength, he knew, was to push them together at the same time he kept them apart. That way, their energy grew. He wouldn't allow them to satisfy their mutual cravings, not when the only reason they "fell in love" was to satisfy him.

Love. What a ridiculous name to call such obsessive desire. If they could feel as he did, the pure joy of manipulating the lives of those weaker than he was, they'd embrace his philosophy in one beat of their pitiful hearts.

But they didn't know—could never know—his pleasures. They could only innocently fall prey to tragedy, shout at fate, try to invoke divine intervention. Their human lives were at his mercy; their souls were his.

Forever.

Giff leaned against the porch railing, listening to the gentle murmur of waves against the sand and the soft rumble of thunder far out to sea. Tonight had been wonderful, beyond even his high expectations. Linda was everything he could have asked for in a woman, even without a spell drawing them together.

They shared many interests, which, of course, could have been influenced by their shared pasts. But beyond the obvious things they had in common, she was thoughtful and intelligent. He'd truly enjoyed talking to her.

He was a lucky man. He would have gone though whatever it took to free their souls, but for once fate had been kind.

And she had a certain radiance about her that wasn't caused by the setting rays of the sun, or the artifice of makeup. She glowed with life, despite the recent loss of her grandmother and the sadness he sensed deep inside. He felt she must be very much alone.

He could relate to that. By choice, he'd been alone most of his adult life. If people knew him too well, they'd discover his past. He couldn't commit to another woman, not when he was destined to love Linda. After his mother died, he'd been without a confidant, someone who spent time with him without asking questions he couldn't answer, or demanding promises he couldn't give.

Linda could be like that, he thought. She could fill the lonely gaps, give meaning to a life lived half in the shadows. She could be his salvation.

There was only one problem.

A sudden burst of wind hit his face, pressed his clothes against his skin and caused him to squint against the deepening night. Thunder rumbled, closer now. Yes, one problem that must be dealt with soon. Finally, and for all eternity.

Chapter Three

It is difficult to say what is impossible, for the dream of yesterday is the hope of today and the reality of tomorrow.
—Robert H. Goddard

The oak bureau was packed with old-fashioned linens, beautifully embroidered and edged with crocheted lace. Quilt pieces rested inside paper bags, along with old instructions cut from newspapers and hand-drawn patterns. Linda remembered some of the items from special occasions, when her grandmother would set a "party table" complete with china and the good flatware. Sometimes they'd only have tea and cookies, but it had always been fun.

When Linda was a child, it had seemed that Grandmother enjoyed the tea parties as much as she. Perhaps she had. Linda supposed that was why this house had always seemed so special—because she was treated as an important, individual person, lavished with attention and love. So unlike her life in New York, with parents who were more interested in their careers than in a home life. Thank heavens for Grandmother, who had given her life some much-needed balance. Linda still didn't feel close to her mother, and her father had died several years ago, an overachiever to the very end.

If she ever had a little girl, she thought as she stroked the lace-edged napkins, she'd have tea parties for her, and set the table with fresh flowers and the good linen. She'd continue to teach, to do research, but she would never make her child feel as though he or she was low on the list of priorities. She'd give her child a sense of the past, a personal and family history that would ground them in their unique reality. Just as she had been taught by her grandmother to go after her own dreams, to pursue her own destiny.

Even though she'd vowed to go through the house and get rid of some items, how could she part with any of these pieces? Each had been carefully stitched by her grandmother or great-grandmother. They were part of her ties to the past, her family. She added a handful of mothballs and shut the drawer.

She yawned and stretched, then struggled up from the floor. Her leg tingled where the circulation had been cut off, and her back ached, either from leaning over the drawer or from the soft mattress. She'd slept deeply for several hours last night, exhausted from her sleeplessness the previous evening, from the large dinner and wine at Giff's house. But sometime in the morning, she'd awakened from another dream—only this time it wasn't a nightmare.

She could feel a blush creep up her neck as she recalled last night's steamy flight of fancy. His face had remained in shadows, as always, but instead of Giff, she'd recognized her long-dead soldier as he'd walked toward her in the night. She'd blended reality with fantasy, she supposed, imagining them on this moonlit beach. Dressed only in a thin, sheer gown, she'd run down the stairs and into his arms, her bare feet skimming across the wet sand. He'd worn a British uniform, the wool cloth still smelling of gunpowder and sweat. But to her, it was the sweetest aroma on earth. It meant he was alive, whole, returned to her from across the Channel. Not dead from a stray bullet or some evil spirit. He'd held her, his heart beating against her breast, then kissed her as a man starving for his soul's nourishment.

He kissed you like Giff, a little voice said, but she wanted to deny the reality. William Howard was her fantasy lover, her ideal man. She closed her eyes at the perfection of the dream. She'd known Gifford Knight only one day, but she'd spent 14 years with the fantasy of William. No wonder she dreamed of him instead. And yet Giff thrilled her as no flesh and blood man ever had, causing her to blend the two in her mind, even though the logical part of her brain knew that she must keep them separate.

She'd torn at his buttons, his belt. Waves had lapped over her feet, splashing against his knee-high boots. He'd slipped the gown from her shoulders, letting it fall into the sea. His chest had been solid, so very warm against her fingers, her breasts. Molding herself to him, she'd soared with pleasure, with their love. Then he'd lowered her to the sand, never stopping the kisses to her lips, her throat. The tide had washed over them, cool against her heated skin, but she hadn't minded. He was alive and she was his, for all time. Finally, they'd experience the perfection of joining body and soul. Finally, after all these years. She'd whispered his name as he settled between her thighs, hot and hard.

"William!"

She opened her eyes and gasped, so caught up in re-living last night's dream that she'd called his name aloud. She blinked against the late morning brightness as she reoreinted herself to her surroundings.

And she heard someone knocking on the door.

Leaning against the oak bureau, her legs shaking and her whole body humming with sexual excitement, she realized that the dream had stopped abruptly—as it always did. There had been no consummation, no incredible release. Only the frustration of never knowing what it would be like to make love to William Howard.

She placed her palms against her cheeks and felt the heat. Whoever was at the door would see the flush. The knock came again, more insistent.

Hobbling on her still-tingling leg, she made it down the hall to the French doors as quickly as possible. She wasn't dressed for company, opting for comfort instead of fashion. But at least the shorts and knit top matched, which was more than she could say for some of her housecleaning outfits.

She didn't have to peer through the sheer lace panels to know the identify of her caller. Giff stood there, a tall shadow against the sun-drenched deck. Her heart started racing again, remembering the kiss last night and the heat of him against her. Was it her dream or the reality of the man before her that caused this new surge of excitement? The two were obviously already becoming confused in her mind. But now wasn't the time to psychoanalyze herself. She smoothed back her hair and hoped that her cheeks had lost some of their color.

"Hello." She pulled open the door, motioning for him to come inside.

"Good morning, Linda." His voice washed over her like the waves in her dream, gentle and coaxing. "I hope you slept well."

He looked so good, dressed in well-creased yet casual khaki trousers and an open-collar, light blue knit shirt that molded against the muscles of his upper chest like a second skin. His dark hair was windblown, his face tan, his brown eyes intense, as usual. His own breathing seemed a bit fast, his nostrils slightly flaring. For a moment it seemed as though he knew what she'd been thinking . . . or even dreaming.

She felt the heat of another blush as surely as if she stood in front of an open oven. Her pulse took off at a gallop. "Yes, I did. I was just . . . cleaning and sorting. I'm sorry it took so long to answer the door."

"No need to apologize. I did come by unexpectedly."

"Yes, well, I'm glad you did." She looked around the kitchen, but the morning coffee was all gone, and she hadn't made iced tea yet. "I'd offer you something to drink, but I'm not sure what—"

"I brought lunch."

"Really?" She glanced at the wall clock. Sure enough, it was almost noon. She hadn't realized it was so late. For the first time, she noticed that he held a large wicker basket, the type that sold in expensive specialty houses for a small fortune. Her mouth watered as she thought about the goodies hidden inside.

"I assumed you would need a break about now. Going through the property of a loved one is very . . . difficult."

Linda nodded. "It is. There are so many *things*. I guess I didn't realize how much one can accumulate over a lifetime—or actually several lifetimes, since much is from my great-grandmother. And each item is special. I don't know how I can part with anything. To think that someone else might use Grandmother's linens for rags or let them decay. If I don't keep this house, though, I'd never have enough room in my house in Evanston to keep what I'd like. Well, I just don't know what to do."

"Why don't we have lunch and discuss your dilemma? I might have a few suggestions."

"That sounds great. I'll just clear off the table." She swept up the mail and morning paper, but Giff stopped her.

"Let's eat outside. The day is beautiful. You should enjoy it."

She smiled and nodded. "I'd like that."

She followed him outside, down the steps and around the house. He moved with such quiet grace, like a natural athlete. She wondered if he'd played sports, perhaps soccer. He had that kind of body. Thanks to her very active imagination and frustrating dreams, she wanted to reach out and touch his shoulders, working her hands down his back to those tightly sculpted buttocks and hard thighs.

Stop it, she told herself. *You're letting your hormones rule. The man brought you a picnic for lunch; he didn't offer himself as a five-course meal.*

Giff spread a blanket beneath the only tree in the side yard, a stubby live oak, then knelt and removed one item after another. Linda peered at each container, hoping that her stomach wouldn't growl and give her away. She'd read somewhere that food was a common substitute for sex. Inside the house, she hadn't been hungry, but now she was ravenous. If she didn't watch it, she'd gain ten pounds after being around Giff only a week. No telling how much she'd weigh at the end of the summer, if he continued to provide such sumptuous meals and stimulating appetizers. *If* she continued to be around him, she reminded herself.

"I took the liberty of ordering a grilled chicken salad for our main course."

"That sounds delicious."

He retrieved a bottle of the chardonnay like the one they'd shared last night and deftly removed the cork.

Linda sank to the blanket, certain that she *was* dreaming this man. Surely she'd switched her days and nights. Anyone this sexy, charming and considerate must be a fantasy.

Shaking her head, she lifted two wine glasses from the basket and held them out. Giff poured, but his eyes seemed to focus only on her. Another blush stole up her neck, and she lowered her head to hide it from him. He already sensed far too much about her. She must be as easy to read as a children's book, but she hoped he couldn't guess her wayward thoughts, her steamy dreams.

"To a fruitful day," he toasted.

She nodded, taking a sip of the wine.

"Have you considered donating any of your grandmother's items to a museum or a local historical society? They'd receive the best of care, and you could share them with others interested in learning about the past."

"I hadn't considered it, but it sounds like a good idea. Actually, I'd only just arrived two days ago to clean out Grandmother's house. I had to get all my paperwork in order in Chicago, then close up my house there after the spring semester."

She watched the strong column of his throat as he swallowed a sip of wine. The urge to move her lips over his flesh was so strong she had to stop herself from acting on it.

"And you plan to continue to live in Chicago?"

She shifted on the blanket, trying to get more comfortable. "Yes. I may decide to keep the house here, though. I've discovered that I want to keep way too much; I wouldn't have room for all of it back in Evanston. And the beach would make a wonderful retreat. Perhaps I could lease it to friends occasionally as a vacation getaway. I'm not sure."

"It means much to you, this house." She watched his eyes scan the three stories of wood, all the way up the attic. The tendons of his neck stood out against tanned skin, and a vein throbbed in a heavy beat. "Wonderful memories . . . and some not so wonderful?"

"Yes," she whispered, pondering the fact that he'd guessed so well. Or was he just good at making general observations, like a fortune-teller? Whatever the reason, he'd hit close to home, and it made her uncomfortable. "Why did you say that?"

"If you spent many summers here as you were growing up, then surely you went through some traumas."

"Yes," she said, thinking of her late night conversations with Gerri about boys and parents, about the Ouija board.

He turned back toward her, away from the past, and smiled. "You must eat."

She filled their plates while he topped off their glasses of wine. The food and drink relaxed her, along with Giff's pleasant conversation about everyday things, including his next book on Saxon England before William the Conqueror. They spoke of nothing provocative. No more mind-reading. Linda leaned back on the blanket and enjoyed the dappled sunlight, slight breeze and mild temperature.

"Tell me about the time you spent here at your grandmother's house."

"Why would you want to know about that?" Linda said, then laughed. "I'm just surprised that you would want to hear about those silly, childhood years. I just remember bits and pieces from when I was really young. Most of the really distinct memories are from when I was a teenager. And a teenage girl is not an interesting specimen of life, I assure you."

"Ahh, I think you are wrong, dear Linda. To understand the woman, a man must understand the past. You are full of hidden treasures that are waiting to be discovered. How can I truly appreciate you without knowing?"

"And will you be around long enough to uncover these surprises?" she said softly.

"Yes, I will. You can be assured of that."

"Cross your heart and hope to die?" she teased, feeling the effect of the wine.

The tenderness left his face. "Why do you say that?" His words sounded flat and cold.

"It's just a funny saying children have. My best friend Gerri and I used it to swear that we were telling the truth. Surely you've heard the expression?"

"Perhaps. I can't recall." The blank looked faded. "Tell me about this friend. Did she visit here with you?"

"Yes, she did, several summers." Linda shivered involuntarily as she remembered the last summer, the eventful night they'd run away screaming, staying out on the beach until her grandmother had called them in. By then, they'd calmed down.

Although Linda had come back to visit many times, Gerri hadn't come with her. That wasn't due to the Ouija board; Gerri had gotten over it quickly—much more quickly than Linda. "We visited together until we were fifteen. After that, we got our driver's licenses and went boy-crazy."

"So what did two teenage girls do at the beach before they became boy-crazy? Tell me about the most vivid memory you have of that time."

She thought about answering, about telling him, but didn't want to blurt out the event that had changed her life. It was a memory that she and Gerri shared, but she'd never talked about it with another person. "Really, I don't think it would interest you."

"You mean you wish I wouldn't pry."

She smiled at his comment. "Very astute. Are you sure you don't read minds?"

He looked up, his face beautifully intense. "I've been told that I can be perceptive. Perhaps I just make more observations than some people."

"Maybe," Linda said, her voice unsure.

"Surely that doesn't frighten you?"

"And if it does?"

He reached out and caught her hand. "You have nothing to fear from me, Linda. Surely you sense that."

"When I'm around you, sometimes I don't trust my senses," she whispered.

"Trust them. Of all the powers in the world, our instincts are the most true."

"But if they're not . . ."

"Your instincts are telling you to trust me," he said, pulling her closer. "My instincts tell me to go slow, or I'll frighten you away. But my body wants you already."

She pulled back, more shaken than ever by his intensity. She could see the truth in his dark eyes, along with the promise of pleasure and the threat of heartache. But she had already confused him with William in her dreams and her fantasies. How could she trust such conflicting emotions, such fickle instincts?

"You do frighten me," she said.

"I'm sorry. I'm rushing you."

She shook her head. "It's not just that."

"Then tell me."

"I . . . It's difficult to admit."

"You can tell me anything."

She doubted that. No man wanted to be compared to a fantasy. No man could ever stand up to the ideal she'd created . . . until now. Perhaps Giff could. But she didn't know him well enough to admit her secret. It was too personal, too sexual. But she had to tell him something to explain why she would be frightened.

"When I was a teenager, my best friend and I were frightened by an incident involving a Ouija board. The experience was . . . intense. There was someone I was communicating with, but we had to stop. The whole thing still seems unresolved to me." She took a deep breath when she finished speaking, half expecting something terrible to happen because she'd admitted such a personally upsetting event. Half expecting censure or disbelief. But Giff didn't question her story, didn't laugh at her fears. He simply sat there, watching her closely.

"Who was this person with whom you communicated?"

She'd never told anyone about William. Only Gerri knew. "A British officer named William Howard. He was killed in 1815."

"Why did you stop talking to . . . him?"

He said the words with such emotion, such longing, that Linda felt shaken. It seemed as though Giff felt her story on a very personal level. She hadn't expected such interest, and the whole idea of talking about that night made her feel a frisson of panic.

She hesitated a moment, repressing a shiver. "Something . . . unusual happened. I really don't want to talk about it now."

"Very well. But I would like to discuss it later, and try to understand if it relates to what we feel for each other."

That's exactly what I don't want to discuss right now, Linda thought. She'd never compared a man she'd dated to William. No one had ever reminded her of him, or had had the same intensity she felt in her dreams. She'd always been able to separate fantasy from reality. Until now.

She sat up and stretched. "I should get back to work."

"You haven't had dessert."

She wasn't sure she wanted to know what other delights he had in store for her. "I shouldn't. . . . "

He reached inside the basket and produced two slices of Black Forest cake.

"How did you know?"

"A woman of your sensuality would naturally love chocolate."

"Are you sure you didn't just read my mind?" she said, half teasing as she reached for a fork.

"I never admit all my secrets."

"Never?" She took a bite of the sinfully rich dessert. Pure heaven.

"I might make an exception for you."

"Keep feeding me cake and I'm yours for the duration," she teased.

"I will hold you to that promise," he said with a fervor that made her look up. He looked as deadly serious as he had yesterday, when he'd said that nothing was too great an expense for her. When he'd claimed that he wanted to know everything about her. Why? Was it just a line, or did he have some overwhelming passion that she couldn't fathom? Whatever, she felt uneasy about the amount of conviction she heard in his voice.

"Don't pay any attention to what I say when I'm under the influence of chocolate," she said, hoping he would take the hint that she wanted to lighten the tone of the conversation. She might be lusting after him, but that didn't mean she was totally at ease with his focus on her as a desirable woman.

"Ahh, backing down already. I must deduce that you are fond of me only because I feed you."

She decided that he'd taken the hint and backed away from any further heavy comments. She would too, she vowed as she took another bite. She'd be charming and witty, and he'd never know how much he disturbed her with those serious comments. "Yes, but what a wonderful basis for a relationship."

"Indeed. I will remember that."

He ate half of his piece of cake, spending most of his time watching her. His passion, held in check, unnerved her, but at the same time her senses felt heightened, poised for some momentous event. Only he didn't try to seduce her, or in any way take advantage of her weakness for him. Was he truly a gentleman, as she'd suspected earlier, or was he a diabolical schemer?

But why would anyone want to scheme against her? It just didn't make sense. Perhaps she was still suffering the aftereffects of that steamy dream last night, or the nightmare the evening before.

"Finished" he asked, looking at her extremely clean plate.

She looked down, surprised that her cake was indeed gone. "Yes. Everything was delicious."

He smiled. "It was my pleasure."

"And thank you for pulling me away from work. Sometimes I lose track of time when I'm going through Grandmother's things."

Giff nodded. "I want you to think about something this afternoon."

She looked at his serious expression. "All right."

"Many cultures, many people, believe that we live more than once. That we have a mission to accomplish in life, and if we don't succeed, we come back."

"Reincarnation."

"Yes, that's one name for it. If your young man didn't fulfill his destiny before being killed, perhaps he has returned."

That was a pretty wild notion, as far as Linda was concerned. How would she even know? How would he know? Still, she didn't want to totally discount Giff's beliefs. "So you believe in reincarnation."

He nodded. "I've studied it most of my life. You could say I'm an expert on the subject. And I think it is entirely possible that destiny played a part in your contacting him."

"Since I communicated with him while I was in my teens, then he'd be no more than thirteen or fourteen now."

"Perhaps. There are other possibilities than physical rebirth. If you'd like, we can explore those explanations."

She frowned. "I'm not good at believing in things I can't see or touch." Besides, she did have a general belief that the soul entered the body between conception and birth, not later in life.

He stood and pulled her to her feet, holding her close. "Just think about the concept for now. We'll have more time to discuss it later."

She hoped Giff wasn't some fanatic. She'd heard stories that some people could be very persuasive, almost charismatic, to sway others to their thinking. Such tactics were often used by religious cults. *Please, don't let Giff be one of those,* she silently prayed. "I'm not sure I want to discuss it."

He searched her face, his eyes fathomless and unwavering. "When you are ready." And then he lowered his lips and she forgot her concerns as he kissed her with all the heady passion of fine wine, with the decadence of dark chocolate, with the promise of a lifetime of love. She clung to him, afraid of the powerful yearnings he brought forth, but knowing that she couldn't let him go without exploring what could be. She kissed him back with all the fire inside her, feeling the unleashed molten heat run through her body.

If any man could chase away her fantasy of William and replace it with memories, it was Giff.

"Tonight," he whispered as he broke the kiss. "At dusk we'll walk along the beach."

She nodded, too shaken for words.

He took her arm and walked her to the French doors. "Until sunset," he said, kissing her hand, holding it tight against his chest, where his heart beat fast and strong. "Lock your door."

"Has anyone ever told you that you worry too much?"

"Never."

She smiled, pulling her hand away from his tender grasp. "I'll see you later."

"Most assuredly."

He waited patiently until she turned the dead bolt and waved him away.

She watched him walk down the beach, the wind rippling through his dark hair, the wicker basket swinging beside him.

He was certainly different, but, oh, that man could certainly kiss.

"Send the dissertation over this line to my computer," Giff said, "and remember that I need it immediately."

His contact at Northwestern—one of many such people he knew from previous research and seminars—would be prompt, Giff knew. Linda's doctoral project, along with other professional and personal information, would be here before the afternoon was up. Technology was a wondrous thing, with laptop computers, fax modems and the like providing an endless supply of facts and figures. And the key to planning any great quest, winning any battle, was information—on friend and foe alike.

Which was one reason he was very uneasy about Linda's trusting nature. She didn't believe anyone would enter her car or home without an invitation. She believed herself to be perfectly safe in this small, isolated community.

She couldn't be farther from the truth. And the fact was, Giff had no concrete information on his foe, had no idea how or when Linda might be in danger, except through the Ouija board. At least she seemed sufficiently frightened of the device, or the events surrounding it, to not use it again.

But surely there were other ways for Mord to appear. There hadn't been a board involved in 1815, or in 1698, or in 1547, or any other time in the past. Perhaps Mord had used the board because an ocean separated the would-be lovers, Giff speculated.

Until he knew more, all he could do was try to make her conscious of security. He hoped she would listen.

He hung up the phone, a sense of barely contained energy flowing through him. Pacing to the windows, he stared out at the Atlantic Ocean, toward England, where this had all began, a thousand years ago.

He'd been a young Saxon farmer when the story had started, in love during that lifetime with a girl who'd captured the hearts of many men. She'd been beautiful, sweet, and not at all ready for the marriage bed, even though every man who saw her wanted her. They'd tried to win her hand, but he had decided he would *make* her fall in love with him. He'd done everything mortally possible, yet still she'd denied his proposals. She'd flirted, smiled but would give him no commitment.

As luck would have it, a sorcerer traveled through the village on his way to the mists of Wales. Or maybe it wasn't luck. Perhaps there was a divine fate that rewarded saints and punished fools. That extoled virtue and denied greed. Oh, he'd paid a price for the eternal love of the girl, only he hadn't realized at the time that the price would be his soul, or that the sorcerer would see her also and become jealous of the wish he'd already granted.

So Giff had loved her in that former life, and she'd loved him because of the spell, but in the end, love hadn't been the most powerful force they'd had to overcome. They'd never said their vows, never shared their love. He had been killed before they could become one in body as well as spirit, and in each subsequent lifetime, the story was the same. They met and fell in love, but their love was never consummated. The joke of a demented sorcerer. The curse of eternity.

Only this time, it would be different. This time he knew what needed to be done. For the first time, he had the information—and the ingredients—to overcome the spell. He glanced toward the closet where his odd-shaped leather bag was stored. Soon, he would need everything he'd learned and more to defeat his enemy.

He forced his thoughts away from the inevitable and tried to concentrate on the present. He pushed aside the lacy flounce of a ruffled curtain and stared at the scenic view of sand and water. The sun shone brightly, washing out the colors of the early afternoon. No one stirred along the beach. People were either hiding from the heat or sleeping off their lunch. It was never crowded here, Giff had been told by the leasing agent, because the property owners wanted it that way. The tourists could go to Hilton Head or Myrtle Beach, but they weren't encouraged to stay along this particular strip of oceanfront. That was fine with him. His walks along the surf with Linda were quiet, solitary times, for sharing and discovering.

The most unexpected discovery of all was how much he truly enjoyed Linda's company. Her quick humor. The times she was quiet and introspective. The way she could relate to his work without prying into his life. Even without the spell, he realized, he would have been attracted to her.

The phone rang then, but Giff let his computer software answer the call. He walked to the shaded interior of the cottage and watched the communication device. Sure enough, the phone number displayed on the laptop's screen was from Northwestern. A sense of excitement flowed through him as the data poured into the computer.

Soon he printed out the faxes of Linda's application, her resume and teaching schedule. Each page he devoured, finding the nuances that made her individual, special. And then the dissertation started coming in the form of a file transfer. He felt the impatience of youth devour his best intentions as he watched the minutes tick away, represented in the form of a shaded rectangle slowly being filled: 50 percent complete, 70 percent complete. He wanted to rush the process, to scream at the computer. But instead he paced and waited, knowing that before long he'd have the major piece of research that had captured Linda's attention, the document that would tell him more about her than any resume or job description.

He was very good at reading between the lines.

A discreet little bell notified him that the file transfer was complete. He opened word-processing software, then imported the text file, noticing for the first time that his hands were not quite steady. That he made mistakes typing. That the mouse darted erratically across the screen.

"Lord Castlereagh and the Establishment of Aristocratic Alliances," he recited from the title. "A Study of Diplomacies in Europe during Reconstruction, from 1812 to 1818." She'd chosen the time period in which William Howard had loved, fought and died. With a smile, he began to read.

The shower felt great, Linda decided, glad to wash off the dirt and grime from decades of old papers, clothes and dusty mementos. Warm water smoothed away the fatigue, leaving her more than ready to see Giff again. He was so different from any other man she'd ever known. More . . . intense, more focused. And much more attractive.

What did he find so compelling—so interesting—about her? she wondered as she dried off. Certainly not her hair, which at the moment lay in wet kinks on her shoulders. Her face, she knew, was pleasant, but had never inspired other men to state their intentions so clearly, so soon. Her nose was too small, her chin a bit too firm. She had nice eyes, but hardly ever used liner or mascara to enhance them. And her body, she thought, looking in the mirror as she finished drying, was compact, not at all willowy like the ideal model's figure. Her breasts were firm and a bit full, her hips round. She didn't cause traffic to come to a complete halt when she walked down the street, but she hadn't suffered any complaints either.

All in all, she was moderately attractive. Well educated. Financially secure. But that still didn't explain Gifford Knight's exaggerated interest in her.

She wanted to know, but how did she ask him without sounding insecure or suspicious? It was a problem she'd have to resolve, and soon, if the pace of his pursuit was any indication of his intention. She'd only met him yesterday, but they'd already had two "dates." She had a feeling that they would end up in either his bed or hers before long, unless she developed much more willpower. This kind of physical attraction was new to her, unlike her earlier infatuations, which had involved talking herself into feeling a mild amount of lust after establishing a relationship.

With Giff, she'd had the urge to get lost in his eyes, melt into his body, from the first moment they'd met. She forgot the little doubts when he kissed her.

She sighed, sure that these thoughts weren't helping her cause. Instead of thinking about his appeal, she should be worrying about his intentions. And tonight, what did he have planned after walking along the beach at dusk? Eggs and bacon at dawn?

"I imagine that if I were to fix you breakfast, dear Linda, we would both be terribly famished. And one would not be enough." She shuddered as she remembered his words from the previous evening. The problem was, she knew he was right.

She rummaged through her closet, wondering

what was appropriate for tonight. Something that encouraged or discouraged? Closing her eyes and shaking her head, she grabbed an outfit. She peered at what she'd chosen: a black, washed-silk, sleeveless jumpsuit. Definitely discouraging if speed of removal were a criterion, but encouraging if one considered the way it molded itself to her body.

So be it, she decided. She'd deal with Giff's advances when, and if, they came.

Minutes later she'd dried her hair, put on some lip gloss and slipped into the jumpsuit. Taking a deep breath, she walked onto the deck. Already the sun was beginning to set, yet Giff wasn't here. Perhaps he'd meant she should meet him again at his house. She couldn't remember. Taking the initiative to find him, she locked her door, slipped the key into her pocket, and trudged barefoot through the hot sand, sandals dangling from her fingers.

A lamp lighted the interior of the cottage with a pink glow, making it appear cozy and inviting. Two large windows faced the beach, reflecting a scene of deep blue sky and pink, fluffy clouds. The door was to the side of the house, Linda knew from last night. She walked onto the porch, but didn't see Giff outside.

"Giff?" she called out, but he didn't answer or appear. Going to the entry, she noticed that the screen door was shut but the door open. Giff sat inside the fussy, dimly lit interior, pouring over papers. More research, she thought, feeling an immediate tug toward the historical texts to which he must have access. She'd give up a year of teaching to read the kind of original material he was able to acquire for his books. She enjoyed the sight of him, so absorbed into the material that he had forgotten the time, even failed to hear her call to him.

She knocked lightly. "Giff?"

He looked up, a flash of what appeared to be panic crossing his face. He immediately stuffed the papers into a folder and stood up.

"Linda, I'm sorry. I forgot the time." He walked across the floral carpet and opened the door, motioning her inside.

"That's all right. I couldn't remember where we were supposed to meet."

"I meant to come to your house, but I'm glad you sought me out."

"More research?" she asked, peering around him at the laptop computer and papers on top of the small coffee table. Electrical cords and a phone line snaked across the carpet.

"Yes, research. Please, have a seat," he said, indicating a chair. "I'll just turn this off and we can take our walk."

She sat on a rose-and-cream-striped horsehair chair and smiled at his quick, sure movements. He did everything well, she thought, from grilling steaks to organizing papers. One of the sheets fell to the floor, and he grabbed it before it fully settled on the rug. To her surprise, it seemed to have the crest of Northwestern on the top. Was he acquiring some data from her university, or was this old research? Or was her mind playing tricks on her?

"Oh, that looked like something from Northwestern." The words slipped out before she could stop herself from snooping into his affairs. It wasn't any of her business, yet she wasn't sorry she'd asked.

"Yes. I'm doing a bit of research."

"I thought you weren't working while you were here."

"It was very impromptu." He looked up and smiled just slightly. "Northwestern has very good research facilities."

"I know." But she still felt uneasy. Was it only coincidence, or could his research be directed at her? No, she was being paranoid, thinking that Giff's actions would revolve around her. With all of his contacts, it wouldn't be unusual for him to have a paper or two from Northwestern.

"Excuse me for a moment," he said, placing the papers and small computer inside, then closing the lid of the briefcase. "I'll just put this up, and we'll be on our way."

He went into another room and she heard a door open and close. In just a moment he was back, smiling and charming.

"Ready?"

"Yes," she said, rising from the uncomfortable chair, pushing the suspicions aside. Whatever Giff was researching was none of her business. The fact that she was suspicious of one piece of paper was no reason to distrust a respected writer.

She smiled at him. "I'm ready."

The pink sunset color had faded from the clouds by the time they walked outside. A few stars twinkled overhead and the crescent moon lit their way. Giff draped his arm over Linda's shoulder, holding her close against his heat. She wanted to turn toward him, to lose herself in his embrace, but stopped herself. This relationship was accelerating rapidly on its own, without her giving it more fuel.

"I'm envious of the research you do," she said softly.

"Envious? Why?"

"Because that's one of the things I love most about history. Reading old journals, finding articles and letters that throw new light on a subject. Like I mentioned before, I spent quite a bit of time with my grandmother while she was ill. I haven't been able to conduct new research since I began my teaching career. Of course, it's still publish or perish, so I'm planning on taking next summer off and digging into the archives."

"Perhaps I can give you some direction on finding specific sources, if you'd like. I have access to a wealth of texts in England and Europe."

"That's very generous of you."

"Not at all. I want you to be happy."

"Giff . . . I don't understand—"

"That I care for you?"

"Yes, but more than that. Why?"

He fell silent, looking down at the sand as they walked slowly. Finally, he spoke. "It's difficult to explain. I've never felt this way about another person. Believe me, I do not accost young women in grocery stores."

Linda laughed briefly. "You didn't exactly accost me. But you have been persistent."

"Too much so?"

"I . . . I don't know. Maybe."

He stopped and pressed her close, looping both arms around her back. "It's difficult for me to go slow, Linda. Perhaps I've been on my own too long, enjoying an easy life. Perhaps I've had my way too often."

"I'm not sure about that, but you certainly seem confident."

He smiled slightly, his shadowed eyes reflecting tenderness. "Do I? I suppose I am."

"You have me at a disadvantage, you know." She snuggled closer, running her hands over his back, loving the feel of power he projected.

"How?"

"You're very accomplished . . . at many things, it seems."

"My cooking skills?" She heard the hint of humor in his voice.

"No, and not your writing ability either."

"Ah, you mean with women."

"You are quick."

"Never with you. With you, I'd go very, very slowly."

Linda felt herself blush. "That's not what I meant! I meant quick as in intelligent, clever."

"And I meant what I said. I'll try not to rush you, but you must know how much I want to be in your bed," he said before she felt the light touch of his mouth on hers. "Inside you," he whispered against her lips.

"Giff, I . . . I don't know what to say." She felt his arousal, hard against her belly. How simple it would be to touch him, to take him inside her and ease their frustration.

"Tell me you want the same thing."

"I do," she whispered, closing her eyes, blocking out reality. Oh, how she wanted to make love to this man. She felt that for the first time, making love would equal or surpass her dreams. That this man would be the flesh-and-blood embodiment of her fantasy lover. But was that fair to Giff, to be compared to someone else, someone who didn't exist?

Until she could reconcile that dilemma in her own mind, she couldn't make love to him. As much as she wanted to experience the overwhelming sensations to the fullest, it wouldn't be fair, to either of them, to risk William coming between them in bed. And if by some chance there was a future for them, she didn't want it to begin with a lie. Now, before her relationship with Giff deepened, was the time to reconcile her feelings for William Howard, for what had happened 14 years ago.

"Something disturbs you. Tell me what's wrong."

She opened her eyes, raised her hand and caressed his face. "You are unlike any other man I've known, Giff. But we are rushing. I don't even know how long you'll be here, what your plans are. I don't want a one-night stand or a meaningless summer fling."

"Neither do I."

"I'll admit I have some issues to work out—and I will, on my own. But ever since I met you, I've felt that you have something driving you. Something that makes you want to pursue me without revealing too much about yourself. I'm not being judgmental, and I'm trying not to be too pushy, but I wish I could feel that what we shared was more balanced."

"Surely you didn't expect me to tell you everything in just two days."

"No, but I want to know more. It's almost like a hunger inside me, to know you better. And I'm not sure we'll have time."

He took a deep breath and settled his chin on top of her hair, holding her tightly. "Then we share the same hunger," he said, taking in a deep breath. "I'll stay as long as you are here."

"You will?"

"I promise."

She wasn't sure why he'd be here that long. It was true that he could do research or write almost anywhere, but hadn't he said that he wasn't writing another book? Yet that the papers inside were impromptu research? She felt like shaking her head at the confusing array of emotions, facts and speculation that filled her thoughts.

Maybe now wasn't the moment to ask what he *was* doing here, with so many other things unsettled. Besides, she'd exhibited more than her usual share of inquisitive behavior since she'd met him. "If you're going to be here for a while, then we'll have time. We can get to know each other. We don't have to rush into bed."

He chuckled from deep inside his chest. "You make it sound like a chore to avoid."

She laughed. "I didn't mean it that way. It's just that—"

"I know. I'm rushing you."

He tilted her chin up, gazed into her eyes for a long time. Then he lowered his lips and kissed her, with tenderness and passion and the promise of many tomorrows. She returned his kiss with equal desire, knowing that she opened herself to possibilities, but also to pain, by accepting him on his terms. But God help her, she wanted him as much as she'd ever wanted anything in her life.

Linda melted into him, clung to his warmth as a chill wind swirled off the waves and blew her hair around them. There is a reason, she thought as he ended the kiss, that he cares for me. That he's here with me. Just give him time—give us time. She held on to that theory as the angry breeze blew off the ocean and whipped through the sand and sea grass, as they walked to her house in silence. As Giff kissed her again and told her good night, watching, as always, until she was locked safely inside.

Damn the modern morality! In ages past they would never have become so intimate so soon. They would have been chaperoned and controlled, with no chance for passion to overrule their heads.

If they kept seeing each other so often, they'd be in bed before anyone came near the attic again, much less touch the board. Damn them!

He'd be trapped, impotent while the lovers consummated their relationship. He wouldn't allow it! Such fury needed a physical outlet, one he couldn't fully express until he had a body. But he could cause nature to quake and moan its misery. The very sea and air about them would show his displeasure at such manifestations of desire.

Love! Bah, they didn't know the meaning of the word. It was lust, pure and simple. They were under a spell, nothing more. Without the magic, they would be two pathetic humans, satisfying nothing more than an itch.

They had no respect for his power, no fear. Yes, that's what they needed. Fear of the unknown. Frightening memories, horrifying possibilities. The woman was most susceptible. She'd been terrified of the Ouija board. Even as he'd taken great pleasure in her responses, she'd turned away. Most people would have been fascinated, would have come back for more. They loved the unknown, the power that came from unexplained events. But not her. She'd run, scared little rabbit.

She'd run again. He'd make her afraid, invade her mind and place doubts about *him*. Anything to keep them apart until he could gain flesh-and-blood status.

Then she'd really have a reason to be afraid. And so would the man.

If Mord had a face, he would have grinned. The man thought he was so wise, so clever. Well, he'd find out that he was no match for a power so elemental, so eternal.

He'd find out the limits of being nothing more than human.

Chapter Four

What we fear comes to pass more speedily than what we hope.
—Publilius Syrus

Linda put down the heavy book and rubbed her forehead. A headache pounded behind her eyes from too much reading; she'd scanned the entire section on parapsychology, demonology and spiritualism. This book, like the others, gave no firm answers, just another author's interpretation of life beyond death. She'd set out this morning to learn more about past lives and evil spirits, but didn't feel any closer to resolving her feelings for William Howard now than she had when she had driven away from the house.

She hadn't really understood until this afternoon, sitting in the public library of Charleston, that there wouldn't be firm proof of contact from beyond the grave. Many of the famous cases she read about in one book were disproved in another. Some of the evidence was compelling, but the skeptic in her made her question the validity of the memories, assertions or regressions of the believers, the people who had supposedly talked to the dead or lived a previous life.

She'd studied books on dreams, hoping to understand her fascination for William Howard and just how her current involvement with Giff might contribute to or confuse that fantasy. Most of the dream books dealt with interpreting symbols. Well, she didn't have symbols as much as she had raw emotion and steamy, unconsummated sex. Just the thought caused a restlessness she knew could only contribute to her current level of sexual frustration. Maybe those dreams simply meant she needed some long-awaited fulfillment in her love life.

Other books dealt with psychic knowledge coming from those already dead, who communicated with the living. One book claimed that reincarnation was tied to astrology. Another described telepathy as tapping into the thoughts and even the subconscious of others, regardless of distance. And of course there were books on Edgar Cayce and an entity called "Seth." Mostly, the books were overwhelming in variety and number; and often written in a style that was difficult to read and understand.

One of the cases really intrigued her, though. In England in the 1960s, a child had died in a boating accident. The father supposedly told the mother that he'd had a premonition that she would get pregnant again soon, and that the baby would be the reincarnation of the dead child. She scoffed at him, but sure enough, she became pregnant and had another son. Soon the boy could "recall" the names of favorite toys or people, and had a special affinity with the family pet, telling his parents things that had happened to the dog when it was a puppy—when the dead child had been alive.

The father had the child regressed through hypnosis, where he told of many past lives. They weren't all documented in writing, but the book claimed that the details were very accurate and compelling. The really intriguing thing from Linda's perspective was that the boy's name was Gifford White, so close to Giff's name. The coincidence of their names really caught her attention, as well as the decade of their births.

Linda's heart went out to that little boy, who had been used to test his father's theories and the spiritualist's claims. Did he ever have a chance at a normal childhood, or see value in himself as an individual? It just didn't seem fair to put that kind of pressure on a child. However, the books she'd read today had confirmed that childhood past-life memories were most accurate when the children were very young, before being influenced by school and friends.

She checked her watch; it was almost four o'clock. She'd spent the day in the library, and still didn't know exactly what had happened that night 14 years ago. And she didn't know what she thought about reincarnation, which Giff had brought up. He obviously felt strongly about the subject, expecting her to consider it seriously. She just wasn't sure about whether souls came back again and again, in either a random pattern or to satisfy some sense of destiny. She wasn't even sure she believed there was such a thing as destiny.

One thing she *had* learned concerned evil spirits, such as the one who had invaded their Ouija board. Several of the texts said that an evil entity had to be invited into the life of a living person. According to the experts, some evil spirits were ghosts of amoral or psychotic people who had died violently. Others were true, elemental evils, the type mentioned in religious and cultural legends like those of Vishnu or Pandora's box. They usually had a link to a ritual, an individual or an object.

What was Mord? A mean-spirited ghost or an evil as old as time? Or had she and Gerri imagined him? She closed her eyes and thought back to that night, remembering the feeling, the fear.

After Mord frightened them with exclamations of "kill," Gerri jerked her hands away, sending the pointer sliding across the board. "Oh, my God, Linda," she said, "this is too weird. Who is this guy? Why does he keep saying 'kill'?"

"I don't know," Linda said, getting up from the table, backing away from the board. "He's evil."

"I can feel it! The evil's still here!" Gerri jumped up, moving around the table as though it might reach up and bite her. "Let's get out of here!"

"Yes," Linda whispered, grabbing her friend's arm

and backing toward the door. Instead of the feeling of fear leaving now that they no longer touched the board, it only intensified, seeming to envelop them. Panic brought forth visions of death. Gerri started to scream, but Linda placed her hand over her friend's mouth, cutting off the sound to a whimper.

She reached for the knob, but it seemed cold and slick, like a glass of icy water. The metallic smell in the air increased, yet it seemed she couldn't get enough air. When she opened her mouth, gasping, the taste permeated her consciousness. Blood. What surrounded them was the smell and taste of violent death, of battles and betrayal and fear.

She jerked at the door, crying, more scared than she'd ever been before. This wasn't a horror movie or a Stephen King novel. This was real. When the knob finally turned, she yanked Gerri into the narrow stairwell, running away from the playful room of her childhood summers and the terror of this teenage inquisition. She ran as though her life depended on it, hand in hand with her best friend, descending the stairs, darting through the sun room and racing down the back steps.

Linda opened her eyes and shivered. The quiet and calm of the library replaced the overwhelming fear, and slowly, she tried to let go of the past. Something felt different, though, a sense of urgency and heightened awareness of the loneliness of the library, the mustiness of the books. Despite the slanted rays of afternoon sunlight, she felt a gloom descend over the shelves and rows. Whispered conversations receded into background noise and she listened to her own heartbeat, which seemed well above normal.

Recall of the experience with Mord flashed through her mind. She tried to force it away from her consciousness, but the old memory hovered in the background, as though it tried to break free again as a terrifying reality. As though just thinking about the past, about the evil, threatened the present.

Linda didn't know whether "Mord" had come with the Ouija board or been "invited" in through Gerri's and her conversations with William Howard, but however it had happened, she couldn't allow him—or it—to return. For now, she had to get away from all these books on paranormal events. And she must never go back to the attic, never risk touching that board again.

She gathered her purse and notepad, her head pounding with renewed vigor as she stood up. Questions swirled through her mind like dark whirlpools. Gifford Knight, who had mentioned reincarnation just yesterday. Gifford White, who had lived through a childhood of case studies. Was there a connection? Suddenly she remembered his comments yesterday about returning to fulfil a destiny. *"I've studied it most of my life. You could say I'm an expert on the subject."* How much of an expert was he? Was it from personal experience, or just a compelling interest?

There were too many uncertainties in her life at the moment. She felt unsafe, isolated, in her grandmother's house. Without close neighbors, which she had in Evanston, she would be more vulnerable to burglars or Peeping Toms. Or just a curious, dark, long-haired man on the beach.

And Giff, no matter how sexy and charismatic, had a very private nature that made her cautious. Well, maybe not when they were together, when his presence overwhelmed her. But at this moment, too many things about him bothered her. She didn't think he would harm her, but she had read stories about obsessive personalities or stalkers, who decided they had a relationship with someone and didn't take no for an answer.

With Giff's potent sexuality and powerful kisses, she didn't really want to say no. But what if she denied his passion? What if he rushed her, or insisted upon the kind of relationship she couldn't accept? She rubbed her forehead, knowing that her fears sounded a bit paranoid. It was just that she had no way to defend herself against that kind of threat, or any other, for that matter. The feeling of nervousness and unease increased, pushing her from the library.

She felt strange, not at all her usual calm, balanced self. She recognized that her thoughts were panicky and jumbled, but she couldn't seem to stop them. It was almost as if someone else were putting these ideas into her head. She wanted to stop the flow of doubts and worries, but couldn't. They kept coming, making her steps quicken along with her heartbeat.

She needed protection, she decided as she hurried outside and was hit with a wave of heat and humidity. The image of her grandfather's World War II pistol, one he'd brought back from Germany in 1946, flashed into her mind. The gun rested in a nightstand drawer, kept inside a velvet-lined case. She didn't know if the pistol would fire, or if it was just for show. Her grandmother must have thought it would scare away a burglar, because she'd kept it close by.

Linda had never owned a gun, but had taken lessons years ago in college, when a campus rapist had the female students in a self-defense mode. He'd been caught before she got up the nerve to actually purchase a pistol.

Now, it seemed as though having a weapon around the house might be a good idea.

Her car was even hotter than the air outside, despite the fact that she'd parked in the shade. Linda fanned herself and wondered if any of her fears would come true. Maybe no one would harm her. Maybe the man on the beach had been harmless. And maybe Giff was just a man who found her very attractive and interesting.

Maybe.

Her hands shook just a little as she turned the key in the ignition. This wasn't like her, she knew, but she felt very vulnerable for the first time in years. She pulled into traffic, heading for the interstate. There was a small gun shop in McClellanville, run by a nice man who was a friend of Mr. Watley. Tomorrow, she'd take the old gun to the shop to see if it was worth having cleaned and repaired. If it was in good condition, she would get some ammunition. That should make her feel a little safer.

At least a gun was something solid. Evil entities and reincarnation—now those were topics with no definite answers, even after a day spent in research. Her heart continued to beat fast, and the air seemed so damned hot and oppressive. She flipped the fan on high and drove north, toward home and the uncertainty that she knew awaited her.

Giff finished reading Linda's doctoral dissertation, a smile on his face. He had found out much about her, from her approach to problems to her own ideas on justice, governing and expediencies. The smile faded when he realized that Linda understood the need for occasional rapid decision-making, yet felt issues should be re-evaluated by a representative form of government at the earliest convenience.

His Linda was a supporter of the common man, a believer in democracy. And she didn't like overpowering men who pushed through their own agenda.

He was guilty of doing just that where she was concerned, and he'd be damned if he could stop the chain of events. She felt he was rushing her; he was. She felt that they should get to know each other better before sharing their love; they should.

But he had no intention of letting her philosophical leanings get in the way of their ultimate goal, the joining of body, mind and soul. That was the only acceptable outcome, and she must be made to accept the inevitability of their love. Once they were committed to each other, then he'd explain. Then she'd understand.

If he lived that long.

The only problem was that he'd begun to feel guilty about deceiving Linda, about holding back the information. When he'd started this quest, he hadn't known what the woman's personality would be. If she was intelligent or kind, beautiful or humorous. He'd loved her, of course, but he hadn't realized how much he'd *like* her.

He switched off the computer and rose, stretching tired muscles. He'd read through lunch, so intent on the subject that he hadn't felt the hunger until now. Linda had left her house after breakfast; he'd watched her drive off. Was she still away? An all-consuming need to know rifled through him, but he tried to contain the impatience. If something had happened to her, he'd know. He felt no great disturbance, only a vague sense of unease.

Closing his eyes and concentrating, he tried to bring her consciousness into focus. *Irritation. Uncertainty. Heat and humidity. Coming home.* Relief washed through him as he realized she was on her way home, driving, no doubt, in traffic, hot and tired. What had made her feel unsure of herself? Or perhaps it wasn't herself that she doubted, but something else. He wanted answers, not more doubts.

Where in the hell have you been all day, Linda?

He would wait until later, then walk to her house. If she wanted, they'd take their nightly stroll. If not, he would convince her to tell him what she'd done all day. Had he truly rushed her, made her run from him? He couldn't allow that to happen.

If she was having second thoughts about their relationship, he would simply change his tactic. She must recognize her love. They must seal their fate.

And June 18th was only eight days away.

Linda stopped for dinner at a small beachside restaurant, but found her appetite lacking. Not like when she was with Giff, who seemed to feed her stomach as well as her fantasies. She didn't want to think about him or anything of substance; she'd thought enough for one day.

She left a half-finished plate of grilled shrimp with pasta and drove away feeling just as vulnerable as ever. She tried to immerse herself in ordinary things, like purchasing a small microwave oven and stopping by the grocery for some frozen dinners. But nothing could totally dispel her feeling of anxiety. She even felt uneasy about returning to the house, a place that had always seemed a wonderful refuge. She found herself driving slowly, seeing the darkness of night as a menace, the calm waters beneath the causeway, threatening.

She pulled into the driveway about ten. The house seemed lonely, isolated, scary. Despite venturing upstairs to the attic two days ago, she no longer felt brave or reconciled to her past. She felt as though the attic pressed down on the house, holding fears inside like the lid of a teapot, holding in the heat and steam until the time was right.

What event brewed inside? She felt it building, steeping as surely as tea leaves in hot water. With a slight fumble, she reached for the keys and turned off the car's engine.

* * *

Giff saw her headlights, heard the crunch of tires on the gravel as she pulled into the drive. *Where have you been?* He wanted to shout the question, to shake her for making him so concerned. He'd been sitting on the warm sand of a dune, watching her house under the cover of darkness, imagining all kinds of scenarios. She'd become lost. She'd had an accident. Someone dangerous had approached her.

And then she slowly drove in, as if no one cared.

She's not used to answering to anyone, he rationally told himself. *But she should be. She should realize how important she's become to me.*

He pushed himself up from the ground, watching her all the while. She paused after opening the car door, the interior light showing her sitting in the driver's seat, hands clenched around the wheel as though she didn't want to leave the circle of light and enter the dark house. Did she sense something was wrong? He couldn't tell. She wasn't reaching out to him mentally at the moment, and the only impressions he received were jumbles of anxiety. She'd pulled inside herself, he realized, as confused as he about what was going on.

He heard the car door slam as she walked slowly to the front door. Her body was an indistinct shadow against the pale gravel and concrete. Then she paused, her emotions suddenly as easy to read as a picture book.

Fear. Upstairs. Don't go near.

He heard her thoughts clearly as she stepped onto the porch. His internal alarm went on alert.

Something was wrong, something Linda couldn't see or hear, but knew was there. With a sudden burst of energy, Giff pushed himself up from the ground and ran toward the back of her house.

Setting her grocery bags down on the counter, breathing rapidly, Linda rushed through the house, turning on at least one light in each downstairs room. She checked the doors and windows, making sure each one was locked. There was nothing else she could do to secure the house. She returned to the kitchen, rubbed her arms with trembling hands, and began to stack the dinners in the freezer. She definitely needed to do something to keep busy.

A panic attack. She had the symptoms, she knew from college psychology classes. She'd seen the reaction in certain high-strung students, who'd let their fear of tests or papers or whatever distort their view of reality. She'd had to counsel them, explain that they needed to understand what the real problem was, then look for a solution to the short-term cause of their anxiety.

But there was no reason for her to feel such fear. She didn't face a pop quiz on calculus, or need to write a 15-page paper on medieval economic systems. This was her grandmother's house—her own house now—and there wasn't anything here to make her hands shake and her knees wobble.

There was nothing here.

She jumped when she heard a knock on the French doors leading to the deck. One of the dinners slipped from her fingers, thudding off the counter and onto the floor. She didn't bother to pick it up. She just stood and stared at the doorway.

The floods on the deck were on, but so were the lights in the den, so she couldn't see outside very well. The knock came again, more demanding this time. Still, she seemed as frozen as the food inside the cartons, unable to take the steps across the floor and confirm her suspicion that Giff was at the door.

Her heart raced as she felt the presence of someone, something, touching her thoughts. *Don't answer the door. Don't be alone with him right now.*

"Linda!" His voice sounded muffled, coming through the wood and glass. But it was Giff. She could see his outline through the shade.

Be careful. Lock your doors. The words were Giff's, but the voice she heard from within mocked him.

Linda grabbed her temples, shut her eyes against the pounding inside her head. Why was she acting like this? What was wrong with her? She wanted to scream in frustration, but didn't. That would only cause Giff to break down the door, certain that she was being murdered slowly and painfully.

"Linda! For God's sake, let me in."

She had to answer the door. She dropped her hands from the pounding in her head. "I'm coming," she called out, hoping he could hear her.

Slowly, she forced herself to cross the room, even though it felt as though she were walking in thick, clinging mud. "I'm coming," she said again.

Finally, she reached the door and touched the knob. It was warm, not cold and damp, as she'd expected. Why had she thought that?

Because the knob to the attic is cold. Because you're frightened. Because Giff is standing on the other side of the door, and you're not sure who or what he is.

"No," she whispered. "I'm not afraid of Giff."

She turned the dead bolt with one hand, then opened the door.

"Thank heavens," he said as he pushed inside.

Linda stood passive for a moment, sensing the panic receding. She closed her eyes and breathed in the scent of Giff, felt the hardness of his body as he held her tightly. His breath seemed ragged as he buried his face in her hair.

"You frightened ten years off my life," he said with such raw emotion that she felt herself melt into his embrace.

"I don't know what happened."

"What did you do today?" he asked, raising his head and gazing into her eyes.

"I went to the library in Charleston."

"Why?"

"Some research." She pulled away, trying to distance herself from him and from his prying questions. What difference did it make to him what she did?

"On what?"

"Damn it, Giff, I don't answer to you. I don't have to tell you everything I did, everything I thought about."

He looked as though she'd slapped him. He

drew back, dropping his hands from her arms. "My apologies. I was concerned."

Linda closed her eyes again and took a deep breath. "I'm not accustomed to explaining myself to anyone else."

"Of course."

"I must have gotten too hot or gone too long without a meal. I didn't feel well today."

"Since you left the library?"

"Yes. Right now, all I want to do is get ready for bed and sleep about twelve hours."

Giff ignored her statement. "Did you meet anyone new today, anyone who upset you?"

"No, not that I think that's your concern." She was getting annoyed with him for being so overbearing. He had no right to assume she would confide her secrets to him. He was, after all, someone she'd met only two days ago. Hardly her nearest and dearest friend, even though she'd believed they could build a relationship based on mutual interests and attraction.

"I'm making it my concern. I can't help but be worried when you're gone all day, then come home upset. You were practically frantic."

She narrowed her eyes and took a step back. "How did you know that?"

He remained silent, staring at her with an intensity that was as unnerving as his silence. Finally, he looked away and expelled a breath. "I know. I heard it in your voice."

"No," she said softly. "I think that what you meant is that you just knew I was upset. You want me to believe that you can sense my moods. That's what you were going to say, isn't it?"

"You don't want to hear what I have to say."

She wrapped her arms around herself. "You're right. I think you should leave."

Giff stared at her. She felt his eyes bore into hers. She felt as though his gaze scorched into her soul. Finally, he turned away and opened the door. The sound of the surf and the breeze from the ocean rushed inside.

"We need to talk sometime soon. I need to explain." As he spoke, he looked into the night. He seemed a million miles away.

Linda felt an irrational urge to go to him, comfort him. That made no sense. She was angry at him for his attitude, not sorry because she'd upset him. It was his own fault that he assumed too much too soon. She clenched her fists at her sides and willed herself to be firm.

"We'll talk tomorrow."

Giff nodded. "You must know that I'm concerned because I care."

She couldn't think of anything to say. She just wanted to be alone, to crawl into bed and try to relax. Thinking about the events today would have to wait. "Good night."

He turned back. "Good night, dear Linda. Sleep well." Then he smiled. "Remember to lock your doors."

Linda couldn't resist a slight smile. "I'll remember."

Giff slipped outside, shutting the French door behind him.

The house was plunged into silence without the

sound of the sea and the ever-constant wind. The scent that was distinctively Giff remained, however, both comforting Linda and making her uneasy. She didn't understand how she could experience such a compelling attraction to him at the same time she felt a deep wariness about their budding relationship.

She turned the dead bolt, locking him out. If only she could so easily control her mind. This morning, she'd had such hope that she could resolve her feelings about the Ouija board, William, and the evil spirit named Mord. But she hadn't resolved anything. In fact, she was more confused now than before.

A bath relaxed her somewhat, soothing her nerves, replacing the unfamiliar feelings of anxiety with familiar scents and sensations. She almost went to sleep in the warm water, the bubbles teasing her neck and tickling sensitive skin and private places. Naked and vulnerable, she couldn't stop herself from thinking about Giff. With the last of her strength, she forced herself to ignore the desire he aroused in her. Instead of just having erotic dreams, now she was experiencing waking fantasies about Giff. Maybe she should have her hormones checked. It seemed as though she was becoming a sexually frustrated "old maid."

She slipped on an old cotton nightshirt after drying off. Her body felt drained of strength and energy after the long day, after spending so much time anxious and perplexed by the lack of real answers. She had to come to terms with her misguided fascination for a long-dead man, yet couldn't. There were no explanations for how she and Gerri had contacted him via the Ouija board. If he'd never lived, she could believe he was a figment of their imaginations. But he wasn't. He'd lived such a short life in a very turbulent period of history, dying just hours before Wellington defeated Napoleon. No picture of him existed, no detailed records. The logical part of her mind knew he was dead. But no book could tell her for sure why she felt he was as real as anyone else alive.

But what was Mord? Who was he? The books weren't clear on that subject either. And she still believed, just as she had 14 years ago, that someone named Mord had killed William. That he hadn't died at the hands of the French, as had so many other soldiers that day. Death by "friendly fire" was a problem in every war, yet the very malevolence she'd experienced with Mord made her believe nothing so innocent as a misfired bullet or poorly aimed cannon had killed William. His death was a mystery, but unfortunately, she could find no clues or evidence with which to solve it.

Her headache threatened again, beginning to pound with each heartbeat. Super-sensitive, she felt each rush of blood through her veins. *Just go to sleep,* she told herself. *Forget William Howard, forget the Ouija board incident. You had many other happy years in this house and with Gerri. Why focus on a few weeks out of all the rest?*

She settled into bed and pulled the covers to her chest, listening to the familiar night sounds to make herself sleepy. Only the night didn't sound ordinary. Instead of the barely audible sounds of waves caressing the sand, tonight they crashed to shore, rushing one after another in a mad dash to conquer the beach, to pull it into the sea. And the night birds were silent, along with the insects who usually serenaded her. The wind blew against the glass, producing creaks and groans throughout the old house.

Linda shivered and prayed that tomorrow would be a better day. She reached over and turned off the lamp, plunging the room into darkness. The house seemed to moan in sympathy to her uncertainties, and her heart continued to pound. It would be a long night, she thought, trying to get comfortable. *If only the dreams would stay away,* she prayed. *Please, leave me alone. Let me rest.*

Mord pushed against the invisible boundaries of his world. If he had legs, he would have stomped them in frustration. He wanted to demand a million answers from the woman. He wanted to know if she was afraid yet, if the dose of fear she'd experienced at the library was enough to make her stay away from *him*.

She should be afraid. He knew what a timid little rabbit she was. It didn't take much to frighten her. Just a healthy dose of something humans considered evil, something they didn't understand.

He wanted to ask if her blood raced and her heart pounded as she drove away from the library. Did she feel very much alive when she ran, when she experienced a strong dose of paranoia and tried to stay away from the house? And what of *him*? Would she stay away from him—for now?

Oh, Mord knew she desired the man's body. His muscle and bone and hair. She fixated on the physical sensations he could provide, simply because he had a human body.

She wanted to sleep, to forget. But he wouldn't let her rest. He wondered how she would like to "make love" to someone else, someone who was more than a mere human.

If he had a body, he'd show her real pleasure—his pleasure. He'd satisfy his craving for her very essence, her soul. She owed him, the fickle, frail human. She owed him for what had happened a thousand years ago. And the man. He owed a debt too, a debt he would soon pay.

Soon, Mord thought. As soon as I have a body.

She sank to her knees in front of William, her eyes scanning the darkness of his face, his expression. All she saw was the blackness of night, the misty image of the man she loved. She wanted to see his features; she needed to almost as much as she needed to share her love. Her hands roamed up his thighs, feeling the solid, warm muscles beneath her searching palms.

"William, make love to me." Waves crashed to the shore as dampness from the sand seeped through the thin material of her gown. She didn't care. She reached for the buttons on his coat, tugging open the wool and running her fingers along the fine, soft fabric of his shirt. He groaned, urging her hands lower, to the strap that held his sword.

She couldn't get it unfastened! Desire warred with impatience. She wanted him naked, as aroused as she, but he wore too many clothes, too many trappings of his uniform.

"Help me," she whispered, and didn't know whether she meant with undressing him or with her almost painful physical need.

He pushed her hands away and jerked open the belt, tossing the sword and scabbard onto the sand. She ran her hands over his thighs, upward to the bulging arousal that pressed against his trousers. He moaned again. She slipped her fingers inside the waistband, working at those buttons, freeing him.

"Yes," he whispered in an anguished whisper when she stroked the length of his shaft, her fingers eagerly testing the size and feel of him. He was satin smooth, hard beyond belief, the length so impressive she had to keep from crying out. It was heaven, to be this close, to know that he would fill her, satisfy her, as no one else could.

She wanted to please him, but he dropped to his knees on the sand and grabbed her shoulders, kissing her with force and passion. She moaned into his mouth as their tongues mated, as she felt such a heady rush that she wondered if she would survive the sensation.

"Make love to me," she whispered again when his lips strayed to her neck, to her throat. "Love me."

"Forever," he murmured.

They sank to the beach together. She felt his weight, his blessed weight, as he pressed her into the sand. Yes, finally he'll be mine. As completely as I will be his. Yes, yes, yes . . .

She closed her eyes as he pushed up her nightdress, as she felt the caress of the wind and his strong hands along her thighs, her stomach, her breasts. "Now, William, please," she heard herself say, the words weak and yet impassioned.

She looked up, still unable to see him. With her fingers she traced his jaw, his brow. His skin felt hot, dotted with a fine sheen of perspiration despite the cool night. She followed the plane of his brow, molded her palms along his cheeks, trying to envision his face.

"Why can't I see you, my love?"

"You know me."

"Yes, but I want to see you."

He pulled the nightgown over her head. His silence stretched out as his fingers cupped her breasts, as his head lowered to take a nipple in his mouth. She closed her eyes and told herself it didn't matter. This was William, the man she loved.

His breath felt hot and moist. She moaned in anticipation, knowing it would be heaven. Knowing he would love her as no one else ever had, or ever could.

She felt the flick of his tongue and almost climaxed. "Now, my love."

His weight lifted as he used one hand to pull at his pants. She moaned at the loss, but knew he would take her now, make her his forever.

Then his fingers turned cold, the breath against her breast icy. Instead of firm fingers that molded her flesh, his hand felt more like talons pressing into her sensitive skin. Her eyes flew open—and she stared into the face of evil.

She screamed, screamed, screamed . . .

Chapter Five

In the drowsy dark cave of the mind dreams build their nest with fragments dropped from day's caravan.
—Rabindranath Tagore.

"Linda, wake up. It's only a dream." Giff sank to the bed and took her rigid, thrashing body into his arms, only to realize that was probably the worst possible course of action. She dreamed of a violation of the worst kind, by an evil she couldn't fully imagine. He couldn't use force to subdue her.

"No! No, no, no—"

"Linda," he said firmly, stroking her face, "wake up. You're having a nightmare.

When she continued to struggle, he felt like crying out in frustration himself. There was only one thing to do.

He closed his eyes and focused on her subconscious, the part of her that dreamt of William Howard and changed him from a faceless lover to the epitome of evil. Mord. He wasn't the one doing this, but he was to blame for making her lose contact with William all those years ago and for trying to enter her life again. Giff wasn't sure how, but Mord's influence was growing, becoming more frightening as the time of reckoning grew near.

"He's gone, love, he's gone," he whispered into her mind. *"I'm here with you. Don't be afraid. I'll always be with you."*

"William?" she whispered.

"Yes, love. I'm here." He stroked her face, her neck. Concentrating on calming her, he took up where her dream lover had left off, stroking her body in long, calming motions. Beneath her sleepshirt, her nipples pebbled, firm beneath the soft fabric. He sucked in a deep breath as his body reacted to her passion. He'd longed for the moment when he could truly make love to her, but now wasn't the time to confuse her dreams with reality. However, there was one thing he could do for her.

He entered her dream, making love to her as William. Both inside his mind and against his skin, he felt her rapid breathing as the last of her fear dissolved, confronted by the heat of her passion. His own response, the shock of becoming mentally and physically aroused so thoroughly, threatened his control. But he knew how Linda loved to be caressed, how she loved his kisses. He made sure she dreamed of those things, that her fantasy was as flawless as possible.

He slipped his hands beneath the shirt, cupping her breasts, testing their weight in greedy hands. Her skin was as soft as satin, firm and smooth. She responded to him with a natural sensuality that made him harden even more. He gritted his teeth and focused on her pleasure.

There would be time to share their love. There must be time before this life was through.

A moan escaped her parted lips as she arched toward his hands. He pulled up her shirt and lowered his head, taking first one and then the other nipple between his lips, sucking as though he could draw life-sustaining love from the fevered buds. Linda reached for him, ran her fingers through his hair, held his head to her breasts as she entwined her legs with his.

He eased one hand down her stomach, feeling her muscles clench as she tried to get closer. She wanted him with a desire that left him aching. He couldn't wait much longer to make her his. Even without fate rushing toward them, he wanted her as a man wants a woman. As a lover seeks his perfect partner. His hand slipped inside her underwear, through her womanly curls.

He stroked a finger through her heat and dampness, feeling the swollen flesh of her arousal. She gasped and raised from the bed, pressing herself more fully into his hands. He thought he might explode.

"Yes, love. Yes," he whispered.

He set a rhythm that she followed, gasping, arching. It took only moments for her climax to start. Giff closed his eyes and entered her fantasy, listening to her scream of pleasure at the same time he experienced her release.

Oh, God, William. Yes, yes, yes!

He'd never imagined . . . he'd never felt anything like Linda's passion. It left him breathless, clenching his teeth against his own threatening release.

Not now. Not like this. He let his mind slip away from hers as he cradled her body to his and tried to calm his thundering pulse. With a shaking hand, he straightened her nightshirt and adjusted her cotton panties.

Her tight muscles finally relaxed. A little sigh escaped her as she snuggled closer. Giff let out a long-held breath and prayed that when she awoke, she wouldn't notice that he was thoroughly, painfully, aroused.

He leaned against the headboard of her bed, pulling her limp body against him. He had to get his mind off making love and back to the problem they shared—explaining how he, William, Mord and Linda were connected. Her ignorance of the alliance caused her too much anxiety, too many dreams and nightmares. Giff knew she was already suspicious of his motives for pursuing her so diligently. And she was suffering from her own doubts and fears about her past and present.

But if he told her too much too soon, she could reject the explanation. She might run, never to fall in love with him, never to release them from this eternal nightmare. That was a chance he couldn't take.

God, how he loved her. How he'd loved her for centuries.

She snuggled closer, rubbing her leg along his, sighing like a kitten.

He stroked her shoulder, resisting the urge to roll toward her, to kiss her full lips and bury himself in the warmth of her body. She was soft and compliant, still responding to the release she'd experienced.

He could slip back into her mind, take up where William left off, and fulfill their destiny before she was even awake. The temptation was as great as his need, but he couldn't take advantage of her that way. She might not return his love when she discovered his deceit. He had no idea what would happen to their eternal struggle if he violated the natural progression of their love, from discovery to commitment to consummation.

"William?" Her voice sounded sleepy, weak and confused.

"I'm here, love."

He watched her face in the dim light, saw her eyelids flicker and a frown mar her brow. Then her eyes opened and she jumped, realizing, no doubt, that she was in her own bed . . . with a man other than the one in her dream.

She screamed and leaped from the bed. "Who—"

"It's me, Linda. It's Giff." He wanted to go to her, calm her fears, but knew it would be best to let her relax and become accustomed to the idea that he was here with her.

"Giff? What are you doing here?" She sounded

both panic-stricken and confused. She tugged at her nightshirt, pulling it over her thighs, stretching it to her knees.

"You had a nightmare."

She pushed her hair from her eyes and eased off the bed, backing up until she reached a table and lamp. He heard her fumbling, imagined her hands shaking. In a moment light flooded the room.

Giff blinked at the brightness, then swung his legs off the bed, away from her. She didn't need to see the extent of his frustration.

"How did you know I had a nightmare?" she asked in a wary voice.

"You screamed."

She remembered screaming, over and over again, as the icy fingers of evil gripped her. She couldn't repress a shudder. It had been the worst dream so far, the most horrible nightmare. If she thought it would return, she'd never sleep again.

And there was no reason to believe it wouldn't recur.

But then she remembered resuming the dream. William had made love to her with his lips and his hands, bringing her to a shattering release that she'd never experienced before. Apparently she'd done more than just dream his lovemaking. Her panties were damp with it. Her knees still shook from the powerful sensations. She imagined that Giff could see her nipples straining against the fabric of her sleepshirt. Was he here when she'd experienced that release?

But had a dream caused her to climax? Had Giff—

"Linda, I just wanted to comfort you."

No, it couldn't have been him. It had been William, all in her dream. She rubbed her temples with shaking fingers. "How did you get into my house?"

Giff stood up, then pulled a key from the pocket of his jeans. "You didn't hide it well. I found it beneath the pot of geraniums on the deck."

His voice sounded calm, controlled, but she heard the slightest bit of censure. No doubt he thought her hiding place extremely unoriginal. Very unsafe. Apparently he was right.

She rubbed her eyes, then pushed her hair back again. "I still don't understand—"

He touched her hands and she jerked. He'd moved so silently that she hadn't realized he was so close. One part of her wanted to let him hold her, to welcome his comfort. But another part of her remained suspicious of his motives and actions. How had he heard her scream, unless he'd been beneath her window?

"I was walking down the beach, worried about you after you sent me away earlier tonight. I stood outside your house. When I heard you scream, I knew I had to come to you."

"Why?" she asked in a small voice, wanting to believe him, but so unsure.

"Didn't you listen to me yesterday?" he said gently. "Don't you believe me when I say that nothing is more important to me than your happiness?"

She whirled away, facing the mirror-like, dark window, but seeing his reflection as he stood behind her. "I don't know what to believe," she cried.

"Believe me, Linda. I would never harm you. Let me keep your nightmares away."

"You can't."

"Yes, I can."

"How? Tell me, how can you do that? You don't even know what they are!"

He remained silent, staring at her with an infuriating yet seductive calm.

"Why do you think you can solve everything?" she asked.

"I don't. I only know that I can help you, if you'll trust me."

"I don't know!"

"Yes, you do." He stepped behind her and placed his warm hands on her shoulders, stroking her arms. She couldn't stop herself from leaning into his solid chest, from closing her eyes and giving herself up to his embrace. She could almost imagine him as her fantasy lover. It seemed as though she could even smell a sexual essence that made her respond on a very basic level.

"Tell me, love," he said.

"Why did you call me that?"

"A term of endearment. Does it matter? I could call you sweetheart or darling, but I prefer to say what's in my heart."

"It's too soon to say such things."

He ignored her comment. "Tell me what made you cry in the night."

"You'll think I'm crazy. Maybe I am," she said with a weak laugh.

"I won't think you are crazy," he said softly. "Whatever bothers you is real, if only in your mind. This nightmare tonight . . . have you had it before?"

"Yes. No. It started out similar to a recurring dream, but tonight it turned . . . horrible. I was so frightened."

"I know, love. I know," he whispered in her ear. "Have you talked about it with another person?"

She shook her head. "No."

"Then tell me. Talking will make it seem less frightening. Keeping everything inside will make it even more terrifying."

"You really want to hear the entire story?"

"Yes."

He turned her in his arms, then nudged her chin so she looked at him. His eyes radiated peace. Calm. She felt as though she must tell him, as though her very sanity depended upon it.

"Very well."

Giff settled on the bed, sitting up against the headboard, his long legs stretched out and crossed at the ankles. "Come, sit beside me."

"I only want to talk."

"Whatever you say. I just want you to be comfortable."

Linda knew she was taking a big risk, cuddling on her bed with a man who had practically broken into her house, who was as mysterious as he was seductive. But tonight she felt no fear, none of her earlier anxiety. She trusted him to keep his word, and to keep her safe.

The result of logic and instinct, or the lingering effects of her dream? How could she judge? She had to follow her emotions.

"Do you remember when we talked about the Ouija board incident?"

"Of course."

"Gerri and I somehow contacted an English officer who had died in 1815."

"Yes, William Howard."

Linda turned to look at him. "You certainly have a good memory."

"I try."

She frowned, turning back so her shoulder nestled against his side, amazed that he remembered a name spoken just once. His arm held her lightly.

"Over the two weeks we talked with him, he became very real to me. I'm not sure why, maybe because I've always loved history more than Gerri. I always thought of him as *my* officer."

"I understand."

"One night, we were talking to William and got interrupted by someone—or something. Gerri and I both felt the most horrible evil, coming through the board, surrounding us in the room. We were scared, but talked to this . . . thing, this evil entity, named Mord until we couldn't stand it any longer. Then we ran out of the room and never talked to William again."

"What did Mord say?"

Linda shuddered at the memory. "He, or it, said that William was dead, and when I asked if Mord had killed him, he said, 'Kill, kill, kill.' "

"And you believe that Mord killed William in real life."

Linda nodded. "Yes, I do. I don't know why, but I truly believe that. You see, when I was in England, working on my dissertation, I researched William Howard to find out if he'd truly lived."

"And had he?"

She nodded. "Yes. That's what's really scary. I didn't make him up. He was real. All I could find out was that he was born in Sussex in 1786 and died at Waterloo in 1815. He was an officer in the Light Dragoons. We lived over a hundred years apart, but he *had* lived."

"And died."

"Yes, that's the tragic part. I know that if he'd lived, he'd still be dead now. But he never had a chance to be really happy."

"Did you discover how he died?"

"No, just that he served in the Peninsula Wars and the Battle of Waterloo under Wellington."

"So you dream about William Howard?"

Linda felt a blush creep up her neck at the thought of telling Giff just *how* she dreamt of William. "Yes, I do."

"And what kind of dreams do you have?"

"Just . . . dreams."

"Scary?"

She fidgeted on the bed, wishing he weren't so close. Wishing he didn't feel so warm, so solid. "No, not scary," she said, knowing her voice sounded reed thin.

"You don't want to tell me."

"You're right."

"Then I must conclude your dreams are rather . . . provocative."

"Well . . . yes. But I don't want to discuss them."

"So you are still rather obsessed with William.

He comes alive in your dreams. May I assume he makes passionate love to you?" Giff said softly, his breath teasing her temples.

"Please . . ."

"Please what, dear Linda?"

"Don't push me to talk about it."

Giff was silent so long that she turned to look at him. His expression was tender yet all-knowing, as though he could imagine every erotic image, every sensual detail of her dreams. "I'm not trying to make you do anything against your will. I won't push you."

She turned away, still flushed, and stared at the wall.

"But what of this evil spirit you sensed? Do you also dream of it? Have you ever felt that it was near?"

"No, not . . . really."

"You hesitated. Are you certain?"

"I've never felt that sense of total evil since then. But earlier, at the library, I felt . . ."

Giff stiffened beside her. "What?"

"It's hard to explain. I was doing some research on spirits and past lives at the Charleston library. You know, you asked me to think about reincarnation, so I did. I decided I needed to know more about the subject."

"What happened?" She heard a sense of urgent concern in his voice.

"Nothing, really. I just felt . . . frightened. I suppose I had an anxiety attack."

"You stayed at the library all day?"

"Just about." She hesitated, not sure how much

to tell him. No longer afraid of him, but reluctant to admit that she'd felt the urge to provide herself with a handgun. "I stopped on the way home and bought some things I needed, like a microwave oven."

"So perhaps this research made you frightened."

"Yes, I think maybe it did."

"And earlier, when I stopped by, were you still feeling anxious?"

She thought a moment. The anxiety had receded after she left the library, then returned when she returned to the house. "Yes, I began to feel frightened again. I had some wild thoughts. I believed you might be dangerous."

"Do you still feel that way?"

She tilted her head back and looked at him, searching his face. "No, I don't."

He seemed to release a sigh of relief. She supposed he didn't like to be considered a threat.

"Tonight, then, you were dreaming of William Howard and ended up having a nightmare about Mord."

"Yes, that's right." Linda yawned, feeling tired from her long day, from the stress of the nightmare and surprise at finding Giff in her bed. "I think I can sleep now."

"Why don't you turn out the light?"

"Why don't you turn it off on your way out?"

"I'm staying with you."

"Giff, no—"

"To keep your nightmare away. To keep you safe."

"But I'm fine now."

"You need to rest," he whispered, laying her down on the rumpled bed. He stood, stared down for a moment, then walked across the room and turned off the light.

"You can't sleep with me tonight."

"Very well," he said, joining her on that rumpled bed. "I'll stay awake. You sleep." He pulled her into his arms, smoothing her hair, stroking her cheek. "Sleep."

She opened her mouth to protest, but couldn't. Lying in Giff's arms felt too right, too comforting. She rested one hand on his chest, feeling the steady beat of his heart against her palm, and closed her eyes. Having him in her bed felt too right, she thought as she drifted to sleep.

His very presence felt very familiar.

Chapter Six

It is the heart always that sees, before the head can see.
—Thomas Carlyle

June 11, 1995
St. Augustine, Florida

Gerri Rogers tossed restlessly in the bed, unable to go back to sleep. The loose-fitting hotel sheets bunched beneath her like lumpy earth beneath a picnic blanket. It hadn't been a dream that awakened her, she knew, but rather a building sense that something just wasn't right. Lying in the darkness, the feeling had intensified rather than diminished.

She lay still, listening to the humming of the air conditioner, the deep regular breathing of Jon as he slept beside her. Other than those familiar sounds, everything was silent. That should have reassured her, she knew, but it didn't. The normalcy of the early morning only heightened the sense that something was wrong.

She decided to get up before she awakened Jon. They'd stayed out late last night, celebrating their engagement with his parents at a seafood restaurant and then at an upscale bar near old St. Augustine. It had been a wonderful evening, filled with good wishes and Dom Perignon. Jon needed his sleep, poor baby, after making so many toasts. They hadn't gone to bed until almost two o'clock, and she'd barely dozed off when she'd had a horrible premonition that something was wrong.

She'd awakened with her heart beating steady but hard, her head aching. She'd yearned for awareness, for understanding, but it lay just beyond her reach, as though sunk deeply in the mire of unconsciousness. Mild panic always accompanied one of these experiences, leaving her slightly weak and restless.

Gerri pulled back the top sheet, then swung her legs over the side. The bedside clock indicated a few minutes past two. She'd assumed it was later. The night called to her, so she walked to the picture window and drew the edge of the drape aside. Darkness cloaked the parking lot with silent, midnight blue velvet. Clouds raced past the half-moon and thousands of stars glittered between them. Nothing seemed unusual.

Yet still, the unease, the edginess, remained.

She thought about her parents, mentally calling

up their images. Was anything wrong with them? Nothing. There was no need to phone them tonight. Besides, all along she'd thought it was a different kind of intuition. Not as sharp as if something had physically happened to someone she loved.

Linda . . .

Days before, a similar feeling had caused her to telephone Linda at the beach house in South Carolina. She had sworn she was okay, but Gerri still wasn't convinced. She knew Linda was sad over the death of her grandmother, but she seemed to be over the initial sense of loss. The sensation several days ago had been sharper, more immediate. Like a threat or a fear.

Gerri knew that Linda's biggest fear came from an experience they'd had when they were teens, something Linda had never forgotten. That was why Gerri had thought of the attic—that Linda had gone back upstairs to the place where they'd used the Ouija board. That damned board was the only thing that could make her feel so intensely miserable.

Linda truly believed that the thing was evil, or at least it had drawn evil to it like a magnet. Maybe she was right. There were certainly many unknown or unexplained things in life. Gerri wasn't so sure about communicating with the dead, however. It was one thing to tune into the thoughts or emotions of a living, breathing person, but it was a different scenario entirely to talk to those already dead. In her opinion, Ouija boards simply helped a person focus the unconscious mind.

She hadn't been to Linda's grandmother's house since the summer when they were 15. The incident in the attic wasn't the reason she hadn't returned. After turning 16 there were just so many other things to do. She'd really dismissed the event from her mind—most of the time. The unusual event certainly didn't give her bad dreams the way it did Linda. She stopped short of thinking that her best friend was *haunted* about what had happened that summer.

Of course, Linda had told her about researching William Howard several years ago. Gerri closed her eyes to the night and recalled how excited Linda was when she returned from England. She'd insisted Gerri come over right away. They'd sat in Linda's tiny apartment and drunk herbal tea while she'd recounted how she'd "found" the long-dead soldier in a dusty journal of military officers who'd served at Waterloo. Linda was absolutely certain that it was no coincidence, that there was no other explanation than talking to the dead.

Gerri wasn't convinced. With Linda's lifelong love of history, she could have read his name in another text and forgotten it, but brought it up from her subconscious while using the board. That made more sense to Gerri than talking to the dead.

The sad thing, Gerri thought, was how Linda clung to the belief that William Howard was some heroic white knight who might magically appear and save her from becoming a lonely woman who buried herself in the past. Oh, Linda wouldn't admit it. Maybe she didn't even realize that was what she was doing. But Gerri knew, and it broke her heart to think that her best friend might never find happiness with a real live man because of a long-dead soldier.

Speaking of real live men . . . Gerri turned back to the bed. Jon had rolled over, kicking the sheet lower as he continued to sleep. She pulled back the drape so moonlight arrowed across the floor, onto the bed. It bathed his chest and abdomen in soft, white light, showing the line of blond hair that disappeared beneath the sheet. She felt her own stomach tighten as she watched him sleep. He was the nicest, most gentle and sexiest man she'd ever known. Absolutely self-assured and content in his career, he radiated happiness. It was impossible to resist his charm; she hadn't even tried from the first moment they'd met. Even if their relationship had developed rapidly from first date to engagement, she could find nothing to complain about. Jon was the right man for her. She knew it as surely as she knew her own name.

If only Linda could find someone so perfect for her. If only she'd forget about William Howard and look for someone here . . . now. Gerri frowned as she thought that Linda was very close to confusing fantasy and reality. That she'd never let go of the past and find happiness in the present.

Even with Linda's mild obsession for a 19th-century Englishman, she was a great friend. They'd gone to the same university despite the fact that their majors were so different. Gerri had missed her terribly when Linda moved to Chicago after getting her Ph.D. They still ran up huge phone bills, met as often as possible, and took a vacation together yearly. It was time to see her again.

She searched her mind for the feeling of unease and discovered that it was gone. Either the crisis had passed or Linda had gone to sleep. The sense of fear must have gone away. Gerri relaxed, content for now to go back to sleep herself. She let the drape slide back down, plunging the room into near darkness, and walked back to the bed.

She eased down to the mattress, snuggling close to Jon. He reached for her, his eyes still closed in sleep, his arms closing around her automatically. Later, when they'd both had coffee and breakfast, she'd tell him about her uneasy feelings concerning Linda. And that they needed to cut their visit in St. Augustine short, to drive to South Carolina as soon as possible.

She hoped her future in-laws didn't think she was a nut, but some things, like lifetime friendships, were more important than good manners.

"Thank you for being so supportive," Gerri said the next day as she and Jon sat beside the pool at his parents' condo. It was quiet this time of day, with so many retired couples resting inside after lunch, or out shopping, or playing their favorite sport. They had the pool to themselves.

"No problem," Jon said, smiling. "I'm just glad Linda is okay. I could tell you were upset this morning. You should have waked me up last night."

"There was no reason for you to lose sleep. If I'd

been really worried, I would have called her right then."

Gerri took a sip of her pink lemonade and recalled the conversation this morning. Linda had sounded a bit distracted, a little flustered perhaps, but basically okay. She'd given off no negative sensations whatsoever, and had told Gerri not to cut her trip short.

Jon had been willing to leave right then if she'd wanted to, but she'd decided to take her friend's word that she was fine. The fact that he was so supportive had touched her deeply. Not many men would volunteer to leave their family with no explanation other than, "My fiancée has this funny feeling." It wasn't as if Jon wanted an excuse to leave; his parents were very nice people. Gerri had liked them instantly.

Yes, the future looked terrific. Good jobs, steady incomes. Health. Plans that meshed. Love. Great sex. What more could a person want?

She reached out her hand and Jon caught her fingers. "Happy?"

"Very," she said softly. "I couldn't be happier."

"We'll go see Linda in a few days."

"I know. This vacation has worked out super. Two vacations, really, for the price of one."

"You don't mind staying at the hotel?"

"Not at all. Your parents are wonderful people, but I'd feel a little funny sleeping with you under their roof."

"I'd feel the same way."

She tugged on his fingers and grinned. "So, did you bring any other girls home to meet Mom and

Dad before they retired to Florida?"

"Never," he replied with playful indignance.

Gerri laughed. "I don't know if I believe you or not."

"Am I not the most trustworthy man you've ever met?"

She turned her head to smile into his eye. "Yes, I suppose you are." A rush of desire filled her at Jon's answering look. Suddenly her one-piece swimsuit seemed too tight, too hot. Her legs shifted along the chaise lounge. "How long did you say your parents would be gone for their golf game?"

"A couple of hours. What did you have in mind?" he asked, his voice lowering to a humorous but suggestive whisper.

She saw herself in his mirrored sunglasses, looking like a woman in need. And she let her eyes trail over his body, tanned and fit, slightly damp from the summer warmth. She wanted to run her fingers through the silky hair on his chest and make him even hotter. "Afternoon delight?"

"I thought you just said that you'd feel funny sleeping with me in my parents' house."

"Who said anything about sleeping?" Gerri replied, leaning closer, stroking his long fingers the way she'd like to stroke the rest of him.

Jon lunged off the chaise lounge, pulling her up so quickly she gasped as she slammed into his chest. She pressed against him, feeling him harden against her belly. She loved Jon's playfulness, his desire to please her.

"Well, well. I suppose that means you're interested?"

"The guest bedroom of this condo has never been properly christened," he said with a sexy growl, his mouth lowering. "And if we don't make it inside in just about thirty seconds, the neighbors are going to get quite an education."

"What kind of education?" she whispered, closing her eyes, feeling his breath against her lips. Her arms closed around his back, her fingers pressing into the firm muscles just below his shoulder blades.

"The mating habits of perfectly normal heterosexual adults. It's a topic that's never been fully explored."

"Then by all means," she said, "let's go exploring."

Chapter Seven

When you love someone all your saved-up wishes start coming out.
—Elizabeth Bowen

Giff eased open the door to the deck, slipped into the gray dawn and locked the door behind him. For a moment he just stared at the key, thinking how easily he'd entered Linda's house. How easily someone else could have entered. A surge of anger flowed through him and he clenched his fist around the key. Linda was his. No one—no thing—would keep them apart this lifetime. He eased open his fist, looking at the key again. She was too innocent, too trusting by far. She needed protection more than she ever realized.

He decided to keep the key until he could get a copy made. He might need to enter the house again, and he couldn't risk the possibility that Linda would hide it better next time. She had been very upset with him for letting himself in, and would probably look for the key later. His fingers closed around the warm metal as he walked down the wooden stairs to the beach.

Overhead, seagulls screeched and circled while small, pale crabs raced sideways across the sand. Waves beat heavily against the shore, as though pushed by the gray storm clouds at sea.

Giff knew the real storm would be here soon, the kind of swirling, dangerous fury that made rain and wind seem calm by comparison. The kind of storm that wasn't produced by the elements of nature, but rather from the depths of hell.

Mord. He was growing in strength, building intensity as he hovered just beyond the conscious, a thin wall away from reality. He'd already begun to infect Linda's mind and invade her dreams. Next, he would seek a physical body for his earthly mission. Like a hurricane gaining velocity over water, Mord would strike with a vengeance, destroying human lives and eternal souls, leaving disaster in his wake.

He must be stopped, this time for good. Never before had Giff—in any of his incarnations—been able to battle him with equal knowledge, with a weapon that could bring him down. On some basic level that Giff didn't understand, he *knew* that Mord mocked mankind, took pride in his advantage of pure evil. Who could comprehend such malevolence? Who could fight such horror and win?

But even in hell, there were rules. Even for the incomprehensible, there was order. Giff knew that order. And in this lifetime, the battle would rage on more equal ground.

He felt fate nipping at his heels, coming closer and closer like the pounding waves of high tide. He began to run, stretching out across the beach, pushing himself to reach the rented house. The two vacant summer homes between his place and Linda's flashed by, along with the faint sounds of wind chimes and the ever-screeching gulls. An exciting urgency pushed him on, until his lungs screamed for air and his calves ached from running through the sand.

He bounded up the stairs and pushed open the door, his heavy breathing disrupting the quiet of the house. Not bothering to brush the sand from his feet or wipe the sweat from his brow, he hurried into the bedroom and yanked open the closet door. Inside, his cylindrical black leather bag leaned innocently in the corner.

Ready. Waiting for the battle.

Running a hand through his hair, taking a deep breath, he reached for the bag. He had an overwhelming need to touch the object, to reaffirm his link to the past. To Mord. To Linda.

He sat on the bed and unzipped the case, pulling out a silk-wrapped bundle. With trembling hands, he peeled away layers of crimson fabric, letting them slide away to the mattress, then the floor. They pooled there like blood, a vivid contrast to the pale, almost flesh-toned carpet.

And then he held it in his hands, the sword that

had killed him. The sword that had taken the life and dreams from William Howard.

The sword that would break the unholy chain of events he'd created a thousand years ago.

When she awoke the next morning, he was gone.

The shock of finding Giff in her bed had faded, replaced by a sense of rightness. He'd been there when she needed him, when the terror caused her to shake in fear. He'd comforted her—nothing more, and although she should be shocked by his presumptive behavior, she felt only peace.

Linda stretched and reached for the pillow he'd rested against, holding it close to her chest. Shutting her eyes to the day, she breathed deep. The white cotton smelled of sun, sand and sea—and virile, dark male.

She knew she shouldn't feel such a sense of loss, but couldn't help it. With Giff here last night, she'd felt safe from the dreams, from the fantasy world that existed only in her mind. Yet his presence provided another source of unease—a desire that she'd never felt for any man except William.

And William was dead—had always been dead to her.

Giff, on the other hand, was very much alive. She'd felt his heart beat beneath her hand as she nodded off to sleep. She'd felt the tease of his lips on her hair, the kiss of his breath on her forehead. As alien the experience of curling up beside a man was, letting him hold her while she slept, she couldn't deny the comfort he provided.

Linda eased the pillow away and swung her legs over the side of the bed. It would be easy, oh so easy, to become accustomed to his embrace, his thoughtful concern. But she also knew that his preoccupation with safety, his mysterious answers to questions and his potent sexuality could smother any long-term feelings she might develop. Now, instead of coming to terms only with her feelings for William, she must also face her attraction to Giff. Instead of solving her problem, she'd simply added another one.

A big one.

She walked downstairs and made coffee, hoping the caffeine would help clear her head. Nothing else had managed to accomplish that trick over the last few days, since returning to this house and facing both the past and the future, in the form of Giff, but it was worth a try.

While the coffee brewed, she unpacked the simple, white microwave oven and set it on the counter. Already, despite its '70s decor, the kitchen seemed more like her own, and she felt less like she was an intruder in her grandmother's house. She'd need to replace the Harvest Gold refrigerator and stove top, along with the fruit-and-vegetable-patterned wallpaper. But that was a project for another vacation. Today she would finish up the master bedroom, sorting through the items in the chest of drawers and all the small, decorative boxes that perched on top like souvenirs from each decade.

First, she needed to take her grandfather's World War II pistol to the gun store. She'd told the owner she'd let him examine and clean it. He had seemed truly interested in examining the old weapon, and she had promised to bring it in. When she recalled how frightened she'd been yesterday, she decided it might make her feel better to have it in the house, just in case.

Hours later, legs folded beneath her on the soft rag rug on her grandmother's bedroom floor, she felt a trickle of tears run down her cheek. She'd found letters, tied in pink and violet ribbon-bound bundles, hiding in fragile envelopes in the back of the lingerie drawer.

Linda had never known her grandfather, the man who'd written these letters during World War II. Yet now she could see how much he'd loved and missed his wife while he'd fought his way across Europe. He'd wanted to know about the most mundane things in her life: dressing their son for school, eating dinner each night behind blackout curtains, driving into town for shopping. He'd worried about their ration coupons and whether any appliances would quit working, since supplies during the war were so limited. But mostly, he wrote about how much he loved and missed her. Even with the subtlety of the past, the natural restraint between men and women, she could tell they were very passionately in love.

Her grandfather had died in the early 1960s of a brain aneurysm, quickly and without warning. Her grandmother had never remarried, preferring to live her life at the beach house in quiet remembrance, surrounded by items from their shared past.

Linda had never understood why until now. She'd never understood how similar her life had become to her grandmother's. Longing for a man who would never walk through the door . . .

Grandmother's memories had been as real to her as the present, but she'd never confused the two. She'd gotten on with her life—something Linda knew she had yet to accomplish. In that way, they were very different.

Wiping the tears from her cheeks, Linda re-tied the ribbons and replaced the letters in the drawer. It was time to get on with her life, to escape the past and march boldly into the future. She was 29 years old, not 15. And Giff was very much alive.

She knocked on his door about three o'clock that afternoon, dressed only in a black one-piece swimsuit and a loose white cotton shirt. Two old beach towels from visits past draped across her arm. She hoped that Giff didn't notice that the heat and her nervousness had caused sweat to dampen her back and forehead.

He opened the door with a flourish that surprised her. In the relative dimness of the interior, he seemed dark, sexy and mysterious—much as he had last night when she awoke with him in her bed.

"Linda. What a pleasant surprise." His gaze traveled over her body like William's hands, tingling and caressing everywhere they touched. She felt her nipples respond, budding against the tight fabric in response to Giff's heated look.

"I . . . ah, I remembered that you said that you liked to swim."

"Yes, a swim would be very . . . refreshing."

She felt that she needed something cooling at the moment. However, he didn't move and she couldn't seem to tear her gaze away. What she saw in his eyes made her remember last night's dream, giving her a vague impression of warm brown eyes heated in passion. She'd never seen William's eyes, or his face. Now her mind was playing tricks on her, imposing Giff's most remarkable feature on her faceless lover.

She closed her eyes and shook her head to clear the image.

"Is something wrong?" he asked.

She opened her eyes and gave him what she hoped was a convincing smile. "No, everything's fine. So, do you have some swim trucks?"

Giff smiled as if he knew what she'd been thinking. *He's not reading your mind. It's only because his eyes are so expressive, because he's so focused on you. That's all.*

"Would you like to come in while I change?" he asked.

"No, I think I'll just wait out here. Get used to the heat."

"Whatever you like," he said smoothly. He eased the screen door shut, then walked silently across the floor, with an inherent masculine grace that made Linda think of other ways he might move. With just as much strength and fluid motion.

"Damn," she murmured, fanning her face. She twirled away and sat on the porch steps. In front of her, the waves rolled in, peaceful and alluring. Two gulls fought over a twisted piece of seaweed, disrupting the hot, quiet afternoon with their squawks. Behind her, she heard a door close from inside the house.

He was stripping off his shirt and pants. His briefs. Stepping into swim trunks. Almost his whole body would be revealed when he walked outside. Would his swimwear be brief and tight, or loose and baggy? Whatever, Linda was sure she'd manufacture some fantasy about what was hidden.

The screen door slammed and she jumped.

"I didn't mean to frighten you."

"You didn't." She kept on watching those damn gulls, half afraid to turn around and see what he wore.

He stood on the step where she sat. "Linda?"

Her gaze shifted in a quarter circle, resting on his tanned feet and muscular legs. Lean, runner's legs. Tan and covered with dark, soft-looking hair. She had an almost overwhelming urge to reach out and see if he was as warm as he looked. She didn't. Instead, her vision roamed upward just momentarily—long enough to realize that his swim trunks, although fairly modest, showed off too much of his body for her peace of mind.

She jerked her gaze away and jumped to her feet. "Race you to the water!"

Flinging the towels to the porch, she took off at a run.

Giff watched her go with a smile on his face. If she'd continued to stare at him much longer, she would have received a real surprise. His swimwear was adequate under most conditions, but not, it seemed, around Linda. He took off at a run, not meaning to catch her, but needing the shock of the cool Atlantic. He'd never been a believer in cold showers, but at the moment, the saltwater equivalent seemed like a very good idea.

As soon as the waves hit Linda's legs, she squealed in surprise. Giff slowed his pace, smiling at her delight as she threw up her arms and kept on running into the surf. She'd surprised him with the visit this afternoon, but as he was learning, she was full of subtle, delightful nuances.

She ran and splashed into the waves, until the water reached chest level. He stared, noting that her nipples beaded beneath the plain black bathing suit that clung like a second skin. He felt another flash of arousal.

"I won!"

"So you did," he said, running into the water. As soon as the waves reached waist level, he dived into the water, letting it wash over him, cooling his body. He swam underwater until his lungs screamed for air, then surfaced, shaking his head.

In just a moment, Linda bobbed up beside him, a smile still on her lips. "You're a great swimmer," she said.

"I swim better than I cook."

"I've already suspected that you're a man of many talents."

The pull of the waves brushed her against him. He reached out with one arm and caught her around the waist as his toes searched for the sandy bottom. He could barely stand here, but braced his legs, pulling Linda against him.

Her smile faded, her eyes darkened as her lashes lowered. He also felt the sexual energy that seemed to flow between them. Last night had changed their relationship, even though she didn't realize he'd been with her inside the dream.

"If I kiss you, as I wish to do, this afternoon will not end with swimming."

She seemed only momentarily surprised that he knew what was on her mind. It was no psychic event. He'd only had to look at her expressive face to tell what was on her mind. Sex. Pure, hot, consuming. That's what she wanted, what she'd wanted for as long as she'd been a woman. Even if she didn't admit it to him, he knew, because he'd felt her passion from afar, and now close up. He'd lain beside her in bed, held her through the early hours of the morning.

Yes, he knew what she wanted. He was more than capable of satisfying her needs, in a thousand ways, if possible, but he had to be certain she was ready. She must want more than his body. She must want to make love, not just satisfy a physical craving.

"What if I said, 'Kiss me anyway'?"

"Then I will kiss you. And I'll want you, and you will want me. What we do about this desire is another question."

"Why does it have to be so serious, such an earth-shattering decision?" she said as she bobbed in the water, brushing against his arousal like a woman intent on torture.

"I want you to be sure. When we make love, I don't want it to be as a result of a nightmare, or a summer fling just because I'm here and you're lonely."

She pushed away from him, glaring, and he knew he'd hurt her. But he had to say what he felt, at least this once. He wasn't going to coerce her into bed, even if that had been his original intention. At one time he might have been able to manipulate and pressure the "unknown woman" he'd come to South Carolina to meet. With that nameless, faceless person, he could have taken her to bed in hopes of beginning to break the spell. Now that he'd discovered more about Linda, he knew deceiving her wouldn't be right. He wasn't sure exactly what would happen when they consummated their relationship, since it had never happened in their previous lifetimes. He wasn't sure what Mord's reaction would be.

But one thing was certain; he wanted to make love with her. Soon, and forever more. But not until she was ready.

He watched her struggle out of the waves, fighting the fierce undertow. She sprinted up the beach, toward the porch of his house. With a clean dive beneath a wave, he swam toward shore.

Linda toweled her hair while she waited on Giff to join her. She knew he would. He had that intense, very "Giff-like" look on his face when she broke away and swam to the shore. Now, as he emerged from the water in those tight trunks and that lean, muscular body, she tried to regain the anger she'd felt when he turned her down.

It's not anger. It's hurt, she had to admit to herself. *Giff is right. We shouldn't rush into bed just because I'm sexually frustrated.* Being honest with herself wasn't easy, but forcing herself to be analytical about her feelings was absolutely necessary. Somehow, she knew that whatever the outcome of this relationship, whether it was a summer fling or a more permanent relationship, she would have no regrets as long as she and Giff were honest with each other.

He walked up to the porch steps, breathing heavily, his chest rising and falling in a ripple of muscle and tanned skin.

"I'm sorry," he said.

"No, you're right," she said, staring him in the eye. "I was being truthful when I spoke, but perhaps not too wise."

"I didn't mean to hurt you."

She shook her head, looking away, giving her hair one more rub with the towel. "You were being sensible. I was acting like a girl, playing with fire."

He stepped closer, his hands resting lightly on her shoulders. She gazed into his eyes, stopping the motion of the towel.

"When we make love, I want you to be certain, to be a woman, not a girl."

"Giff, I am a woman."

"I know. But sometimes, when we are . . . emotional, we act on those emotions without thinking. I want you to consider what has grown between us these few days. Soon, the time will be right. We will both know it, and we *will* make love."

"Yes, I know we will," she whispered, melting into the dark depths of his eyes. His presence was so compelling, so intense, that she lost a bit of herself when they were together. What would it be like to lose herself completely to his passion? She shivered as her imagination took over. But then she remembered that she was supposed to be an adult, to seriously consider the next step. Letting lust rule her thoughts was not the way.

"Why don't we sit down and cool off?" she said, tying the beach towel around her waist.

"Good idea." Giff walked up the steps, holding out his hand.

She placed her fingers in his, letting him lead the way to the table and chairs on his porch. Unlike their first "date," when he'd cooked out, the sun was still shining brightly and there were no romantic candles, table setting or wine.

"I have iced tea made," he said as they pulled the chairs into the shade and sat down.

"I'd love some."

"Sweetened?"

"Of course."

He grinned at her reply, then walked inside. Apparently the strong, sensual feelings they'd shared were once again on hold. For now, that was best. Alone, Linda knew she could think more clearly, deal with her reactions to his sexuality.

Within minutes, he brought out two sweating glasses.

She took a long drink. "This is great."

"Tell me more about what you teach. All I know is the subject of your dissertation."

"I seem to have a special affinity for the years of the Napoleonic Wars. I teach a junior-level course on war and diplomacy, a study of the strategies used by politicians and military men, and how thin the line was during that period. I also teach a senior-level discussion course on a variety of historical topics, at my discretion usually, that relate to current events."

"And do your students develop an appropriate appreciation of the various eras?"

Linda laughed. "Usually not. As a matter of fact, they think I'm a little strange for getting so involved in the past. Maybe they're right. Gerri, the friend I told you about, always said I should have lived in another age, since I found it so interesting."

Giff smiled to himself. Without knowing it, Gerri had keyed in on one of the strongest aspects of Linda's personality—her past lives. Since her relationships in her previous incarnations had ended unresolved, she felt a strong link to the periods in which she'd lived. The strongest, of course, to her most recent life as Constance.

"Are there any other periods of history that you find particularly intriguing?"

"Yes, I find the religious climate surrounding Cromwell's rise to power very interesting. Some people consider it unusual that England had only one civil war that resulted in the institution of another type of government—and the overthrow of the monarchy. I find myself amazed that the monarchy was re-instituted in such an unstable political environment."

"Yes, or even a very different monarchy. As time passed, I think the English preferred to believe that Cromwell was not the winner of the war, and that the monarchy survived intact."

"We do seem to overlook some of our history. The beheadings, for example. They seemed so long ago, almost as though they're fairy tales and not part of our past. And the fact that England was governed from France for centuries, with visits by the king and a disdain for the Saxon people."

Linda seemed to consider him thoughtfully for a moment, taking another sip of tea. "Is that why you write? To make people see the humanity and commonality of our history?"

"I really hadn't thought of it in those terms. But I suppose you could say that I feel compelled to share the past with my readers. I want them to get a more accurate picture of life and death, and how little human nature has changed over time."

"I think you do a wonderful job. I still don't understand how you get such a realistic, all-encompassing grasp of life during any time in the past."

Because I've been there, he answered silently. Of course, she wouldn't believe him. She'd been skeptical of the subject of reincarnation when he brought it up two days ago. So he fell back to his pat answer. "Research."

"So you've said. I still think that there's something special about your grasp of human history and conflict that gives your books a special life."

"I thank you for the compliment, but I don't believe I can explain exactly how I write my books."

"Oh, I don't expect you to. Just don't stop writing!"

Giff smiled. "I'll do my best to continue to live up to your standards."

Linda finished the last drops of her tea. "I'm going back to my house. I'm a salty mess."

"You look fine," Giff said. She looked young and carefree, the earlier, serious conversation erased from her open, honest expression.

She fluffed her curly hair in response and grimaced. "I think some shampoo and conditioner is definitely in order."

"Will you have dinner with me later?"

"I'd love to," she said, tilting her head to the side, smiling. "Give me enough time to shower and shampoo."

"I'll be down around eight."

"Perfect," she said, rising from her chair. With another smile and a wave, she skipped down the steps and across the beach to her own house.

Giff rose and collected the two glasses. She'd no doubt think about what had nearly happened this afternoon, about what they'd discussed. She'd form an opinion, one way or another, about whether she was ready to make love. Perhaps he'd been a fool to stop their passion so abruptly, but he'd been compelled to listen to his heart.

And his heart said that he wanted to make love with Linda O'Rourke, not defy the spell with his soulmate. For the first time in his life, the conflict seemed very real, very personal. All of a sudden, the possibility of losing the battle hit him like an unexpected punch to the gut. Losing the battle meant never seeing Linda again, not just losing his life.

Suddenly, his war with Mord seemed more real, more imminent. June 18th was only seven days away.

"Let's go somewhere different tonight," she said.

Giff watched Linda as she stood on the deck, the golden-pink sunset bathing her face in light. Her eyes were wide, her posture telling him she was slightly tense. "Anywhere you'd like," he answered. There was something different about her tonight. Something more sensual, with an undercurrent of awareness that flowed between them like radiant energy, stronger than it had ever been before. Apparently she'd considered what they'd discussed and made a decision. His heart rate picked up as he realized what conclusion she'd reached.

"There's a casual restaurant up the beach," she said, pointing with one sandal. "It's built on a man-made pier. They have the best fried shrimp in the whole, wide world."

He smiled, wondering if she was thinking about how well they fit together on that small bed of hers, how their hearts seemed to beat as one. Or how she'd looked at him earlier today, their wet, aroused bodies brushing together. Was she wondering if he remembered as well? "That's quite a recommendation. Should we walk or drive?"

"Walk, if it's okay with you."

"Why don't we take a flashlight," he suggested. "It will be dark when we return."

Linda gave him a faint smile, a nervous little look, as she quickly turned and entered the house. In a moment, she returned with her purse and a large black flashlight. "I'm ready."

They walked slowly up the beach, hand in hand, listening to the gulls and the waves. He could become accustomed to this kind of quiet companionship, Giff thought. The only thing that would make the scene perfect was if they were going back home later to make love, to lie in each other's arms until dawn. To forge a bond stronger than any spell.

If Linda had decided to trust her feelings, as he sensed she had, he hoped she didn't regret that she would be giving herself body and soul. If there was any other way to break the cycle and live, he would pursue that course. He regretted using Linda to free them from the spell, but it must be done. And he must remember the strength of his enemy. Mord had always won, lifetime after lifetime. If Giff could not defeat him, he would be dead by this time next week. Linda would grow old without finding true love, and they would repeat the cycle again and again.

Evil entities, Giff thought bitterly, made relentless enemies once they were involved in the lives of mortals.

"Giff?"

"Yes, love."

"How did you really know I was having that horrible nightmare last night—early this morning, I should say."

He sighed and looked down at the sand, even

though he knew she watched him. She wanted answers, but now wasn't the time to reveal everything. She just wasn't ready for the entire truth. He didn't dare risk frightening her away.

"Before you say anything, I just want you to know I don't buy that story that you heard me from below, outside the house. There's no way."

He stopped and turned toward her, pulling her body against his. Her breasts rested lightly against his chest, her thighs shifted and meshed with his. "Have you ever heard of people who have a psychic sensitivity to each other? You might have heard stories of a spouse who sensed that their mate was in trouble, or a mother who knew their child was in danger."

She leaned back and looked him in the eye. "Of course. As a matter of fact, my best friend does that to me all the time."

He was surprised at that, but tried not to let it show, since he'd been prepared to introduce the subject slowly and convince her gradually. "What does she do?"

Linda shrugged. "She seems to know when I'm upset, angry. Sometimes when I've had a really bad day, or a nightmare, she'll call. Once when we were in college, I became ill with bronchitis and had trouble breathing. She rushed back to the dorm from a date and took me to the campus clinic." A look of dawning comprehension crossed her face. "You're telling me that you can do the same thing?"

"Yes." He wasn't about to tell her that it worked only with her. He didn't have an idea how she would react; she could just as easily decide he was crazy as she could assume he was her soulmate.

He searched her face as she considered his claim, but it was obvious from the frown on her brow and the narrowing of her eyes that she wasn't ready to believe him. "Maybe you were already inside my house before I screamed. You could have guessed I was having a nightmare. Later, you could have devised this explanation."

He pushed down a small surge of anger at her skepticism. "I don't make up stories."

"You're a writer."

"Of historical fiction, not melodramas."

"Point taken. So, you weren't creeping up the stairs to seduce me."

"The thought hadn't crossed my mind," he said with mock outrage. In a softer voice meant to soothe, he said, "Actually, I could claim I was waiting for an invitation."

Linda laughed. "And I'm fairly certain that you wouldn't have accepted my invitation if it was offered last night. You were, and continue to be, a true gentleman."

Giff tried not to grimace at the heroic image she'd created for him. He wasn't being that noble. As a matter of fact, he realized, he'd been selfish from the beginning. It was a sobering thought, one he chose not to dwell on at the moment.

"So you're serious about sensing my moods?" she asked.

"Very." He was also serious about making love with her—soon.

"Amazing. To think I know two people who are psychic."

"You believe me?"

"Of course. It's the only explanation that makes sense."

Giff couldn't resist smiling at her youthful willingness to accept his words. "I'm glad. This kind of . . . gift . . . doesn't occur too often. You must be very special to have two people sensing your feelings."

"Well, I'm not sure I want anyone roaming around inside my head—you can't do that, can you?"

"Absolutely not." Not all the time. Not without more of a bond between them.

He felt her let out a sigh a relief.

"Good. Then I suppose being concerned for my well-being is okay. Of course, it does make me a little uncomfortable whenever Gerri calls and asks what's wrong. I'm not sure it will be any easier knowing that now I'll have two people worrying about my state of mind."

"I'll always be concerned—for your happiness and your health."

"That's sweet, to say that you'll *always* care, but—"

"I'm perfectly serious, love. I have no intention of walking away."

She pulled back, frowning, looking into his eyes. "And if I asked you to leave?"

He felt himself stiffen before he could stop the automatic, gut-wrenching vision from invading his mind. No, she wouldn't do that. Even though she'd panicked after visiting the library, she wouldn't just decide not to pursue a relationship. They were perfect for each other, destined to be together.

"I must believe you won't," he finally said softly.

"Only if you did something that made me push you away."

He wondered what she meant. Did she expect him to turn into a serial killer? A sex maniac with odd fetishes? He didn't understand her reservations. With little time left, how could he convince her that he was her destiny, and that he would do everything in his power to be worthy of her love? He couldn't come out and say that he'd be everything she'd wish, that he'd do whatever was necessary to make her fall in love with him.

Instead, he touched her cheek, looked into her eyes and hoped that later, she would forgive him for deceiving her. Because even if she tried to push him away, he wouldn't go far. He couldn't give up his goal.

"Fair enough," he said finally.

She fell silent and pulled away from the circle of his arms, walking again toward the pier that he could now see in the distance. Warm lights beckoned from the restaurant windows and the whole world seemed tinted orange from the setting sun.

You're mine, Linda, whether you realize it or not. And I'll never let you go.

Linda knew some of the people seated at the restaurant. Mr. Watley was there with his wife and two grandchildren, and the hardware store manager said hello. This, she realized, was her first real social date with Giff. It was difficult to believe that they'd become so close so soon, when all they'd done was eat two meals together and walk along the beach—not counting that scene in her bedroom early this morning.

She felt close to him, unusually attuned to his moods and fascinated by the various aspects of his personality that were being slowly revealed. She was falling for him without knowing if she was being wise. But she hoped that he was the man who could make her forget her fantasies and focus on reality.

"I haven't been here in ages, but I discovered it was still open the other day when I drove by," she said. "It's a Sunday night tradition in the community. My grandmother used to bring me here often."

"You still miss her, don't you."

"Yes, very much. She was a wonderful person," Linda said, taking a seat at a small table near the glass windows, overlooking the ocean. It was difficult to explain to anyone how much she'd needed her grandmother, a woman with endless hugs and stories, who made the best fried chicken in the whole world. A plain, down-to-earth woman, not at all like Linda's busy, preoccupied parents.

Time had seemed to stand still during those summers when Linda visited the beach house, as though life would go on forever if only the sun continued shining and the waves still beat against the shore. But it wasn't so. Grandmother had died in an artificially lit hospital room while snow and ice pelted the windows. The end was neither fitting nor just for such a life filled with sunshine. And not at all fair.

"What is it? You look so sad."

Linda shook her head, gazing out at the water. "Nothing . . . just remembering." She tried to smile, to lighten the mood, but knew she fell short as Giff continued to look concerned. "I'm okay, really. Even though she's been gone for about six months, I haven't *really* dealt with it until now. The knowledge that she'll never be there again, that we'll never have another summer together, makes me sad."

"As it should," he said, taking her hand. "The past can never be recaptured once it's gone. But the future can hold new experiences, and new memories will be made. Our pasts shape our futures, but we can never go back."

She looked at him closely, noticing the intensity that had come into his face while he spoke. He wasn't just talking about her grandmother, about missing someone who was dead. But what did he mean?

"I'm sorry," he said. "I should be saying something to cheer you, not becoming philosophical."

"That's okay. I want to know more about you, remember?"

"I assumed you'd be more interested in my taste in movies or music than my thoughts on the hereafter." He smiled and took a sip of water.

"Everything. I want to know it all."

"And I told you it would take some time to learn that much."

"I'm patient."

"I'm not," he said, holding her gaze.

She felt her insides start to sizzle when she realized what he meant. Waves of heat pulsed through her skin. She half expected—half wanted—Giff to lose control, to haul her over the table and kiss her senseless. She wanted to lose herself forever in his dark eyes, but the waiter arrived, cheerfully explaining today's specials. Linda pulled her hand away and sat back, putting some space between herself and Giff.

They ordered dinners and wine, then turned back to each other. Linda felt the intensity dissipate in the cool air of the restaurant. Once more, he was firmly in control of his desires.

"Are you making progress sorting your grandmother's things?" Giff asked.

Linda took a sip of water, searching for her own composure. "It seems so intrusive, but I owe it to her to take my time and decide the fate of each item."

"I'm sure she wanted you to. Otherwise, she would have disposed of them herself or left them to another relative."

"I'm just about the only one that's left. I'm sure she would have willed it to my father, but he died several years ago. My mother was never close to Grandmother."

"What does your mother do?"

"She plays the violin in the New York Philharmonic. She's very dedicated to her career."

"I see."

"She always felt more comfortable in that environment than home baking cookies."

"There's room for both, don't you think?" He reached over and held her hand, stroking his fingers across her knuckles. His gaze held hers, open and admiring. Linda had the absurd idea he was about to propose, which caused a nervous giggle to escape.

She clamped her other hand over her mouth and turned away from his sexy, dark looks. "I'm sorry." She turned back to face his questioning expression. "Yes, I believe there's room for both."

"When you marry and have children, will you want to continue teaching?"

"I haven't given it much thought." She shrugged, hoping he would take the hint and keep the conversation light. Contemplating a "relationship" with Giff was one thing; talking about marriage and family another. "Probably."

He raised her hand and kissed it. "You should think about it."

She drew in a deep breath. Surely she was reading more into his words than he meant. She needed some clever line to get the conversation back on track, she thought, searching her brain. "Is that one way of saying that I'm not getting any younger?" she finally said, trying her best to laugh away his intensity.

"I would never be so bold," he said, smiling in return. "I just believe you should think about it."

Thankfully, the waiter brought their food then: a heaping platter of fried shrimp and scallops for

Linda, a grilled filet of swordfish for Giff.

"Would there be anything else?" the young man asked, but Giff declined, serving the wine himself.

"By the way," Linda said after swallowing her first bite of shrimp, "do you still have my key? I noticed it wasn't under the flower pot."

Giff reached inside his pants pocket. "Here it is," he said, placing it in her palm. "You should think of a more original hiding place."

"I know," Linda said, raising her eyebrows and giving him "a look." "I've learned my lesson."

"Good."

She was glad the issue was resolved. At least Giff wouldn't be an unexpected visitor in the middle of the night. Of course, she could always invite him in. . . .

"Does the food live up to your expectations?"

"It's great. If I eat all this, you'll have to carry me home."

"The idea has merit," Giff said as he slowly smiled, never taking his eyes off her face. "Eat up."

Linda laughed and dug in, savoring each morsel on her plate, thinking of each bite as but an appetizer to the main course, which sat across from her with wicked dark eyes and the promise of a meal she would never forget.

No! He wanted to scream in frustration. He forced all his energy against his boundaries, but he was still trapped, unable to enter the physical plane.

They were going to "make love." Lust, there was only lust! Mord felt her passion, felt the man's answering desire. He'd done his best to keep them from giving in to their passions, used the last of his strength to hold them apart with fear and uncertainty. Yet they hadn't listened. They wanted to satisfy their cravings for each other.

Damn them! He would find a way to get out of his limbo. And when he did, he'd find new ways to make them suffer for ignoring his wishes.

If he'd had a fist, he would have beaten them unconscious. He would not be ignored. Especially by mere humans.

Chapter Eight

Only passions, great passions, can elevate the soul to do great things.
—Denis Diderot

She was, in fact, too full of the delicious dinner to walk back through the shifting, thick sand. Since there were no cabs around this small town, Giff paid the owner's son to drive them home. Laughing, carefree, and relaxed, Linda leaned against Giff's shoulder, tilting her head back and reaching for the stars as the teenager's souped-up 1970s Pontiac convertible roared down the two-lane road. Giff's right arm rested across the back of the seat, but she felt his hand, lightly touching her shoulder.

"This is fun," she said, unable to keep from feeling like a teenager herself. "A sexy date in the back seat of a classic car."

"Is that what I am?"

Linda laughed again and rested her head on the curve of his shoulder. "Definitely. The sexiest date I've ever had—in or out of a convertible."

"Thank you," he said very seriously, which only made her laugh more. He was, without doubt, the most intense man she'd ever known. But that was only part of what made him sexy. He had a dry, intelligent sense of humor. And he was mysterious. Maybe even dangerous—to her libido and peace of mind.

Tonight, she felt ready for danger.

Giff leaned forward. "Turn off here," he said to their young driver.

The bump of the car going from asphalt to gravel made Linda sit up straighter, but Giff didn't let go of her. In fact, his hold seemed to tighten.

The car slowed, then stopped at the front door. The motion-sensitive fixture flicked on, flooding the front of the house and the drive with light. Linda blinked, her eyes adjusting to the change. The heavy throbbing of the engine broke the silence.

"Thanks for the ride," Linda said.

Their teenage chauffeur jumped out and opened the passenger door. "No problem."

Giff followed Linda out and handed the young man a folded piece of currency.

"Thank *you,*" the young man said, grinning, stuffing the money in his jeans pocket.

Linda stood beside Giff on the front porch as the car roared off. In a few seconds, she could hear the sounds of the insects and the faint pounding of the surf.

This was the moment to gather her courage, the time to make her big move. "Would you like some coffee?"

"I'd love some."

She unlocked the door, thinking that this was the first time she'd entered the house through the front since arriving here a week ago. It looked different from this perspective, more of a dignified Victorian lady, with lacy white trim over crisp blue wood, rather than the informal back side, which resembled a weathered old beachcomber.

Giff held the door open as she stepped inside. The front door featured a beveled glass insert, and a fern stood tall on a stand just inside the small foyer. Light from the porch filtered through the frosted and cut glass, giving the entryway a magical appearance.

Giff looked around, glancing inside the front parlor. "Nice."

"Grandmother liked to have a more formal place, somewhere she could play the piano and serve tea and cookies. But we lived in the back of the house, there and the upstairs."

"I like them both. It's good to mix the old and the new."

Impulsively, she took Giff's hand and led him through the dark hallway toward the kitchen. She smiled to herself. He'd seemed surprised at the gesture. Maybe he thought she was intoxicated from two glasses of wine. It wasn't so. If she was a bit tipsy, it was from his presence and the naughty thoughts he provoked, not from over-indulging in spirits.

She flipped on the light. "I'll have the coffee made in a minute."

Giff drifted off as she measured coffee into the wire basket. In a moment she heard music float in from the den, recognizing the stirring, haunting soundtrack from *Age of Innocence.*

"Love the music," she called out. She could see Giff's silhouette against the windows as he stared out at the beach. He looked utterly alone, troubled somehow. A flash from the movie raced through her, a vision of Daniel Day-Lewis's character, battling both himself and his society, alone in his fight to create love from desire. In the end, he'd lost the woman he adored, but gained a respectable life, full of decency but void of passion.

She could identify with that character. The difference was that she'd tried to create passion without desire. She'd tried to make love before, but had only achieved sex, failing to attain true intimacy with a man because . . . she didn't know why. After a few relationships, she'd given up on finding a man that stirred her like the one from her dreams. She'd begun to believe that men like that just didn't exist. That she'd created an illusion not based at all in reality.

Then she'd met Giff.

Other men she'd known couldn't hold a candle to her fantasy lover, William. She'd never consciously compared them to William, simply because there was no resemblance. But with Giff, she felt differently. He had the same passionate intensity, the same effect on her senses. She wanted him with a physical yearning she'd never felt before.

Making love to him might fulfill her fantasy, once and for all time. But should she try harder to separate Giff and William in her mind? She'd already decided to live for the present, not the past. And even though she agreed with Giff that the past shaped the present and influenced the future, she believed it wasn't healthy to continually confuse the two men in her mind. She was with Giff, not William, even if the intensity of feeling was so similar.

She tore her eyes away from his still form and plugged in the coffeemaker. Gripping the cold tiles of the countertop, she wondered if he could sense how much she wanted him right now. If he could feel her strong emotions as he claimed he could.

Yes. Make love to me. Make me burn.

She stared at the water as it slowly bubbled through the filter. She listened to the soft gurgle, wondering why she couldn't hear her own blood as it boiled through her veins, heated by desire.

The overhead light flicked off, but she wasn't frightened; she was excited. She knew who had done it. With a silent breath on her neck, a heated nearness all along her back, Giff pressed against her, pushing her gently toward the cabinets. the rounded edge of the tile crushed against her pelvic bones and stomach while Giff's hardness pressed into the cleft of her buttocks. Her heart beat faster and faster, until she was sure he could feel the heavy throbbing all through her body. Until it seemed as jarring, as erratic, as the coffee perking just inches away. Hot. Boiling.

"Linda," he whispered. "I want you."

She closed her eyes and gripped the tile even harder. She was on fire. His lips touched the space behind her ear where she'd pulled her hair up earlier. Without hesitation, she rolled her head back, against his shoulder, giving him better access.

With lips and tongue he tasted her skin, with gentle nips he claimed her neck. She'd never thought of teeth as tools of arousal, but by the time he nuzzled the collar of her dress across her shoulder, she knew they were wonderful. Everywhere he touched sent sparks of awareness shooting through her body, colliding in the tips of her breasts, ricocheting down her abdomen to explode like tiny fires between her legs. She felt empty there, wanting the same pressure that she felt near, but not near enough.

She wanted more. She wanted all of him, filling the void she'd lived with so long.

Her legs buckled, but he pressed closer, moving his hands beneath her arms, sliding upward to caress her aching breasts. His palms molded her, teased her, until she felt supported only by the tug of his fingers on her nipples and the throb of his arousal, pressing between her legs.

The pleasure was unbearable. She cried out, ready to beg him to stop, pleading for him to continue, but could only utter an anguished moan.

"That's it, love," he whispered against her hot, damp neck. "Let go."

She spun around, taking his mouth in a bruising kiss, holding him so tightly she was sure they'd be crushed together. He returned her passion, lifting her from the ground, supporting her weight on greedy hands that moved from her buttocks to the back of her thighs. Her legs crept upward, until they locked around his waist. Until she pressed into his arousal, leaned back and screamed her passion.

The night exploded in light, colors she'd never seen before, pleasures she'd never dreamed. The fire burned brighter for an instant, but didn't fade and die. It glowed, ready to be fed more tinder. Throbbing with renewed desire, ready to be ignited in other ways.

"Make love to me," she whispered, opening her eyes, wondering if she was still in her grandmother's kitchen in South Carolina. It took her eyes a moment to focus in the darkness, to find his face and see the intensity of his expression. Only then did she realize she was sitting on the kitchen table, her legs still locked around his body, his hands supporting her back. The smell of coffee and just a hint of warm arousal filled the room.

"I am," Giff said softly.

She saw smoldering, unfulfilled desire in his eyes, felt it in the tenseness of his body. They hadn't removed a stitch of clothing. Of course he hadn't found his own release. He'd given to her; now it was her turn to make him scream, to give him the same. Together, yes, together this time, just like in her dreams.

She tried to unwind her legs, to get off the table, but he simply scooped her into his arms. She held tightly to him, placing kisses wherever she could reach. His skin tasted sweet with the salt of desire. When she raked her teeth across the straining tendon on the side of his neck, he shuddered and bumped into the door facing.

"I want you as I've never wanted another woman," he said, breathing heavily.

"Then make love to me now . . . here." Linda slid from his arms, leaning into him on shaking legs. She grabbed his shirt, pulling him from the doorway, backing toward the large, overstuffed couch in the den.

"Upstairs," he whispered, before she kissed him again.

"No. Here. Make me your woman here, not in that girlish bedroom upstairs."

"Yes," he said, following her down to the soft cushions. "Yes."

She sank lower into the softness, pressed close by Giff's weight. Soothing music flowed around them. She noticed for the first time that the room was filled with a faint, yellow light. Looking around, she saw lit candles on the mantle, flickering like ageless, romantic beacons to lovers lost in a sea of desire. Just as she was lost.

His hands worked the row of buttons down the front of her dress, until he'd opened just enough for her to remove it.

"Let me," she said, slipping her arms free, raising her hips as he skimmed the material from her body. She felt no hesitation, no shyness around Giff. If he wasn't the man of her dreams, he was as close as heaven would allow. And she wouldn't—couldn't—worry about comparisons now.

He ran his hands over her body as if memorizing it with his fingertips. She'd worn nothing underneath the dress but a clinging body suit, thin and edged with lace. Giff's eyes seemed to glow as he shaped her, molded her breasts, reached behind her and lifted her from the couch and sat her in front of him, straddling his lap.

He kissed her deeply, with so much hunger Linda was lost to his passion. His lips consumed her. His tongue claimed her. The fires he'd ignited earlier burned again, stronger than ever. Without breaking the kiss, she reached for the buttons of his shirt, impatient to feel his bare skin against hers. He seemed to feel the same way, lowering the straps of the bodysuit over her shoulders, down her arms. Just as she jerked his shirt free from his pants, he pulled the bodysuit to her waist and crushed her against him.

It was heaven, his sleek, hot skin against hers. He felt lean and hard, his muscles tight bands across his chest, his back sculpted of flesh and bone.

"Not enough," she said breathlessly.

He pushed her back onto the couch, kissing her face, her neck. His hands grabbed the bodysuit and pulled it from her roughly, leaving her totally exposed to his eyes. And they looked, oh, they looked, blazing a trail across her breasts, her stomach, the junction of her thighs. He feasted on her with a hungry gaze, then devoured her with his hands and mouth and until she thought she would go quite mad.

"Now, Giff, now," she moaned, more excited than she'd ever been before. She realized that she'd never made love before. She'd never felt this way, even in her most erotic dreams. Tears came to her eyes, blurring her vision as he pulled away.

"No, don't leave me."

"My clothes, love."

Yes, she'd forgotten about his clothes. His shirt hung from his shoulders, and his slacks, once crisply creased, were wrinkled. She ran her hand up his leg as he fumbled with his belt. Beneath her fingers, he was solid and muscular. She wanted all of him, sliding her hand higher until she traced his hardness, pressing against the cotton as though it might break free, fill her hand. Fill the lonely ache inside her.

"Hurry."

He eased the zipper down. She looked into his eyes and saw the same hunger she felt. She remembered her dream, on the beach with William, touching his arousal. Suddenly the tears returned, threatening to spill down her cheeks. Giff's face swam before her, then dissolved until she couldn't see his features any longer.

She shut her eyes, stretched back against the soft cushions and waited with breathless impatience. She heard him fumble, then heard the unmistakable tear of foil. Then he was upon her, pressing her once more into the soft cushions, warming her with his heated skin, kissing her tingling lips until she couldn't think any longer. She opened her legs, felt him mold against her as though they'd been made for each other. He rested against her hot, swollen dampness.

"Remember, love. Remember this always," he whispered before plunging inside.

She arched from the couch, impaled in wonder and sensation so intense, she cried out. He was everything she'd ever wanted, a fantasy come to life. His breath came hot and heavy on her neck, his hands grasped her buttocks and urged her on. Their rhythm pushed her deeper into the softness of the cushions, pushed him deeper inside her, until she became wild and free for the first time in her life.

"Yes, love. Yes."

It came over her then, a release so intense she lost all control. She felt herself stiffen. Fire shot through her. He surged within her, swelled in his own passion, called her name.

And she cried out her answer. *"William!"*

Chapter Nine

Fate often puts all the material for happiness and prosperity into a man's hands just to see how miserable he can make himself.
—Don Marquis

Linda floated in a warm mist, a feeling of complete satisfaction permeating her body. Making love with Giff had been more than she'd expected—more than she'd dreamed capable of feeling. She'd never experienced such pleasure before, not in her real life or her dreams of William.

William!

She'd called his name. Oh, my God, she'd called out his name in her moment of passion. She felt herself stiffen involuntarily. Resisting the urge to get up and bolt from the room, she forced herself to lie still. What did Giff think? He must be furious. That was why he was so quiet, lying heavily atop her, just waiting for her to open her eyes. A shiver a real terror raced through her as she imagined the look of angry condemnation in his face.

But when she did open her eyes, she saw only an appearance of equal satisfaction, almost a triumphant smile and a possessive gleam in his dark eyes. He looked like a man who'd just made wild, passionate love.

"Giff?" She could hear the trembling uncertainty in her voice. That made her feel weak and vulnerable, but she couldn't help herself. This went beyond embarrassment, far beyond using the wrong fork with salad.

"Yes, love?"

"Are you okay?"

"I believe that's supposed to be my question," he said with tenderness.

"But are you . . . happy?"

He smoothed a strand of hair back from her face, his gaze bathing her in sweet promises she couldn't begin to believe. "I've never been happier."

She looked away from his face. Perhaps he hadn't heard what she'd said. Or maybe she hadn't really said it aloud. Maybe she'd just imagined committing such an unpardonable sin. Yes, that was it.

"I'd hoped you would be as happy as I," he said.

"I am. I'm just . . . confused."

"Whatever it is, we can work it out."

She still felt horrible, but his words meant that he hadn't heard. Or if he had, he was gentleman enough not to notice. Of course, there wasn't any guarantee that she wouldn't say William's name at an equally inopportune moment in the future. She seemed to have no control whatsoever whenever Giff touched her.

"I'm not sure this is something that can be 'worked out.' "

"What we did was right, Linda," he said with finality and the assurance of a totally self-confident man. Not the kind of man whose ego would be personally devastated by a woman calling another man's name in passion. But neither was he the kind of man who would welcome such an indiscretion.

"It was wonderful," she said finally, meaning that with all her heart and soul. Nothing had ever been so perfect, so right.

"Making love was our destiny. Do you believe that?"

"Destiny? I do if you mean that we were attracted to each other from the start."

"And if I don't? If I mean destiny in the larger sense, that we were meant to be together?"

"Giff, don't." She closed her eyes, fighting the pain he caused by bringing up the future. A future she couldn't comprehend. They had this summer; her mind simply wouldn't comprehend any commitment beyond August. When the fall semester started, she planned to be at Northwestern.

"You don't want to face our feelings, but they're real. I noticed it earlier, at the restaurant, and other times. You avoid the truth, but what we shared proved we are bound."

"We've only known each other a few days. That's the truth I see."

"A few days can be a lifetime," he said holding her tightly, looking at her with such an intensity that she became frightened of his conviction.

There was no arguing with him, no moderation in his beliefs. Still, she had to try. She wouldn't be coerced into accepting another person's thoughts. She had a brain and it had begun to function again. "It's not a lifetime! It's less than a week."

"Let yourself believe," he said fiercely. "Feel with your heart. You'll know I'm right."

She pushed at his shoulder, wiggling out from beneath him. He didn't try to stop her, but he didn't help much either. "You know what it sounds like to me? Male manipulation. You think you're right and therefore I must be wrong." She found her dress at the foot of the couch, grabbed it and pulled it over her head.

"That's not fair, love."

"I'm not your love!"

He rose from the couch like a naked warrior. An angry one, from the hard glint in his eyes. The candlelight no longer made the room appear romantic and cozy. Now the atmosphere seemed heated, warmed by an almost unholy glow that seemed to radiate in his gaze.

"You are my love. You always were and you always will be."

Linda whirled away, unable to look at him and not remember the incredible pleasure he'd given her. The passion they'd shared. But even then, he'd controlled her. He'd skillfully brought her to the peak twice. He was a wonderful lover, but that didn't mean they were "destined" to be together. Sex wasn't love. She'd known that always.

The very idea of destiny frightened her—and not because she didn't care for him. She did. But his ideas seemed radical, almost obsessive. Once before she'd wondered if he could be the kind of unbalanced, stalker-type person who wouldn't take no for an answer. Who wouldn't stay away. He'd implied that they were involved in some preordained relationship.

She didn't want that; she wanted to be loved for herself, not because of some master scheme in Giff's mind. All she'd ever wanted was to find a man who stirred her heart, who didn't make her think she was missing something incredibly important. Now she'd discovered the element that had always eluded her in past relationships, but the man who had given her such complete joy was now revealing his wild, obsessive philosophies. She had to reason with him, to make him see that there were other explanations for their passion.

"I don't believe in the same things that you do," she said quietly. "I believe we make our own destiny. I don't believe we're puppets in some bizarre play already written."

"I'm not saying we lack free will. But some things are bigger than the reality in which we find ourselves. Sometimes," he said with dark intensity, "there *is* such a thing as fate."

"So fate brought you to South Carolina? You just decided Mr. Watley's grocery store was a good place to meet your destiny?" She shook her head, not wanting to hear more, but wanting him to admit there was another explanation. Something that would convince her she hadn't just made love to a crazy man.

"Yes, in a way, that's correct. It wasn't fate that brought me here, however; it was you."

"Me? What did I do?"

"You called to me."

She took a step back, clutching the fabric of her dress, becoming more frightened. "I did no such thing. I didn't even know you before I met you in the grocery!"

He stepped forward, not allowing her retreat. "You know me, Linda." His voice drifted over her with a hypnotic melody she couldn't resist. His hands held her upper arms in a grip that didn't hurt, but still felt as binding as steel. She couldn't move, couldn't run away.

"Look deeply into my eyes, into my heart, and tell me you don't know me."

She looked. She couldn't stop herself from gazing into his dark eyes, flickering with candlelight, burning with the strength of his convictions. Was she looking into the soul of madness? Into the dark depths she searched for truth, for hope, but her vision swam. Damned tears. Why did her emotions betray her when she really needed reason?

She blinked and continued to stare. Suddenly her vision cleared and she saw the darkness of night, the twinkling of a million stars, the loneliness of a stretch of beach, and a man. *William!* her mind screamed. He walked closer, then began to run. Her heart swelled in welcome. He was here.

And then she realized that she could see his face. For the first time, it wasn't a blur. She ran toward him, frightened yet certain she must know the truth.

Inside her mind, she called out, "William!"

He came closer, closer. She strained to see his face, to finally know her fantasy love. Then he stood before her, reaching out. Calling her.

He was Giff.

"No!"

"Yes," he said, holding her shoulders. "If you can't believe your heart, believe your eyes. Believe what your body told you, only moments ago."

"You're not him! He's dead." She twisted, but he held her fast. "You're not a ghost."

"No, I'm not. I'm a flesh-and-blood man, as real as any. And I am your destiny, just as you are mine."

"No."

He let her go when she struggled again. She wanted to run out the door, to get out of the house and never face him again. What she'd imagined in his dark eyes frightened her more than the Ouija board, more than Mord or anything else in her life. She began to shiver, to feel cold inside. She backed up until she felt the rough bricks of the fireplace.

"I want you to leave," she said as calmly as possible.

"Don't ask that, love. That's the one thing I cannot do."

"And quit calling me 'love.' "

"That I will not do."

"Damn it, Giff, I'm tired of playing mind games with you."

"This is no game." He walked toward her so fast, she barely had time to brace herself. His eyes seemed fierce, burning with fires of anger, not passion. "This is deadly serious."

"Don't threaten me. Don't you dare try to scare me into compliance."

She stared back at him, into the dark depths of his eyes, and suddenly she no longer felt only her own confusion and fear. She actually felt his anger and frustration. She sensed his growing need to control, to secure, and the strength of his emotions made her stagger. Her knees buckled, but he held her by the arms, staring into her eyes.

"What have you done to me?" she whispered.

"I've made you mine. Forever, Linda. That's the deal."

"No!"

He shook his head. "Yes. It's done."

"Get out!" She wrenched herself away and ran into the kitchen. She didn't have her grandfather's gun, but a knife should work against a madman. She yanked open the drawer and let her hand curve around the heavy wooden handle of a carving blade.

When he didn't follow, she stalked slowly back to the den.

He was pulling on his pants. The expression on his face looked tired, dejected. Not at all the face of a delusional lunatic. She felt the pain inside his mind, the confusion and fear he tried to hide. The knife she'd raised in self-defense lowered, until it dangled from her fingers. He didn't want to harm her. But he had. . . .

"This isn't finished," he said softly as he slipped on his shoes.

"I don't want to see you again, Giff."

"I'm not crazy, Linda."

She didn't answer, but stood there and stared, her heart pounding even as it threatened to break in two. Finally he turned and walked to the back door.

"I know this has been a shock. I'm willing to give you a few days, but we must talk soon."

She shook her head. "Good-bye, Giff."

"Good night, Linda."

The door shut with a soft whoosh of sound. The knife clattered to floor. In a few seconds, she ran to the windows, watched him walk down the steps to the beach. He looked defeated for the first time. She'd never realized, until now, how alive and vibrant he'd always seemed before.

Stop it! she told herself. *Quit feeling sympathetic toward him. He took your weakness—William—the one thing you admitted to him, and turned it to his advantage.* He must have realized how emotionally vulnerable she was at this time, after losing her grandmother and having those frightening dreams. All he'd done was helped her create her own illusions, then try to convince her they were real. She didn't understand why she'd imagined feeling what Giff felt, knowing his innermost thoughts, but that was probably just part of the delusion she'd suffered.

Well, she wasn't crazy. She knew what was real.

William Howard had died in 1815. She'd talked to him on the Ouija board just 13 years ago. So even if there was such a thing as reincarnation, which Giff had mentioned, he could only be 13 or so years old now. Not in his mid-30s. Her research at the library had confirmed her beliefs; the soul reincarnated at or before birth, not at some point in a person's adolescent or adult life.

There was absolutely no way he was William.

With one last look at the rumpled couch, she fled upstairs, to the safety of that girlish bedroom.

He felt such pure rage that he writhed in unfulfilled hate. They'd satisfied their lust, for the first time ever. He wanted to strangle them with icy fingers of death, but he hadn't the strength to reach out that far.

At least they'd argued. Their anger gave him power and hope that all was not lost. The man would not give up, not after tasting her passion. He would be back, with trite explanations and apologies, and she, weak female human that she was, would accept him back.

Humans! How he hated their weaknesses, their passions. How he craved the strength of their fears. He would use the sexual act against them, making their ultimate separation and defeat even more satisfying. They would rue the day they decided to defy him.

Soon, he would have a body. He would no longer be restricted to raging within this void. Soon, he would vent his anger on their meager flesh and bone. And they would see how unsubstantial humans really were.

Until then, his frustration roared. And nature gave thunderous voice to his anger.

The next day it rained, fitful storms that lashed the windows and seemed to rage along with Linda's tears. She curled up in her bed and watched the water pelt the window, looked into the grayness beyond the glass and cried for things that could have been. She poured out her heart, her dreams, and when the rain stopped, it seemed as though a flash flood had washed away everything that was dear. It seemed that the emptiness inside her would never be filled.

The next morning she decided she'd mourned enough for the death of her childish fantasies. She pulled herself from the sanctuary of her bed and threw herself into sorting and cleaning the old house. She made up a guest bedroom for Gerri and Jon, then tackled stocking the pantry and refrigerator for company. She kept herself so busy that she hardly had time to think about Giff.

She went to the gun store, paid for the cleaning of her grandfather's gun and bought ammunition, which she stored with some trepidation in a drawer near the French doors. Despite her earlier vacillation about having a gun in the house, it made her feel better to know she could defend herself. Against who, she wasn't sure. Even if Giff turned out to be her enemy, she didn't believe she could actually shoot him.

She told herself she didn't miss Giff, but that wasn't true. She missed him when she paused to listen for his knock on her door, or when the wind whispered to her at night. When she looked out at the beach, she imagined that she saw him standing there. She couldn't pass by the couch in the den without re-living the way she'd given herself to him, body and soul, for those fleeting moments. Her breath would catch and her heart would skip a beat. And the kitchen . . . that was the worst of all. A heated blush stole up her neck every time she had to work at the counter or sit at the table.

She told herself she wasn't really dying of need. That she just imagined his voice inside her head, calling to her, wanting her. That she wouldn't desert all her principles and run down the beach to his house.

If he was still there.

She'd been happy, she told herself over and over, before he came into her life. Perhaps not ecstatically so, but at least content. *Resigned,* a little voice said, to her single, celibate status, but she ignored the comment. She could be perfectly happy without a man to complicate her life. Especially not this particular man, who felt that he'd claimed her, or found her, or some such nonsense. He'd obviously been living in the past too long, researching history. He'd begun to sound like a mythical feudal lord.

She was no prize to be won. She was an independent woman of the 90s. There was no such thing as destiny.

She told herself that all day, but at night, she dreaded going to sleep. For to sleep meant she'd dream, and now, in those dreams, she saw Giff as her fantasy lover. Giff as the man she'd waited for all her life. Giff as her one true love, returning to her from a long journey.

She'd run to him, cling to him, return his kisses with equal passion. And they'd sink to the sand, make love as the waves broke around them, and she'd cry out her fulfillment, over and over. For now she knew what she'd been missing.

William, she'd shout, and Giff would answer her with smiling, dark eyes that promised eternity.

She was going mad.

She knew she appeared a sight, with dark circles under her eyes and a haunted look that would cause anyone to run the other way. *I've got to pull myself together before Gerri arrives. I know I can't lie to my best friend, but she can't begin to understand how I feel. She can't be burdened with all my pain.*

Four long, lonely days had passed since she'd asked Giff to leave. It was a relief when she heard a car pull off the road onto the gravel drive. She ran to the front door and looked out the beveled glass to see Gerri, waving from the passenger seat of a shiny white convertible.

A wave of joy washed through Linda as she watched the happy couple drive up. Finally, here was someone with whom she could share, someone who would understand and not immediately ask too many questions. She threw open the front door and ran down the steps, hugging Gerri as though she hadn't seen her in years rather than months.

"I'm so glad to see you," Linda said, sniffing

back a fresh batch of tears.

"I'm glad to see you too," Gerri said with a crooked smile and misty eyes. "Don't cry! You'll have me blubbering like a baby."

"I'm sorry. I can't help myself. They're happy tears."

Gerri held her shoulders and pushed back. "You're okay?"

Gerri could always tell when Linda tried to fool her. "No, but I'm much better now." She sniffed and looked away, her watery gaze colliding with the tall, sandy-blond-haired man standing by the fender of the car. His skin was tanned and his eyes turned up at the corners, as though he laughed often. "You need to introduce us, Gerri," she said.

"Linda, this wonderful, gorgeous man is my fiancé, Jonathan Moore."

Linda swiped a hand across her cheeks. "It's nice to meet you, Jonathan. I'm so glad you could come for a visit." She offered her hand.

He smiled and shook it. "I've wanted to meet you for some time. Besides, Gerri insisted we come right now."

Linda turned back to her friend. "I'm glad you did."

Gerri frowned. "Something else has happened?"

Linda couldn't answer. Not right now. "Come on inside, you two. I have lemonade and cookies."

"Just like the old days," Gerri said, grabbing her purse and urging Jon up the steps. As she passed by Linda, Gerri whispered, "We'll talk later."

Several hours later, Linda relaxed on the deck with Gerri and Jon as the sun set behind the house. Gerri and Jon sipped wine coolers and talked about their careers, a topic they obviously loved and Linda could barely understand. The corporate and financial worlds were far removed from her academic life.

"We've decided on a Christmas wedding. Do you remember when we were girls, how I wanted to have red dresses for my bridesmaids? Well, now I can."

"That's great." Linda looked down the beach, wondering if she'd see a dark figure walking among the waves at dusk.

"And we both have the week between Christmas and New Year's off, so we can honeymoon then," Jon said.

"We've talked about a scuba vacation," Gerri said. "Jon suggested Belize, but I'm not sure."

"You can't beat the dive sights," he said.

"But the accommodations!"

"You always did hate to rough it," Linda observed.

"I assure you, I haven't earned any new scouting badges lately, especially in New York City. Come to think of it, maybe they should give one for hailing taxis in Manhattan in the rain."

Jon laughed.

Linda smiled. "I'm sure you'll find a good compromise," she finally said, taking a sip of her wine cooler. She barely tasted the sweet drink. She kept thinking of the dry chardonnay Giff had served. So different.

She shook her head, blinking several times.

"What's wrong?" Gerri asked.

Linda looked up, surprised at having been caught daydreaming. "Nothing. I . . . I have just a tiny headache. Probably the sun I got earlier today."

"Maybe we should go in," Jon suggested. "I'm sure you've had a long day."

"I'm fine," Linda said. "Really. I'm looking forward to tasting those hamburgers."

"I'll get them on the grill," he said, rising from his chair. "The coals should be hot by now."

She watched him walk to the portable grill. Jon was a great guy, as "perfect" as Gerri had said. Tonight, he'd volunteered to cook out to save Linda the hassle of preparing dinner. She appreciated the thoughtful gesture. Her energy level hadn't been too high the last few days, even though she'd pushed herself to clean and sort.

"I'll be back in a minute," Gerri said, gathering up the empty bottles and heading inside.

The pleasant, usually mouth-watering aroma of searing meat drifted through the air. But Linda wasn't as hungry as she'd been lately. When she'd smelled the grill heating up, she'd thought about Giff and their first date at his house. Her appetite had deserted her, gone just like Giff's overwhelming presence.

She knew that soon, probably later tonight,

she'd have to tell Gerri what was bothering her. About Giff. About his claims to be her fantasy lover. Linda was glad that Gerri respected her need to take her time. Revealing intimate secrets was not something that came naturally. In truth, Linda admitted, she'd had few to reveal before now. And nothing as serious as her brief but passionate relationship with Giff.

In a few minutes, Gerri returned with two fresh bottles and the platter of lettuce, tomato, onions and buns. She placed them on the table and sat back down.

"We're hoping to buy an older house in Connecticut within five years. Jon and I both feel we may be able to work away from the city for at least part of the week by then."

"That's nice," Linda replied automatically.

"And it will be better to raise a family in the country."

A family. Linda looked from Gerri to Jon, seeing the future stretching before them in years of happiness. She felt like crying again. At least Giff had used protection. There would be no "mistakes" from her ill-fated liaison with him.

No smiling little Giffs, no curly-headed little girls running through the old house.

She looked up to see Gerri's questioning gaze. "I'm sorry. What did you say?"

"I asked if we could help you do some sorting tomorrow."

"That's not necessary. I'm coming along fine."

"But we want to help. We can't just sit around and let you work."

"I'll take some time off. We can lie on the beach."

"You'd burn to a crisp. No, let us help, at least part of the day."

Linda thought about it. Once Gerri decided to do something, it was virtually impossible to change her mind. And there was one area of the house that she'd dreaded sorting and cleaning.

"Well, if you insist. I've done most of the downstairs rooms, but I haven't tackled the attic yet."

Gerri took a drink from her wine cooler. "Have you been up there again?"

"No, just that one time when you called."

"What's this about the attic?" Jon asked, placing a platter of burgers on the table.

"That's where we used to play when we were kids," Gerri answered, passing around plates.

Linda handed flatware to everyone. Her friend obviously hadn't confided their encounter with the Ouija board to her fiancé. Of course, Gerri had never been as affected by what they'd done as Linda. "Gerri used to come with me during the summers when I visited my grandmother."

"Well, I'll be glad to volunteer for any heavy work. I need the exercise after days of eating in restaurants and at my mother's house."

"Sure," Gerri said. "The attic will be fine."

Linda could only nod. The meat tasted like sawdust in her mouth.

Later that evening, Jon excused himself and went upstairs to read. Linda was sure Gerri had asked him to, because as soon as he'd climbed the stairs, she followed Linda into the den from the kitchen and launched into an interrogation.

"What's happened, Linda? You look like you lost your best friend, which is impossible, of course, because here I am."

"How about I lost my newest friend," Linda replied, trying for a light tone and knowing she failed miserably. She tucked her feet under her in the comfortable recliner, having already decided she'd never sit on the couch again.

Gerri pulled a chair close to the recliner. "Who was it?"

"A man I met the day after we talked the first time. I just turned around in the grocery store and there he was." Linda shrugged, looking out the windows at the darkness. It hurt so much to talk about Giff. "He'd rented a house a few doors down the beach. He's a world-famous author of historical fiction."

"You can bore each other to death with dusty old history facts. Sounds like a perfect match."

"Yeah, I suppose it does. Only it wasn't." Even if making love with him had been as close to perfect as she could ever experience.

Gerri placed her hand on Linda's arm and leaned close. "I'm sorry. Do you want to talk about him?"

"I didn't think I had a choice," Linda said, trying again to joke. "You know how persistent you can be."

"I worry about you."

"I know. And thanks for being concerned." Linda leaned her head back and closed her eyes.

"How to begin—I don't know. Should I start with Giff—that's his name—or William?"

"You mean William as in the one we talked to on the Ouija board? Your fantasy man?"

"The same. You see, I told Giff about William, and now he thinks he's him."

"Wait a minute! Are you saying this guy thinks he's an English officer who died in eighteen-something? Is he crazy?"

Linda opened her eyes and leaned forward. "I don't know what to believe, Gerri. Giff is . . . very intense. He's attractive, articulate, interesting. He's charming and mannerly. But he's almost obsessed with security. He keeps telling me to keep my doors locked. He says a person can't be too careful. But then one night, when I was having a bad dream, he just showed up in my bedroom."

"You don't mean he just magically appeared? Tell me you don't mean that."

"No, not magically. He used a key that I hide under the geranium pot on the deck. At first he told me that he'd heard me screaming, but later he admitted that he can sense my moods and feelings, just like you. I believed him, but later . . ."

"What is it? What happened?"

Linda squirmed in her chair. She didn't want to tell Gerri that she'd made to love to a man she'd just met. Yet how could she explain Giff without telling it all? "Four nights ago, we went out to dinner. Afterwards, I invited him in for coffee and . . . well, one thing led to another and we . . ."

"Made wild, passionate love?"

Linda nodded.

"So, it was terrible? What happened to make you so upset?"

"It was wonderful. And then he acted very . . . possessive . . . as though it was all just a pre-ordained event that I had no control over. He said it was destiny, that we were bound together. He was so intense. It scared me, Gerri."

"This guy sounds weird. But what does he have to do with William?"

"This is really embarrassing."

"You can tell me." Gerri leaned forward.

"I think I said William's name when I . . . you know."

"Right then?"

"Yes, and Giff didn't even comment. He acted like that was perfectly normal for me to call him by another man's name. Maybe for some bed-hoppers it is, but not for me!"

"Of course not."

"I think he hypnotized me or something. I looked into his eyes and saw my regular dream with William, only this time I could see his face. And he was Giff."

"Oh, Linda, that is scary."

"I told him to leave, that I didn't want to see him again."

"And he left?"

"Yes, but he said it wasn't over between us. He insists that we're destined to be together. It's just a matter of time."

"You've got to be firm."

"I think Giff might be one of those obsessive, stalker-type personalities."

"Has he bothered you since that night?"

"No, but that doesn't mean he'll stay away. As a matter of fact, he said that he could only give me a few days. That it wasn't over between us."

"Well, at least he hasn't kept bothering you. That's a good sign. Maybe he'd had a little too much to drink that night, or . . . something."

Linda shook her head. "Not Giff. He never loses control. Even when he—"

Gerri held up her hand. "I get the picture. Of course it bothers you that he wants to be in control all the time!"

"I've been on my own for years. If I'd wanted a man around to give me orders, I could have found one. This goes deeper than just being bossy. Giff's not just spouting philosophy. He's intense, Gerri. Really, really focused."

"Have you talked to the police?"

"Why? He hasn't done anything criminal."

"Well, no, but he's scared you. And he got into your house without your permission."

"But he did that because I was having a nightmare."

"Now you're defending him."

"Damn."

"I know I'm only hearing part of the story, but it sounds to me like you did the right thing. You don't need a guy like that messing up your life."

"You're right. It's just that it all started out so perfectly." She'd had such hopes, such dreams, even if she was reluctant to believe that their relationship would last beyond the summer.

"The worst affairs often do," Gerri said. "Sometimes I think the best ones start out with horrible first dates or big misunderstandings or anything to make the two people look absolutely mismatched."

"Is that how it happened with you and Jon? You didn't tell me there was a story behind how you met, only that you'd had a date with the new guy upstairs."

Gerri smiled. "Yes. Jon was moving into his apartment, one floor up, and he lost control of a big stack of boxes. I was bringing my bike up the stairs and almost got bowled over by an avalanche. It was pretty irritating at the time. I felt like a clumsy fool, dodging boxes and losing control of my bike." Gerri laughed. "It bounced all the way down the stairs, making a huge racket. Jon felt as foolish as I did. We ended up laughing about it and going out for a beer after he moved in. One thing led to another, and here we are."

"That's a great story." Linda wished she could garner more enthusiasm, but she couldn't, even for her best friend. And she hadn't even told Gerri everything, about how those empathetic feelings of Giff's anger and frustration had crept into her mind, how she could still feel him calling to her, pulling her toward him.

"I'm sorry," Gerri said. "I can tell this guy really got to you. Why don't you just try to forget him? He's obviously one card short of a full deck."

"Maybe."

"Of course he is. After all, he didn't tell you anything new, did he? He just used your own words and twisted them around."

"You're right," Linda said, wishing she was

more sure. "But what if there is some truth to what he says? He talks about reincarnation and believes my story about Mord."

"Oh, don't even get me started. I don't want to think about that night before I go to bed!"

"I'm sorry. It's just been on my mind a lot lately."

"Well, now you have some company to take your mind off those depressing things. We'll have a good time and get you laughing again."

Gerri stood up and held Linda's hand, giving it a little squeeze. "You'll be fine. Just give it some time. When you get back to Chicago, this whole episode will seem like a distant memory."

"I hope you're right." Linda looked up at her friend, knowing Gerri truly believed that if you didn't think about something, it wasn't real. Well, maybe she was right. At the moment, however, Giff still seemed too near, too fresh in her memory.

"Good night. Don't get me up too early."

Linda smiled. "I won't."

As Gerri's footsteps faded away, up the stairs, Linda stared into the darkest corners of the room, those silent places untouched by the single lamp that burned beside her chair, and prayed that Gerri was right. That Giff's claims meant nothing. Because deep down inside, she had a horrible fear that he'd been telling the truth.

Chapter Ten

Evil enters like a needle and spreads like an oak tree.
—Ethiopian Proverb

They were finally here. The woman's friends. Two people who could release him from this void. But which one?

If he used the woman, he would gain great satisfaction from giving this scenario a real twist. They wouldn't be expecting aggression from a friend. A best friend who understood the woman's fear of the Ouija board. And the man wouldn't want to fight a woman. He thought himself too noble.

Weak humans.

But there could so much more satisfaction in taking over the body of the man. He was a fine speciman of humanity, but without rage or anger of his own. He needed passion, needed to use this strong body to fulfill its potential.

Yes, the man would be fine. But first, he needed to go to the attic.

If Mord had hands, he would have led the man up the stairs. Since he didn't, he'd make some subtle suggestions. By this time tomorrow, Mord would have a body.

A strong body ready to serve a new master.

"I'm worried about her, Jon," Gerri said.

He looked up from his book. "What do you mean?"

"I'm afraid she's in love with that strange man."

He set his book on the nightstand. "What strange man?"

"Oh, the one she met several days ago at the grocery store. I'm so worried."

Jon folded the corner of a page, then carefully closed the book. "How strange is he?"

"I don't know. From what Linda said, he sounds like a macho control freak with one foot firmly planted in a fantasy land. She says he's intense and obsessive. On the other hand, it's hard to believe Linda would be attracted to him if he wasn't . . . okay."

"I don't want to interfere with your relationship with Linda, but if it would make you feel better, I could have a talk with this guy."

Gerri sat down on the bed and hugged Jon. "That's sweet. I don't think it's necessary. They apparently had an argument four days ago. Linda told him she didn't want to see him again. If he'll just stay away, she'll get over him. She'll go back to Chicago in August, or before, and return to her normal life."

She rested her head on Jon's shoulder as his arms came around her.

"I know I've just met her, but she seemed rather distracted tonight," he said. "Kind of sad too. Do you really think she'll forget this guy so quickly?"

"Oh, honey, I don't know what to think. I've never seen Linda like this before."

"Then I guess it's a good thing we came to visit."

"I'm glad you didn't object to us leaving St. Augustine early. I know you're not used to my intuitions."

"But I believe them. I believe in you."

"You know something? You're the nicest man," Gerri said, stroking his jaw. "And I'm glad I fell in love with you."

He pulled her across his lap. "Just don't think I'm too plain vanilla because I'm not intense and brooding."

"I've always had a real fondness for vanilla," she said, leaning into his kiss. "Real fondness."

Sounds of laughter drifted down the stairs, floating through the air like an old, seldom-played song. A half hour ago, Jon and Gerri had walked upstairs, hand in hand, dressed in comfortable-looking clothes, to tackle the attic. Linda had warned them it would be dusty and boring, but apparently they were having too good a time to notice the dirt.

Linda shook her head and smiled. Lovers! She couldn't imagine what they were doing up there. Or maybe she could. The thought caused her smile to fade.

Damn Giff anyway. She couldn't even think about her friends without him intruding in some way. He was driving her crazy, and he hadn't even been around lately. He haunted her thoughts, invaded her sanity, with memories of their growing relationship. If she closed her eyes, she could see walks at sunset, a lunchtime picnic beneath a shade tree. She remembered the way he'd made her feel with just a look, the way she'd melted at his kisses. And they way she'd given herself to passion so freely, with such joy and abandon.

Instead of her yearning diminishing over time, she felt even more edgy. She missed him terribly, especially when it seemed he called to her. Was that reality or just another fantasy? She couldn't tell. All she knew was that she didn't want a man who believed he was destined to be with her. She didn't want someone who was so obsessive that he gave her no options, never asked for her beliefs or opinions.

She wanted a real relationship. She wanted to be loved for herself.

Her brief, extraordinary affair with Giff was over now. If she kept telling herself that, she might just make it through the summer.

"Here, let me help you with that," Jon said.

Gerri heaved the cardboard box onto the card table. "That's okay. It isn't that heavy." She looked at the variety of games and toys thrown haphazardly inside over the years. "It looks like mostly kid stuff, probably some of Linda's old things. I doubt there's anything worthwhile."

"Then let me look through there while you see what's in this old chest. I think there are old dresses and hats. Something might be valuable, but I'm not too good a judge of women's things."

"Oh, I wouldn't say that," Gerri said with a grin. "I remember last night you were particularly complimentary about that new nightgown."

Jon grabbed her around the waist and pulled her toward him. "That's different. Besides, who was *in* the nightgown interested me than anything else, even that sexy perfume you were wearing."

They kissed, long and slow. Even though they'd made love last night, both of them thoroughly satisfied, she felt desire well up again. At this rate, they wouldn't be of much help to Linda. Not only would they never finish the attic, but if she walked in on them, she'd be reminded of her unhappy affair with Giff.

On the other hand, if they were discreet, Linda wouldn't see or hear them.

Gerri broke away and rested her head on Jon's shoulder. "I'm glad this is one of the last few boxes. We're both sweaty and dirty, and I could really use a shower."

"I'll come with you. We need to save water."

Gerri laughed. "Get back to work, then. I'll race you downstairs as soon as we're finished."

"That's the best offer I've had all day."

Gerri sat on the floor and started exploring the

1950s-style dresses. Each was folded neatly, and most had matching pillbox and net-style hats, and colored cotton gloves. "These are so funky, Jon. Do you think I'd look just like June Cleaver if I tried one on?"

"I doubt it," he said, looking up from sorting puzzles and board games. "But if you find any genie costumes, you could dress up like Jeannie. I assure you that unlike that dim-witted astronaut, I'd know what to do after I rubbed the bottle."

"Very funny."

"Say, look at this. I haven't seen one of these in years."

Gerri swiveled around. "What is it?"

Jon carried his find to her. "A Ouija board. My sister had one of these when she was a teenager. We teased her about it all the time."

He held out the board to Gerri, but she didn't want to take it. The last time she'd touched that thing, she'd been scared to death. Linda had never gotten over her experience with the board "Those things can be a little weird," she said slowly.

"Don't tell me you believe that you can talk to spirits through this?" Jon said, his tone mocking.

"No, I . . . I don't know. But something strange happened one time when Linda and I used it."

"Girls have such vivid imaginations."

"I'm not sure we imagined it."

"Sure, and next you'll be telling me you performed seances at that card table."

"Not exactly," she said, eying the innocent-looking board with distaste.

Jon laughed at her expression and waved the

board around her, making ghostly noises as he teased, "Watch out for the creepy-crawlies."

"Jon, don't!" He dipped the board lower and lower, until she had to throw up her arm to keep it away from her. "Quit."

He stopped his teasing, but kept smiling. "Okay, but I still say you take all this hocus-pocus too seriously. It's just a board game." He put the box down on the card table and was silent for a moment. "Look, right here it says it's for entertainment purposes only."

"Yeah, sure it is. All I know is that Linda and I both got scared by that thing, and I don't want to have anything else to do with it."

He put it aside. "Maybe I should take it back to New York and see if it will give me any insight into future money markets."

"Maybe I should just bash you over the head with it."

Jon laughed. "So, are you finished?"

"Let me fold these dresses back into the box. I'm sure Linda will want to give these away to someone. She mentioned museums and theater groups."

"These games are all sorted as to kind. Linda will have to decide if she wants any of the toys."

"She probably won't. I'm sure there's a children's home or a charity that will want them."

"I'll pack them back into the box and mark it, then."

"Well, throw that Ouija board away. I know for a fact that Linda will go ballistic if she even sees the thing."

Gerri finished sealing the old dresses back up and labeling the contents of the box. She pushed up from the floor, stiff from sitting there so long. She was also ready to get Jon out of the attic, to take advantage of his teasing mood.

"I'm ready for that shower now," she said provocatively, a little pink pillbox hat with delicate net stretched over her forehead and eyes. A sagging artificial rosebud partially obscured her vision. Did women actually wear these things?

"Oh, Jooon."

He stood staring down at the card table, at the Ouija board that still rested on it.

"Jon?"

"What?" He finally looked up. He seemed distracted.

"I said I'm ready for a shower." She wagged her eyebrows at him.

"I'll be down in a minute." He looked back down as though the board contained all the secrets to the universe—as thought it was perfectly normal for her to wear an old pair of knit shorts, a crop top, and a funky pillbox.

She removed the hat, tossing it on top of the box of dresses. "Are you okay?"

"Sure. I'm fine." His voice sounded as though he were far away.

"I thought you were going to join me," Gerri said, trying to interest him in something beside the creepy device.

"I will."

She watched him for a minute, then turned away. She didn't take his lack of interest personally. In her experience, men picked the strangest times to get moody. And then they accused women of being temperamental. "I'll see you downstairs then."

"Okay."

Gerri frowned as she walked down the narrow stairs to the second floor. She hoped he threw the darn thing away. If Linda saw it, she'd have a fit. That's all she needed on top of her obsessive neighbor and their disastrously brief affair.

It was a good thing she and Jon had come to visit Linda, Gerri thought as she grabbed clean clothes from the guest bedroom. She paused beside the dresser, where an old school photo of Linda perched like a typical grandmother's treasure.

Linda needed her here right now, to get over that man and pull herself back together. Gerri touched the photo with her fingertips. "Before I leave, I'll have you laughing just like the old days," she vowed. Then she gathered up her clean clothes and walked into the bathroom.

Before she turned on the water, she paused. Jon wasn't going to join her. She hoped he'd come down from the attic and out of his strange mood.

The rush of blood, the sensations of skin, the feel of air expanding lungs. Mord felt it all as he eased into the body of the man named Jonathan Moore. Up through his fingertips and arms to his mind, which seemed enormously suitable for settling the destiny of the "lovers"—once again.

This man was intelligent and without much

guile. His mind did not spend much time concocting schemes and deceptions. Too bad. He would have been well-suited to a devious lifestyle, with his looks and brains. But his lack of subterfuge made him all the more receptive to manipulation. It should be easy to guide him toward the pleasures of fear and pain.

But first, Mord needed to become fully integrated into the flesh. To learn again how the body responded, what it was capable of doing. It had been too long since he'd felt the heady rush of sensations that could be perceived by humans. He looked forward to enjoying taste, one thing he particularly missed in the void. Meat and spices, sweet and bitter. Even the taste and smell of blood. Such ecstasy!

Pathetic creatures though they were, humans had some enjoyable characteristics. They spent their lives craving and satisfying their needs, and their desires were so many, so varied. Food, warmth, security—and sex.

Mord wondered exactly what this body craved. What its basic needs were. It would be interesting to see how each could be fulfilled.

He needed to practice patience. It had been so long. He wouldn't let the physical sensations rule. The woman needed to pay for her poor judgment. And the man—he would suffer and die for his greedy pursuit of the woman.

No one kept Mord away from his goal. Especially not a pathetic human. Especially not now that he had such a fine body to use.

* * *

Linda fixed a big, old-fashioned supper that night, using her grandmother's fried-chicken recipe and adding mashed potatoes and fresh green beans. For dessert, she'd bought a peach pie—and some low-fat ice cream to top it off.

"Every little bit helps," she reminded Gerri after telling her about the dessert.

Jon was late getting to the table, but looked refreshed and cool in a mint-green pullover shirt and chinos. His hair was still damp, slicked back from his forehead in a different style than he'd worn before.

"Dinner looks great," he said, sitting beside Gerri. His manner seemed more formal, less relaxed. "You look very nice too," he said to his fiancée. "I like that dress."

"Thank you," she replied, looking at him with a strange expression on her face.

Linda didn't understand what was going on between the happy couple. Gerri looked almost uncomfortable around Jon, which was really unusual, from what Linda had seen so far. They'd seemed so perfect for each other, as though they never had an argument or disagreed. Of course, she knew that was a simplistic view. No one was that happy all the time.

"I thought tomorrow we might take a little side trip. Can you suggest any site we might like that would be fairly close?" Gerri asked.

"Myrtle Beach is nice. It's a little more oriented toward tourists and visitors than we are, and you could easily drive there and back."

"Sounds good. What do you think, Jon?"

"Whatever you'd like is fine. Linda, can you get away?"

"I'm not sure." For some reason, she wasn't certain she wanted to spend the entire day with a recently engaged couple. Her pain over losing Giff was still too raw. As often as she reminded herself that it was for the best, that he was not the right kind of man for her, she couldn't stop thinking about him.

At night, she could almost swear she heard him call to her. She recognized sorrow and longing, but knew deep down inside that it was her own desires that she experienced. Just because he claimed to sense her emotions didn't mean he could inject his own feelings into her mind. Whatever had happened that day, after they'd made love, must have resulted from stress and heightened awareness. She'd imagined the intensity of feeling. He hadn't really changed her, or claimed her, by making love.

"Oh, Linda, you should come," Gerri said. "We'll have a great time."

"Maybe. I . . . may have some workmen coming by. I'll have to check." She'd made up the excuse on the spur of the moment, but it sounded good.

They dug into the meal. Although everything tasted good, Linda didn't eat with her customary gusto. She'd lost her appetite, she knew, and it didn't help to realize why. She missed Giff. He'd been a wonderful dinner companion. Whenever she remembered their times together, the rest of the world seemed to fade momentarily.

The sound of lips smacking in delight pulled her

back to the present. Surprised, she watched Jon tear into a drumstick. As a matter of fact, he seemed to have a near-fascination with the food. He closed his eyes and savored each bite. He even licked his fingers after touching the chicken. His appetite seemed enormous. Surely one didn't work up that much of a hunger by looking through old things in the attic.

Gerri also seemed confused by Jon's table manners, but other than the slight peculiarity, he seemed charming, if a bit distant. Yesterday he'd been more friendly and outgoing. Today, he was almost blandly nice. That would been more than acceptable in many men, Linda realized, but she sure had enjoyed his former wit and laughter. She suspected Gerri was thinking the same thing.

This is one time I'm glad I don't share Gerri's ability, that I can't sense her thoughts as she can sense mine, Linda thought.

"Would anyone like coffee with their dessert?" she asked when Gerri finished her meal.

"If it's not too much trouble," Jon said.

"I'll help you," Gerri volunteered. "Jon, why don't we have dessert on the deck? Would you set up the chairs?"

"Certainly." He placed his napkin beside his plate and smiled as he rose from his chair. "Excuse me."

Gerri and Linda gathered the plates and flatware.

"I don't mean to pry, but is something wrong with Jon?" Linda asked as soon as they were alone.

"I'm not sure. He's been acting strange ever

since we finished in the attic."

Linda stiffened. "What do you mean—strange?" Surely, after all this time, there couldn't be anything there that would affect a person. After all, she hadn't experienced any eerie sensations after she'd ventured upstairs that second day. The oddest sensations had been on the stairs, and the cold doorknob. Some of that had been in her mind.

"You know. Distracted, too polite. Just not himself."

Linda suddenly remembered some of the text she'd read in the library last weekend. Stories of strange possessions. A chill raced through her and she involuntarily shivered. Could she believe any of those tales? Could she afford not to? After all, she and Gerri had been involved in a supernatural occurrence 14 years ago.

Mord. Just thinking his name made her shiver again. It made her imagine horrible things that could cause a change of personality. "Almost like something's taken over his body," Linda whispered.

"What?"

"Gerri, you didn't find the board, did you?"

Her friend's silence answered the question. Gerri looked almost guilty.

"You didn't touch it, did you?"

"No . . . but Jon did."

"No!" Linda whispered.

"Linda, don't get all upset. That's not why he's acting strange."

"Are you sure?"

"Well, no, but I'm sure that a Ouija board

doesn't act like a pod from *Invasion of the Body Snatchers*."

"I'm serious, Gerri."

"So am I. I think Jon's just distracted. I know he's acting a bit out of character, but that could be due to a number of factors."

"Like what?"

"He could be worried about the markets. Maybe he's thinking about a client. Maybe he doesn't feel good."

"Or maybe he touched the damned Ouija board and something's happened to him."

"Linda, listen to yourself!"

Linda sat on a kitchen stool and rubbed her temples. "I don't know what to think, Gerri. I have this terrible feeling. I can't explain it. All I know is that I felt very much like this at the library last week when I went to research reincarnation and evil spirits and things like that. I got to thinking about Mord and suddenly I had an awful feeling. I was nervous, hot and paranoid."

"Remember that I called you, right? And we decided it might have been a panic attack. Nothing scary. Nothing unusual."

Linda looked up. "I can't explain it, but I don't believe that's all there was. It was too real."

Gerri walked over and put her arm around Linda. "Look, you've been under a lot of stress, with losing your grandmother and having this brief but bad affair with this Giff guy. It's no wonder you're having panic attacks."

"I'm not crazy." Even as she said the words, she remembered Giff making the same claim. She still wasn't sure she believed he was completely sane. But could she be certain she was rational?

"Of course you're not nuts. But Linda, try to look at this objectively. Giff says he's really William; you think Jon's been possessed by a Ouija board. You admitted that you're confused. Maybe this is just your mind's way of telling you to slow down."

"I think my mind is telling me to be careful." She remembered Giff's warnings to lock her doors. To be cautious. "No," she whispered as tears welled up behind her closed eyelids.

"Linda, what is it?"

"I don't know if I'm going to get over this one, Gerri. I can't shrug him off like I did when I got jilted in the eleventh grade."

"Of course you're going to get over him. You're just tired. You've been working too hard. Tomorrow, we'll all have a nice day together. Relax, see the sights. Things will look better then."

Linda looked up. Gerri was obviously concerned, getting herself all worried. One of them being upset was enough for now. Linda knew she had to pull herself together, before she ruined Gerri's vacation.

"You're probably right. I'll try my best."

"That's better." She handed Linda a tissue. "Now, blow your nose like a good girl."

Linda smiled at Gerri's teasing. "Yes, ma'am."

"Let's get that coffee made. I can't wait to taste the nice, fattening peach pie and the diet ice cream."

Linda wadded up the tissue and threw it at Gerri. Sometimes, a best friend was just what a person needed to take her mind off problems that couldn't be easily explained or solved.

Giff sat on the sandy dune, watching the setting sun bathe Linda's house in orange, turning the blue paint nearly purple. Soon it would be dark, time to sleep and indulge one's fantasies. Would Linda dream of him again, of the passion they'd shared and the lives in which they'd touched?

A breeze whispered through the sea grass, making the dried blades rustle and the green blades sing. Inside the house, lights came on in the kitchen, then the dining room. Linda was preparing dinner, he supposed. He sat still and watched. Soon he saw her, a dark shadow near the kitchen sink, moving back and forth. In a moment, he saw her more clearly as she sat a dish on the table. Her friend Gerri entered the room, helping serve the meal. As the sun slipped lower and the darkness spread, he could see their features more clearly in the bright interior light.

Linda was smiling, apparently enjoying this visit from her friends. Giff felt a stab of jealousy as he watched the two women laugh, so at ease. He wanted that kind of closeness with Linda. But he'd tried too hard, pushed too fast, that night they'd made love. She'd fought against the destiny he knew rapidly approached. He couldn't blame her. Looking at the situation from her point of view, which he'd done over the last four days, he understood her reluctance to get involved with a man obsessed by fate.

If only she knew. If he could only make her understand the truth . . .

The man, Gerri's fiancé, entered the room, causing both women to turn. He looked like a fine, upstanding yuppie: driven to succeed, to dress correctly, to have the perfect life. He wondered if the man had ever faced hardship. Giff doubted it. This one looked as though he'd been born to the good life.

At least Linda was surrounded by her friends. She would be safe, at least for now. They still had two days; apparently Mord wasn't going to show himself until the last minute. Giff hadn't a clue as to how Mord might appear in this lifetime. He still needed some portal or invitation to get back into their lives. Anything negative or evil could initiate his presence, even if done innocently by a person, such as Linda's use of the Ouija board when she was just a teenager. Giff imagined that an item used for great evil could become a device, or perhaps something like a crystal ball or even Tarot cards, if used with harmful intent. So far, Giff hadn't sensed or seen such a person or device, which was the one reason he felt Linda was relatively safe at this time.

But he would continue to watch. He would continue to try to reach out to her. The idea that she could easily dismiss him from her mind wasn't the issue; he wanted her to think about him with the same devotion that he felt for her, to re-live the moments they'd shared and the passion they'd experienced. If he could make her remember, then he had a chance to win this twisted game of fate. He had a chance to live.

Remember me, Linda, he said silently, willing her to hear his thoughts.

He watched them sit down to dinner. For a moment, Linda paused, hands on the table beside her plate, staring out the window in his direction. He knew she couldn't see him. He was too well hidden in the shadow of the dune, the setting sun at his back. But she could feel him. And she could remember.

Chapter Eleven

Evil events from evil causes spring.
—Aristophanes

After slipping into a new ivory and lace nightgown, Gerri dabbed perfume on each wrist. Somehow, she was going to get Jon to snap out of his zombie-like state and revert back to the man she loved. If something was bothering him, she wanted to know. In the five months they'd known each other, she'd never seen him this distracted.

She looked at her reflection in the bathroom vanity, checking for wrinkles on her pale skin, worry lines or signs of stress. She saw nothing unusual, just the few gray hairs that she pulled regularly from her black shoulder-length hair. Jon had always said he loved her hair.

Had she put too much pressure on him lately,

asking him to leave his parent's house in St. Augustine early to make this trip to South Carolina? But it hadn't seemed to bother him at the time.

She shook her head. This was no way to start their future together.

As soon as she entered the guest bedroom, she felt his eyes on her, even in the partial darkness. All the lamps were turned off, and only the nightlight Gerri had in each room provided illumination. The room seemed very cool, as though the air conditioning was set too low.

"Jon?"

"I'm here."

She heard the mattress squeak, then saw his silhouette as he walked toward her. He looked tall and powerful in the meager light.

She stood still, rubbing her arms where goose bumps had suddenly risen. "I'd like to talk if you feel like it."

"Later." He reached for her. His hands felt even colder than the chilly air as he pulled her close.

"Your hands are freezing!"

"Then you can warm them," he said as he embraced her tightly.

She pushed against him, but his arms were solid bands. "You're awfully persistent tonight, aren't you?" she said, trying to keep the mood light.

"Why shouldn't I be?"

"No reason. You just seem different. I thought we could talk about it."

He laughed, but then the sound died away, leaving silence. "Maybe you'd like it different. Maybe you were bored with the same old Jon every night."

"You know that's not true."

His hands roamed down her back, pulling her closer to his aroused body. "You don't want to spend the whole night talking, do you? There are far more interesting things to do."

She tried to push away from his chest. "Really, I'd like to—"

Her reply was cut off as his mouth covered hers, swooping down like a bird of prey on an innocent lamb. He seemed ravenous, plundering between her lips, grinding his teeth along hers until she tasted blood and some form of alcohol. Was he drunk? He'd never acted this way before.

He wasn't seductive; he was almost punishing. And she wasn't the least bit aroused. "Jon! Stop it. You're scaring me."

"Does that excite you, Gerri? Would you like to play a little game?" He hauled her closer, then kissed and suckled along her neck until she knew she would have marks the next day.

Her heart began to beat rapidly. She couldn't get enough air into her lungs. "No! Jon, stop!"

"You can't come in here wearing a gown like that, smelling like a ripe offering, and expect a man to stop. Women like that are teases, don't you know?"

"No. I'm not a tease." Especially now, when the last thing she wanted was more of his attention.

"Let's pretend I'm a plundering pirate and you're the spoils of war."

"No—"

He cut her off again, kissing her until she thought she'd gag from his demanding mouth and tongue. One hand slid to her breast, kneading it roughly before rolling the nipple between his fingers. With his other hand he held her tightly against his arousal, so tight she couldn't move.

"You like that. See how you respond."

"No, I don't. I'm not enjoying this. You're hurting me."

"There's a thin line between pain and pleasure."

"No."

"It's been so long," he whispered against her neck.

"It's been less than a day!"

"An eternity."

He raised her by the upper arms and tossed her to the bed, falling with her, his weight pinning her like a drugged butterfly. The mattress groaned in protest, the headboard squeaking in an ageless rhythm.

"Don't do this, Jon. Not like this."

His mouth fastened on her breast, sucking through the satin until the peak was hard and painfully distended. His hands dug into her hips, shifting her more fully under him until his arousal pressed tightly between her legs.

"Beg me for it, Gerri. Ask me."

"Please, stop!"

"Wrong response. I'll have to be more persuasive. I thought you'd like our little game."

He jerked up her gown, then his fingers dug into her thighs. She resisted, but he pulled her legs apart and pressed his weight more fully into her.

"Jon, I'm going to scream if you don't stop. I swear I will."

"I'll stop your screams. I'll make you scream."

He laughed at that remark, his alcohol-laced breath cool on her damp skin.

She twisted beneath him and tried to strike out, but he held tight. She'd never been so frightened in her life. No one had ever treated her this way. Nothing in her past months with Jon warned her that he could act so cruel.

"You know you love it."

He wasn't playing a game. He was serious. "No! Stop right now."

His response was to buck against her. She felt his penis, heavy and strong, against her inner thigh, and knew a higher level of panic. He was going to rape her. The man she loved was totally out of control. His teeth bit down on her shoulder. She cried out.

"None of that," he said, slipping a hand over her mouth. "We can't have a party if we're interrupted."

Gerri twisted with the last of her strength, thrashed her head from side to side. All that came through his painfully tight fingers were small moans.

"That's better. Maybe next time I'll tie you up. You'll like that."

She bit down on the fleshy part of his palm, as hard as she could.

He drew back, raising his injured hand, looking very surprised at her actions. She took advantage of the moment to roll away, falling off the side of the bed.

"Help!" she screamed as loud as she could. "Help me . . ."

Chapter Twelve

All your life you live so close to truth, it becomes a permanent blur in the corner of your eye, and when something nudges it into outline it is like being ambushed by a grotesque.
—Tom Stoppard

Linda leaned against the deck railing, unable to stay inside the house when she knew Jon and Gerri were making love. She'd heard the unmistakable noises, the muffled sounds, just after Gerri finished in the bathroom. It didn't take a genius to figure out what was going on upstairs. She wasn't a prude; they were both adults, and sex was perfectly normal. She didn't resent their happiness, but she had to admit that she felt painfully envious of their relationship.

Two people, so much in love. She sighed and

looked out at the beach. If only . . . but her wishes were nothing but leftover dreams, and even those had been distorted by Giff. She'd lost her fantasy man, her long-dead hero. He had become so mixed up with Giff's image that she no longer drew a crazy kind of comfort from her imaginary lover.

She'd been wrong to think that Giff was the man to make her forget William. If only she'd known before they made love, if only she could have guessed how very complicated her life would become as a result of Giff's arrival. His passion felt more like possession, as if he'd changed the very essence of her soul by making love to her. Otherwise, shouldn't she be able to forget him, to feel anger instead of longing?

She sighed deeply and blinked her tired eyes. As much as she needed rest, she needed the night more. A steady breeze from the ocean tangled her muslin gown and robe around her legs, and blew her curls away from her face. Small, puffy clouds raced through the sky, skimming over the waning moon and moving on. Her nails curled into the deck railing, holding her still, providing a touch of reality in a world gone painfully awry. She leaned into the wind, feeling like a schooner, sailing into an unknown ocean, depending on ever-changing winds and currents with no charts or maps.

She wasn't sure how long she stayed there, but soon felt tiny pinpricks of awareness across her skin. Her stomach muscles contracted against the empty, sinking sensation. She blinked, focusing on the beach in front of her. A man, silhouetted against the moonlit waves, stood on the damp sand. If he hadn't been dressed in white, if his hair were longer, he could have been the one who scared her last week.

She knew this man was Giff.

Energy pulsed through her like electricity flowing through a circuit. Her heart began a rapid beat. Her palms began to sweat. Was he here to spy on her, or had he come to talk? Or was he here for some other reason?

Her heart cried out, "Run to him," but her common sense said, "Be careful." She wasn't even sure at that moment that she wanted to talk about what had happened after they'd made love. But she did want him to say something that would make her understand, after the sleepless nights and tears. He stood still for long moments, his posture tense and unyielding. She could only stand on the deck and wait for him to make the first move.

Then he slowly shifted from his rigid posture, resigned, she supposed, to facing her. He walked slowly toward her, hands in the pockets of his cotton slacks. In the harsh illumination from the newly installed floodlights, he looked tired, his face thinner, his eyes bleak. He did not appear happy to see her.

When he reached the steps, he paused. "There are some things I need to explain."

She nodded, confused and shocked by his reserved mood. He seemed almost . . . humble.

He walked the rest of the way up the steps, then stopped in front of her on the deck. Even bathed in the softer light from inside the house, she saw lines of fatigue around his eyes and mouth.

"I've missed you," he said softly.

His words cut through her misery, right to the nerve. She held herself back even though she wanted to be enfolded in his arms and tell him that she'd missed him too. To please come back to her, stay and make love to her. But she couldn't. She didn't trust herself to speak, because all those words might come rushing out. And she'd already learned that her senses were totally unreliable where Giff was concerned. She couldn't give in to what she felt, because that was exactly what he wanted her to do, what he'd asked her to do, over and over—to trust her instincts.

He reached for her hand. She looked down and noticed that his fingers trembled ever so slightly. Then his warm, gentle grasp enfolded hers, and she allowed him a moment to just stand there, a rush of feeling so strong that she was sure he felt it coursing between them.

"Let's sit down," she said softly, then led him to the deck chairs.

He turned a chair so they faced each other before sitting down. His nostrils flared and he breathed deeply. He seemed to be feasting on her, the sight and smell of her nourishing him in some indefinable way. Linda could almost feel his emotions, as tangible as the salt air and sandy grit on the deck.

"About a week ago, you saw a man on the beach. A man dressed in black. He frightened you."

"Yes," she whispered. "His hair was long and

wild. I thought he might be dangerous."

Giff took a deep breath. "That man was me."

He paused and looked closely into her eyes. Linda wondered just briefly why she wasn't surprised, but she didn't have time to analyze her own feelings as he began to speak again.

"I'd just driven in from Savannah. It was late, I was tired, but too keyed up to sleep at the small motel down the beach. So I went for a walk, looking . . ."

"Looking for what?" she whispered.

"For you. I know you didn't believe me the other night when I tried to tell you this, but it's true. I felt drawn to this coast, pulled by your presence. I didn't know who you were or where you were exactly, so I followed my instincts. I flew to Savannah from California, where I'd been working on a film project."

"Giff, you have to know how crazy this sounds." Her heart began to pound faster as she absorbed his story and searched for the truth.

He nodded, looking away at the sea. "I know. I realize that to you, to anyone else, the claim sounds . . . odd. It's just that I've lived with it most of my life. I've always known, it seems, yet you don't."

"Don't know what?"

"That there *is* such a thing as destiny. That it's bigger than our mortal lives, stronger than our free will."

Linda sat back in her chair, trying to distance herself from his overwhelming presence. "I can't believe that."

"I want to show you. If you'll allow me the opportunity, I'll prove what I say."

"How can you prove something as vague as the concept of destiny?"

"By showing you our lives, our pasts."

"I know what my life is—what it's been."

"Yes, this life. But what about the past life, and the one before? What about going back to the time when we first met, a thousand years ago?"

She pulled her hand away. "You're talking crazy again."

"It's not crazy, Linda. Surely you've heard or read of past-life regression. You could be regressed and see the truth. Everything you say can be written or recorded, in case you don't remember when you wake up. I'll write down what I know, who I've been and the names you've had. After you've been regressed, you'll see how our lives have touched, time after time. You'll have the proof you need."

"I don't know if I believe—"

"I'm not asking you to believe everything right now. I only want this chance."

"And if I can't be regressed? If my version of the past is entirely different from yours?"

"It won't be," he said with a serious finality that frightened even as it intrigued.

"Even if I do get regressed and our stories are similar, that doesn't mean I believe that our relationship is some ordained event over which I have no control."

"The only thing that matters to me at the moment," he said wearily, "is that you're willing to try."

"I don't know."

Giff wiped a hand over his eyes, frustration written on his face. When he spoke, his voice was soft, yet hinted at his conviction. "Your name was Constance in your past life. We were engaged."

Her pulse started to race as she recalled a Ouija board session, just before Mord had stopped them. She and Gerri had just gotten the board out and were discussing William. Even now, after all those years, the scene came back to her as fresh as if it had happened yesterday. She closed her eyes, blocking out the waves and wind, concentrating on the past, on the stuffy, hot attic and the slick feel of the board beneath her fingers.

"I'll bet he was handsome," Linda said with a sigh, gazing upwards as though she could see their long-dead yet newly discovered friend. "Since he was an officer, he'd probably be dressed in a red and white uniform, with gold braid and brass buttons. And he'd ride a prancing horse and carry a sword—"

"Linda, you're doing it again," Gerri complained. "Let's just contact him and see if he can tell us anything else about how he looks. I can't believe he's all that modest. I mean, last night he wouldn't even tell us if he had a girlfriend!"

"If he loved someone, she'd probably be a fiancée or a wife. Gentlemen back then didn't have 'girlfriends.' Besides, he's an honorable man. They don't brag," Linda informed her more down-to-earth

friend. "You really should read about the culture of that time, you know."

"Okay, Miss History Teacher," Gerri responded while rolling her eyes, then laughed. "Let's get on with it."

Linda positioned the board exactly in the center of the table, then locked eyes with Gerri. They placed their hands lightly on the pointer as they had so many times before, waiting for that magical moment when their spirit friend would begin to reveal himself.

"William Howard, this is Linda. Are you there?"

The pointer seemed to hover a moment above the board, then moved swiftly to "yes."

"Would you answer some questions for us?"

Again, the pointer hovered and moved to "yes."

"William, this is Gerri. We want to know about your girlfriend."

"Gerri," Linda whispered fiercely, "don't say that! And you're supposed to ask a question."

"Well, I just want to know," Gerri whispered back, leaning forward. "Okay, I'll make it a question." She sat up straight and closed her eyes for a moment, thinking of how to get him to answer. "William, were you in love with someone?"

The pointer hovered, moved back and forth, and finally, slowly, moved to "yes."

"I knew it," Gerri whispered triumphantly.

"William, was the woman you loved alive when you died?" Linda asked.

Again, the answer was "yes."

"What was her name?" Gerri asked, obviously getting involved in the subject.

The pointer began to spell and Linda read off the letters. "C . . . O . . . N . . . S . . ."

A gust of wind caused the wind chimes to sing out, breaking the spell of the past. Linda opened her eyes. "Constance," she whispered.

"Yes," he said, leaning forward. "You remember?"

"I remember the Ouija board."

"Yes, the questions about William Howard." His voice held a hint of surprise and so much enthusiasm that Linda felt her own heart race.

She answered cautiously, despite his infectious excitement. "I remember asking . . . I don't remember *being* someone else."

"Think about this, love. How is that the questions you asked the Ouija board and the answers I have now are so similar? There's no coincidence here." He reached for her hand again, gazing deeply into her eyes. "It's real, Linda. I'm real, and I—"

A scream split the night, a horrible sound of terror.

Linda felt icy dread shroud her body as she jumped to her feet. "It's Gerri."

Giff ran into the house on Linda's heels, ready to defend her against whatever—or whoever—had caused the scream. But the frightened woman stumbling down the stairs, wild dark hair and even wilder eyes, wasn't the threat.

"Gerri," Linda gasped, hugging the crying woman, "what happened?"

"Jon . . . he . . ." She cried all the harder, her

red fingernails digging into Linda's shoulders. Bruises ringed the woman's upper arms, impressions of strong fingers, Giff thought.

"Gerri, please, tell me what happened. Should I call a doctor—or the police? Do you need to go to the emergency room?"

"I don't know. I don't think so," Gerri replied.

So this was Linda's best friend, the one with whom she'd shared the Ouija board. Giff had seen her from a distance, smiling and relaxed on the deck. Laughing with Linda. He'd felt almost jealous as he'd watched the two, comfortable with each other from years together.

Giff wanted that same acceptance, that same warmth. Yet he'd been too bold, too sure of himself after Linda had given herself so freely. He'd almost ruined his one chance at happiness.

Gerri's tearful wail broke into his thoughts. "Jon . . ." She didn't seem to be able to finish what she needed to say.

"Who is Jon?" Giff asked softly.

Gerri and Linda both jumped at the sound of his voice. Linda turned around slowly, and Gerri kept hold of her arm.

"Who is he?" Gerri asked in a shaky voice.

"This is Gifford Knight."

Gerri's eyes became even more round. She seemed frightened, rather than upset, once again. "The man—"

"Yes," Linda said quickly.

Giff wondered what Linda had told her friend to evoke that type of response. Had she said he was a crazy neighbor, a mad seducer of women?

A nut who believed in reincarnation and destiny? He cursed the fact that he didn't know *how* Linda saw him. He only knew that when he touched her, she responded with instinctive acceptance and passion, and that knowledge gave him hope that he hadn't destroyed his one chance at breaking the eternal bondage.

"Who is Jon?" Giff asked again.

"Jonathan Moore, Gerri's fiancé," Linda answered.

"Is he upstairs?"

"Yes . . . in the guest bedroom," Gerri said, burying her head against Linda's shoulder. As her hair slipped to the side, Giff noticed purple bruises on her neck and teeth marks on her shoulders. He tensed, a rush of anger going through him like a bolt of lightening. No sane man, no one who claimed to love a woman, could have made those marks.

"Has he ever been this rough before?" he asked, knowing that the question would upset both women, but needing the information. He'd seen the blond-haired man from a distance also, and he'd seemed reserved, polite even. Not a madman who would victimize his fiancée. But who knew what demons lurked beneath the surface of any man?

Linda glared at him. Gerri sobbed harder.

"I'm sorry to ask, but I need to know what we're facing," Giff said.

"No," Gerri finally answered. "He's never been like this. He's always so . . . kind."

"He seemed fine this morning," Linda added.

"He'd been drinking, but didn't seem drunk," Gerri declared. "I don't know what happened. He's been acting strange ever since we sorted through those things in the attic."

Giff stiffened, alarm bells sounding in his brain until he was deafened by the shrill noise. His muscles went rigid. He felt like clutching his head, screaming, cursing until he was hoarse with it. His first instinct was to grab Linda, run into the night like a coward who balked when the first shell exploded in battle. Damn it, he wanted to *live*.

It had happened. God, it had finally happened. The sense of impending doom he'd felt, the final confrontation that he knew would come, was upon them. He'd been right about the date, about the significance of the dates. June 1815. June 1995. Dates coinciding with days of the week, with the lunar cycles. His month to meet destiny.

"Giff, what is it?" He barely heard Linda's voice through the discordance inside him. She grabbed his arm. "What's wrong?"

He shook his head, not willing to say the words aloud. He had nothing here with which to defend himself or the women. Nothing that would stop the evil that was now Jonathan Moore.

As if summoned by the conversation, the man in question strolled down the stairs as though he didn't have a care in the world.

Gerri took one look at him and started crying again. Giff had the impression that Linda would have physically assaulted Moore if she hadn't been supporting and comforting her friend. Instead, she glared at him and said, "You pig. I want you out of my house."

"It was a mistake," Moore said smoothly, one shoulder lifting casually.

Giff wondered if he was always this suave and detached, or if this was a new aspect of his personality—one of Mord's traits. He'd ask Linda later, after he talked to Moore.

"A big mistake. You can't treat people like this and expect to be welcome," Linda said with venom.

"I'm sorry, I—"

"Get your things packed and don't bother us again," she ordered.

Giff had never seen her like this, and was surprised by the strength and loathing he heard in her voice. Her gentleness and calm had been replaced by a fierce protectiveness for her friend, as though the arm she'd placed around Gerri's shoulders could protect her from the world. But she didn't know who—what—she was confronting. To encourage her defensive instincts now could be a disaster. Besides, *he* was here to fight this battle. It was because of him that this possession had occurred, and his own instincts told him to face his enemy now, before Linda complicated the strategy with her own agenda.

"Linda, why don't you fix Gerri something hot to drink," Giff suggested. "I'd like a word with Moore."

Linda looked at him as though startled that he'd interfered. Didn't she realize how responsible he felt for her? Surely she must be able to sense, especially now, that he would protect her with the last drop of his blood.

Then Linda looked at Gerri, who was so obviously upset and physically battered. With one last glare at Moore, she said, "We'll be in the kitchen. No male heroics, no fighting in my house."

"Of course," Giff said. "Moore?"

"I just want to explain," he said calmly. Too calmly. "I didn't mean to harm—"

"Go to hell," Gerri said weakly.

"My thoughts exactly," Linda said as she tightened her arm around her friend, turned her back and escorted Gerri into the kitchen.

Go to hell. Gerri's words were ironic. For Mord, that would be like returning home.

When the women were out of hearing, Giff stared at the man before him. They were about the same in height, although Moore might have a few pounds on him. Moore appeared to be slightly younger, around 30. But the evil that possessed him was ancient, as old as time itself, if some of the theories were correct.

"So, you've managed to find a way into her home."

Moore looked away casually, his gaze traveling around the room. "Yes. Surely you've heard. I was invited to spend some time here with my fiancé."

"Don't play innocent with me. We both know I'm not talking about—or to—Jonathan Moore."

"Do we? But that's who I am."

"That's who you appear to be."

"Appearances, in this case, aren't deceiving. I'm an investment banker in New York."

"You're the lowest form of life ever created."

Moore laughed, moving a few steps away. His fingers trailed over a fragile porcelain lady, her skirts spread as though she danced alone. "Usually those epitaphs are thrown at lawyers, not bankers."

"I don't suppose it would do any good to warn you away from her."

"From Gerri? Hardly, since she's my fiancée."

"I'm talking about Linda. You will not have her, not as long as I can draw a breath." Giff felt a red rage fill him at the thought of Mord claiming Linda. It was all he could do to stop himself from strangling Moore. But that wouldn't solve the problem. It wouldn't kill Mord. He'd simply find another body to possess, now that he was unleashed.

There is a way, though. Be patient. Giff told himself this even as he watched Moore's eyes narrow, his lips turn up slightly in a mockery of a smile.

"Now why would you think I'd have an interest in her? She is rather a cute little thing, all cuddles and curls—except when she's angry, of course." He picked up the figurine, his thumb tracing the delicate curves of the porcelain woman's breasts while he stared into Giff's eyes. "Are you the insanely jealous type?"

"Yes."

Moore placed the dancer back on the table and smiled. "Then I suppose it bothers you a great deal that I'm staying in the house."

He said it so coolly, so smugly, that Giff reacted from pure rage. He doubted Moore even saw the punch coming. By the time he must have felt it, he was already sprawled on his back, propped up by his elbows, rubbing his jaw.

"That answers my question." Just as soon as Moore said the words, he sagged to the floor, as limp as a deflated balloon.

Linda rushed to the doorway, concern in her eyes. "What happened?"

"He made one remark too many," Giff said.

"You hit him?"

"Apparently." Giff noticed, for the first time, that his knuckles ached from the unaccustomed impact. "I haven't practiced in some time, but fortunately, he didn't move any faster than a punching bag."

Linda looked at him with a worried expression on her drawn face. "I never thought of you as violent. And I told you no fighting!"

Giff walked toward Linda, touching her cheek with one finger. "This was hardly a 'fight.' I'm not a violent man, but I can only be pushed so far. Moore exceeded those limits, with Gerri . . . with you."

He looked deeply into her eyes, his words from days ago echoing in his mind. *You're mine. I'll never let you go.*

She stared at him a long time, her gaze wide with dawning awareness and a touch of fear. The bond was still strong, and he was sure she'd heard his thoughts almost as clearly as if he'd spoken them aloud.

"I'm going to take her upstairs to my bedroom,"

she said slowly, as though she needed to soothe him.

He almost laughed at the thought. He could not be calmed this night, not when his enemy lay just inches away.

But Linda didn't know that. She had yet to realize how evil and determined Mord could be, even if she had guessed what made Moore act as he did. At the moment, he couldn't explain it all to her, so he nodded. "Stay together. Lock your door. Get some sleep."

"I can't just leave Jon down here. What if he wakes up?—"

"Leave him to me. I'll stay and watch him."

She looked again at the prone form. "You won't do anything . . . rash?"

"Like tie him to a cement block and throw him into the ocean?"

Linda nodded, completely serious.

"No, nothing like that," he said, smiling slightly at the dilemmas she faced; she despised Moore, but didn't want him harmed. She feared Giff, but took comfort in his presence. "I'll simply make sure he understands that he can't treat women that way. That he can't come into your home and assault people."

"Gerri said she thought he'd been drinking."

"Perhaps. That's no excuse."

"She's looking for explanations. She loves him."

Giff felt a new burst of anger fill him. "Yes, I suppose she does. And he'll use that to his advantage," he said softly.

"What?"

He shook his head. "Never mind. I'll explain it all tomorrow."

"More stories?"

"The truth, love."

She shook her head. "I don't understand what's going on—what happened in the attic, what you said outside earlier, and what I feel at the moment. But I can't deal with anything else right now."

"Later, when you're not so tired."

She nodded, then sighed deeply. "I'm getting Gerri upstairs."

He hoped that she would be able to rest. Her fears were real, but perhaps she could put them aside for a few hours. "I'll be here. Don't worry."

She turned and walked back to the doorway of the kitchen. "I should worry, you know. A few days ago I never wanted to see you again. I was sure you were crazy."

"And now?"

"Now I'm not sure which one of us is crazy."

Giff smiled. "You'll understand it all. Later, love."

She returned to the kitchen, probably to get Gerri, without arguing with him. For that, he was grateful. As much as he wanted to be with Linda, to care for her and soothe her fears, he needed some time alone also. His own thoughts were spinning rapidly, and he needed to analyze this new situation with Moore.

Giff pulled Moore across the floor until the man leaned against the couch in a half-sitting position.

Perhaps the women wouldn't notice him when they passed by.

In a few seconds, Linda was back, her arm around Gerri. "Good night, Giff. Wake me if anything happens."

"Nothing will happen. Not tonight, anyway." The time wasn't quite right. The date wasn't the same. Not yet.

She gave him a puzzled look at his cryptic answer, then walked up the stairs.

He'd gone too far. He knew that now that the body of Jonathan Moore was slumped in defeat. When he awoke, his jaw would be sore and his head would hurt. More sensations to digest, but far less enjoyable than frightening the woman named Gerri.

Oh, that had been glorious. To use sex against her when she did enjoy it so. He knew she did—this body he inhabited knew she did. That was why it was so difficult to control. He'd wanted to plunge inside her with a type of madness that was pure pleasure. He'd wanted to hear her scream in fear and in denial of her own satisfaction.

But he had gone too far. He must remember to exert caution. He'd been surprised that the man knew him so quickly. Of course, the man thought he was so clever, researching his past lives. All that meant was that he knew he would die soon.

The man had gained the woman's trust. That was bad, an unfortunate obstacle that would be overcome with time and skill.

They thought they could save themselves. Fools!

They only postponed the inevitable. The outcome was set, had been set, for a thousand years. No human knew how to defeat an elemental force. Oh, some had won temporary victories. Some, who studied the ancient texts, who believed in what couldn't be seen.

These "lovers" only dragged out their own fate. So be it. He would enjoy his time in this body, in their world. In the end, he would kill the man, perhaps even take the woman by force. Their fear and hatred would keep him alive as he slipped back into the void. Until he could break free again.

Yes, he would be more careful. They would hardly know he was here.

And despite the fact that Moore was unconscious, Mord made him smile. It felt so good to be in control.

Chapter Thirteen

When you are in love you are not wise: or, when you are wise you are not in love.
—Publilius Syrus

Gerri concentrated on taking one bite of food at a time, watching Jon consume his breakfast the next morning with a yellow and purple jaw that was obviously tender. His manners were even worse today than they'd been last night, although when he caught her watching him, he seemed to slow the pace and wipe his mouth. Or maybe he was having a hard time because his jaw was sore. She didn't know. She wasn't going to ask. She wasn't even sure she cared.

Anger and confusion fought for control in her mind—about his current nonchalant attitude—about how he'd hurt and disappointed her last night. Now he acted as though nothing terrible had occurred.

She'd refused to be alone with him. She and Linda had spent the night in Linda's room; then they'd stayed together, even while dressing and putting on makeup. Words didn't come easily between them; it seemed that they both felt awkward about what had happened, unable to comprehend why Jon had turned into such a cruel monster.

A cruel monster who, at this moment, was still her fiancé.

Gerri wondered if she'd deceived herself before about Jon. Had there been a mean streak hiding beneath his easygoing personality? Had he secretly resented their "normal" sex life? Had she lied to herself for months about how "perfect" he was?

She didn't know if she'd been a total fool. Jon was probably the only one who could tell her, and she didn't think she would believe anything he tried to say. He *had* tried to talk to her earlier, catching her alone in the kitchen while Linda went back upstairs, but Gerri had felt so much panic and deep-seated pain that she'd run away. She still wasn't ready, but she couldn't avoid finding out—or facing—the truth for much longer.

Jon seemed to be a totally different man from the one who had attacked her last night. He sat across from her now, taking careful bites of toast and scrambled eggs. Other than his colorful jaw, he looked . . . normal. He finished his coffee and gazed at her over the rim of the mug. She looked away. She didn't want to encourage conversation yet.

Gerri glanced out the window at the beach, letting her thoughts drift back to a half hour ago. Linda's friend Giff, the one who might be crazy or obsessed, had stayed all night, until Gerri and Linda walked downstairs this morning. Apparently he'd watched over Jon after punching him in the jaw and dumping him on the couch. Giff had appeared tired, but radiated such intense energy that Gerri had stepped back after walking into the den, uncomfortable around him. He'd looked at her with interest, but not pity, as though he understood something she didn't. Then, with a tender look at Linda, he'd slipped out the French doors, saying he had things to take care of.

Gerri supposed she should be shocked at Giff's involvement in her problems, but it was apparent that despite Linda's earlier doubts, she still cared for him and respected his opinion.

The whole incident—the attack, the denial, then Giff's violent reaction to Jon—just didn't make sense. Maybe, Gerri thought, she was crazy, but if so, she wasn't the only one in this house.

"Gerri, sweetheart," Jon said, breaking into her swirling thoughts, "yesterday afternoon is fuzzy. I remember feeling strange after coming down from the attic."

"I don't want to talk to you right now."

"Then please just listen," he said, speaking faster. "Maybe it was all the dust. I might have taken some allergy medicine, like an antihistamine. Then later, I got a strong urge for something to drink. I found a bottle of brandy in the sideboard and poured myself a glass."

"It must have been more than one, to make you act like you did," Gerri said dryly, dropping what was left of her toast to the plate. Jon *never* drank too much. He'd explained that he was concerned that he might offend a potential client or reveal something that he shouldn't. He was a most thorough, meticulous man; he never let himself get too carried away, and his restraint was one of the many things Gerri had loved about him.

"I don't know how many I had, but it must have been a lot. I honestly don't remember anything that happened in the bedroom."

"I find that hard to believe," she said, finally looking up.

Gerri watched Jon, saw the bewilderment in his face and came to the conclusion that he really was baffled. She glanced at Linda and saw similar confusion—and some sympathy—on her friend's face.

"I love you, Gerri," he said softly. "I'd never intentionally hurt you."

She pulled back her hair, revealing the marks on her neck. Then she raised the short sleeves of her cotton sweater, showing the bruises there. "Does this look like it felt good?"

"No, of course not. But I'm telling you, that wasn't me! I'm not like that."

"I don't want to interfere, Gerri, but I think he's telling the truth," Linda said.

"Gerri, please, you've got to believe me. What happened last night—it will never happen again."

"Can you promise?"

"Absolutely. If necessary, I'll never touch another drop of liquor as long as I live. I never want to hurt you. I know I must have done it, but I can't believe it happened."

Gerri finally closed her eyes and nodded. She'd looked for a long time to find "Mr. Right." She didn't want to believe she'd been a fool, that she'd been deceived about his character. Besides, it was inconceivable that Jon had become an actor worthy of an Oscar in a few days; she was sure he was telling the truth now She didn't want one incident, however awful, to ruin their chances together.

"Okay. I'll forgive you. Maybe it was a combination of alcohol and drugs. I don't know. I just believe that you wouldn't do something like that on purpose."

"Never."

She looked up. "But Jon, listen to this. If you *ever* treat me like that again, you'll get more than a punch to your jaw."

"Well, I'm glad that's settled," Linda said, pushing back her chair. She grabbed some plates and walked toward the kitchen.

"Let's get away from the house today, try to forget what happened," Jon said, reaching for Gerri's hand.

She was reluctant to let him touch her, but she knew she'd have to start somewhere. She couldn't imagine not touching the man she loved. He cradled her hand gently, as though he knew what she faced in trusting him again.

"Maybe that would be best," she said. "We could

go up to Myrtle Beach, like Linda suggested last night."

He smiled. "I'd like that."

Linda walked back in and Gerri asked, "Would you like to go with us? We're going to Myrtle Beach for the day."

Linda frowned and seemed to search for something to say. Finally, she shook her head. "I don't think so, but thanks for the offer."

Gerri got up and began to gather her dishes. "Why not? We'd have a great time. It would be a good idea for you to get out of the house."

"I didn't sleep too much last night, and I've developed a whopper of a headache. I think I'll just pull the shades and take a nap while you're gone."

"You're sure?" Gerri walked into the kitchen with an armload of margarine and jelly jars.

"The question is, are you sure?" Linda asked in a serious tone of voice.

"Yes. I've thought about it. Jon and I have talked about it. If I can't trust him . . . well, I'm not sure what happened last night, but I believe Jon when he says it was a combination of medication and alcohol. He's not a violent man."

"He might not be, but what if—"

"Please, don't say it. Jon's fine now. We're going to have a nice day and forget last night."

Linda frowned.

"Why don't you come with us? You can see for yourself that he's okay."

"No, thanks. Go ahead and have a good time."

Jon strolled into the kitchen, carrying his dishes. "When would you like to leave?"

They decided to leave in a half hour. Gerri helped Linda clean up the kitchen while Jon made sure the car was unpacked and ready for a short trip. Things seemed to be back to normal, but Gerri kept getting alarming vibes from Linda, who wouldn't admit what she was feeling. A headache, she claimed, but Gerri didn't think so. She believed the unsettled feelings centered around Linda's relationship with Giff, and despite her best friend's assertions, she supposed Linda knew it too.

Gerri absolutely refused to believed that Jon's behavior had anything to do with their visit to the attic. After all, the Ouija board was just a device that had focused their thoughts and dreams. Maybe it was more than a board game, but it didn't cause Jon's cruel behavior.

A mere board couldn't do that.

Chapter Fourteen

Unless we remember we cannot understand.
—Edward M. Forster

Linda snuggled deeper into the soft beige sofa where she and Giff had made love. Her vow to avoid this piece of furniture now seemed childish, especially after seeing Giff last night. She'd wanted time to explore her feelings for him, the intense attraction coupled with the fear, but there hadn't been time, not with Gerri's much more immediate problems to face.

Linda had dozed erratically throughout the morning, and still felt groggy with sleep. She was exhausted from the mostly sleepless night with Gerri, from worrying about her friend's health and happiness. In the light of day, without Jon's bizarre behavior to make her suspicious, she wondered what had really happened last night—and earlier, in the attic.

Breakfast this morning hadn't provided any answers; it had only confused the issue. Jon's normal and contrite mood, his apology and partial explanations, made last night seem even stranger. She still felt torn about leaving Gerri alone with Jon, but perhaps giving the two of them some time alone to work out their problems would be the best solution.

It was still impossible to believe that the mild-mannered, good-looking man at the breakfast table was the same person who had terrorized Gerri last night and caused Giff to react so violently.

Giff. When she closed her eyes, she remembered the passion they'd shared on these cushions. Even though it had been several days, she still smelled his scent. When she shifted her weight, she sunk lower, enveloped by the softness, and felt cocooned by his arms. And if she let herself imagine, she felt the press of his body on hers, the blessed heaviness of his hardness filling her with anticipation.

She jerked awake, fighting the desire. Not wanting to crave him like food and air, but knowing that he was never far from either her conscious or unconscious thoughts. Feeling his emotions inside her head, imagining him whisper seductively to her. It was as though he hadn't left her, as though he'd been with her all the days since they'd made love.

Who was he, really? There was no way he could

be William Howard reincarnated. It had only been 14 years, and unless Giff had spent the first 16 years or so of his life without a soul, she couldn't believe he had William's. So how did he know so much? Why did he claim destiny was responsible for their attraction?

She sighed and rolled to her side. Could she even say that what he felt for her was attraction? Rather, it seemed more like obsession. Perhaps he was a reluctant lover, a man who felt destiny pushing against his own free will.

She felt sure that if they'd met under different circumstances, she'd still be attracted to him. They had much in common, with their backgrounds in history. And she admired his work. On a personal note, he was compelling, handsome and interesting. Of course she'd find him attractive.

But would he say the same thing of her? She was not classically beautiful or endowed with the most marvelous figure. She supposed she could most accurately be described as "cute," but did intense, highly motivated, English-born men go for "cute"? There was the common interest in history, yet he didn't seem at all inclined to discuss that with her. As far as conversations, most had involved his questioning of her background, her plans. She believed that that was entirely motivated by his view of destiny, not by any real interest in her as a person.

How did he know about the question to the Ouija board, and the answer that had started to spell "Constance"? That had to be more than a good guess. Constance wasn't that common a name. She'd admitted that she believed he could sense her emotions, just as Gerri could, but was it possible that he really could read her exact thoughts? No, that was crazy. Every mind-reading incident she'd ever heard of had been dismissed as a parlor trick. Without proof, Giff's assertions were no more than an illusion—magic tricks by a master schemer.

But *why*?

She flopped to her back again, her headache returning from all the unanswered questions. All she knew for sure was that she didn't want a relationship based on his need to satisfy fate.

The house was so quiet, the midday sun blocked by drawn shades. Outside, even the surf sounded subdued, as though it knew she needed to rest. Soon, her eyelids drifted closed and she gave in the demands of her tired body.

She awoke with a start, all senses on alert. Had Jon and Gerri returned? She felt she was no longer alone, and the feeling that she was being watched made her heart pound faster. Opening her eyes slowly, she rotated her head, hoping that she'd just had a disturbing dream. That she was still safely alone in the house.

Then her eyes collided with the dark, shuttered gaze of Giff.

"You," she breathed.

He rose like a panther from the chair where he'd been sitting, fingers steepled and eyes intense.

"You scared the daylights out of me."

"I didn't mean to frighten you," he said, sitting beside her hip on the couch. "You needed to sleep."

"How did you get in here?"

He held up a key. The same one, she suspected, that he'd used to get in the other night when she'd had the horrible nightmare.

"Give me that," she demanded, reaching for the traitorous metal.

He slipped it into his jeans pocket. "Not yet. I may need it again."

"I'll change the locks if I must. You can't just let yourself in anytime you wish."

"Believe me, I don't," he stated, reaching for her hair.

She should have jerked away, she told herself. But his fingers were warm on her cheek where he smoothed away several strands. "I love your hair. It's so alive, so beautiful."

"I suppose I have hair just like Constance," she said, unwilling to let him believe she was totally gullible, ready to welcome him with open arms just because she'd been so willing the other night. That had been a mistake, she realized looking back. At the time, it had seemed perfect.

"No, nothing like hers, really. I remember it being much more pale, thinner and straighter. I never saw it down, but I imagine it was quite long."

"What do you mean, you never saw it down?" she asked, playing along with his Constance fantasy.

"We courted in the presence of her family. I

never had the opportunity to see her any other way than fully dressed, ready for a ride, a ball, or tea."

"You and she . . . never . . . ?"

"Made love?" he finished. "No, we didn't. You and I have never made love before, in any of our past lives." The look on his face changed, becoming more tender. Softer, with the harsh lines erased. More handsome. "The other night was a first for us both."

Linda scooted to the end of the couch. "This conversation is getting a little crazy again." And she was in dangerous peril of giving in to his seductive charm.

"Only because you don't believe me. Because you won't listen to the truth."

"Your version of the truth often sounds a bit bizarre," she said.

"But it isn't. It's actually very simple. The problem is that you haven't heard the whole story. I realized that last night. I've been telling you portions, but we're always interrupted before I can finish, or you aren't ready to hear more."

"That sounds conveniently like an excuse. Have you given this more thought and come up with a complete scenario?"

His mouth thinned and his eyes looked harsh in the muted light. Linda felt a building anger coming from inside him, along with frustration like nothing she'd ever experienced before. She didn't want to feel his emotions, and had no idea why she could do so. But she had a sneaking suspicion it had something to do with making love the other night. From the moment they had joined physically, they had also bonded mentally.

"I'm not making this up. You can confirm the names and dates by research, if you wish, but I'm hoping that once you listen to the entire story, you'll believe."

"So you say I can research all this?"

"Yes."

"And you have excellent sources for research, don't you? I suppose once I told you about William Howard the first time, you could have done a little research on your own. You could have found out more about him than I know. You could have discovered that the woman he loved was named Constance."

She watched a tick in his jaw. "I could have. But I didn't."

"So you claim." She paused when he didn't comment. "That evening at your cottage. Was that really 'research' on your computer, that sheet of paper from Northwestern, or was it something I'd really hate, like snooping into my life? Damn it, Giff, you've invaded my life! Now I can't even have a fantasy without you claiming that it's part of some past life or destiny."

"How would I have learned about your dreams? How would I know that the other night, you were dreaming of making love to William on the beach? You were aroused, Linda, beyond anything you'd experienced before. He was ready to consummate the act, ready to make you his forever. But then the dream changed, didn't it?"

"Yes," she said softly. But then her chin came

up. "You could have figured that out on your own from what I said."

"But would I know that at the moment William was to make you his, your lover changed? His hands became cruel claws. His breath was cold on your neck. You looked at him and knew him for what he was, Linda."

"No!"

"Yes! He was Mord. And you began to scream."

She closed her eyes and put her hands over her ears. All the terror of the dream rushed back. She rocked herself back and forth, hating Giff for being right. She'd never told him that. He'd described it to the very details that had her crying out in fear.

"He's gone, love, he's gone." She heard the whispered words in her mind, just as she'd heard them in her dream. *"I'm here with you. Don't be afraid. I'll always be with you."* Then she felt Giff's arms around her, holding her close to his heart, stroking her, just as he had in the dream. He'd saved her from her nightmare by making her believe that William was with her, making love to her. And she'd climaxed, in her dream . . . and in Giff's arms?

The memory made her blush, made her pulse race wildly. But she shuddered at the knowledge that he really had been inside her head, guiding her dreams, reaching to her subconscious. And she could feel his emotions, connect with his conscious mind.

"Oh, God," she whispered, burrowing into his

shoulder. "There really is something strange going on here."

"Not strange," he said gently, his breath ruffling her hair. "Not when you know why and how. The only strange part is how it all started."

She felt as though destiny had indeed thrown a suffocating blanket of fate over her when she pulled back to see his face. With a heavy heart, she asked the inevitable. "How did it start?"

That she trusted him enough to let him try the regression was amazing, Giff thought. He'd wanted to prove it all to her, and this was the easiest way, but when she'd agreed to let him use hypnosis, he'd felt his heart skip a beat. She didn't completely trust him, he knew, yet she believed he wouldn't harm her. After all she'd been through in the last two weeks, that was a major victory.

It was a start.

"Just sit comfortably with both feet on the floor. Try to relax," he coaxed, watching her closely as she sat in a winged-back chair in the den. He'd drawn the drapes, turned the ringer off on the phone, and lit several candles. The scents of lilac and honeysuckle drifted through the air.

A soft, oversized T-shirt in pale blue draped over Linda's shoulders and breasts. Her legs were covered by a pastel floral cotton skirt. Beside her, a tape recorder hummed away, but other than that slight noise, the house was totally quiet.

"Um-hmm," she replied, eyes closed, her squarish, capable hands resting on the arms of the chairs. Not clutching. None of her body language indicated that she was frightened.

"Just listen to my voice," he said, and proceeded to count backwards from ten, putting her in a deep state of relaxation.

"You're in a meadow, Linda. The day is beautiful. It's spring and the grass is green and thick. Birds are chirping. The flowers are blooming. Do you see the flowers?"

"Yes."

"What color are the flowers?"

"Yellow. Pink."

"Good. Now walk across the meadow. The sun is shining and the grass tickles your feet. You feel very relaxed and happy."

Linda giggled. "Little blue flowers," she whispered.

"That's right. Beautiful flowers."

A soft sigh and an even softer smile escaped her lips.

"Up ahead there's a door, sitting in the meadow. Do you see the door?"

"Yes."

He took a deep breath. "Behind that door is your past life, Linda."

"Okay."

"I want you to open the door."

She frowned briefly, but apparently was doing what he said.

"What do you see?"

"A big, red brick house. There's ivy on the walls."

"Where are you?"

"I'm in the garden."

"And what is your name?"

"Constance Gail Alden."

"Is anyone with you?"

"Yes. Amelia is here, and William."

"Who is Amelia?"

"She's my sister," Linda said in a tone that implied the question was foolish.

Giff knew from his research that Amelia was her twin sister, but he wasn't going to tell Linda about that. He wanted her to come to her own conclusions.

"And who is William?"

Her face softened. "He's my betrothed."

"What does he look like?"

"He's tall and has brown hair and brown eyes. And he's wearing his uniform, the one with the short jacket and gold buttons. He's the most handsome man I've ever seen," she said, her voice giving credence to her words.

"What does Amelia look like?"

"She looks like me, of course!"

"Tell me. I can't see her."

"She has blond hair and blue eyes. She's not too tall. Papa says she's pretty."

"So you must be pretty too."

"William says I'm beautiful," she said proudly.

"What is William doing?"

"He's talking about returning to his brigade on the Continent. I don't want him to go." Her mouth turned down in a slightly pouting frown.

"Is he leaving soon?"

"Yes."

"Do you love him?"

Her expression changed, her face relaxing into

a genuine smile. "Very much. We're going to be married when he returns. My father is giving us one of the family estates. It's in Kent, near Dover. I love the sea."

"I want you to leave the garden. The meadow is still there, just beyond the hedge. Can you see it?"

"Yes."

"Good. Walk into the meadow."

"Okay."

"Do you see another door?"

"Yes, I see it."

Giff sighed and thanked God Linda was so trusting and responsive. Most subjects took several sessions to regress, he'd learned over the years from his own regressions and from watching others. He couldn't remember when he wasn't being hypnotized, questioned or studied. It was a part of his life, the one he'd left behind in England. But Linda was totally cooperative for an adult, obviously ready to face her past lives.

"I'm there," she said in a singsong voice.

"Open the door."

"What do you see?"

"A kitchen. We're making bread. It's so hot!"

"What does the kitchen look like?"

"Dark. Smoky. Everything is dark and dull."

"What is your name?"

"Myra."

He took her through two more lifetimes, until she became obviously tired. By then he was also exhausted, but filled with a sense of elation that they'd been so successful. He stopped the regression with both relief and reluctance. She could have revealed so much more, but she had enough information on the tape to keep her head spinning for days. It wasn't necessary to go all the way back to that first lifetime when they were joined. That one, he knew, would be particularly difficult for her.

The session had been painful for him to endure, even more devastating when he realized how responsible he was for the set of events that kept recurring lifetime after lifetime. As difficult as it was for him to face the facts, he could only understand that initial incident from his viewpoint. Linda would give her insight into what had happened.

As much as he wanted to know all the circumstances, including what she'd thought of him during that lifetime, he wouldn't push her. To regress too much could be harmful, psychologically and physically draining. She was already under an extreme amount of stress.

It would get worse before it got better.

"I'm going to count backwards from ten," Giff said. "You will come slowly awake. When I reach the number one, you will be completely awake and your eyes will open. Ten, nine, eight . . ."

Giff counted and watched the growing awareness on Linda's face. Her nose twitched; she shifted slightly in the chair. Her legs were probably asleep, he thought. She seemed tired, but not overly.

He only hoped she would accept what he'd asked her to recall.

"One."

Linda's eyes opened. She blinked, looking around the room as though surprised to be here. She uncurled her legs and winced.

"Do you remember anything?"

"I remember a meadow," she said slowly, carefully.

"Yes, I used the meadow to relax you. Do you remember opening the doors in the meadow?"

She frowned, rubbing her temples, staring at the floor. Then she looked up suddenly, enormous distress clouding her sea-green eyes. The expression on her face was painful to see, stripped bare of everything but the truth. He knew that she'd remembered, without playing the tape, without him having to coax her.

She remembered. He felt the truth like a slash across his soul.

"Oh, my God," she said, then staggered from the chair.

He rose also, standing in front of her and holding her arms as she weaved slightly. "It's okay."

"No," she said in a anguished tone. She looked into his eyes, and all he could see was the raw pain of an open wound. "It will never be okay again." Then she ran from the room before he could stop her, bounding up the stairs as though the hounds of hell chased her.

Chapter Fifteen

I like the dreams of the future better than the history of the past.
—Patrick Henry

Linda heard Giff pounding up the stairs behind her, but she didn't care. She had to get away from the room, from him, from everything. It was true. It was all true.

She was just another incarnation of the wealthy, spoiled Constance; of Myra, the cook's assistant who'd loved the lord's youngest son; of Alice, a merchant's daughter who'd been promised to the Church but fell in love with an Irish rebel; and Sarah, a Jew who loved a Gentile. All their lives had centered around the man they'd loved, and none of them had had any chance for creating a life outside the bounds of this damned obsessive . . . fate.

Even now, after the regression was over, new images bombarded her mind with the same rapid cadence as her footsteps as she ran along the hardwood hall. In each lifetime, the early and unexpected death of the man she'd loved. The horror of losing him, before they could marry or consummate their love. Feelings like she'd never experienced assaulted her, making her head swim with tangled images and patterns.

A sob escaped her, even though she pressed her lips together tightly. How long had these entwined lives gone on? she wondered as she ran into her bedroom and slammed the door. She'd gone back through several lifetimes, and each time, Giff had been there as an image inside her mind or an actual flesh-and-blood man. Oh, he'd looked different, but she'd known him nonetheless. The intensity, the single-minded pursuit of her affections, were the same. She stood in the center of her bedroom and shivered, hugging her arms with unsteady hands.

Giff had been right all along; there was such a thing as destiny.

And she was only a tiny, meaningless pawn in the bigger game of obsessive love and death. She could fight against it, she could deny it, but she'd keep coming back, again and again, to love the same man. The knowledge left her weak in the knees. She sank to her bed, curving into a ball as though that simple action could shield her from harm.

Nothing could protect her. She had no free will.

Even now, fighting against the idea that she'd been destined to meet Giff, she knew that she'd fallen in love with him. How could she not? She'd been half in love with William Howard most of her life; Giff had always reminded her of the fantasy lover, the long-dead soldier. Her attraction to Giff had been immediate and unwavering. Even when she had been frightened by him, she'd still wanted him. Now she knew why; she had no free will. Bitter knowledge, it sat like a hateful pill in the center of her tongue, making everything sour with the taste of defeat.

He knocked on her door, but she didn't answer. He probably wouldn't go away, but she didn't want to encourage him to enter her room so that she could see the truth in his eyes again, as she'd done the night they'd made love. She'd looked into the brown depths and seen William, but she'd rebelled against the truth. Now she could deny it no longer.

She heard the knob twist, then Giff's voice close by, quiet and steady. "Linda?"

She didn't roll over, didn't look at him. "Call me whatever you want," she said bitterly. "It really doesn't matter."

"You're hurting, but I don't understand why."

She rolled over, swinging her legs over the side of the bed. "Can't you? Doesn't it matter to you that we have no free will? That we can't just meet someone else, fall in love, get married and live happily ever after? One life. That's all I wanted. I didn't ask for eternity with you!"

"No, you didn't," he said with so much tenderness that she sat perfectly still and stared.

"What do you mean by that?"

"You didn't ask to become involved. We didn't go back that far in the regression, but I will tell you that I started the alliance. It's all my fault that we were linked."

"Gee, I don't know how to thank you!" she threw out, knowing she was being sarcastic, that he hated it, but not caring at the moment. Pushing herself from the bed, she paced across the room. She might love him, she might still desire him, but right now she wanted to lash out. Giff was the obvious choice.

"I know this is a shock to you, finding out about your past lives, but try to understand that we have a chance to change the past . . . and the future."

"What does that mean?"

"In each lifetime when we found each other and fell in love, something tragic always happened."

"I know."

"What?"

"I just . . . know. After the regression, I could still remember things. Things that didn't happen during the regression. They just keep . . . coming."

Giff stared at her, his dark eyes glittering against his tan.

"I don't know why the men—you—died. Are you saying the deaths weren't natural or accidents?"

"Hardly," he said bitterly. "Yes, we were ill-fated lovers, but there was nothing 'natural' about my deaths. They were all due to treachery, betrayal, even murder."

"Murder?"

"In this past life as William Howard, I was murdered by my cousin Jeffrey." Giff paused for a moment, his gaze burning into hers. "The date was June 18, 1815, a Sunday."

Tomorrow is June 18th. A Sunday. Icy tendrils of fear snaked through her soul. She shuddered, remembering feeling the evil of Mord through the Ouija board, knowing instinctively that the entity had somehow killed William. "Where were you? What happened?"

"We were at Waterloo, thick in the fighting. Jeffrey and I had purchased our commissions together, served together in the Peninsula War. I knew him so well, since childhood. I trusted him with my life, and in the end, he took it."

Linda closed her eyes, recalling the descriptions of Waterloo that were so real, she *had* to believe in William when she was 15. When she opened her eyes, she took a step toward the window, looking out at the ocean. "But why would he turn on you like that?"

"Because he wanted you also, loved you as Constance. At first it was good-natured rivalry, but when you accepted my proposal during a leave before we pursued Napoleon on the Continent, he became even more jealous. I didn't notice the small changes at first, but now I realize them for what they were. Jeffrey's appearance changed, his manners deteriorated. He became controlling and manipulative. He was overcome by evil, and in the end, I lost everything."

"The sadness I felt when I talked to William . . ."

Giff took her arm and gently turned her to face

him. "Linda, you and I aren't the only two souls linked."

She narrowed her eyes, trying to read his shuttered expression, believing she already knew the answer. "He drops another bombshell," she said aloud. "Who else is involved?"

"Not who—what. Mord."

She wasn't surprised, but just saying it aloud made the knowledge more horrifying. "Then he is here."

"You've felt his presence?"

"I'm not sure if I *felt* him. I thought maybe I was imagining things when Gerri told me yesterday that Jon had acted strange all afternoon, ever since touching the Ouija board. She accused me of having a panic attack, because I suggested he may have been possessed."

"You were right. Apparently the Ouija board is the conductor through which you, Gerri and Mord are linked. I suspect that Mord gave some subtle suggestions that you use the board, since we were physically separated by the Atlantic." Giff paused, then continued. "In a way, we're linked also, but not physically."

"Then how?"

"When you first used the board and talked to William, you were, in fact, talking to my subconscious mind."

"What do you mean?"

"I was asleep. I was twenty years old when you began communicating with me, but I knew from when I was a small child that I'd had past lives. When we talked through the board, the conversations appeared to be dreams. That's all I thought they were at first. Then I realized you were reaching out to me; I recognized *who* you were. I knew from general impressions that you were near a beach, but I didn't know which one. I sensed that you were American, which accounted for the time difference."

Linda sat down on the bed, her mind reeling. So that's how he could be both William and Giff at the same time. One while he slept, one while he was awake. She had so many questions that she didn't know where to begin. "You said you knew about your past lives. How?"

"My father believed I was the reincarnation of his son who had drowned. Apparently he was right."

"Gifford White," Linda whispered.

"You knew?"

"I read about the case in one of the books I researched. Why did you change your name?"

"I was too famous. People didn't take me seriously. Although I didn't bear any physical abnormalities, I was a freak. Do you have any idea how difficult it is to function with that kind of notoriety?"

"I can't imagine. I remember thinking at the library that it must have been horrible for you as a child."

"It was not an ideal childhood, even though my father didn't intentionally thrust me into that type of circus atmosphere. And yet, if that hadn't happened, I would never have known about William Howard, or you as the woman I'd loved in my past lives. When I had the dreams, when we communicated through the Ouija board, I would have dismissed them as just interesting but meaningless fantasies."

And she would have continued to believe that William Howard was her own peculiar voice from the past, totally unexplained. "Then we have the Ouija board to thank."

"In a way. I believe that somehow, we would have connected without the physical presence of a board. Since my father was an American with ties to New York, and you are from New York, I have to believe we were fated to meet. The fact that I stayed in England complicated the logistics. Perhaps we would have met at a social event, or been introduced by friends if I'd been raised an American. But who knows?"

"By using the board, though, I also connected to Mord."

"He would have used another means to get us together later, when you were older. After all, we were fated to meet, just as Mord was destined to intervene. As soon as he sensed our connection, he interfered with the communication. By frightening you, he broke it off. Sometimes his actions don't follow the conventional thinking of a human mind, but that's to be expected, since he's anything but human. Perhaps he didn't realize how young you were. I suppose he assumed you would continue to contact me, but you never did."

Linda shook her head. "I was too frightened. To Gerri, it was a scary incident that she soon forgot.

But to me, it was more than just a horrible episode I could push aside. I felt the evil, I felt the pain of being severed from you. I never got over it, just as I never forgot my fascination for William. I suppose from that summer night on, I never really had free will. I loved the idea of the tragic, heroic soldier. I wanted to find you, but I was afraid."

"I waited to meet you again in my dreams. I hoped all my life that you'd try to contact me again. Occasionally I would sense your dreams, but never your conscious mind. The knowledge that you were real kept me hoping and planning, even when I thought I might be a little crazy for believing I knew about the past and could predict our future."

All that time, he was waiting for her. Yet for many of those years, before her research, she'd assumed William was a personal fantasy. And what a fantasy he became as she grew older. Her face heated at the thought of sharing her erotic dreams with Giff. "You knew I dreamed of William through the years?"

Giff smiled, a slow, seductive slant of his mouth and a lowering of his eyes. "Very interesting dreams," he said softly. "But most unfulfilling. Do you know how many mornings I woke up in a very . . . agitated condition?"

Linda felt her blush intensify at the image. She'd also awakened aroused, but to know she'd caused another person to be in the same situation was startling, to say the least.

"Just think how we could have relieved our suffering if only we'd known each other then." He leaned toward her, passion flaring in his eyes.

"I was a bit young when it all started, remember?"

"Oh, yes, I know. You didn't have the dreams then. But later, I could have finished those fantasies of yours."

She held him close, wanting him with a rush of desire that left her breathless. She had another memory, of last Sunday night, when he'd fulfilled her as no other man ever could. "You did, the first time we made love. But I need more than a fantasy. I need—"

She never got to finish her words. His mouth swept down, covering her even as his body pressed her against the mattress. Closing her eyes against the heady rush of passion, she returned his kiss, clinging to him, knowing he was real, but believing the fantasy as well.

Knowing that he could be gone tomorrow. Knowing his words were true, that they'd never lived happily ever after. She pushed the pain aside, hiding it deep where it wouldn't interfere with the moment. Later, she'd dig it out, but for now, there was no time for unhappiness.

If all they had was one more day, one more chance to make love, then let it be the best. Their first time had been a flash fire. This time would be a slow burn.

She let her hands roam freely, feeling each muscle and bone and sinew beneath the confines of his clothes. When that wasn't enough, she pulled his shirt from his jeans, running her hands inside the waistband, wanting to feel his buttocks clench as he pressed into her.

With a burst of strength, she rolled him over so he lay on his back and she straddled him. His eyes showed surprise and excitement at her boldness. Her own heartbeat began a rapid pace as she molded her hands over his chest, ribs and stomach.

I love you, she wanted to whisper, but knew she couldn't. Destiny drove him, had driven him all his life. But she had fallen in love with him without knowing about their entwined fate. Perhaps she had sensed it. Perhaps she was also guided by something more powerful than free will. In her heart, she knew she loved him for what he was, who he was. And she wanted to show him how much.

She unbuttoned the shirt, then swept it from beneath him, throwing it to the floor. Her eyes roamed his solid, bare chest, seeing his heart pound beneath the muscle, the small male nipples bead with desire. Her tongue and mouth followed, tasting him, making him moan as she succumbed to each impulse to touch, to drive him mad. The first time, he'd been in control. She wanted him wild this time, so aroused he lost the ability to be precise and careful. She wanted him as crazy for her as she was for him.

Her hands found the snap of his jeans, the zipper that concealed the object of her quest. While her tongue traced a path down his stomach, she watched his eyes darken, then close. She slid lower on his body as the metal rasped and his breathing quickened. His legs shifted, then opened, and she settled between them. Carefully, she peeled apart the jeans, pulled down the dark briefs, and exposed him to the daylight and her seeking fingers.

She teased, traced his length and circled his breadth, blew against his tip with feather-light breaths, and finally, when he gasped her name and trembled, she took him into her mouth and tasted heaven.

"Enough," he moaned later, when she'd explored the ways she could please him. She looked up to see his eyes, burning with a force so strong it made her tremble in response. Then she realized she felt his passion inside her mind, feeding her desire. Her legs tensed involuntarily, and she felt the wetness of her own arousal.

She knelt, knowing she looked wanton, reveling in the fact that she held such power over another person. With shaking fingers, she took off her top, then reached behind and unsnapped her bra. Her nipples beaded tight, feeling the caress of the warm air and imagining his mouth instead. She watched him, his eyes roaming, heating her with a fiery gaze. Her skin became moist, overheated and flushed, and she touched the waistband of her skirt, pulling it lower. The friction of her clothes aroused her, the air and his eyes caressed her, until she thought she might again climax before he entered her. But she was determined to hold on to the passion, to experience it fully with him.

She pushed her skirt and panties lower. He watched, his eyes narrowing as each new inch of flesh was revealed. She knew he saw his own erection, standing proud, just inches away from where she knelt. The clothes slipped past her curls, down her thighs. She supported herself on hands and knees, over him, her breasts touching his penis. He exhaled, closing his eyes briefly. When he opened them, she felt only the heat of his gaze on her flesh.

Naked, she inched her way up his body, fighting the urge to impale herself on his organ and ride him fast and hard. But she wanted more. She wasn't through with him yet.

He caught her around the waist, holding her tightly, while his mouth closed over her breast. He sucked, hard and thorough, on the nipple until she almost collapsed on top of him. But his hands held her above him. His tongue flicked, again and again, until she began to squirm. She lowered her hips, touching his erection with her belly, rubbing against him to torment him as he did her.

"Now," she gasped.

"Not yet," he said, his breath hot.

He took the other breast, sucking it until she cried out. Then his hands moved lower, to cup her buttocks, to squeeze until she knew that if he didn't let her sink onto him, she would explode from the pressure. "Please," she whispered, going with his rhythm, clenching her muscles until sweet agony made her plead.

"Now," he groaned, guiding her toward his waiting shaft, positioning her above him. She wanted to plunge, but he stilled her movements as the tip teased her, entering slightly. She fought him, but he was strong, making her wait, making her take him slowly, sliding down until she gasped when their bellies touched, when he was fully inside her.

He started the rhythm, moving slowly, rubbing her most sensitive spot, then withdrawing. But it wasn't enough. She'd forgotten that she wanted him to lose control. With a surge, she pulled herself upright, still joined, but sitting atop him. Her eyes raked him as her hands did the same. She massaged the muscles of his chest as she moved over him, faster and faster. His eyes closed; he fought for control. She knew she couldn't take much more. Her own climax fast approached, but she wanted to see him shake the veneer of sophistication just once. She wanted to prove that she had control over something in their crazy lives. Inside her mind, she screamed the words—*wild, free!*

His eyes snapped open and he cried out, a feral sound that echoed off the walls of the bedroom. With a twist, he pulled her beneath him, his hands hot and heavy. She'd have bruises tomorrow, but she didn't care. He'd lost control, lost it all. For her.

Fierce. That's the way he looked above her, framed by the girlish canopy. Sweat beaded on his brow. He stretched her arms above her, lowered his mouth and kissed her deeply, without respect or restraint, his tongue plunging just as he moved inside her. Quickly, hard. She caught the new cadence, wrapped her legs around his and closed her eyes.

It came, a burst of brilliance that stopped reality. Nothing penetrated the void but his shout and the feeling of him swelling inside her, bursting with life. She hovered there, feeling everything, never more alive. The blackness descended, sprinkled with a million pinpoints of light, and the certainty that she was held, loved and safe.

Giff collapsed, knowing he'd never experienced what he and Linda had just shared. She'd pushed him past the point of reason, of endurance. He'd lost control of himself and the situation, but it seemed that was just what she wanted from him. He wasn't sure why she'd wanted it that way, but he was willing to give her anything.

When he could move, he turned his head and kissed her cheek. She smiled. With reluctance, he tried to move away, since he knew his weight must be crushing her. But she held him tighter, kept her legs wrapped around him until he felt himself stir again.

"What are you up to, wench?" he teased sleepily.

"I have over ten years of acute sexual frustration built up, and it's all your fault. I know a good thing when I see it—and feel it. I'm just holding on to what is mine."

"And I'm yours?"

"So you say. At least, for the moment."

"For longer than that, sweet Linda."

"Do you have any idea why we were able to make love this time, when we never have before?"

"Only theories. I think that because I was aware of the past lives and the situation, I took a more active role in changing the normal course of events. And, of course, the morals of today are different. A hundred and eighty years ago, you were never allowed out of sight of a responsible adult. There was no way I could have seduced you in the short time we had together."

"Whereas today I'm a brazen hussy."

"Don't change," he said, gliding his hands down the slope of her back to her nicely rounded bottom. "There are definite advantages to living during this period."

She stretched, rubbing against him. "I suppose I should let you up."

"If you don't, we're going to be in this bed for quite a bit longer. Are you up to it?"

"I think the question is, are you?"

She clenched her muscles, squeezing him, so that he felt the rush of blood and the erection that slowly filled her.

"I think you are," she said breathlessly.

"We should talk."

"Yes, we should." She moved, setting a slow pace that made his breath catch.

"You're trying to control me again."

"Is that so bad?"

"No, not bad."

She reached up and kissed his jaw, then his lips. "We didn't use any protection."

"It's okay."

He stopped moving. "What do you mean by that?"

"I just mean that I probably won't get pregnant right now, but if I do, it's okay."

"Okay?" He felt confusion and, with it, just a touch of anger. He did not like to be confused; he didn't handle surprises well, yet this woman was a constant source of unexpected twists and turns. "What do you mean—okay?"

"Don't be angry. I've never thought about having a child before. But Giff, I want your baby."

He closed his eyes against the rush of emotion; he refused to put any more defining name to what he felt. He'd never thought about creating a child with Linda, concentrating instead on creating a relationship with her. And, of course, on defeating Mord. Never had he considered what would come after the final confrontation. If he lived . . .

"Giff, are you upset?"

He opened his eyes. "No, I'm not upset. I just . . . you've done it again. Made me lose control. Made me crazy with longing. To create a child with you would be the most wonderful thing I could ever imagine."

"Then make it real," she urged, pulling his head down for a kiss.

"Today was nice," Gerri said, leaning back against the headrest of the convertible and glancing at Jon. She was a little surprised that she'd been able to forgive him after last night, but he did seem back to normal. He'd been polite, interested in the sights, and had honestly tried to make the day a good one.

"I enjoyed it too."

"Do you feel okay?"

"Perfectly fine," he said, flashing her a white-toothed grin set off by his tan face.

He looked fine. Dressed in crisp tan slacks and a mint green pullover, he seemed exactly what he was: a successful, young, confident man without a care in the world. She wished she could be sure that the events of last night would never be repeated. Just the thought of his obsessive, sinister actions made her cringe.

"Why the frown?" he asked.

She looked back at him. "No reason. Just a tiny headache," she hedged. "Probably too much sun."

"Yes, it is bright here."

"No more so than St. Augustine."

"That's right. It was hot and sunny there too."

Gerri turned back to watching the road slip by. That was an odd comment. He'd grown up there, yet he sounded as though he was just realizing the fact that St. Augustine had a tropical climate.

"I hope Linda got some rest today," Jon said lightly.

"I'm sure she did. With no one to bother her, she probably slept most of the day."

"I hope you're not too tired."

Gerri felt herself stiffen before she could stop the reaction. Jon's comment wasn't that suggestive, but she had the image of him trying to make love to her later. She didn't know if she was ready for that yet.

"I'm a little tired. And like I said, I have a bit of a headache."

Jon sighed as if in sympathy. "Too bad. Maybe

Linda and I will have to put you to bed early. Do you think she'll stay up and entertain me?"

"Depends on what you have in mind," Gerri said coolly. "She won't sing and dance for you, if that's what you mean. And she doesn't play a musical instrument."

Jon laughed. "I suppose we'll just have to talk."

"Just make sure talking is all you do." Gerri resented the surge of jealousy his words provoked, but she couldn't control the response. Linda had an innocent sexuality that she didn't even realize. Men responded to that, all kinds of men. Even engaged ones.

"Do I detect a note of jealousy?" Jon asked, then chuckled. "Linda is an attractive woman."

"Yes, and she's my best friend."

"Speaking of friends," Jon said, his demeanor changing, "what do you know about this friend of Linda's—Giff?"

Gerri shrugged. "Not much. She met him when she came down here for the summer. He's renting a house nearby."

"What does he do?"

"He's a writer. Historical stuff." Gerri laughed sadly. "At first, I thought he'd be a perfect match for Linda, with both of them fascinated by history. But their relationship didn't work out."

"Then they're no longer involved?"

"I don't know." Last night, it had seemed as though they were involved. Giff had taken over like a man perfectly comfortable giving orders. And Linda had followed his lead, as though she was happy to do his bidding. That wasn't like

Linda, but Gerri didn't know if that was because of the incident last night or because of her feelings for Giff. Until they had an opportunity to talk, she just didn't know.

"Linda deserves someone special," Jon said harshly. His eyes narrowed against the blowing wind and sunlight.

What an odd thing to say. Jon barely knew Linda. Why would he sound so interested in her relationship with Giff? Or with anyone?

As a matter of fact, why was Jon even thinking about Linda?

Gerri looked out the car window, watching the pines and tall grass beside the road whip by. Her involvement with Jon had always been so straightforward. Her friendship with Linda had been simple and true. Why were things suddenly getting so complicated, so . . . strange?

Linda slipped from the bed later as Giff drifted to sleep. She needed some time alone. It was almost three o'clock in the afternoon, and Gerri could be home at any time, but Linda wanted a hot shower and a cold drink first.

She grabbed a casual cotton dress from the closet and some underwear from the dresser, and made her way quietly to the bathroom. The water felt wonderful, but it cleaned away Giff's scent, and the smell of their lovemaking. If possible, she'd hold on to the memories forever.

Even if a cruel, evil fate snatched him away.

Her heart missed a beat. The pain inside her was almost unbearable.

Tears filled her eyes, ran down her face as swiftly as the shower spray. How would she ever live without him, now that she knew their shared past? Now that she realized what a chance there was that he could be killed. What had he said? *Treachery. Betrayal. Murder.* That's what faced them. Not the stuff of happily ever after.

She slumped against the shower wall, feeling emptiness she couldn't define. Her hand drifted to her stomach, where she felt the void most acutely. If she were lucky enough to have Giff's child, a part of him would live on. She would have her own tiny piece of history, a baby created from a man who had pursued her for a thousand years. A man who had never said he loved her, only that they were destined to be together.

Anger had spoken earlier, when she'd lashed out at Giff because they had no free will. Looking back to when she first met him, she questioned whether fate or Mord or any outside influence affected her attraction to Giff. She'd never believed in love at first sight, but she realized now that such an immediate case of lust and sense of familiarity was a good start. She honestly believed that she would have fallen for Giff without past lives or the intervention of an evil entity. And she wanted him to be her destiny, her future, regardless of the past.

If what he'd said were true, they'd never shared a bed before. Because Giff was aware of the past lives, he'd been able to intervene with fate, or Mord, or whatever master plan guided their lives. That meant this lifetime was different from the others. If one thing could change, maybe the final outcome would be different. But how? What needed to be done? Did Giff even know?

She sniffed away her tears, then finished washing. Suddenly she felt tired, as the sleepless night, interrupted nap and hours of lovemaking caught up with her. She sagged against the shower wall.

"Want some company?"

Chapter Sixteen

What we call despair is often only the painful eagerness of unfed hope.
—George Elliot

"Giff! You scared me." Her morose thoughts and lethargy deserted her as adrenaline raced through her body.

"Who did you expect?"

"I thought maybe Gerri had gotten home. I thought maybe Jon . . ."

Giff's expression sobered. "I wouldn't leave you alone in the house with him."

"You were sleeping," Linda admonished.

"Very lightly." He stepped out of his briefs and into the shower.

"I was just getting out," she said warily.

"I'm not making a pass," he said, slipping past

her under the warm water. "I'm taking a shower."

"Hmpf." She wasn't sure she believed he was innocently taking a shower. But then, they had made love to the point of exhaustion.

"Very articulate," he said with a smile.

"How can you joke? We're facing a major crisis."

"Let's be clear," he said, reaching for the soap. "*I'm* facing the crisis. You are watching from the sidelines—safely away from the action."

"How can you say that? I don't even know where the sidelines are! Besides, what happens affects me too."

"Of course it does. And that's why I need to concentrate on defeating Mord."

"How can you defeat something than can invade bodies, terrorize people and—"

"Linda, I know how to defeat him. For the first time, I have what it takes to end his involvement in our lives forever."

"What is it?"

"It's complicated. I'd rather not explain it now."

"You don't want me to know."

"Let's just say that it would be to both of our advantages if you remain ignorant."

"You're afraid I would say something."

"Not really. But I don't know what kind of control Mord may exert over you. The less you know, the less you could reveal, either accidentally or by him tapping into your thoughts."

"He can read my mind?" Linda grabbed Giff's arm. "Tell me he can't do that!"

Giff turned off the water. The sudden silence

seemed oppressive. "I'm not sure of the extent of his power."

Linda reached for a towel, her thoughts in turmoil. She'd asked him this before, but needed confirmation. "Can *you* read my mind?"

"Not exactly. Before we made love, I could sense your general emotions, sometimes pick up on a thought. Nothing consistent or coherent." He grabbed a towel and began to dry himself. "Since we made love the first time, our bond is more powerful. I feel a much stronger sense of your conscious thoughts. But no, I can't actually read your mind."

She was thankful for that much at least. She didn't like the idea of someone else inside her head.

"You're relieved," he said.

"I thought you said—"

He tipped her chin up. "I didn't claim that I couldn't read your expression. And you have a very expressive face." He kissed her quickly on the lips.

"I've sensed your emotions too," Linda admitted. "Usually when they're very strong. It's kind of frightening."

"Yes, I suppose it is. I remember the first time I became aware of you, through my dreams. I'd never felt that kind of bond with anyone else, and it was rather shocking. I'm glad we have that ability. Because of our bond, I sensed your dream that night when I came into your bedroom. I only intended to ease your terror, but I became so involved in your needs, your passion, I couldn't leave you aching. I could feel your frustration as acutely as my own."

"Why didn't you just tell me the truth?" She felt disappointed that he hadn't trusted her. He'd kept secrets; he still refused to tell her everything.

"I didn't think you were ready to hear it. If I'd told you then that I could sense your emotions and get vague impressions of your thoughts, you would have refused to see me again, or had me arrested as a dangerous psychotic."

"Maybe you're right. It bothers me that you haven't been totally honest."

"I did what I thought was best at the time, mostly to protect you from Mord."

Linda stepped from the shower. "Can't you tell me something about him? Something that will help me understand what we're facing?"

"Mord is an elemental evil, I believe. He has existed forever. He will exist forever."

"Then how can we possibly defeat him?" Fear of the unknown caused her to shiver. She'd felt Mord's evil presence, sensed the danger of being influenced by him. The idea of prevailing against something so inhuman, so eternal, was impossible to consider. She reached for her dress, clutching it in front of her.

"I will not defeat him. I must simply disassociate his existence from ours."

"Giff, that sounds like you're saying he should just go away." His casual, seemingly unconcerned attitude made her nervous. Didn't he realize the danger?

He looked up from toweling his feet. "Yes, I suppose it does."

"Giff!"

He smiled, then laughed. She hadn't heard him laugh before, and the foreign sound echoed through the bathroom. Despite her worry, she felt giddy with the sound, as though it opened entirely new worlds to explore. As though he had revealed a different side of himself.

Of course, he hadn't. Her good mood was simply the effect of an afternoon of sex, the release of tension. It wasn't a turning point.

"The most important thing we can do right now is act normal. Go about your regular routine, but be aware of where Jon—or Mord—is at all times. Don't allow yourself to be alone with him."

"Linda! Are you in there?"

Gerri's voice came floating down the hall, nearby enough to cause Linda to pause and stare at Giff. He looked back, totally naked, completely unconcerned, one eyebrow raised as if to ask her, "What did you expect?"

Gerri rounded the corner of the bathroom just as Giff knotted the towel around his hips.

Linda concentrated on chopping tomatoes for the dinner salad, but couldn't resist glancing at Gerri every now and then to make sure her friend was okay. They hadn't had a chance to talk much since Gerri had returned to the house—and found Linda and Giff in the bathroom. She didn't know how Gerri felt about that, or how her day in Myrtle Beach had gone.

Linda wasn't looking forward to explaining her newly revived relationship with Giff. Two days ago Gerri had seemed relieved to know that the brief affair was over, agreeing that it was for the best, that Giff sounded more than strange. *How could she think he was anything but "one card short of a full deck" after everything I said?* Linda thought. She'd painted him as a nutty, obsessive guy. Now she knew differently.

When Gerri had surprised them in the bathroom, she hadn't said a word to Giff, just stared at his towel-wrapped body as if she'd never seen a man before. Then he'd politely excused himself, padded back down the hall to Linda's bedroom and gotten dressed. Minutes later, as Linda had finished dressing and putting away the wet towels, he'd walked back down the hall and asked Gerri if Jon was acting normal today. When she said yes, Giff had kissed Linda briefly and said he'd be back shortly.

Linda supposed that meant he was inviting himself to dinner. Which was fine with her. She wasn't looking forward to sitting across the table from Jon, knowing he'd been possessed by something evil.

How could she continue to act normally when she knew what was controlling Jon? Or was Mord in control all the time? Did he sleep or fluctuate in strength, or just grow more powerful? She considered herself a very level-headed person, but this experience just did not fit in with the logical, pragmatic approach she preferred. The fact that it was history in the making did not make her comfortable. She liked to prove theories, to discover new facts and to do so in an orderly process. She wasn't the kind of person who jumped into the water without knowing the depth, yet that was just what she was doing with Giff. This time, it really was sink or swim, if Giff could be believed about the confrontation with Mord.

What was she thinking! Of course she believed Giff.

"So, you and Giff have made up," Gerri said.

"In a manner of speaking."

"What does that mean?" Gerri asked, pausing in the process of tearing up pieces of lettuce. "I thought you believed he was nuts. Then he showed up last night, and I didn't know what to think."

"I'm glad he came by last night. And no, I don't believe he's crazy."

"What about his claims that he's William?"

Linda dropped the pieces of tomato on top of the lettuce. Explaining all this to Gerri would be almost impossible. She wouldn't believe it, Linda knew. But still, she had to try. "He is William, Gerri. And I'm Constance, his fiancée."

Gerri's jaw dropped open. "You mean you're pretending—"

"No, I mean we're reincarnated."

Gerri gave her a sideways glance, her eyes narrowed in thought. "How do you know that? Has he talked you into believing something weird?"

"He didn't have to talk me into anything. This afternoon, he regressed me through many past lives. In the last one, I was Constance Alden, William Howard's fiancée."

"You're subconsciously making that up because the Ouija board started spelling the name."

Linda shook her head. "No, I remember it. I saw myself sitting in an English garden with my sister and William before he went to war. We were going to be married when he got back and live by the sea. You know how I've always loved the ocean? Well, I was the same way then."

"That just proves that this regression is a hoax. He prompted those memories, Linda. You're just giving yourself the same traits in this supposed past life as you have in the present."

"No, Gerri, he didn't plant the memories. He even recorded it on tape, so if I didn't remember, I'd have a copy. You can listen to the tape if you'd like. And he took me back several more lifetimes. In each one, I was in love, but the love always ended tragically."

"Linda, I don't believe in this hocus-pocus, past-life stuff. Just because I can sense when something is wrong with you doesn't mean that I'm gullible to every strange character who claims you were in love with him in the past."

"It's not like that, Gerri. I can tell this is true."

Gerri hugged Linda. "I know you think it's true, but Giff is just really good at deceiving you. He obviously wants a relationship."

"But why? He could have any woman in the world. You've seen the man. He's handsome, successful, sexy as hell. Why would he focus on some boring history professor from the Midwest?"

"Don't put yourself down like that."

"I'm not putting myself down; I'm stating facts." Why couldn't Gerri see that Giff's explanation made sense? That he was acting from a compulsion fed by destiny? But maybe Gerri couldn't see because she had never been that closely involved. The frustration grew inside Linda. She knew the truth, as instinctively as she knew Mord was evil.

"You're blind if you think men don't find you attractive," Gerri said.

"Gerri, I don't care how other men see me! I only know that the minute Giff and I met—actually, it was even before that—but anyway, he let me know he wanted me. And it wasn't casual, Gerri. He didn't want a little summer fling. He went after me," Linda said, hitting her chest with her index finger. "Me. That just doesn't make sense without the explanation of why."

Gerri shook her head. "You're blind."

Linda sighed. "There's more that I need to tell you."

"At the moment, I have my hands full with a fiancé who has as many moods as my engagement ring has facets, and a best friend who thinks she's the long-lost love of a crazy man."

"I know this sounds weird, but listen. There's a reason for Jon's actions. He's—"

A loud crash from the dining room shattered the night. Linda stopped talking, a shiver of cold racing down her spine. Mord. She felt him as thought he'd just stroked a long, cold, bony finger down her back.

Gerri rushed to the doorway leading to the dining room. "What happened?"

Giff watched the slight, malevolent smile fade from Jonathan Moore's face as he bent down and retrieved a broken piece of pottery. At least the face was Moore's; the expression was all Mord's. It was all Giff could do to stand, fists clenched at his side, while he observed the game that Mord played with all of them.

"Jon, what happened?" Gerri asked from the doorway. She had a flustered expression on her face that probably meant she and Linda had been talking. Giff wondered what Linda had told her—and what Gerri had believed.

Linda walked into the dining room, right behind Gerri.

"Sorry, Linda," Moore said smoothly. "I seem to be clumsy tonight."

She looked at the broken flower pot, the dirt and the uprooted fern. "That's okay," she said in a very neutral tone of voice. "I'll just put the plant in another container."

Moore started to step forward, but Giff walked around him, cutting off his approach to Linda. He didn't want Mord touching her.

"I'll help you," Giff said, squatting beside her and picking up pieces.

"You don't have to."

He stopped gathering the broken pottery and looked into her eyes. Worry, fear, but also strength radiated from her gaze. "I want to."

She looked back toward the floor. Silently, they

gathered the large pieces and carried them and the fern into the kitchen.

"He stopped my conversation with Gerri," Linda whispered when they were alone, standing side by side at the sink. "I think he can read my thoughts."

"Perhaps. Maybe he was listening from the doorway. I'd just arrived as he bumped against the plant stand."

"I didn't believe for a minute that it was an accident."

"From now until this is finished, nothing will be accidental. Don't trust anything he says or does. And don't be alone with him."

"Yes, I know."

"Did you speak to Gerri?"

"I tried. I told her about us, about the past, but she doesn't want to listen. She thinks we're both crazy." Linda deposited the plant into another container, patting the soil around it in a loving manner.

Giff looked back across the room to the open doorway into the dining room. Gerri and her fiancé were in conversation as they swept the broken shards and spilled dirt onto some newspaper, but Giff couldn't hear their words from this distance. "She'll find out soon enough that he can't be trusted. I only hope that he doesn't harm her before I can confront him."

"Do you think he will hurt Gerri?" Linda said, washing the dirt from her hands. "I can't just stand by and let him—"

"We can't do anything yet. Mord hasn't completely taken over. If I try to sever his hold on

Moore, Mord will simply go somewhere else, lurk around for another possible host. As it is now, at least we know where Mord is, even if the person he's chosen is not acceptable to you and Gerri."

"Who else could he chose?"

"Gerri, for one. What better way to hurt you than to take over the body of your best friend? You would never harm her, and Mord knows that. He could terrorize you and feel perfectly safe."

Giff felt Linda's shudder as his arm brushed hers. But mostly he felt the ripple of fear go through her soul. She knew she couldn't hurt Gerri. Could she stand by and watch Moore wounded or destroyed, knowing this would also hurt Gerri? Giff didn't know the answer to that question. In the end, the outcome might be determined by Linda's loyalty—to whom she would be loyal and to what degree.

He had done everything he could to ensure her feelings for him. He'd even experienced some surprises of his own: Linda's warmth and caring; her intelligence and strength; her brave acceptance of both good and evil. He hadn't expected to revel in the emotions she stirred. At the moment, he didn't have time to explore the new sensations. But later, if he lived, he planned on spending a lifetime examining the fact that even without the spell or past lives, Linda was the perfect woman for him.

All he could do at the moment, however, was reassure her. "I'll do my best to make sure Jon isn't seriously injured."

"*Seriously* injured? Not injured at all would be a better promise."

"I can't promise that, love. In order to break the contact, I must draw blood."

"Could we just leave?" she said in a small voice. "Is there any way to run away from Mord?"

His heart went out to her, because he recognized the desperation she felt. "No, love, we can't. He's a part of our relationship. Until I sever the bond, there's no way to be safe."

Linda shivered again. Giff cursed the fact that he'd told her anything about what he had planned. He wrapped his arms around her and pulled her close. "Don't think about it. Tomorrow, Mord will be stronger. He will push for a confrontation, or he will use treachery."

"Do it now, when he's weak. Do it before I beg you to stop."

Giff closed his eyes, feeling her pain and uncertainty as surely as his own. "That's not the way it works. He and I must be equal adversaries, each aware of his own role. There's still too much Moore influencing his actions. When Mord becomes stronger, he'll push Moore aside and be truly integrated into the body. Then and only then can I challenge him, or accept a challenge from him. Remember that tomorrow is the day I believe this will occur. To push fate beyond the boundaries would be foolish. I'm not sure what the outcome would be, or if I would be able to break the chain of destiny."

"And you want this over. You want the link to be severed."

"It has been my life's work," he said, pushing a strand of curling hair behind her ear. "You'll never know the extent of research I conducted to find the answers. Some of it is theoretical, since we're dealing with an evil entity. But from what I've learned, I have the keys."

"Will you tell me what they are?"

"No. Again, if you know, Mord might be able to get that information from you, by directly reading your thoughts or by trick. I can't take that risk."

"So I'll be ignorant of this plan of yours, except to know that it involves blood. I'm supposed to carry on, just like everything is fine and normal, until you launch your assault."

He heard the catch in her voice and again felt her pain. "I know it's difficult—"

"You don't know how much. You don't know how I worry about Gerri, about you. I want to know everything, but you won't share that with me. You want to be in control."

"It's not a question of wanting to be in control. I'm the only one who can break the bond."

"Why?"

"Because as I explained, I was the person who started it. A thousand years ago, out of selfishness and my own insecurity, I began this nightmare. If I had trusted, if I'd avoided the lure of the easy fix, we wouldn't be in this situation."

"That's right," Linda said, wiping her eyes with the corner of a paper towel. "We wouldn't be here at all."

"What do you mean by that?"

"That we would never have met. That there would be no . . . attraction between us."

"We don't know that. How can we tell what

would have happened without the spell? But I believe we would have found each other, perhaps even before now. Perhaps from the very start, we would have lived long, healthy, happy lives."

She pushed away from him, her eyes revealing a wealth of hurt and anger. "And maybe, just maybe, we wouldn't have been in love at all."

Giff frowned, confused by her angry words. She was looking at the negative aspects of the bond, not the positives. He wished there was something else he could say to make her consider other possibilities.

Before he could comment further, however, she grabbed the salad and marched into the dining room. "Let's eat," she said with forced cheerfulness to Gerri and Jon, and Giff cursed his own inadequacies in dealing with Mord.

Soon, he vowed. Soon, it will be over.

And he was answered by an evil laugh that echoed throughout his mind. *"Soon, soon, soon,"* the sinister voice said, peeling forth in a baneful litany.

Chapter Seventeen

Evil is unspectacular and always human
And shares our bed and eats at our own table.
—W. H. Auden

"I'm going up to bed," Gerri said to Linda, Giff and Jon. The clock on the mantle said it was only 9:30, but she felt stressed out. She didn't want to worry Linda with her problems, though. Linda had enough on her mind right now, with her relationship with Giff, Jon's erratic behavior, and the fact she was staying in her grandmother's house. Despite the fact that Linda didn't talk too much about her grandmother's death, Gerri knew it still bothered her.

Gerri came up with a plausible excuse. "I think I got a little too much sun today."

"Do you need some aspirin or anything?" Linda

asked, concern evident in her voice. "I could go up with you."

"No, I took something earlier. Thanks anyway." Gerri rose from her chair in the den and picked up her glass of tea. "I'm going straight to bed. I'll see you guys in the morning."

"Good night," Linda said. She looked as though she wanted to say something else, but Gerri supposed she didn't because either Jon or Giff were here. Having men in your life really did complicate things.

Giff, as usual, appeared brooding and dark as he sat beside Linda on the couch, one arm resting along the back, right above her shoulders. He seemed so protective, but Gerri knew that there was a thin line between concern and manipulation. She wasn't yet sure which Giff was, but she didn't trust Linda's assessment of his character. Despite what Linda believed about this past life connection, Gerri wasn't buying it.

Jon was being charming, saying the right things, making polite conversation. She should have been relieved, but instead, she felt restless, unsure of herself. Somehow, Jon just didn't seem *right,* even though she couldn't place her finger on what was wrong. She'd often said he was perfect, but she'd been half joking. What she'd meant was that he was perfect for her. This Jon seemed so perfect, he was robot-like. The spark of teasing and humor that had made Jon so lovable was gone. And she had no idea if he would ever get it back.

"Would you like me to come upstairs with you now?" Jon asked.

"No," she said quickly. Too quickly, she realized. Linda and Giff both looked at her with concern. "I mean, I need to get ready for bed, and this headache is pounding. You can stay downstairs as long as you like."

"Whatever you wish," Jon said, smiling. "I hope your headache is better soon."

"I'm sure it will be fine tomorrow. I just need a good night's sleep."

"If you need anything—anything at all—you know where I'll be," Linda said. Giff folded his hand over Linda's as if signaling that he'd be with her. Gerri wasn't sure if that made her feel better or worse.

"Of course. Well, good night."

The stairs seemed unusually steep. *It's because I'm so tired,* she told herself. But that wasn't all. She didn't relish facing Jon when he finally came up to bed. Perhaps she should have requested that he sleep in another bedroom. It was too late now—unless he attacked her as he did last night. Then he wouldn't have to worry about sleeping at all. She'd be ready for him this time. A can of pepper spray rested just under her pillow.

She'd washed her face and put on an extremely modest nightgown when she heard his steps, coming slowly down the hall. A few of the old boards creaked. He seemed to pause outside the bathroom door, then move on. Only then did she realize she'd been holding her breath.

The lamp on the nightstand was on. Jon had pulled back the quilt and sheet and was lying down when she came into the room.

"Feeling better?" he asked.

"A little," she said, her tone guarded. She slipped into bed on the other side, rolling toward him despite her attempts to stay near the edge.

"Small bed," she said, repositioning herself.

Jon chuckled. "I won't bite," he said. "I got the message loud and clear. You aren't interesting in having sex tonight. Don't worry. Everything is fine."

She looked at him, knowing she was frowning but unable to stop the automatic expression. "Good. Because I really don't feel up to another confrontation."

"Me neither," he said, then yawned. "What do we have planned tomorrow?"

"I'm not sure. Linda and I didn't get to talk very much tonight."

"Giff is around her constantly," Jon said, disgust practically dripping from his voice. "I doubt he leaves her for a second."

"I'm certain he'll go back to his house tonight," Gerri said weakly.

"Surely you don't believe that," he replied, scoffing.

"It's really none of my business what he does, as long as it doesn't hurt Linda." She wished Jon hadn't brought up Linda again. Based on his comments earlier and his concern for her now, Gerri wondered if Jon had second thoughts about the engagement. Was he so attracted to Linda that he'd act obnoxiously toward his fiancée? But that didn't make sense. Linda would perceive him as just as obnoxious, defeating his purpose. But why did he act so jealous? The whole idea made her head pound harder.

"He doesn't seem like the stable sort to me," he said. "I think she should reconsider her relationship with the man."

"You didn't feel that way two days ago. You didn't seem to feel strongly one way or the other." She couldn't keep the chill out of her voice. Jon was beginning to get on her nerves like never before. They'd always been so compatible.

"I've changed my mind."

That's not all that's changed about you, Gerri thought. *How about your personality? That's undergone a major overhaul.* But she didn't want to get into an argument tonight. She only prayed that whatever was bothering Jon would be resolved soon. This was not the man she'd agreed to marry—and she had no intention of continuing the engagement if he didn't revert to his old, normal self.

"I'm really tired, Jon. I don't want to discuss Linda and Giff any longer."

"Very well." He switched off the light and rolled to his side of the bed. "By the way, I think it would be nice if the four of us did something together tomorrow. We don't want Linda to think we're unsociable guests."

"I'm sure she doesn't think that."

"Still, I think a group activity would be nice. After all, we're at the beach and the weather is quite cooperative."

"You mean like a swim or a cookout?"

"An excellent idea. I'd love to go swimming."

Gerri was surprised by his reference to planning something tomorrow. With things as tense as they were, she wasn't sure anyone would enjoy an activity. But they had to do something. Perhaps some physical action would disperse some of the pressure. "Sure. A swim sounds fine. I'll talk to Linda."

"Wonderful." She heard him get settled, but knew he wasn't sleepy. He was lying on his back, staring at the ceiling, if she wasn't mistaken. What was he thinking?

She wished she knew what was wrong. She was beginning to get an awful suspicion that things would get worse before they got better.

Chapter Eighteen

Fear is a kind of bell . . . it is the soul's signal for rallying.
—Henry Ward Beecher

Sunday, June 18, 1995

Giff was on his third cup of coffee, Linda her first, when Gerri and her fiancé came downstairs the next morning and walked out onto the deck. Moore looked smug, Giff thought, as though he kept a giant secret that he was dying to tell. Gerri looked somewhat rested, but there seemed to be pale shadows beneath her eyes. At least she didn't look terrorized or abused, like she did that first night he saw her. Giff was very concerned, however, that she had refused to take Linda's warnings seriously.

If she didn't know that Jon was possessed, then she wouldn't take his threat with the grave degree of concern it required. Giff suddenly realized that he'd become concerned over Gerri's safety, concerned for her as an individual, not just as Linda's friend. He'd been so intent on his goal that he hadn't taken time to consider the humanity of his actions, except where they concerned Linda.

That still had to be his major concern, but he felt his heart thaw slightly as he realized the impact these events had on other people. Now, on what might be the last day of his life, he felt more alive than he had in years.

"Good morning," Linda said to Gerri. "Did you sleep well?"

It didn't take any mind-reading abilities for Giff to know the anxiety beneath her innocent words. *Did Jon act strangely? Did he hurt you? Did you argue?* All those questions were going through Linda's mind, because she'd expressed as much to him aloud, just minutes ago.

"I slept fine," Gerri answered. "My headache is all gone."

"That's great."

Linda was the one who'd had a restless night. She'd tossed and turned, mumbled in her sleep, and had fleeting dreams of Mord. Giff had interceded, touching her mind, telling her it would be fine. That no one could hurt her. But in his heart, he'd known that those were his wishes speaking. Logically, he had to acknowledge that there was a chance Mord would prevail. Despite everything that Giff had learned, though he was as prepared as he could be for this confrontation, things could go wrong.

And he knew that if he did die trying to defeat Mord, Moore would be freed, unlike the previous lifetimes, when they'd been unaware of the possession. Mord wouldn't stay in that body, since Linda was already aware that he was evil, that he had tried to hurt Gerri. But he would find another body, and this time he'd be more subtle. He wouldn't alarm her. Just as he'd done when he took control of Jeffrey's body in 1815, Mord would be charming and try to win her affection.

Because that was his goal: to steal her love, to destroy the true feelings between the souls of the lovers, whether in the bodies of Linda and Giff, or Constance and William, or Myra and Richard, or any number of others in past lives. Mord wanted the true love to die, and he'd do anything to achieve his goal, including killing Giff and making himself the new object of Linda's affection. Even though Mord obviously couldn't inhabit a human body forever, he could stay long enough to complete the spell. And Giff, because he'd never been aware of the evil presence until this lifetime, had never had a goal beyond love.

"How about a swim after breakfast?" Gerri asked. "Jon made the observation last night that we haven't done anything together—the four of us."

Giff looked up at Moore, wondering why he'd made the suggestion. Had he specifically mentioned swimming in the ocean? Accidents happened in the water, and it was difficult to tell why, in many cases. Giff didn't like the idea at all.

Moore smiled blandly, apparently willing to let Gerri do his talking.

Linda looked at him too, then turned to Giff. "What do you think?"

"The water may be too cold here for Gerri and her fiancé."

"It shouldn't be," Gerri said. "We got in the ocean in St. Augustine, and it was great."

"It's a fine day," Moore finally said, smiling more broadly.

A fine day to die. The words echoed in Giff's head until he felt dizzy from the sound. He didn't want to die. He wanted to live, to have children and be loved. To grow old beside the woman of his dreams.

Linda looked at Gerri. "Why don't we have a light breakfast. Then we can check it out later this morning. Get yourselves some coffee, and then we can fix some toast and cereal."

Gerri and Moore went back inside. Linda turned to Giff. "Are you worried about getting in the water, or the four of us doing something together?"

"We're all good swimmers."

"Yes, but something's bothering you."

Giff had to smile. "Now who's reading minds?"

She smiled back. "Okay, it's a feeling. Or maybe I'm reading your body language. You're not exactly subtle in your dislike of Jon."

"He's not really Jon, love. You must remember that. He's been taken over—almost completely, if my guess is right."

"Then the confrontation will be soon," she said, her expression suddenly sober.

Giff nodded. "Most likely. That's why I'm concerned about this request to go for a swim. I have no doubt that was *his* idea, not Gerri's. He has something planned, but I'm not sure whether he wants to separate us or simply get us all in the water for another reason."

Gerri and Moore returned before Linda could reply. They sipped coffee and Gerri talked. Giff watched Moore, who smiled at Giff's scowls. And all the time, the tension inside him built. His heart raced, then subsided. He felt the flush of heat, then the chill of cold. Nerves, he thought. And the more tense he became, the more certain he was that this day would test his abilities—and those of his foe.

Gerri, Linda and Moore brought their breakfast outside and sat at the table on the deck. Linda had fixed toast for Giff, but he wasn't very hungry. Not nearly as much as Moore, it seemed. Giff watched him pile toast with strawberry preserves, then take a huge bite, letting the red fruit ooze from each side of his mouth. He looked over and smiled, the strawberries suddenly appearing to be blood-red in the morning light. Then slowly, he wiped away the preserves with his fingers, licking each one, seeming to savor each taste. Mord fed on fear as much as Moore's body required food. Giff looked away. He'd lost his appetite.

Moore's table manners reminded him of how Jeffrey had changed. There was something about the taste of food that Mord truly loved—or craved. Evil entities surely couldn't "love" anything. Whatever the cause, it made Giff slightly ill to watch him eat.

As Linda and Gerri cleared away the dishes, Moore sat back in his chair, the perpetual smug grin on his face.

"You're not enjoying yourself, Gifford."

"I'm not here on vacation."

Jon laughed. "Well said. Still, it wouldn't hurt to pretend you're having a good time, if only for the sake of the women."

"Why?"

"Oh, you really have lost your sense of humor. But then, you never were much fun. Always taking our little challenges so seriously."

"Rather like a life-and-death struggle," Giff said dryly.

Mord laughed again. "Yes, I suppose to you it is. To me it's just another interlude. Just a bothersome little detail in an eternity of chaos."

"Will Moore still be there when you leave?"

"Who knows? I may be able to stay here longer than usual. Good body, strong and fit. Women like handsome men like this."

"She'll never love you."

"Linda? Well, perhaps not. But we both know she won't have you, now don't we?" Mord chuckled again, then set his chair down with a bang. "This is a new twist, you knowing about me. It was also a twist that the two of you were physically separated. Something had to be done to get you together, but when I realized how young she was, I became angry. I'm afraid I frightened the poor child away. She wouldn't touch the Ouija board again, so I couldn't get to her. I was going to use her friend, but she wouldn't touch it either. Silly women. Jon was the only one who didn't know about that night." He leaned forward on his elbows, across the table. "So here I am."

"I was expecting you."

"Yes, I suppose that you were, if you know about the past. But being forewarned is not enough."

"I'm aware of that."

"If you're under some misguided notion that you can destroy me, I'm afraid you will be sadly disappointed. Briefly, though. I won't let you suffer long, I promise."

"How very benevolent of you. Are you mellowing with age? I remember the last time. You didn't inflict a wound that caused a quick death. It took me almost an hour to die on that cold battlefield, listening to the cries of my fellow soldiers and their horses. Did you stay and watch, or leave for England?"

"Oh, I returned to camp. The battle was over by seven o'clock. When I discovered my poor, dead cousin, I just had to accompany his body back to England. And I had to console his grieving fiancée. It didn't take too long to gain her confidence. She was a very emotional young woman."

Giff raised from his chair, anger stiffening him. He wanted to lash out at the evil that sat across from him, but knew idle threats and physical violence were useless. Mord would only feed on those emotions, using them to his advantage to become more powerful. Giff eased back into chair.

"Will Linda need consoling, do you think?" Mord asked.

Giff ignored the question. "How long did Constance grieve?"

"Oh, she was no fun whatsoever. She moved into that house her father was going to give you as a wedding present. She walked the beach and cried, refused to go out or move to London. I gave up on her after a few weeks. It was obvious she thought of your loyal cousin as a friend, nothing more."

"She lived a lonely life. Never married," Giff said. He knew that from his research. "You didn't win that battle, Mord. She never loved another man. Neither will Linda."

"Well, she may never fall in love again, but these times are different. Surely she'll need some consoling. Perhaps in the future, I'll visit her. Not as Jon. She doesn't like Jon any more. But as another man, someone she doesn't suspect. A little romp in the bed does wonders for the grief-stricken."

"You'll never touch her."

"Don't bet your life on that." And with that remark, Mord burst into peals of laughter, leaning back and cackling like the insane, evil entity that he was.

"What's so funny?" Gerri asked as she and Linda walked onto the deck.

Giff silently glared, but Mord quit laughing and said, "Giff just told me a humorous story. He can be quite amusing."

Linda seemed alarmed. She knew, Giff realized, that the showdown would commence soon. Her eyes showed distress. Her complexion was pale. "Maybe we should go into town, catch a movie or something," she said.

"No! Let's have our day at the beach," Moore said, standing. "Gerri, why don't you and Linda get your suits on? Giff, do you own some swim trunks? This isn't St. Tropez, you know."

"I'm aware of the proprieties," Giff said coolly.

"Then run along. Get ready." And Mord laughed again.

"Giff?" Linda asked.

"Stay with Gerri and get changed. I'll be right back."

The water of the Atlantic *was* cold, Linda realized as it lapped around her calves. It seemed even colder than when she and Giff had gone swimming several days ago. Maybe it was because of what she knew now. She'd lost her innocence about the past, the present and the future, and the knowledge left her chilled.

Fate was sweeping them forward, like tiny sea creatures caught in the waves that flowed to the shore. If Jon—or Mord—wanted to go swimming, she should have resisted. But if Giff had serious doubts about going along with the idea, he would have said something. He would have made up an excuse or simply refused. He hadn't. Even now, he was changing into his trunks to join them in the water.

Linda hadn't wanted to go in yet, saying they should wait for Giff. But Jon had insisted they should relax and have fun. Gerri had grabbed her hand and pulled her into the shallow water. Then she'd run into the waves, screaming like a child just as she'd done when she was younger.

For just a moment, it had seemed like old times.

Then Linda remembered the expression of pure hatred on Giff's face, the maniacal laughter of Jon—or Mord. She knew that something would happen soon. None of them could survive the suspense much longer. Surely now Mord had completely taken over Jon. That meant that Giff could confront him.

It also meant that Giff might be dead soon. That they would never have that future that had seemed so possible only a week ago. She touched her hand to her stomach, wondering if they had created a child. It would take weeks to find out. Weeks that Giff might not have.

A large wave broke where she stood, splashing her with cool salt spray. She shivered and walked farther into the water, trying to keep her gaze on Gerri, who was about 25 yards out into the ocean. Jon swam toward her, perfectly at ease in the waves, a natural athlete.

Where was Giff? It had been about 15 minutes—not too long, but long enough that Linda worried about him. Surely it didn't take more than a few minutes to pull on some swim trunks and return to the beach. And Giff was always saying that she shouldn't be alone with Jon. Didn't he see the danger of Gerri being alone with him, now that he'd become completely taken over by Mord?

The sound of screams and splashing diverted

Linda's attention to Gerri. Alarmed, Linda watched arms stretch up from the waves and water splash. Then she heard Gerri's giggles, and knew that she and Jon were merely playing, like two children in the water.

But that didn't ring true. Why was Jon pretending to play? If he was possessed by Mord—which he seemed to be—he wouldn't be playing unless he had some ulterior motive. Like trying to lull everyone into a false sense of safety. And as Giff was always saying, you couldn't be too careful.

With one last glance back toward Giff's house, Linda waded deeper into the water. She had to get to Gerri, to warn her without letting Jon know that they were wise to his tricks. Of course, he probably knew. He was no doubt playing with all of them, enjoying the fact that they were scared to death of what he'd do next. Of how he planned to destroy Giff.

More screams and giggles erupted. Surely Jon wouldn't hurt Gerri. That wouldn't serve any purpose. It was Giff he was after, and, Linda thought, her. For some reason, he wanted to hurt her, almost as though he was punishing her for some imagined wrong. She didn't know why; she wished she'd asked Giff more questions at the time they were talking about it. The knowledge had been such a shock that she hadn't tried to understand all the "whys." She'd been too busy trying to assimilate the "whats."

But Linda was sure that Gerri wasn't a target; she didn't have anything to do with this centuries-old feud. Jon must be just playing around, for whatever reason. Gerri was too sweet and trusting, but she wasn't stupid. She wouldn't let their water play go on for too long. She wouldn't get herself into a dangerous situation. Linda kept telling herself that as she struggled out from the long, sloping beach, pushed and pulled by the waves and the strong undertow.

She stopped for a moment, not sure why, but then realizing that it was absolutely quiet. No screams, no giggles. Just the rush of water and the cry of the gulls. Panic rushed in, fear for herself and for Gerri.

Suddenly she felt a tremendous pressure on her chest, almost as if someone were crushing her. She bent over, sputtering when a wave broke near her face. The urge to run out into the water was as strong as the pain and pressure inside her. She had to get to Gerri!

"Gerri!" she called as loud as she could.

There was no response. She started to call again, but another wave rushed over her, filling her mouth with salt water. She choked, turned away from the waves and coughed so hard that it felt as though her lungs would burst. Pain ripped though her throat as tears blinded her. Struggling, gagging and gasping, she could think only that she had to get to Gerri.

Jon was killing her, just yards away, and Linda knew she was helpless.

"Gerri!" she called weakly, struggling against the waves.

Suddenly she felt an arm around her middle. She turned, expecting to see Giff, wanting him to save Gerri. But the arm around her was as cold as the icy Atlantic. And the face was Jon's.

Giff ran to his rented house, rushing to get back quickly before Mord could separate Linda and Gerri. Giff believed that as long as the two women were together, Mord wouldn't act. He thrived on human emotions, and to isolate individuals and conquer them with fear was his modus operandi. The bond between Gerri and Linda was strong, and together they would feel more invincible. Separate, they would worry about each other, thus feeding their fears—and fueling Mord's strength. Giff had to trust in that bond, that they would stay together no matter what Mord tried.

Giff ran up the steps and pulled the key from the pocket of his jeans, unlocking the door quickly. There were a few other things he had to do beside change clothes. He walked swiftly though the small house into the back bedroom, and opened the closet door.

The black leather case was where he'd left it, leaning against the wall, hidden by other luggage and a hanging garment bag. To anyone else going through his belongings, it would appear to be a traveling case for a rifle or shotgun.

But it wasn't. He lifted it from the closet and laid it on the bed. Soon he would need the unique power of the instrument. This time, he wasn't learning the skill or practicing. He unzipped the case and removed the blood-red, satin-wrapped bundle.

Peeling back the layers, he stared at the gleaming steel of the sword. A military implement, the weapon of an officer and a gentleman. It looked so cold and deadly lying there amongst the red satin, but Giff also thought it held a certain innocent beauty. Like a deadly snake, its power to destroy was only in contact with flesh. And Giff knew what that sword felt like as it plunged into a body. As it severed tissue, nerves and blood vessels. As it pierced vital organs and left a mortal wound.

This was the sword that had killed him in 1815. And now it would destroy his link with Mord.

Giff had spent eight years tracking down the sword. He knew what it looked like from his regression, but he had no idea what had become of it after the Battle of Waterloo. He suspected that his cousin, possessed by Mord, had returned with it to his home in Brighton. Giff traced the genealogy of the family, reading wills for any mention of a family sword, a piece of the famous battle. Finally he found a reference in a document filed in 1898, by his cousin's great-great-grandnephew. The sword had been sold at auction to Chester Thurgood, a military memorabilia collector and dealer in London. Thurgood had kept excellent records of his sales, Giff discovered, when he visited the current owner of Thurgood's business, a fellow named Matthew Gooding. Gooding allowed Giff to review all the old sales receipts, and he soon discovered the sword had been sold to a nobleman who was restoring an ancestral estate in Sussex. Luck had been with Giff, because he'd found the sword hanging on the wall of Viscount Whiteburn's great hall, near other weapons and shields from centuries past. None of which, Giff believed, had anything to do with the viscount's family.

He'd paid a ridiculous sum for the piece, but it had been worth it. Armed with the sword, years of research, and the words to a spell he'd researched in some obscure monk's texts on ancient pagan rites, he was ready to defeat Mord.

Giff hefted the sword, testing the now-familiar weight with his arm. He'd trained for three years, learning to use the weapon skillfully. It was unlikely he'd be involved in an actual sword fight, but he wanted to be prepared for any outcome. And with Mord, one never knew.

It was time. He placed the sword on the satin, ready for use. Since he couldn't carry it down the beach or leave it at Linda's house, he hoped he could lure Mord down here, so their final confrontation would be away from the eyes of Linda and Gerri. A private battle, to death or freedom. He only hoped the outcome would be freedom—his from the spell and Jon's from the possession. He could only hope that they didn't die in a futile battle against evil, because then, Mord would win.

Giff opened one of the dresser drawers and found a pair of swim trunks. He'd been swimming often in the ocean, late at night after Linda was safely inside her house. The cold water refreshed him and temporarily relieved his lust for her. Besides, the exercise was good, keeping him in shape for the battle to come. He pulled off his jeans and stepped into the trunks, leaving on his cotton shirt for later—after Mord quit playing his silly games.

Suddenly he felt bolt of panic. It came from Linda, he knew, but it didn't seem to be her own fear. She was afraid for someone. *Gerri!* The word screamed inside Giff's head like a sudden thrust of a sword. Something was wrong, terribly wrong. Giff ran from the house, at an angle toward the beach, towards the screams that echoed inside his head.

Linda struggled against the arm that encircled her. "Let me go!" she screamed, even as more salt water splashed into her face and mouth. "I've got to get to Gerri."

"She's gone under. There's nothing you can do."

"No!" Linda fought him, but he was so much stronger. His head was above the waves, his body firmly braced against the undertow. She raked her nails against his arm, kicked with her legs until she couldn't kick anymore. "Gerri!" she screamed until she was so hoarse, no sound would come forth, until the water almost drowned her.

He dragged her from the ocean as tears screamed down her face, as salty as the waves. She tried to fight, but all she could think of was, "It's too late." Gerri was gone. She waited to feel the emptiness, but it wasn't there. She couldn't grasp the reality that her best friend was dead.

"Stop fighting me," Jon said, but his words weren't harsh. They sounded oily-smooth, not thick with emotion, not like a man who had just lost his fiancée.

"You freak! Get away from me."

He pulled her the rest of the way from the water,

then let her go. She sank to the sand, exhausted from her struggles against the waves and Jon. Or Mord, she should say. Why should she continue to call him Jon when she knew not a speck of humanity remained in that body?

"You won't even try to go get her, will you?" she accused. "She's out there!" Linda pulled herself to her feet, unsteady, avoiding his hands as they tried to assist her. "Get out there and find her body!"

"It's no use," he said calmly. "She's gone."

"She's not gone," Linda cried, striking him in the chest with her fists. "You killed her."

"It was an accident."

"You killed her, just like you killed William."

He grabbed her wrists, stilling her with hands as cold and strong as iron bands. "Don't start accusing me, Linda. You'll regret it."

"Giff—"

"Ha." Mord laughed sarcastically. "He can't do a thing. Don't you know that? He's never been able to do anything."

"He will. This time, he can."

"Oh?" Mord's eyes narrowed. "And what does he have planned?"

Linda tried to twist away, but he held her easily. "Leave us alone!"

"I can't do that," he said smoothly. "Tell me what Giff has planned, and perhaps I'll be nice."

"Never!" she screamed, searching the beach. Where was Giff? Had something already happened to him? But no, she hadn't felt the same sense of loss as she did when Gerri . . . If something had happened, she'd know. She only felt her own panic, her helplessness in the face of such a great evil.

She saw movement out of the corner of her eye. Jerking her head around, looking past Jon—Mord—she saw someone struggling from the waves, someone—

"Gerri!" Linda screamed the word, then twisted away from Mord as he turned, as startled as she.

Giff pulled Gerri from the water, then picked her up and flung her over his shoulder as he walked slowly from the ocean. Linda ran to him, slowed by the shifting sand and ankle-deep waves. She couldn't get there fast enough.

"Giff!" she called, running as hard as she could.

She touched Gerri's arm, searching for her wrist, for her pulse. "Is she—"

"No, I don't think so." Giff laid her facedown on the sand, then put his arms beneath her breasts and pulled. A gust of water and a fit of coughing followed. Gerri retched, spitting up salt water, then coughed so hard it hurt to listen. But to Linda, it was the most wonderful sound in the world.

"She's alive," she whispered to Giff, looking at his exhausted, concerned face. "You saved her." Linda turned back to stare at Gerri, supporting her head with trembling hands.

"She'd gone under, but I could see her red bathing suit just beneath the surface. I didn't know then if she was still alive, but when I pulled her up and got some of the water out, I thought I felt a pulse."

Gerri moaned then and tried to roll over.

"Let me," Giff said. He gently raised her to a half-sitting position, wiping the hair and water from her face. "Linda, run to the house and call 911. I'll be right behind you."

She stood up, her exhaustion a distant memory. "Mord did this."

"I know. Go call 911. I'll deal with him later."

Giff watched Linda run up the steps to the deck, then into the house. He picked Gerri up, cradling her shaking form against his chest, and followed Linda's sandy footsteps up the stairs. Before he went into the house, he looked around the beach. Mord was nowhere to be seen.

"Jon . . . tried . . ."

"Don't try to talk," Giff said in response to Gerri's hoarse whisper. "He can't harm you now."

Gerri closed her eyes, her head rolling toward his chest. Giff could tell from her convulsive shakes that she was silently crying. He wished he could convince her that it wasn't Jon who had attacked her, that it was an evil entity that had taken possession of him, but from what Linda had said, Gerri wouldn't listen.

Later, when she'd recovered from this near drowning, he would explain. Or, if he wasn't able, then Linda could tell her the whole story, and make her understand that her fiancé was not the monster he seemed to be.

Linda opened the door for him as he walked across the deck. "They're on their way. It will be about ten minutes."

Giff nodded. He walked into the den and placed Gerri on the sofa.

"How is she?" Linda asked, hovering over them.

Giff straightened. "She's weak, but better."

Linda sank down beside the sofa. "Gerri? Can you hear me?"

Gerri rolled toward Linda's voice and opened her eyes. "Linda?"

Linda gave her a gentle hug. "I knew you'd gone under. I tried to get to you, but . . . I couldn't."

"Jon tried—"

"No, it wasn't really Jon. You mustn't think that. Jon has been taken over by Mord."

Gerri shook her head, her brows drawn together. "No," she said weakly.

"It's true, Gerri. I tried to tell you the other night, but you wouldn't listen. You must believe that it isn't Jon. It's Mord."

Gerri tried to protest, but she ended up coughing again.

"Linda, I think you'd better talk to her later. She'd in no condition to hear this now."

"She needs to know. She must understand."

Gerri's eyes were closed, her breathing even, as if she'd drifted off to sleep. Giff leaned down and raised Linda to her feet. "She will, love, she will." He hugged her close. "Let her rest and heal. Then you can tell her everything. She'll listen."

Tears glistened in Linda's eyes. "I looked for you, but you didn't come."

"I'm sorry. I thought you and Gerri were together on the beach. I needed to get something ready . . . for later."

"What do you mean?"

"Don't worry about it."

She broke from his embrace. "Don't treat me like a child, Giff. If you have something planned, let me know. Let me share it with you."

He shook his head, his emotions in turmoil. Telling her what he had planned would only make her worry. He wasn't even completely sure it would work. After all, the plan was based on theories, his own and those he'd researched. If he was wrong, then he'd be dead . . . again.

And the cycle would continue.

"You're going to face him soon, aren't you?"

"I must. Next time he tries to frighten you, separate you from Gerri, or come between us, he'll be more ruthless. He's been toying with us so far, but soon he'll be more deadly. I can't wait for that. I can't risk your life."

"So you'll risk yours."

"I have no choice."

She flung herself at him, and he held her fast in his arms. A feeling came over him, a love so strong, it made tears come to his eyes. He buried his face in her salt-smelling hair, holding tight, wishing he had the ability to stop time. If only they'd been together longer. If only they'd shared more of their lives, of their dreams. They'd never discussed what they'd do in the future, because he never knew if they'd have a future. But, he realized as sirens blared in the distance, they should have talked about their hopes.

He should have told her he loved her days ago, and often since. Now, when it might be too late, he realized that he hadn't been at all fair. He'd been too focused on his goal, not concerned enough about her needs.

He pushed away slightly so he could look into her face. "I love you," he whispered. "And I'm sorry for . . . all this. For Gerri's pain and your involvement."

Tears streamed down Linda's cheeks. Her face seemed pale, anguished. He wanted to comfort her, but knew of nothing he could say.

"I love you too," she finally whispered. The sirens wailed, louder now. "For whatever reason, because of you and me, or who we were before, I love you." The ambulance ground to a halt on the gravel, the siren dying with a final, weak groan. "Even without the damned spell, I'd love you."

His lips touched hers with all the love he had in his heart, trying to put a lifetime of passion and commitment into one kiss. Her mouth opened beneath his, and his tongue mated and danced until they were both breathless. Linda shivered, clung to him as though she would never let him go.

But she must. He broke the kiss, held her by her arms and gazed deeply into her eyes. He looked into her heart and felt love, fear and a terrible sense of frustration. There was no doubt that she knew what he was up against, and hated the fact, almost as much as he, that it was unavoidable.

The paramedics pounded on the door.

"I'll let them in. You stay with Gerri."

The minute he opened the front door, the entire atmosphere changed. Two men rushed in, one carrying a medical bag of sorts, the other a respiration device, he guessed. "She's in the den. This way." He led them down the hallway. Suddenly the house was filled with noise and activity. No longer were he and Linda alone in their own world.

Linda had been kneeling beside the sofa, holding Gerri's hand, when the paramedics walked in. She rose and backed away from the couch. Almost immediately, Gerri cried out, "Linda."

"I'm here," she said, rushing around and leaning over the back of sofa.

The two men worked over Gerri, taking her pulse, measuring her respiration. All the time, Linda held her friend's hand, telling her she would be fine.

In a few minutes, the paramedics brought in a stretcher and announced that they were ready to transfer Gerri to the hospital.

"Who's going with her?" one of them asked.

"I am," Linda said, looking at Giff. "I have to," she said, as if explaining.

"I know," he said. And he did. He understood that she had to leave, to get out of the house and take care of her friend. She would walk away, and he might never see her again. And she knew that. It was best that she was gone when the final battle came. Giff felt that although Linda tried to keep a brave face, she was torn apart inside, worrying about him, about Mord's power and Jon's innocent life.

"I'll do my best," he said quietly, standing before her. He touched her cheek, gazed deeply into her eyes, and tried to let her know that his love for her would transcend whatever happened. Even if he was no longer alive when she walked back through that door.

"Be careful," she said, trying to smile through her tears, her words mirroring his own entreaties.

He nodded. "I will."

"Miss, we need to go."

Linda looked around at the paramedics, at Gerri on the stretcher and then back at him. With one last, weak cry, she whirled away and followed them out the door.

Chapter Nineteen

How does one kill fear, I wonder? How do you shoot a spectre through the heart, slash off its spectral head, take it by its spectral throat?
—Joseph Conrad

Giff walked onto the deck after Linda left, looking over the beach and sea, trying to find a sign of Moore. Footprints . . . many footprints: some running into the surf, some headed down the beach toward his rented house. He couldn't tell which ones were his and which ones belonged to someone else.

He went back into Linda's house and prowled the rooms until he was sure Moore wasn't inside. He felt full of impotent fury, at Mord, at himself, at the situation. At last he'd found Linda, made her his, given his heart to her, and there was no guarantee that he would live to see her return from the hospital. He wanted to shed his self-control, learned from many years of training and discipline, and smash something.

When he looked at his hands, they were shaking. This wouldn't do. To face Mord, he had to be calm and steady. Giff turned to the sofa, the place where he'd made love to Linda, where they'd sat and confronted Moore last night, where Gerri had lain almost drowned. The cushions were damp from her swimsuit and hair, but he didn't care. His own shirt and swim trunks were dry by now from all the walking he'd done. He sat on the sofa, elbows on his knees, hands clasped between. Closing his eyes, he concentrated on the words he needed to defeat Mord.

He wasn't sure how long he sat there, but soon a calm descended upon him, steadying his hands and quieting his mind. His past lives played in his head like snippets of movies, each with a different cast, but guided by the same warped director. Giff focused on Mord, envisioning the scenario that must occur to break the connection forever. The chant, the weapon, the blood . . .

His head jerked up and his eyes opened. The sword! He'd left it in his house when he ran onto the beach. He'd been so concerned about Linda that he hadn't gone back to get it. Damn! It was the absolutely crucial element to his probable success. How could he have been so negligent as to leave it out of reach?

"Looking for this?" a haunting voice said from behind him.

Giff felt the whoosh of air before he turned. He pivoted away from the couch, but the sword came down on his upper arm, slicing his skin. He didn't feel the pain, but knew that would come. Immediately he felt the heady rush of adrenaline, which would give him the strength and endurance he needed to succeed. At last, the battle had begun, he thought with grim excitement.

But first he had to get away, to get a weapon of his own. And he must feel no anger, show no fear. If he gave Mord any more strong emotions to feed upon, the entity would only become stronger and more determined.

"Very lax of you to forget a weapon," Mord said, holding the sword up and studying the blood on the blade. "You must have been terribly distracted."

"Someone nearly drowning does that to me," Giff said, backing away to the center of the room. Mord lurked behind the couch, but began to circle that piece of furniture. Soon there would be nothing between them.

"This does look familiar," he said, studying the wrapped wire grip and engraved knuckle-bow. "If I'm not mistaken, it's from William's cousin."

"That's right." Giff eyed the fireplace, the tools resting beside it. He needed some time to plan a defense, to distract Mord. "Jeffrey was his name."

"Ah, yes, Jeffrey. A fine body. So you tracked the sword down. That must have been a time-consuming and expensive proposition." Mord lowered the blade and advanced, making awkward circles. "I don't suppose you did it out of nostalgia."

"Not exactly." Giff backed toward the fireplace.

"If you have some absurd idea that using this sword on Jon's body will make me go away, you're going to be very disappointed—right before I run you through."

"Do you think I'd reveal my plans?"

Mord laughed. "Of course not. I'm just stating fact. Besides, I doubt if you would kill Jon's body. Gerri and Linda would no doubt hate you for that."

Rage filled Giff, but he tamped it down. Now was not the time to think about possible outcomes, or be taunted. He'd do what he had to do to break the cycle, but murdering Moore wouldn't accomplish that goal. He clenched his jaw and backed up further, until he felt the brick of the hearth hit the back of his calves.

"Just as I thought," Mord said smugly. "You have no intention of killing Jon. So, what good is the sword? A mystery . . ."

"Don't worry about it. If I'm correct, you can't really die."

Mord raised one eyebrow, circling closer, making greater sweeps with the sword as if he was testing his own abilities, or that of the blade. "Very astute. Did you figure that out yourself?"

"I'm very good at research," Giff said, his fingers touching the cold metal rack that held the fireplace tools.

"Yes, I imagine you are. You probably read all sorts of folk tales and myths about evil beings. I wonder how much you believe."

"Enough to know what I'm up against."

Mord laughed. "Do you think so?" He advanced, holding the blade out straight in front of him. It gleamed in the afternoon sun, filtered through the windows to Giff's right. "This body isn't trained in fencing or swordplay. It's a good strong body, but as I said, not trained. That would have given you a little advantage . . . if you had the sword." Mord laughed, the sound sinister in the silent room. "But since I have the sword, I'm afraid this contest will be rather one-sided."

He lunged quickly, catching Giff off guard, nicking his shoulder lightly with the edge of the tip. Giff recoiled automatically, almost going off balance when he realized he couldn't back up anymore without stepping onto the brick hearth. His fingers closed around the handle of what he hoped was the poker.

"It's going to be very amusing to kill you twice with the same weapon. Very unique."

"Don't bet on it," Giff said, raising the fireplace tool.

"Ah, so we are going to fight. An uneven match, to be sure, but I had nothing better to do with the women gone."

"Terrorizing women does seem to be your specialty."

"Well, it's all very confusing. This body," he said with a sweep of the sword in an arc around him, "is accustomed to sex. Jon was apparently a very randy young man. And Gerri is certainly attractive, if a little thin. I'm afraid the combination of

Jon's desire and my temperament wasn't very accepted. She wanted nothing to do with a little rough sex."

"You never did know how to win a woman on your own. That's why you have to take them by force or coercion. That's why you don't have a body of your own, isn't it, Mord?"

His face closed, taking on a countenance of fury. "You sniveling human. You know nothing."

"I know about you. You're a failure in the mortal world—you never could succeed with even the most simple evil tasks. You have a nasty disposition, which carries over into whatever body you inhabit. And the rules are that you can't stay in any one body long."

"I'm crushed that you have such a low opinion of me. But keep in mind that however ineffective you believe me to be, I'm infinitely stronger than you."

"Not necessarily true. Just like every other entity, you have your weaknesses."

Mord lunged, but he was too slow. Giff moved to the side, and the sound of the sword striking brick echoed throughout the room.

"You won't live long enough to discover them," he said as he repositioned his body.

"Your biggest weakness is that you really can't stay away from the mortal world. You keep coming back, messing with our lives, interfering with our destiny."

"It amuses me to become involved in your petty lives."

"Small pleasures for small minds," Giff said tauntingly.

Mord lunged again, this time connecting with Giff's forearm. The two previous cuts had begun to sting, sharp reminders of how deadly the sword was. And how intent Mord was on destroying him.

"I don't think I'll toy with you too long. I find I'm growing bored."

Giff backed toward the more open area by the French doors. "Bored or worried?"

"Don't flatter yourself," Mord said, advancing steadily.

"And you should be careful not to become overconfident."

"You won't kill this body," Mord said smugly. "Linda would never forgive you."

Linda . . . where are you, love? Are you safe? Stay safe. Stay away.

Linda thanked the off-duty EMS paramedic, who'd been kind enough to give her a ride back to the house. She'd had a horrible feeling as she'd sat ineffectually in the waiting area, hoping for a good prognosis for Gerri. The unease had built until Linda had paced the room, anxiety similar to her panic attack at the library pushing her toward action.

Giff was in trouble. The thought had raced through her mind until she couldn't think of anything else. The condition of her best friend had paled in comparison to her immediate concern for Giff. She must do something. She had to get to him! She'd raced back to the emergency entrance, where she'd spotted the nice young man and asked for a ride home.

Now, as she stood on the front steps, she was only partially relieved to see that the door was locked. That didn't mean Giff was safe. In fact, she thought she heard voices from inside the house. Perhaps Giff was doing nothing more than watching television in the den.

Somehow, that scenario didn't ring true.

With careful, quiet movements, she pulled the key from her purse and unlocked the front door. Immediately a chill wind assaulted her and a feeling of fear washed over her. *Like the attic,* she thought. *Mord was here!*

Stealthily, she walked down the hall toward the den, the voices becoming louder. The sound of metal against stone or brick made her stop, her breath catching. They were fighting! A fight to the death.

She hurried, still trying to be as silent as possible. But it was difficult when it seemed her heart pounded loud enough for anyone in Myrtle Beach or Charleston to hear. Surely Giff and Mord could detect the deafening beat. What if she distracted Giff? She had to help him, not be the cause of any injury . . . or worse.

"You won't live long enough to discover them." She heard Jon's voice, rife with Mord's evil inflection. She swallowed the cry that threatened to escape, giving away her presence. With one hand on the wall, she crept forward.

She listened, clinging to the shadows of the hallway, as Giff taunted Mord, saying things that were bound to make him angry. Why? Couldn't he defeat him cleanly, quickly? Did he have to make Mord's evil even more dangerous?

Linda peered around the corner. What she saw caused a sob to escape her lips. Giff stood, legs apart, expression grim and defiant, holding nothing more than a fireplace poker—the same one she'd used as a possible weapon when she'd been frightened by the man on the beach. *It's not enough!* she wanted to scream. Not against the deadly, highly polished, red-stained sword held by Jon—or Mord.

Tears sprang to her eyes as she saw Giff's tattered shirt, blood streaking his arms, staining the ripped cotton on his shoulder. *Oh, love, be careful. I can't bear the thought of living without you. Not now, when we've found each other after all these years.*

"You won't kill this body," she heard Jon say in such a smug tone that she wanted to strangle him herself. "Linda would never forgive you."

Anger swept over her, erasing the tears, the fear for Giff's life. Jon's back was to her as Giff circled toward the French doors. Giff needed an advantage, something that would cause Mord to become distracted or off balance.

With a burst of strength, she launched herself across the room.

Giff heard—and felt—the sound of Linda's sob from the hallway, but didn't look toward her. He had to maintain his concentration. Becoming distracted by her presence would only tip the outcome in Mord's favor. Instead, he kept his voice steady and said, "As you observed, it isn't my intention to kill you."

"Then I'll finish our little fight. I hope you said good-bye to your true love." Mord's evil laughter echoed in the room.

Giff had only a moment to react with heart-stopping fear to the sight of Linda, hurtling across the room at Mord's back. Mord obviously didn't sense—or see—her. And Giff could do nothing, not even yell, which could cause deadly consequences.

"You evil son of a bitch," Linda screamed as she hit her target.

Mord whirled, an eerie cry escaping lips stretched tight in a feral grimace. Linda's arms clamped tightly around his neck, he sliced with the sword, but found only air.

"Now, Giff! Get him now!"

"Linda, no!" Giff could tell what Mord was about to do before Linda could react. With a roar of anger, Mord backed quickly into the room divider separating the den and kitchen. The sound of Linda hitting the waist-high countertop reverberated throughout the room. Her pain and fear echoed in Giff's mind.

Giff rushed Mord, hoping he would drop his defenses for a moment so he could strike out, incapacitate at least his sword arm. Mord twisted, shoving Linda into the dividing wall. Giff swung with the poker, aiming at the arm that held the sword. If he could break it . . .

With a cry, Linda's arms loosened. She dropped

away, bending double as she sagged to the floor.

Mord twirled, and Giff's blow fell ineffectually through the air.

"Two against one," Mord said with anger, his voice cold. "And I thought this was going to be a fair fight."

Giff raised his weapon, preparing to strike again, but with a burst of speed, Mord reached out and grabbed Linda's arm. She staggered awkwardly to her feet.

"If you're going to cheat, I must also," he said, draping the sword across Linda's chest and neck as he pulled her against his body.

"Let her go. If it's a fair fight you want, let her go and come after me."

"Giff, no! He doesn't fight fair. You know that."

Giff's throat tightened at the pain he saw on Linda's face and felt inside his soul. It wasn't just the physical bruises. She'd tried to save him by risking her own life. He wanted to hold her tight against him at the same time he wanted to yell that she was foolish. That she'd endangered the only person he'd ever love. That his life meant nothing unless she was safe.

But he said nothing, silently following Mord as he backed across the room. Now, more than ever, Giff knew he must defeat Mord. He couldn't allow Linda to come to harm, to be at the mercy of Mord.

She didn't struggle. Her eyes were wide with fear, her body tight against Mord as they continued to retreat. The stairs loomed directly behind them. Mord looked back very quickly.

"I think we should have a reunion upstairs," he said, grinning malevolently. "What do you say?"

"I say that you should let her go. Fight me. I'm the one you hate, not her."

"Oh, I'm beginning to get a healthy dislike for our object of desire." Mord used the flat side of the sword to caress Linda's cheek. "As I said, Jon is apparently a randy young man. I believe I'll take advantage of his natural abilities after I get rid of my competition. I never did bed you, did I? Always such a fiercely loyal wench. Even to the memory of a dead man."

Linda cried out, the sound echoing throughout the still house. Mord backed up the steps, then stopped and brought the sword lower, until it rested against the tip of Linda's breast.

"Yes, I'll have to take you by force, but have you I will. Perhaps in the attic, on that smooth, hard floor. Perhaps in that childish bedroom of yours, tied to the bed. Perhaps both places and more."

"Never," Giff growled. He felt such impotent rage that for a moment he was blinded by anger, consumed with hatred. *Stop it!* His lifelong training held him in check, bringing the paralyzing fury under control. *That's just what Mord wants. He feeds on your emotions, your hatred. Don't give him the weapon he needs to defeat you.*

Mord continued backing up the stairs, the sword against Linda's throat. "Come on, Gifford. What are you waiting for? Would you like to watch me take your lover? That can be arranged too. Your death might be slow and painful. You could live long enough to see her suffer."

"You'll never have her."

"I'll kill myself before I let you touch me that way," Linda said fiercely.

"You two can be so dramatic," Mord said with an evil chuckle. He paused again, about halfway up the steps. "What's stopping you?" he said, staring at Giff.

That's right. Make him wonder. Keep him off balance. A voice inside Giff's head calmed him, gave him the resolve he needed. He focused on the spell-breaking chant, whispering the words in English. "Blood and souls together in evil intent."

"What's this? Reciting poetry at a time of crisis?" Mord's evil chuckle drifted downstairs.

"Love and souls eternal in the best creation."

Keep him off balance.

As though Linda heard his thoughts, she gave a small cry and collapsed, just as if she'd fainted. But Giff saw her open eyes, the stony determination on her face. Mord was forced to either give up his shield or try to hold on to her body, letting the sword drop away momentarily.

He chose to keep his shield, grabbing for Linda even as she launched herself backward against his knees. In a scramble for control on the steps, they both stumbled. Linda rolled away, then righted herself and raced downstairs.

Mord regained his balance, then arched the sword, his head thrown back and another scream echoing off the ceiling. "Damn you!" With a cry, he paused on the stairs, as though not certain which direction to go. Up, toward the attic, or down, to face his human foes.

Giff barely acknowledged the fact that Linda rushed past him. As long as she was safe, he didn't care where she went. He concentrated on Mord, on getting him back downstairs. For some reason, Mord wanted to go to the attic. Maybe he needed to be near the Ouija board in case Moore's body failed him. Giff wasn't sure of the logistics, but felt certain there was a valid reason.

And if Mord wanted to be in the attic, Giff wanted him downstairs.

Mord divided his attention between Linda and Giff. Apparently, Giff thought, she was doing something of interest, but he didn't dare look away from Mord to find out. Quickly, when Mord wasn't looking, Giff pivoted to the side of the stairs, reaching through the carved newels with the poker.

With a satisfying, solid connection, the hook buried itself into the calf muscle of Jonathan Moore's body.

Mord screamed in pain. Giff jerked, pulling the leg out from beneath him.

With a clattering of the sword and a thud of the body, Mord tumbled down the steps.

Giff leaped onto the outside edges of the steps and jumped the rail. The sword lay on the worn carpet runner, gleaming brightly in the dim interior. His fingers fitted naturally through the knuckle-bow, sliding around the grip like a familiar handshake. Immediately, he felt a flow of energy and strength enter his arm. *This time, I will not fail.* He recognized the truth even as Mord struggled to rise from the bottom of the stairs.

"You won't kill this body," Mord said, looking up the stairs, his words not quite steady.

Sword ready, Giff descended. The chant began to echo in his head. Victory was near.

From the corner of his eye, he saw Linda, then heard a drawer slam. She turned, a revolver held in her hand.

"He might not kill you, but I will," Linda said with a voice both soft and steely. Giff watched Mord, gauging his reaction to Linda's threat, even as he heard the distinctive click of a firing mechanism being drawn back. Still he didn't look away.

Mord awkwardly rolled his head to the side, watching Linda approach. "That wouldn't be a good idea," he said. "Gerri would never forgive you."

"And I would never forgive myself if something happened to Giff."

"You don't believe I can be defeated by mere bullets?" Mord said in a scoffing tone. But Giff realized that beneath the swagger, the evil, there was concern. If Moore's body died, he might be in trouble. He could be banished to wherever evil entities resided when not tormenting humans—probably another dimension—or he could have some time to search for another body. Giff didn't know the rules. He didn't want to trust the unknown aspects of this new scenario. Breaking the curse was their best chance for a life without Mord's malignant influence.

"I'm perfectly serious," Linda said. "I don't want to shoot, but I will. I've had this gun cleaned and I know how to use it."

"Linda, don't," Giff said calmly. "If you kill Jon's body, Mord will still be loose. He might find someone else to host his evil, someone that we don't know." He paused, sending her a mental message to be careful. *Stay back, stay away.*

"I'm not going to stand by and do nothing, Giff," she said, her voice suddenly shaky. "I want this to be over. I want to be safe."

"You will be, love." He stepped closer to Mord, the sword tip lowered. He was lucky in one regard. His blood already coated the tip of the sword. He needed that to cast his own spell. "He's not going to kill me."

"Don't believe him," Mord said. "There's no way he can win. A mere mortal against me? I don't think so."

I love you, Linda. If something happens, remember that I love you always.

Giff stopped near the bruised and battered body. He knew that Linda kept the gun pointed at Mord. He knew that Mord was confident he couldn't be killed, but confused and concerned about this turn of events. Obviously, he was so concerned that he didn't try to leave the body, or pursue another attack.

With a smile and a cry of triumph, Giff arched the sword over and directly at the chest of the body that housed Mord.

Astonished eyes stared up at him. He pressed the blade to the center of the sternum, resting against the solid bone there, barely pricking the skin.

He heard Linda's swift intake of breath, felt her

confusion and fear. He saw Mord's expression, also registering confusion. Apparently, the combination of injuries and indecision had temporarily debilitated him.

With a swift slice, he cut the skin of Moore's upper chest. As long as Mord was integrated into this body, he was part of the physical plane. And since he was part of it, the spell, which Giff had researched and then written in Old English, should work.

He prayed it worked.

Blod and sawol ba in yfele ingehygde feded
Lufu and sawol ece in thaet beste *ge*sceap
Toberste thone bend be Mord bannen
On thissum daege min ytemestes deathes
Send him fram uncere wyrde
Be mine willan, mine sweorde, min blode

Suddenly an expression of pure rage overcame Moore's face. The body heaved, shuddered and momentarily lifted from the floor. Giff removed the blade just in time to keep it from pressing more firmly into the chest. And he hazarded a glance at Linda. She'd lowered the gun and stared in rapt attention at the sight of Mord's anger.

A howl that seemed to come from the bowels of hell ripped from Jon's throat, but Giff knew it was Mord's way of expressing his disbelief. He hadn't expected Giff to know about a counterspell, much less piece together the link with the weapon of death. And, Giff remembered, a wise man once said that all knowledge is power. Wise words indeed.

Moore's body contorted, writhed and then went slack. Suddenly a chill wind whirled around the room, a hurricane of unnatural fury. Papers and magazines flew from the tables and crystal teardrops chimed like fearful bleating sheep. It seemed as if the entire room was caught in a vortex of unworldly rage, as though even the sunlight and shadows were sucked up and away.

Linda cried out. Giff opened his arms and she ran to him, shivering, burying her head against his bloody chest.

The wind howled, swirling around them, then seemed to rise through the ceiling like a tornado retreating into the clouds. Tinkling crystal gradually stopped, papers settled softly to the carpet. The den was left silent and disheveled, like the aftermath of a storm.

Giff lowered his head, resting against Linda. Suddenly he felt drained—mentally and physically. He'd lost blood; it still dripped from the slices on his arms. His hold on Linda slackened, even though he wanted to keep her close.

She looked up, worry etched on her features. "Is it over?"

"It's over," he said softly.

From the end table she grabbed an embroidered table linen—one her grandmother had probably stitched—wadded it up, and pressed it to the wounds. "What did you say to him in Old English? I could only make out some of the words."

He recited the chant in modern English. "Blood

and souls together in evil intent. Love and souls eternal by the best creation. Break the bond by Mord proclaim. On this the day of my last death, send him from our future. By my will, my sword, my blood."

"How did you know . . ."

He stopped her from asking more questions by easing slowly from her arms, sliding down onto the wood floor, leaning against the solid, wing-back chair. His hands shook as he placed the bloody sword beside him. Only then did he look into her eyes. She seemed blurry and far away.

"I think you'd better call 911 again."

Chapter Twenty

We are shaped and fashioned by what we love.
—Johann Wolfgang von Goethe

Linda paced the hospital waiting room, her arms wrapped around her. Ever since Mord had left Jon's body, swirling around the room in a chilling storm, she'd been cold. So very cold. Even Giff, when she'd leaned against him and he'd held her briefly, had not made the icy fear go away.

She wondered if she'd ever be warm again.

The doctors hadn't let her go into the emergency room with Giff. She wasn't a relative, they'd explained, and they had some routine tests and medical procedures to perform. *Get out of here while we sew him up,* Linda translated their comments. Even Giff had seemed willing to part with her, saying it would be best if she waited outside.

At least he was talking again. He'd frightened her to death when he'd almost passed out on the floor of the den.

It appeared as though the only useful function she could now perform was completing about five sheets of paperwork. She didn't even know most of the answers, such as Giff's date of birth, his address, his doctor's name. Was he allergic to anything? Did he have a family history of any serious disease? Was he on any medication?

It brought into focus her lack of knowledge about Giff, despite the fact that she'd fallen in love with him, made love with him. She felt foolish to leave so many blocks blank. By the time she'd completed what she could, she'd needed to get away. So she'd gone to the gift shop and purchased a shiny, cheerful balloon, then taken the elevator to the floor where Gerri had been taken after being admitted.

Linda checked with the nurses' station, then walked quietly down the tile hallway. The door to 412 was half-open. The setting sun bathed the shadowed room in rosy light. Gerri was the only person in the semiprivate room, wearing a mint-green hospital gown and lying still beneath a sheet.

"Gerri?"

She turned her head, then smiled crookedly in welcome.

"Linda," she rasped. She swallowed and winced.

Linda rushed in and poured a glass of water from the plastic decanter. "You sound horrible."

"Salt water," Gerri whispered after taking a drink. "Hoarse."

"I understand. You don't have to talk. I just wanted to check on you."

"Blood . . ."

Linda looked at herself, the dried splotches on her shirt. She was sure she looked a sight, and hadn't even thought about how this would affect Gerri. When Linda had left the house, her only concern had been Giff's health. Now, she needed to explain *whose* blood had soaked her shirt. And why.

Linda sat beside Gerri on the bed. "There was a fight at the house after you left," she began.

"Jon?"

"He's going to be fine. Actually, this is Giff's blood. Jon . . ."

"What?" Gerri's hand closed tightly around Linda's fingers.

"For the past two—no, two and a half days, Jon has been possessed by Mord, just as I tried to tell you."

Gerri shook her head. Linda could see the pain in her eyes, pain from not believing that something else had caused her fiancé's erratic and nearly deadly behavior, while at the same time being unwilling to accept that he could have acted that way on his own. She was caught between two explanations; one made no sense to Gerri, but the other was too painful to believe.

"Gerri, it's true. I know you don't believe me, but listen. Mord began to take over when Jon touched the Ouija board in the attic. He'd been waiting for one of us to touch it again. He wanted you to be the one, so he could inhabit your body, taunt me and kill Giff, knowing that I wouldn't be able to harm my best friend. But you wouldn't touch it. Jon became strange right after that. You told me so yourself. Gerri, he would have raped you!"

Gerri shook her head again. "Not Jon."

"I know that wasn't Jon. It was Mord, living out his evil through an earthly body. He had none of his own. He's a spirit, what Giff calls an elemental evil. He said Mord has always existed, and will probably always exist."

"Then Jon . . . still possessed?"

"No. Giff knew the spell that would break Mord's involvement in our lives. He had to draw blood."

"Where is Jon?"

"Downstairs in emergency. He has a small gash on his chest where Giff had to prick him with the sword."

"What sword?" Gerri rasped.

"Are you sure you should be talking this much?"

Gerri tightened her grip on Linda's fingers.

"Okay, but let me tell you the story. Just lie there and listen. Don't argue and don't ask questions until I'm finished."

Gerri relaxed back to the mattress, then nodded. Her eyes, Linda noted, were full of equal measures of skepticism and curiosity.

Linda began to speak, telling her again about Giff, about his real name and background. She explained how they had been linked, reminding Gerri about the past-life regression. Linda knew that Gerri doubted the spiritual realm, even though she had psychic abilities that she accepted as just the way her mind functioned. She didn't want philosophical discussions about her premonitions, nor did she want to speculate on what caused them. To Gerri, her gift just *was*.

Linda gave a detailed account of the fight, which she'd seen from the hallway, then the den as she went for the gun. If she'd harbored any doubts, they'd fled after seeing Giff and Jon—no, Mord—circling each other.

"So Jon is downstairs under observation, and Giff is still being treated," Linda concluded.

Gerri nodded, a frown between her brows.

A nurse bustled into the room with her stethoscope bouncing against her amble breasts. She smiled at Gerri. "Visiting hours are almost over. I need to get your stats."

"Get some rest," Linda said gently. "I'll come back as soon as I can."

As she walked back down the antiseptic-smelling corridor, Linda worried that Gerri's emotional wounds from being attacked twice and almost killed by her fiancé would take much longer to heal than any physical ailments. Perhaps if she could fully accept the strange, supernatural turn their lives had taken, it would make it easier to understand what Jon had been through. Only then could she forgive him for the pain he'd caused.

Linda took the elevator back down to emergency, only to be told by the receptionist that the doctors were still working on Giff and she'd just have to wait. She poured herself a rancid cup of coffee, sat across the room from a woman and boy and watched a sitcom re-run on the television.

Giff and Jon had been in the emergency room for over an hour when a young, dark-haired, green-garbed doctor came to the doorway. Linda jumped to her feet.

"Miss O'Rourke?"

"Yes?"

"I understand that you completed the paperwork for Jonathan Moore and Gifford Knight."

"Yes, I did. Please, I need to know how he's doing."

She meant Giff, but the doctor obviously wanted to talk about Jon. "Mr. Moore's condition is stable. He's resting, but seems disoriented. He's not certain how the wound occurred."

He obviously wanted her to fill in the blank. She wasn't going to volunteer anything, especially the fact that Giff had stabbed him.

The young doctor sighed. "Anyway, his cut is superficial and has been taped. We think it would be best to admit him."

"I agree." Jon needed to be observed. He'd no doubt feel confused, but she couldn't be responsible for his recovery at her house. Not when her main concern was Giff. "But I really need to know about Giff—Gifford Knight."

"I didn't treat Mr. Knight. I'm sorry."

Linda resisted the almost overwhelming urge to grab the man's lapels and insist that he go find out, that someone tell her something. "Look, I've been waiting forever to find out what the hell's going on in there. Now I want to talk to the doctor who treated Giff. If someone doesn't tell me how he's doing in the next five minutes, I'm going in there and find out for myself!"

After all, if she'd been foolish enough to face down an evil entity with a 1940ish German revolver, she would certainly burst into an emergency room and insist on some answers.

The doctor turned on his heel, marching back into the emergency room.

She walked to the heavy, metal framed windows. Outside, a glorious sunset painted the sky orange, pink and purple. Giff would have loved to walk along the beach tonight. They could have held hands, run from the big, errant waves and watched the sand crabs skittle across the beach.

She wasn't sure they'd ever take another walk, hold hands or make love. The spell was broken. She and Giff were no longer destined to fall in love, only to end in tragedy. Mord was out of their lives forever. But did that mean that Giff had no feelings for her?

She flopped down on the utilitarian couch. How many nervous people had sat here, anticipating news of their loved ones? She could almost feel the negative power radiating from the furniture of the room, making her edgy, unsatisfied with the waiting, with the uncertainty of her future. Giff was injured—she didn't even know how seriously—and she had no idea what he was thinking.

The fact that she could no longer sense his emotions, his thoughts, scared her so much she wondered why she wasn't shivering. In a week, her perception of reality had changed. Her idea of what was "normal" for her, for Giff, was forever altered. If reality changed again and she had to go back to believing that there was no one special out there for her . . . well, she wasn't sure she could do that.

She wanted Giff, wanted a chance for him to fall in love with her normally, without the pressure of an eternal curse. She wanted to see if he could possibly love her as much as she loved him—without the damned spell. And the doctors wouldn't even let her inside the emergency room.

She rested her head in her hands, staring at the brown tweed carpet with coffee stains and a path worn almost bare by others who had waited for news. *I will not cry again*, she told herself. She'd cried enough in the last ten days.

Suddenly she saw two feet in front of her. Long, elegant, bare feet. She looked up into Giff's face.

"Are you ready to leave?" he asked, his expression closed.

"They're releasing you?" She was shocked to see him standing here, much less ready to go home. He'd lost so much blood. He'd been so weak.

"I told them I was leaving." He said it as though it was a perfectly logical thing; tell the doctor what you're going to do.

Linda stood up, touching his unbandaged arm. His face was slightly pale. Adhesive patches peeking from the sleeves and the vee where his cotton shirt was unbuttoned. "Are you sure you're okay? Your cuts—"

"The doctor took care of them. Most were on the surface."

And some were deeper, she finished to herself. Linda frowned. She wasn't sure she should take him from the hospital, but knowing Giff, if he wanted to leave, he'd go with or without her. She picked up her purse. "We'll have to call a cab."

"Already taken care of," Giff said.

She could tell he was tired. He hadn't smiled, or even really looked at her since he'd walked into the waiting room. Maybe he didn't want to be around her. Perhaps he couldn't wait to get back to his rented house, pack, and get back to his real life in New York or England.

No. That's your insecurities talking. You're tired and edgy yourself. She took a deep breath and nodded. "Let's go."

A cab waited beside the emergency room entrance. Night was falling; purplish-gray clouds skittered across the indigo sky, and the lights outside the hospital had come on. It seemed unbelievable, Linda thought, that so much had happened since breakfast.

Giff carefully lowered himself into the back of the cab and rested his head against the seat. He took her hand, but he didn't speak. Linda leaned forward and gave directions to the driver, then settled next to Giff. Close but not touching. She didn't want to hurt any of his wounds, and he seemed oblivious to her attention anyway.

The silent drive took about 20 minutes. She thought perhaps Giff had drifted off to sleep, but just when her anxiety increased, he said, "Don't worry. I'm just very tired."

She held on to that hope as he paid the cab driver and she unlocked the front door. The house smelled musty and was silent as a tomb. When she stepped into the foyer, everything looked so *normal* that it seemed as though she'd been away for a long time. As though none of the events of the last few days had really happened.

Giff walked up beside her, took her hand, and silently led her through the hallway. They didn't stop as they went through the den, but Linda saw the mess from the swirling wind and the fight. There were drops and splatters of blood on the wood floor and the area rug. One of her grandmother's favorite embroidered linen runners lay on the floor, soaked with Giff's blood. She vaguely remembered pressing it to his arm before calling the paramedics.

"I'm sorry about the . . . lace thing," he said. "It's probably ruined."

She looked at him, wondering how he could imagine that she cared about that piece of material. But then, he'd always been considerate, understanding her desire to hold on to the past. "It doesn't matter," she said softly. "All that matters is that you're alive."

Giff looked deeply into her eyes. For a moment, she thought she saw a spark of desire—or love. Then fatigue won out and he gently pulled her toward the stairs.

He went directly to her room, and didn't stop until he reached the yellow gingham-covered bed. His eyes seemed so weary. "I need to rest. I want to sleep with you beside me. If you'd rather not . . ."

"I want to be with you," she said without hesitation. "Why would you doubt that?"

"You have a choice. I don't want to pressure you any longer."

She broke eye contact and moved around him, pulling down the bedspread and top sheet. "Don't be silly," she said as she walked to the other side of the mattress and did the same thing there. She glanced at his intense expression. If he wasn't so tired, she thought, he'd probably argue with her. But for now, he remained silent.

"Come to bed," she said, sitting down, patting the spot where he'd rested last night. "We can talk later."

He sank to the mattress, closing his eyes almost immediately. But his hand reached out, searching for hers, and she took it, snuggling into the double bed beside him.

He wrapped his arm around her, pulling her close. Within moments, she heard his deep, regular breathing. Outside, the waves rushed to the shore, the occasional night bird called, and the wind chimes sang their lilting melody. Everything seemed so terribly normal. Linda closed her eyes, fighting back tears and uncertainty, and tried to sleep.

Giff woke just before daybreak, when the world outside the window seemed cloaked in blue-gray mist, half-waking and fighting the dawn. Linda slept beside him, her hand resting in his, her bottom nestled against his hip.

His heart swelled when he realized that this was the day he'd waited for all his life—the day he was free from the curse. He recalled a trite saying, "Today is the first day of the rest of your life." At least, it had always seemed trite. This morning, it seemed the most brilliant statement he'd ever heard.

He was a free man, but did that mean he was also free of Linda's love?

How could she love him when she realized how he'd used her? He'd tried to tell her before, to explain his actions. She'd been confused and hurt then, but had still loved him. Now that the spell was broken, would she feel the same way? Or would she want him out of her life, gone like one of her grandmother's items that had some sentimental value, some good memories attached, but no longer belonged in her life?

She'd been wonderful last night, calm and quiet, as though she'd understood the extent of his exhaustion. The wounds had taken their toll, but that wasn't all of it. It was as though all of his energy had been focused on defeating Mord, with nothing left.

His life had been centered on the past, with the present providing a way to make a living from his first-hand, personal knowledge of history and the means to search for the woman of his young dreams. He'd never thought about the future, never envisioned the morning after the final showdown. Suddenly it seemed so clear; he'd concentrated so hard on the exact sequence of words and deeds needed to defeat Mord that he'd never dared to hope.

Linda stirred, rolled to her back and continued to sleep. He eased his arm from beneath her and propped himself up on one elbow, watching her. Her eyelids fluttered. The expression on her face changed from quiescent to earnest, her lips moving, smiling, then frowning. Her brow furrowing, then relaxing. Her cheeks flushed. She always did blush so charmingly.

He wanted to know what she was dreaming, but dared not violate her privacy again. Not for mere curiosity. Not to satisfy his own needs, when he'd done so much already to compromise her future, her happiness.

She smiled in her dream; then her eyelids fluttered more and her head tossed on the pillow. Her body shifted restlessly beneath the covers; she was still dressed in the blood-splattered shorts and shirt she'd worn yesterday when she'd accompanied him to the emergency room. She seemed agitated now, a frown on her face. Her breathing quickened. And then she cried out, "Edric."

He stopped breathing for a second . . . a minute. She'd called out his name from the first time they'd known each other, almost a thousand years ago, before William the Conqueror had fought his way to victory in England, when Christianity was young and belief in magic still prevailed. Her name had been Willa, and she'd been the most beautiful girl he'd ever seen.

How superficial that attraction seemed now. He remembered a line from John Donne that he'd memorized, just for the purpose of reminding himself of his folly: "Love built on beauty, soon as beauty dies." After finding Linda and discovering the beauty inside her, he finally felt the full impact of that truth.

She slumped back against the pillow as though exhausted from her dream. Slowly, her eyes opened. She looked at him for a long time without speaking. And then she said, "I remember," with such surprise and joy that he felt tears form in his own eyes.

"Your name was Edric and you were young—too young, by today's standards, to want to marry."

"Yes," he said hoarsely.

"You courted me, brought me wildflowers, wrote poems. I never let you know how I felt."

"You were young also. Probably too young to wed."

"But not too young to fall in love," she said with quiet certainty.

"Because of the spell—"

"No," she said, laying her hand on his cheek. "The spell had nothing to do with it. I loved you."

Giff closed his eyes, wishing he could believe her, but thinking that she'd confused her feelings. "The sorcerer—"

"Had nothing to do with how I felt," she finished. "I remember when he came to town. He was middle-aged, with a gray-streaked beard and bad teeth, and I was scared. I wanted to run to you, but my father wouldn't have approved. So I watched as you talked to the sorcerer. You looked up at me across the town clearing and I saw it in your eyes. I felt it in your soul. You wanted him to cast a spell."

"I was afraid."

"You were young," Linda repeated. "I should have told you that I cared for you. Instead, I flirted and teased, as though I had all the time in the world."

Giff rolled away from her patient, understanding eyes, and sat on the edge of the bed. Was she so forgiving that she'd make excuses for his behavior? He ran his hands through his hair. Didn't she see that he'd invited the evil into their lives a thousand years ago, just as she'd innocently allowed it to re-enter through the Ouija board 14 years ago?

"You should have had a lifetime of happiness," he said. "Instead, you've had an eternity of unhappy lives, Linda, because of what I did."

He felt her weight roll toward him. "I've also known love, even though it was lost to me. I learned."

"You should have learned that destiny is fickle," he said, knowing the bitterness he felt seeped into his voice. "What we love can be taken away in the snap of a finger . . . or the thrust of a sword."

"Yes, but the point is that we loved."

"The point is that I screwed up our lives. I forced you into these cycles, caused you centuries of grief. I did that!"

"You made a mistake."

"A mistake is when you break your Aunt Bertha's favorite vase. What I did was invite evil into our lives."

"You didn't know that—"

"I knew enough to stay away from someone who offers an easy answer to my problem. I knew he was bad, that what I was doing was wrong, but I was too greedy to see past the wanting."

"You were in love."

He whipped around. "Yes, I was. A love so fierce, so single-minded, that I stopped at nothing to have you."

She shook her head, staring at him. "I don't believe that's what happened. You didn't know what would result from your request for a love spell. It wasn't your fault."

"Of course it was."

"Giff, it was Mord who approached me later. I remember the lust in his eyes, the awful fear he made me feel. I would have nothing to do with him. In fact, I believe I ran to you because I felt safe in your arms. That's when he decided. I could see it in his face, the anger. I felt his rage. He wanted me, but had already performed the spell for you. It was Mord's ungodly revenge that caused the grief, not you."

Giff wanted to believe her, wanted to forgive himself. He'd lived with the knowledge for so long, but had never paid the emotional toll until now. The past, catching up with him, putting both his present and future happiness in danger, cut like a new dagger in an old wound.

"Let me help, Giff," Linda said softly. "Let me share this with you."

"I can't ask that of you," he whispered.

"You didn't ask. But I'm offering. I know it's bold of me to say this, but I think that we have the basis for a relationship. We've gone through so much together. We both love history. We're both lonely at times, and we enjoy the quiet as well as the fun things in life."

"The past would be between us. Don't you think I know how you must feel? I've used you, Linda. I sought you out, seduced you—used you to free myself from Mord's spell."

"You freed *us* from Mord's spell, at the risk of your own life."

"What good is a lifetime if I can't use what I've learned in the past?"

"Until a few days ago, I never thought about having more than one lifetime for any purpose. Reincarnation was some nebulous concept from a philosophy course. But I do believe one thing, and that is that we've both matured throughout our lifetime. I'm not that same shy, reluctant girl that I was as Willa. You're not the impetuous youth I knew as Edric. We've grown up. Now it's time to take the next step."

"The next step?"

"Yes, as adults. Learn about each other. Think about the future, not the past. I want a chance with you."

He was afraid to ask, afraid that his pounding heart would give out before she answered. But he had to know. "A chance to fall in love with me?"

"Oh, Giff, I already love you. I tried to tell you—it's not the spell. I've loved you for a thousand years. Don't you understand?"

He framed her face with shaking hands. "You love me?"

"Yes," she said, nodding, smiling through misty eyes.

He framed her face, working his fingers though her hair. "I never thought I'd hear you say those words again. I never thought you'd forgive me."

"There's nothing to forgive."

He felt the ice around his heart melt, the hollowness inside his soul fill to overflowing. Warmth flooded him, just like the first rays of sunshine that filled the room with light. "All my life, I focused on one thing—changing my fate," he said. "You were a faceless, nameless person, bigger than life, yet not quite real. Now, you are my life. I was lonely before, but could never find the companionship I craved. At times I grew frightened, yet I couldn't allow myself to become frozen by fear. Until I loved you, I never knew what a cold, empty shell my life had become. Now I could never go back. You showed me how to love.

"I love you, Linda. And I swear to you, if I have forever in your arms, at the end of time, I'll still ask for one more day."

She rose to meet him, and he kissed her with all the love in his heart, holding her tightly, fusing together their souls in a spell that needed no sorcerer's help, in a destiny they would build anew, in a love that would last an eternity.

Chapter Twenty-one

Destiny grants us our wishes, but in its own way, in order to give us something beyond our wishes.
—Goethe

Wednesday, June 21, 1995
Coastal South Carolina

Twilight stretched across the beach like a giant, lazy cat. Gulls, painted pinkish-orange by the setting sun, glided overhead and squawked, looking for a last bite of food before retiring for the night. This was the most peaceful evening Linda could remember. At last, the future lay before them like an unpainted canvas, unplanned and unexpected. Together, they would create their own fate, be guided by their own love.

She stood beside Giff on the firm sand, her fingers gripped securely, her heart just as safe in his capable, loving hands. Three days had passed since the confrontation with Mord, since Gerri's near drowning and Jon's hospitalization. She looked to her right, where Jon stood beside Gerri. They weren't holding hands, but at least they were together. At least they'd started to talk and were trying to understand what had happened.

Gerri had been dismissed from the hospital on Monday, with orders to take it easy for a few days. Linda knew that before she'd signed out, she'd visited Jon in the psychiatric ward of the small hospital, where he'd been admitted for observation.

The doctors had no doubt assumed he was on drugs or crazy. Since he wasn't sure what had happened to him, he probably did seem unstable. But Giff had smoothly told them a story about a feigned sword fight that got out of hand, about over-the-counter antihistamines, too much sun and a few drinks. Linda had repeated the story to the police, who wanted to make sure that assault charges weren't necessary—from either Giff or Jon. And Gerri, bless her heart, had gone along, although she still didn't seem too certain about Jon's possession by an evil entity.

The police had finally decided that if neither party wanted to press the issue, they couldn't prosecute. The doctors had seen no further sign of violence or disorientation in Jon, except that he couldn't remember parts of what had happened for the past several days. That was consistent, they'd claimed, with temporary memory loss caused by drug and alcohol combinations. Linda knew they'd been reluctant to release him, but couldn't come up with any other excuses for keeping him in the hospital. They'd released him into her care, with warnings for him to stay off all medication, stay out of the sun and not drink another drop for several weeks.

Jon had readily agreed, obviously needing explanations more fervently than the physicians.

Last night Linda, Giff and Gerri had sat down with him, repeating the story of Mord, from the first Ouija board encounter to the final fight. Jon didn't want to believe; he was even more skeptical than Gerri. But in the end, it had been the only explanation that made sense. With a businessman's pragmatism, Jon had finally accepted their answers. It was also obvious that he didn't want to believe he had actually gone temporarily insane, tried to rape and then drown Gerri and attempted to kill Giff with a sword he had no knowledge of using. There had been no drugs, no significant use of alcohol and no other reason why a "perfectly normal" man would do such things.

Gerri hadn't totally forgiven him, Linda knew, and she felt almost ill whenever she thought about their past happiness. They'd fallen in love, been so well matched and sure of the future. Now, Jon's unintentional actions came between them like a brick wall, built piece by piece over the last few days. Linda wasn't sure how long it would take to tear down the wall, or even if it could be torn down.

Gerri had come to South Carolina to share her

happiness with Linda. And Gerri had been so certain that Linda was in trouble—emotionally or physically. Instead of saving her friend, she'd had her own happiness almost destroyed. That was a bitter pill for Linda to swallow. She would do whatever possible, she vowed, to help Gerri regain her love for Jon, and feel the same confidence in the future that she'd had when she arrived.

The same confidence Linda now felt with Giff.

"Ready?"

She looked into his eyes, seeing a dark glow of contentment that had never been there before. Intensity still radiated from him, but a different kind. The kind that came from inner strength, from happiness and love.

"I'm ready."

He handed her a box of matches as a monarch is handed a scepter.

"Gerri? Jon? Are you ready?" she asked.

They stepped forward, eyeing the makeshift raft and box with as much loathing as they would a nest of rattlesnakes. "Let's do it," Gerri said. "I want this thing out of our lives for sure—forever."

Linda nodded. They all stepped closer until waves lapped at their feet and they sank further into the sand. Giff held the wooden planks, careful not to touch the contents of the box, while Linda held up a match.

"I feel I should say some last words," she said. This did seem like such a final, extreme act.

"How about 'good riddance,' " Gerri murmured.

"Giff, do you have any final words?"

"No. I said my piece when I broke the curse. Mord is gone."

He was, Linda knew. Out of their lives for good. But the Ouija board had remained in the attic, a reminder of the way the evil had entered. A possible portal through which Mord could return. She wasn't willing to take that chance, no matter what Giff said.

"Just do it, Linda," Gerri said fiercely. "We should have destroyed it years ago. I should never have bought the damned thing at the garage sale. I shouldn't have used it."

And, *she* shouldn't have either, Linda knew, even though Gerri didn't say the words. It had all seemed so innocent at first, such fun. They'd all learned the hard way that even the most harmless events could produce deadly results, if not pursued for a virtuous reason. In a past life, Giff had let his insecurities and his lust rule his head, but he'd been young and impetuous. Linda had let curiosity of the dark unknown guide her use of the board. Gerri had wanted to hide her head in the sand, to believe nothing paranormal had occurred. And Jon. He was probably the most innocent person of all, yet had been used as a pawn by Mord. Maybe because of his goodness. Linda didn't know; it no longer mattered. Mord really was gone. She felt that throughout every cell of her body.

"Okay," Linda said, taking a deep breath.

She and Giff waded into the surf, the raft bobbing in the waves between them. She held the match and box high, so it wouldn't get wet. Luckily, the water was calm, as though it had been ordered especially for this occasion. When they were almost waist deep, Giff stopped.

"I think this is far enough out," he said. His gaze scanned the beach and the sea. No other living soul could be seen, along the beach or the dunes. No one except Gerri and Jon would witness their actions.

Linda dragged the match across the sandpapery strip, watching the spark ignite. She slowly lowered the glowing wand as the reflection danced across the water, magnifying it a thousand times. The sight was mesmerizing, fascinating. Inside the box, the Ouija board seemed to stare back at her with accusing eyes, asking her why she was doing this. She had a strong urge to pull the board from its final resting place. It was, after all, her first link to William. Like a withered prom corsage that she couldn't throw away, she wanted to hold on to the symbol of the memories.

The paper caught fire in a burst, spreading flames in a red-gold wave to the cardboard. She barely felt Giff's hand on her shoulder, urging her away. Then she blinked and the spell seemed to be broken.

"You don't need the board. You still have your memories. You have me."

She smiled. He was right, of course. She'd never faced the board before because she didn't want to face the memories of that night. Fear. Betrayal. But they, like her past lives, didn't need physical reminders. For the first time, she felt truly free.

He pushed the raft further out, where it bobbed

on the waves and burned with unholy enthusiasm. The smell of charred wood and paper drifted to her as though washed in by the waves. Flames reached for the twilight sky, pointing toward the sliver of moonlight in the east. And she walked away, hand in hand with Giff, toward the peace of the beach.

They emerged from the waves. Gerri and Jon stood close to each other, staring at the pyre.

"It's over," Linda said, lightly touching her friend's arm. "It's really, truly over."

Gerri turned to her, her eyes unfocused at first, then troubled in the waning light. "I always thought it was odd that you fixated on William and that damned board. I thought it was some psychological problem, caused by your parents or your serious nature. I never dreamed it was real, that there was a cause for your . . ."

"Obsession?" Linda finished with a smile. "You can say the word. I realize now that I was obsessed. So was Giff. We were halves, trying to find each other, trying to make a whole."

"It just makes you feel so . . . shaken," Gerri said. "I thought I had all the answers. I thought my life was so *normal*."

"It was. It will be again."

Gerri shook her head. "I'm not sure."

"I am," Linda replied, hugging her best friend. "You just need time. Your view of life tilted. Give it time to right itself. Don't push it."

"I won't," Gerri said, her voice small and filled with tears. "I promise."

Linda hugged her for a long time. Night fell. The lights near the wooden steps came on. Finally, she pulled back and looked at the sea. The dying embers of the box still bobbed in the waves, glowing red against the dark water.

"Let's go inside," Giff suggested.

Arm around Gerri, Linda walked up the steps, across the deck and into the house. The men followed, not talking.

Once inside, she made coffee while everyone sat, almost as if by unspoken agreement, in the den. Within minutes she poured steaming mugs for the four of them and carried the mugs to the coffee table on a brass and wood tray.

"What will you do now?" Gerri asked, reaching for the coffee.

Linda smiled at Giff. "We're leaving for Chicago in a couple of days. I want to introduce Giff to my other house. He said we could live there, but I thought I'd wait for a final answer until he's seen the place."

"It's a monstrosity," Gerri said with a slight smile.

"I love it," Linda replied.

"I'm sure it's fine," Giff added. "Besides, if Linda loves it, it can't be all bad."

"Did she tell you about the leaking turret room? Have you ever tried to decorate a round room with a drip in the middle?"

"Leaks can be fixed," Giff said, taking a sip of his own coffee. "We'll do whatever is necessary."

"Actually, I offered to move if he really hated it."

"You mean move away from Evanston?"

"No, just get another house." Linda laughed, feeling unburdened. "Giff can live wherever he likes, since he writes. My job is at Northwestern, so he's giving up his apartment in Manhattan and moving in with me."

"As in living in sin?" Gerri teased.

Linda was glad her friend's sense of humor had returned. "No, we talked about that too."

"I proposed," Giff corrected her. "In a most romantic fashion, if I do say so myself."

Linda blushed even as she smiled. On one knee beside the bed, naked as the day he was born, looking sexier than a man had a right to, he'd proposed. And she, caught in a weak moment after making love at dawn, had instantly accepted.

"You seemed to find it romantic at the time," Giff said in mock outrage.

"Stop it," she said, trying to suppress a full-blown laugh. "We'll talk about it later." After accepting his proposal, he'd fixed her an enormous breakfast: two eggs, bacon, toasted bagels with cream cheese and fruit preserves. And just as he'd said that first time they met, she was very hungry. One egg, over easy, would not have been enough.

"Congratulations," Jon said. Linda was relieved he'd finally joined in the conversation. He'd been very quiet since coming home.

"Thanks," Giff replied.

"Gerri, I have something else to tell you," Linda said.

"What?"

"I had another dream last night. Ever since Giff regressed me, it's like this flood of memories have been released."

"Are you sure these dreams are reliable?" Gerri

asked. Linda knew her friend's innate skepticism was talking.

"Yes, I think this one especially. It explains so many things."

"Like what?"

"Like why we have this special friendship. How you can read my emotions so clearly."

"Tell me."

"In my immediate past life as Constance, I had a sister named Amelia. She wasn't just my sister, but an identical twin. When I dreamed last night, it finally became clear to me; you were my twin."

"Me? Have a past life?"

"I think most people have lived before," Giff explained. "At least, that's the prevailing theory. There are young souls and older souls. Yours is apparently linked to Linda's."

"Do you really think so?" Gerri asked Linda.

"Yes, I do. I saw you and me together in the dream. It was kind of surreal, but we've always had a connection in life. Not always as sisters, but always someone close."

"If that's true, it does explain a lot," Gerri said thoughtfully. With a sudden smile, she added, "I guess that means I'm going to be Giff's sister-in-law, so to speak."

Linda laughed. "So to speak. Not bad for an only child."

"Three only children," Giff added.

"Not bad at all. Have you set a date?" Gerri asked.

"No, but we will soon," Linda replied. "I thought we could have the wedding in New York so you and Jon can attend, in addition to Giff's friends and Mother. I wanted to check with her first. You know how her schedule is," Linda said with dry humor.

"Yes, I know." Gerri also knew that Linda's mother wouldn't put anything ahead of her performance schedule. Even her only daughter's wedding. That was the way she was, though, and Linda had accepted it.

"I wish Grandmother could have lived to see me married," Linda said sadly. "She really loved a good wedding. You could always tell which person she was—the one crying more than the bride's mother. I'm sure mine would have been a large-box-of-tissues event."

"I'm sure she's watching," Giff said softly.

Linda felt the sting of fresh, happy tears. "I'm sure she is too. And I'm sure she's happy that we're going to keep the beach house."

"I wouldn't think of parting with it," Giff said. "I've found I'm rather attached to things from the past."

"Me too," Linda said, smiling at the man she loved. The man with whom she had earned the right to spend eternity. "Me too."

His fury knew no bounds. It was unthinkable that a pathetic human could defeat him in a battle to the death. How had the man learned the counterspell? Had a sorcerer assisted him? But no, there were no men of magic left on the earth. They'd all died long ago, before humans began to believe in their own eternity.

If he had a head, it would be pounding in pain. If he had fists, he would have pummeled some object, some person into a shapeless mass. But now he had nothing.

He watched them burn the Ouija board, watched the flames and smoke rise from the funeral barge in a pagan rite designed to send the dead on their way.

Well, he was already in his hell. The man had won this battle. Mord knew he must abide by the counterspell; he was out of their lives forever.

But there were other lives, other people who would call to him. Until they did, he would stay in the void. And remember the pleasure and the pain of humanity. And wait.

Epilogue

If you have built castles in the air, your work need not be lost; that is where they should be. Now put the foundations under them.
—Henry David Thoreau

November 1995
Coastal South Carolina

Giff paused from carrying their suitcases inside the beach house and watched his wife as she stood between the den and kitchen, looking at the new cabinets, floor and appliances. "It's wonderful. Even better than I thought."

"Yes, I think so too," Giff said, trying to keep the humor out of his voice. Linda had taken to renovations like a duck to water. Her house in Evanston had been almost completely redone, from the old, screeching plumbing to the new roof. The turret room no longer leaked.

She walked into the room, running her hands over the custom oak cabinets, trailing her fingers across the faux marble countertops. "It looks very . . . nineties, yet I can see how the antiques will blend in nicely."

"You don't miss the Harvest Gold appliances?"

She pulled open the doors on the new side-by-side refrigerator/freezer. "No," she said, grinning over her shoulder at him. "Not one bit." Her expression sobered. "It's *our* house now, isn't it? Not Grandmother's house, or even the same place I visited as a child. *Ours*."

Giff placed a hand on her shoulder. "Yes. But I'm sure, from what you've told me about her, that she would have approved."

"I know she would."

As he carried their luggage up the stairs, a flashback hit him as it did every time he entered this house. Jonathan Moore, possessed by Mord, holding the sword to Linda's throat as he stood on these steps. That image would stay with him forever, but they'd put it behind them. Giff could even say that he and Moore were friends, playing racquetball and sharing a few mugs at the local pub when Linda and Gerri visited each other.

Giff set the bags down in the newly decorated master suite—the room Linda hadn't seen yet. As a matter of fact, this was the first time they'd been able to spend more than a weekend here since the summer. Linda had five days off from Northwestern for the Thanksgiving holiday. The remodeling work had been started earlier in the fall, when nervous energy had driven him to complete a new project.

Awaiting the birth of one's firstborn son would do that, he observed.

"Giff?"

"Up here, love."

He heard Linda's footsteps on the stairs, then down the hall. "What are you . . ."

She paused in the doorway, then walked inside, stopping on the Aubusson carpet that covered the center of the hardwood floor. He watched her gaze sweep over the refinished oak furniture. Soft coral walls matched the quilt on the king-size bed, and custom drapes duplicated a colonial style they'd admired during an historic-home tour. "It's beautiful! When did you do this?"

Giff looped his arms around her from behind, pulling her against his chest. "Do you remember that trip I told you I was making to New York to visit my publisher?"

"Yes, the one where I asked you to bring back a dozen street-vendor beef hot dogs?"

"That one," he said, smiling into her hair. He'd had to pay a small fortune to air-express a dozen of the requested items to Chicago, coordinating the delivery with his flight from South Carolina so he could bring them home in person to her. Her smile had been worth the effort.

"So you were really at the beach house, arranging all this?" she said, her hand sweeping around the room."

"Yes. You're sure you don't mind that I surprised you?"

"No! You've done a beautiful job. I've never seen a four-poster bed that large."

"After making love in that tiny bed in your old bedroom, I figured we could use one a little larger."

"There's a new doorway," she said, pointing to the interior wall next to the closet.

"Another surprise. Go ahead," he said, urging her forward.

He opened the door and waited as she walked inside. "A nursery!" She laid a hand across her gently rounded stomach. Her eyes glistened in the dim light. "It's wonderful."

Giff smiled again, relieved that she liked the changes. He knew he'd stepped out on a limb by ordering the remodeling without Linda's consent. After all, this house was hers by right and because of her memories. And their son would visit here with them, would sleep in that crib and probably draw with crayons on those walls. Although Giff felt as though he'd known Linda forever, he'd discovered that living together provided new opportunities to learn each other's likes and dislikes. He wasn't complaining; he'd thoroughly enjoyed them growing together as a couple. A part of him was still hesitant about doing something this large without her knowledge and approval.

As he watched her smile wistfully and run her fingers along the spindles of the crib, he decided he'd succeeded in making her happy.

They'd already decided to name their son William Howard Knight. When Will grew older, he could have another room, down the hall. And, Giff thought, if he could talk Linda into another round of morning sickness and bloated ankles, perhaps they'd have a little girl in the nursery next.

"I've been so busy learning to be a wife and an expectant mother that I hadn't thought much about the beach house." She walked back to where he stood in the doorway, hugging him around the waist. "I'm glad you're a considerate husband. And, I'd like to add, being wealthy is also one of your greatest assets."

Giff pulled her close, enjoying the feel of her fuller figure. "Once I accused you of only loving me because I fed you. Now I see that your tastes have changed. I have to remodel homes to gain your affection."

"That depends on how hungry I am at the moment. I still love it when you feed me."

As if their son knew he'd been replaced as the topic of conversation, he began to kick vigorously. "I think he approves of his new room," Linda said with a grimace. "Do you think I can put up with another three and a half months of this?"

Giff raised an eyebrow. "It's a little late, isn't it? We should have thought of that back in June."

Linda's smile faded and she touched his cheek. "I don't recall that we were thinking much of the future at that particular moment."

"No, I suppose we weren't. But that's all behind us."

She nodded and rested her cheek against his chest. "I wished for your child, though. I think someone up there was listening."

Yes, they were blessed. Sometimes, he lay beside Linda watching her sleep. He was a very lucky man. The fact that their son had been conceived the day he'd regressed Linda, the first time they'd made love without protection, was a bonus.

With Mord out of their lives forever, they were truly free.

"I hope Gerri and Jon are having a great time in the Caymans," Linda said, pulling away and taking his hand. She walked back through the master bedroom.

"I'm glad they finally agreed on a place for the honeymoon."

"They had a rough time of it," Linda said, her tone serious and introspective. "I still feel guilty because of what happened last summer. I wish—"

Giff squeezed her hand as they started down the stairs. "Don't feel guilty. You did nothing but invite them for a visit."

"I know. But when I think of how close both Jon and Gerri came to dying, it makes me sad and angry." Linda walked to the couch and sat down, looking up at Giff as he settled beside her. "They were so happy before, and after the ordeal, it took them months to recover from the brutality Mord caused."

"But they overcame the memories. Their loved thrived, even if it did take them some time to discover each other again."

"The wedding was beautiful," she observed.

"You looked beautiful as matron of honor," Giff

said softly, stroking her hand. He didn't think he'd ever seen her lovelier, except perhaps at their own wedding in July.

The ceremony had been performed in a small, historic cathedral in New York, and the reception at Tavern on the Green had been attended by friends and family. Linda had tried to keep it small since they'd rushed the date, but her mother had turned into quite a supporter, surprising her by helping with both the arrangements and the guest list. Linda said that she felt closer to her mother now than ever before. Perhaps her pregnancy had something to do with the change of the mother-daughter relationship. Whatever the cause, Giff was grateful.

"Thank you again for the changes. The kitchen, the bedroom, the nursery . . . they're all just wonderful." Love shone from Linda's eyes as she looked into his eyes.

"For you, dear Linda, anything," he said, leaning forward, kissing her tenderly. "Whatever you desire, whatever I can do to make you happy, you have only to ask."

"All I ask for is your love. And this lifetime together. Growing old, watching our children become adults. I can think of no greater gift. If we come back, if we're bound by love and not by spells, then so be it. But for me, forever is not my dream. Here and now, with you, is all I can desire."

She closed her eyes and took his lips, sealing their love, bonding them together as a family, with hope and dreams to last an eternity.